"Before we head out, there is something I need to get out of the way before it distracts me any further," Justin said.

She met his gaze before he finished his sentence. Her lips were parted and he took his opportunity. Lowering his mouth to hers, he brushed his lips against hers. She tasted perfectly sweet and enticing. His hand moved behind her head and he adjusted her and deepened the kiss. As he dipped deep into her moist heat, a growl escaped him when her tongue danced around his. Not only did she respond to the kiss, but when her fingers ran up his arms to his shoulders, sparks ignited inside him that created an even stronger urge to do more than just kiss her. A hell of a lot more.

A car drove by and honked, and Grace jumped. Justin turned to see the back of the car before it disappeared but didn't recognize it. Returning his attention to Grace, he focused on the way her curls twisted beautifully into the clasp confining her hair behind her head. When he stepped back, the view was beyond perfect. Her hair was slightly tousled, with more curls falling loose around her face, and her lips were wet and slightly swollen.

She licked her lips and then brushed her fingers over her mouth.

He gripped her chin, tilting her head so she'd look at him. "We're not done," he informed her.

"Oh." She cleared her throat and then pulled away, turning and hugging herself as she hurried to his truck.

Tall, Dark And Deadly

LORIE O'CLARE

St. Martin's Paperbacks

This is a work of fiction. All of the characters, organizations, and events portrayed in this novel are either products of the author's imagination or are used fictitiously.

TALL, DARK AND DEADLY

Copyright © 2009 by Lorie O'Clare.
Excerpt from *Long, Lean and Lethal* copyright © 2009 by Lorie O'Clare.

Cover photograph © Shirley Green

All rights reserved.

For information address St. Martin's Press, 175 Fifth Avenue, New York, NY 10010.

ISBN: 0-312-94341-5
EAN: 978-0-312-94341-7

Printed in the United States of America

St. Martin's Paperbacks edition / April 2009

St. Martin's Paperbacks are published by St. Martin's Press, 175 Fifth Avenue, New York, NY 10010.

10 9 8 7 6 5 4 3 2

To my three boys, Andy, Jonathan, and Luke, who are always there with advice on plots, characters' names, and lots of understanding when I'm chained to the computer writing for hours on end. I'm the most blessed mother on this planet and I love all three of you very much!

Acknowledgments

I wrote the first draft of this book over ten years ago while on a trip to the Tetons. At the time, my critique partner, who wasn't published back then either, fell in love with this book. Years later, she still had faith in this story, and my writing, and gave me that push to get it published. Thank you, Shadoe, for always being there for me.

To the Smut Sluts, you know who you are, for your continued support and for keeping my morale up. All of you are wonderful!

This book wouldn't have come to be if it weren't for my agent. Roberta, you have had faith in me from the very beginning and that's meant more to me than you'll ever know.

Of course, Mom, you've been my number-one fan from day one, even when you informed me you had to skim certain pages of my books. I love you for that and for being there first in line to buy any book I released. You're the best and I hope I'm half as good a mother as you are.

Most importantly, to all of you, who reach out and buy this book, and enjoy this story as much as I did. If you've ever seen the Badlands, or if you ever have the chance, stand very still and stare at that rugged land. You'll experience what I experienced when this story came to me. Rugged and untamed, yet land to be respected. It's named simply "Badlands" yet there is something so beautiful, so peaceful and serene about them.

It's not every day you run across people like Grace Jordan and Justin Reece. They are so close to my heart, for their imperfections as well as their perfections, just like the land they live by. I pray they become lasting friends for you, too, as you read *Tall, Dark and Deadly*.

Lorie O'Clare
www.lorieoclare.com

Tall, Dark
And Deadly

Prologue

There were two kinds of women in the world—those you screwed and those you married. It wasn't a rule he'd made up. It was simply how it was. Some women were best at raising children, keeping a presentable home and life in order. Others were best on their backs, offering pleasure, and taking it like the good little sluts that they were. They were two separate breeds. If a woman possessed one of those qualities, she sure as hell didn't possess the other.

He didn't need a wife. And the sluts, well, they were only decent after being properly trained, altered from how their parents and society told them they should be. That was how it was with women; they needed to be told how to be. If it wasn't him doing it, then their mothers, or their fathers, their friends, books they read, teachers, someone else, would be telling them how to act, to dress, to behave.

It might as well be him.

He walked down the stairs quietly. "Grace?" he asked, keeping his tone calm, sedated.

She jumped nonetheless, spinning around and damn near tilting his laundry basket over. His folded T-shirts and underwear teetered before she slapped her hand over the top of the clothes, while adjusting the basket against her hip. "Master?" she hissed, her blue eyes wide.

He hated that look. Pure guilt. "Are you supposed to dry my T-shirts in the dryer?"

Grace glanced at the basket, which now trembled in her

grasp. He yanked it out of her hands and tossed the basket to the side, watching her closely for any signs of disapproval or resentment that he'd just spilled his clean clothes on the basement floor. "I asked you a question, Grace."

She straightened. Her training really was in force better than any of his other sluts' ever had been. "Master, your T-shirts are line dried on the wooden dryer and your underwear dries in the dryer." She never pulled her gaze from his.

He nodded, then turned to stare at the overturned basket and folded clothes on the floor. "Were those T-shirts hung on the wooden dryer?"

She licked her lips, like looking guilty would lessen her punishment. "It's cold outside right now. I thought you wouldn't want to wait that long for your shirts to dry."

"You thought."

"Yes."

"You disappoint me, Grace," he said, lowering his voice.

Grace stared at him, hating him with every ounce of blood pumping through her body. *T-shirts. Fucking T-shirts.* She sucked in a breath, and dropped her gaze to the basket that still held half of his clean laundry. *Fucking prick! You've got better things to do than beat the crap out of me over T-shirts.*

"I'm sorry, Master," she said.

"You are, Grace. You are sorry—pathetic," he hissed.

She cringed, knowing without a doubt at that moment it was going to get bad.

"You've been with me five years. Five years you've lived in my home, in my fucking mansion! And look at you. You spoiled fucking brat," he howled, his voice echoing off the walls.

Grace didn't look up. Somewhere upstairs a baby started crying. Grace's insides hardened, positive Master's screaming probably had woken Rachel from her nap. Rachel—the baby Grace had given birth to and who was immediately taken away from her. Her beautiful daughter whom she wasn't allowed to touch, or mention, or ever ask questions about.

Master bent over and picked up the basket, scooping the

clothes into it, and then handed it to her. She searched his face quickly, wondering for the thousandth time if possibly a morsel of compassion existed in his soul. If he even had a soul.

"Drop the basket upside down." Rick wouldn't let this go unpunished. Grace, of all of his sluts, challenged him more than any of the others ever came close to doing. He knew it was the only reason he'd held on to her this long.

Grace never took her eyes off of him when she slowly turned the basket upside down, let all the clothes fall to the floor, then dropped the basket on top of them. She hated him; it was clear on her face. Before he was done with her she would beg for his love. Beg to please him. That was what a good slut did. And once he had her to that point, he would know his work with her was done.

Then he would kill her. Like with all the rest. It was a slow process, although most didn't take as long as Grace.

"Is there anything else you'd like?" She turned and walked away from him.

As much as he loved the view of her bare ass, the marks from her last spanking almost faded completely, and the way her thigh-high stockings hugged her long, slender legs, Grace never allowed him a moment of pleasure. With her it was always discipline.

"Yes, actually there is," he snarled, grabbing her arm and spinning her around. "A bit of fucking appreciation would be nice."

Grace teetered on her high heels but balanced herself without reaching for him. "I thought since I was done with laundry I'd get started on your supper."

Of all things—thinking. They were sluts, damn it. They didn't think—they fucked!

"I'm not sure what to do with you." He let go of her and put his hands on his hips.

"Master?" she whispered, raising her gaze to his face and looking at him with intense blue eyes—bedroom eyes.

"Grace," he rumbled.

Her blue eyes darkened, showing her outrage. She breathed

heavily, the tight corset she wore pressing her breasts together and causing them to rise and fall. An incredible view, if he didn't say so himself. Corsets were the most incredible invention, designed to restrain a woman. The tighter the better, containing her, presenting her to him with the fucking kick-ass view the small garment offered.

He didn't look away but let her see that her actions, as well as her attitude, would cost her dearly. He would punish her for acting up, and the thought of it made his dick hard as steel.

If Grace could kill Master, she would do it. She wasn't sure if she hated the look he gave her right now more than the way he gazed at her after beating her. Right now his dark eyes were venomous. The black leather mask he wore—always wore—concealed the rest of his face, which she was sure was probably grotesquely deformed. The devil would be ugly.

He planned on torturing her. Storming away wouldn't make the pain any worse. Pain was pain; there weren't any levels anymore. Master ejaculated to humiliation, torture, and abuse. Grace knew from experience her next move wouldn't sway the events that would follow over the rest of the night. Master intentionally picked a fight with her so he could torture her. There wasn't any winning with the beast. And someday, maybe soon, he would pay dearly for it.

She wasn't going to stand here, letting him get to her, when all he did was glare at her while his dick grew hard against his leather pants. Turning again, she willed her legs not to tremble and managed to walk toward the stairs with her head held high.

"Grace!" Master made her name sound like a curse word.

There wasn't any point in turning around. If he were going to beat her, at least she would make it to a room that was carpeted and didn't have a cement floor.

"Grace!" he yelled, his sickening tone bellowing throughout the basement.

Grace made it up the stairs, her stomach churning as the sound of Rachel crying grew clearer. Her high heels clicked against the stone floor when she headed down the narrow hallway toward the kitchen. During the times Master left her alone, she'd managed to learn her way around parts of his large mansion where she wasn't allowed to go. He continually changed locks, which continually sabotaged the plan she fought to remain patient to implement.

Ever since Rachel was born and he yanked her away from Grace, informing her coldly that sluts weren't mothers, her bitter hatred toward him had consumed her like a life-threatening poison. "Don't give him this power," she scolded herself, pacing the length of the room. If she lost her ability to think clearly, Master would win. He would know he'd finally taken her mind, too.

Grace gripped the marble countertop and stared down at the long bright red fake nails he insisted she wear. Taking a moment, she did what she always did to regain control of her emotions. She tried remembering her life before she came here. Her parents, her uncle, the home she grew up in, over the years she fought to keep those memories from fading. Then slipping out of her heels, she slipped the straps over her fingers and padded out of the kitchen stocking footed, praying Master would remain in his personal rooms long enough for her to make her move.

There wasn't a woman on this planet who didn't crave pleasing a man. Some of them came by it naturally. Others, once shown the pleasures of submitting, learned what to do to get him off. Grace knew how to please him. Storming off like she had control of her own actions proved she simply might not be trainable.

"There's always a first," he growled, unlocking the door to his private section of his home. Tonight couldn't happen again. Grace usually obeyed him without question. If a woman could be perfect, she would come close. Unfortunately, he admitted to himself, they couldn't be. They were imperfect creatures, continually in need of instruction and correction. But usually training didn't take too long, and Grace had been with him for years. Tonight, though, tonight she would learn how defying him would destroy her world. He would show her—he would take from her what mattered to her more than anything. That fucking brat she gave birth to would die.

And it would all be her fault. He would make sure she knew that.

"No slut defies me—ever." He stormed into his bedroom and entered the small sitting room off of it. Carefully removing his leather mask, he placed it on a small table and reached for the large picture album on the shelf above the table. "The problem is I've held on to Grace for too long."

He felt the itch, knew what it meant, and understood he could only keep the craving at bay for so long. Lately it was starting to consume him, make him antsy, and that would make him sloppy. Like tonight.

He chuckled when he pictured her expression after he exploded over his T-shirts. Grace disobeyed simple instruction and needed to be reprimanded, but it was the craving growing inside him that made it so easy to explode.

It was time to travel, take long walks, and search for his next slut. He would know when he found her. The carefully applied makeup—signs she adored her body would mean she wanted him to also. And then would come the training, the part he loved the most, watching understanding glow in their eyes when they let go of the lies and false education their world had inflicted upon them.

"There's nothing wrong with being a slut." Running his fingers over the leather cover on the album, he opened it slowly. "Once you understand that sexual pleasure is the ultimate gift you have to offer, you're finally free of all the bullshit everyone stuffed into your head. And that's when you're mine."

He chuckled over the simplicity of manipulating the world around him. Every time he found a slut, it was like waiting to pick fruit from the tree. You had to know when it was perfectly ripe or the fruit would be no good. It was a very methodical process, one he'd perfected over the years.

Although spending time with memories had its place, there were things to do. If he allowed Grace's actions to go too long without punishment, he wouldn't be able to endure the pain. Already his balls tightened against the base of his shaft, his urge for release becoming a distraction. Distractions made a man weak, something he would never be.

Grace wasn't in the kitchen. His supper hadn't been started. The level of punishment she'd earned damn near made him light-headed. He would spend at least a day of intense sexual torture, inflicting pain and hearing her scream while he fucked her in every hot, tight hole she had. He would whip her while she sucked his dick, bind her, spread-eagled, and apply nipple and clitoris clamps.

Picturing her body jerking from the pain, knowing how smooth and moist her flesh would feel under his palm while he administered punishment after punishment, just about made him come. As soon as he saw to her immediate punishment, the ultimate act that would permanently free her mind and make her his, then they would leave here and he could put to play everything he fantasized about right now.

In the pantry, off the kitchen, the two small gas cans were slightly dusty. He picked them up and glanced at the canned goods on the shelves. More dust. More reasons to punish Grace. He stalked out of the pantry, through the house, and up the stairs toward the nursery. He would soak the floors but then wanted Grace by his side when he struck the match. Maybe he would make her strike the match. Not many experienced giving life and taking it away within the same year.

"Wait a minute," he said, putting his hand to his mouth as the vapors from the gasoline filled the room. "Why isn't the brat making noise?"

He didn't plan on drenching the room the brat slept in with the hired nanny who made sure she didn't make too much noise. The rooms around her igniting in flame would suffice. But usually she screamed or made the strange whimpering sounds that babies always made. Very seldom was the brat quiet.

The sensation hitting him as he increased his pace to the bedroom created prickles, like icy fingertips dragging down his spine.

"Master?" Grace's soft voice purred, her sultry tone ironically assaulting his senses.

But when he turned around, there wasn't time to react when she threw the match.

"Burn in hell, motherfucker!" she screamed.

Flames ignited between them, her body wavering as the heat quickly grew unbearable.

"Grace!" he screamed, watching as she clutched that brat and turned, running away from him.

Chapter 1

"Copy that." Lt. Grace Jordan held the two-way radio to her lips while resting her elbow on the roof of her squad car. She lowered her gaze, fighting to concentrate. The longer she stared at the god-awful scene, the more her mind started fucking with her.

"There's nothing on file," Christy Briggs, the RPD dispatcher, repeated.

Grace let her finger off the toggle button of the two-way microphone. The curly cord stretched to its limit where she stood next to the open driver's side door. "I can't believe there's never been a rape before in Rockville, South Dakota."

"There have been. They just don't get reported," the dispatcher offered, speaking a bit too comfortably over a two-way radio for Grace's comfort.

"Ten four," Grace said, lowering the radio. She'd question Christy about what she just said when she got back to the station. God, anyone could listen in on a two-way.

"Rockville is a small town. We might be in the Badlands, but that doesn't mean we have a high crime rate." Lt. Eugene Bosley paused at the front of her car. "All that means is that if there are any rapes, they aren't reported."

"Huh," she muttered, pushing a stubborn strand of hair that wouldn't stay with the others behind her ear. "That's what your dispatcher just said."

"She's your dispatcher now, too." Bosley's grin seemed out of place on the moonless night that made everything seem darker. With a brutalized and very dead body not twenty feet away, smiling about anything didn't fit the setting. He watched her move the strand behind her ear and rubbed his fingers together, like he ached to do it for her. "Everyone knows Margaret Young disappeared, but her mother won't file a missing persons report so we can't investigate. She's convinced Margaret will come home on her own. My bet is she looks like this one here, if not worse, right about now." He thumbed in the direction over his shoulder.

"Lovely image," Grace grumbled, letting her gaze shift to the body on the ground behind Bosley. Already yellow tape surrounded the crime scene and every squad car owned by the Rockville, South Dakota, police department had to be parked around them.

It was a bitch learning this antiquated system Rockville used. Grace bent over into her car, put the two-way back on its clip on the dash, and reached for her flashlight. Officers were all over the crime scene. Grace wouldn't let lack of technology botch up her investigation. She prayed the cops with her new department were better trained than the equipment they used or they'd trample over any possible evidence before she got a chance to bag and document it.

"Time to rely on old-fashioned intuition," she ordered herself.

"On what?" Bosley was right behind her when she straightened. His Clark Kent good looks were as out of place in this morbid scene as his jovial manner. "Stick with me. I'll show you the ropes, sweetheart."

"I've seen rape before." She knew more about the despicable act than anyone in this town would ever know. "Have we gotten ahold of her parents yet?"

"They're on their way now," Bosley told her as he walked by her side over to the body lying behind the Dairy Queen.

Grace looked around the dark parking lot and across the street at the courthouse. Amazing that someone could do something this horrendous in the middle of town and get away with it. Grace wouldn't ever get the stomach for this—

no matter how many grotesque things she'd learned humans were capable of over the years. She turned, putting her hand over her mouth, and squatted in front of the young girl lying partially naked on the asphalt.

"Looks like she was pretty," Grace said, adjusting her latex gloves before reaching to move a strand of blonde hair from the victim's face.

"April Monroe. Age eighteen. Graduated from Rockville High but not employed. Marla works over at Stop And Go. She's locking the place up and should be here soon." Bosley stood over April, his matter-of-fact tone flat, sounding bored.

"Is she okay to drive over here?" Grace asked. She stared at the halter top strap that was pulled halfway down the girl's arm and at her shorts, which were twisted around her ankles.

"The Stop And Go is just down the street." Bosley patted Grace's head as he remained standing next to her. "But I think she's got a ride bringing her."

Grace nodded, ignoring the sensation that he petted her like she was some kind of fucking pet. Instead of growling at Bosley to keep his paws to himself, she shifted, moving away from him and focused on April.

With nothing more than distraught parents calling dispatch because their babysitter wasn't there when they arrived home, and then an idle passerby spotting the body while cutting through the parking lot heading home after his shift, Grace didn't have shit to go on. They confirmed April was the babysitter for the Harrises and had sat on previous nights without any problems. The Harrises didn't find anything out of place, but Grace planned to make their home her next stop.

"So April vanishes from her babysitting job and no one saw a thing," she mused. Grace touched April's chin, noting the makeup that April probably had taken care to apply. Now it was smeared around her eyes and black lines smudged down her cheeks. Her lips had bright red lipstick smeared across them like she had fought off being kissed repeatedly. There was bruising around her mouth as well. "And this other girl, Margaret Young, she just vanished, too?"

"You're comparing apples to oranges here." Bosley looked irritated and waved off her confused expression. "Margaret was trash. Even her mother knew it. April on the other hand . . ."

"Was? Knew? You're referring to Margaret as if she's already dead.

"It's hard saying with a girl like her."

"If April was such a good girl, then why is she lying here dead?" Grace hated labels and insinuations. They were often inaccurate and they were bad investigation techniques.

"I'm good, darling, but I'm not that good." His smile gave her the chills.

Grace looked away from him, but not before letting him see her disgust. "Is the M.E. on their way?"

"Starkey should be here any minute. I put a call in to his house myself," Bosley said. "The M.E. is just Robert Starkey."

Rockville wasn't a big town, which was part of the appeal in accepting the position here. She would learn her way around soon enough. "Do you know if April ran with kids she went to high school with?" Grace did know that there was only one grade school and one high school in Rockville.

"You think someone she went to school with did this?" Bosley asked incredulously, like he didn't believe it to be the case. He walked around April, focusing on Grace but then shifting his attention to April when Grace looked up at him. The radio beeped in the car and he walked over to answer it.

Grace trained her flashlight over April. It would be hard to speculate anything until after the autopsy. Not knowing anything about the teenage girl, other than she once was very pretty, Grace did know there wasn't anything April could have done to deserve dying like this.

"Bruises on her right and left arm, a very obvious fat lip, possibly a broken nose. Right eye is swollen shut," Grace said to herself, making mental notes for now on April's condition. "Her hands are crossed over her pelvic bone, one over the other," she continued, and then glanced around her, looking for someone with a camera. "Bosley," she yelled. "We need pictures."

Two officers standing over by the yellow tape appeared to

be doing nothing more than watching and talking among themselves. Fine with her. They couldn't fuck anything up if they stood back.

Lifting the hand that rested, palm down, over the wrist above April's other hand, Grace looked at the victim's fingernails. They were painted a dark red and several were broken, proof that they were her real nails and not fake. Even though April no longer felt any pain, Grace was gentle when lifting the fingers to her nose. She avoided touching the swollen, bruised parts of April's wrist when she breathed in the scent, trying to figure out what April had last touched.

"Weird," Grace mused, expecting to inhale the metallic smell of blood or dirt but not the strong smell of cologne. The other hand smelled the same, as if April had sprayed her hands with mens' cologne before she died. Either that or whoever she had fought off was drenched with cologne.

Grace placed the hands over the pelvic bone again and noted that April was partially shaved and trimmed and the curly brown hair was matted and flattened, one indication that she'd been raped and the hair smashed as another body pressed against that part of her.

Grace stood, walking toward the victim's feet, and then scanned the parking lot for shoes. "The bottoms of her socks aren't dirty." Grace shot the flashlight beam around the parking lot and then glanced toward the street when someone pulled into the lot. "If that were the case, then she was carried here; otherwise her socks would be black from walking across the asphalt."

Bosley got out of his car and headed toward Grace but then pointed at a dark brown car that pulled up and parked in the street on the other side of the yellow tape. "Starkey is here," Bosley called out, and headed to the car. "I'll get your camera, Grace. Hold on."

Grace glanced back at the young girl, lying faceup, her head tilted like she had tried searching for stars. Her makeup-stained eyes were swollen and closed. "There aren't any stars out tonight, anyway," Grace told the dead body. "You shouldn't have died like this. I'm sorry," she whispered, guessing the amount of pain the girl possibly had endured during her last few minutes of life.

For a moment Grace knew the same amount of pain, and as she clutched her neck, her vision blurred on the dead girl lying on her back while memories of torture and abuse flooded her mind. There were too many monsters on this planet. Today she had the power to take them down, even if it was one at a time; whoever did this to April Monroe would pay. And if something similar happened to Margaret Young, regardless of what anyone thought of her, she deserved the same justice.

Grace stood, blowing out a breath and grabbing her wits when she focused on Bosley and the man next to him as they approached.

"Grace, this is Robert Starkey, our medical examiner. Grace just hired on. She's from D.C." Bosley rocked up on his heels, like he was proud of her or something.

Starkey nodded seriously. "A big-city cop might be a good thing on the force. Would you look at this," he said, done with introductions and all business. "What kind of jerk would do this to a child?"

"A very sick one," Grace commented, returning her attention to April. "Looks like she was beaten pretty badly. I'm not sure what the cause of death might be. I don't see bullet wounds."

"Let's turn her over," Starkey said, and two younger men, their uniforms indicating they were the ambulance driver and technician, moved in quickly, sliding to their knees and then easing their hands underneath April. Blood covered her backside and filled the air with its putrid, metallic stench. Starkey squatted next to Grace, who matched his position. "Lordy, Lordy," he said, making a tsking sound with his tongue while pulling on latex gloves. "This is bad, really bad," he muttered.

"She bled out internally?" Grace asked, moving when Starkey leaned over the body. It looked like the blood had pooled over April's ass, and as they rolled her over, it now seeped to the ground, the black foul fluid turning Grace's stomach. "Did he stab her down there? I can't even tell."

"Get a gurney," Starkey told the ambulance attendants.

Then giving Grace his attention, he took his time straightening while pulling off his gloves. "We usually don't have crimes this violent around here. But I'll do a full autopsy and have all your answers for you then."

Grace nodded, covering her mouth when she inhaled, feeling her stomach turn when she couldn't block out the stench that now hung too heavily in the air. "I noticed the bottoms of her socks are clean. Someone either carried her here or was holding her and she kicked off her shoes."

Bosley was snapping pictures but stopped at Grace's comment. "Find her shoes and we might know what direction she came from."

Starkey and the ambulance attendants moved in around April. Another car tried entering the parking lot but couldn't around the emergency vehicles. The officers loitering along the yellow tape turned when the driver of the car simply put it in park and then jumped out, immediately wailing loudly.

"No. April! No!" the woman screamed, unable to get past the yellow tape when the officers standing there stopped her. Her wails turned to brokenhearted sobs as she covered her mouth with her hands. "It can't be. It can't be," she continued crying.

"Is that April's mother?" Grace asked when Bosley nodded. Grace left the ME, wanting to hear his initial speculation, but knowing she needed to talk to April's mother as well.

"I'm Lieutenant Grace Jordan," she said when she reached the woman.

"I'm Marla Monroe," a woman, possibly in her mid-forties with dyed blonde hair and make-up streaming down her face from tears, said, and then grabbed the yellow tape between them. "I need to get in there."

"Marla, you can't enter the crime scene." Bosley moved around Grace and put his hand on the woman's shoulder, although she didn't seem to notice. Her expression was twisted horrifically. "You let me take you home and we'll get your car driven over there for you. Come on now. This isn't how you want to remember your daughter."

Grace didn't know anyone in Rockville, but when Marla

turned and started crying in Bosley's arms, when he stepped over the yellow tape, she guessed they knew each other pretty well. There wasn't anything Bosley could say to ease her pain, though.

Grace turned and stared at the girl on the ground, at her lifeless body. It was like Grace could hear April's final screams, feel the girl's willingness to do anything—absolutely anything—to make her assailant stop.

Grace knew that level of hopelessness, of acceptance of whatever might be done to her. And she knew the despicable taste that came with submitting to a monster and willingly doing whatever he wanted. God help them if there was a monster like that here. Chills rushed down her spine when she turned and faced Bosley and Marla.

"Whoever did this," Grace said, feeling the hairs on the back of her neck stand. "I swear to you I'll catch him."

Marla's eyes were moist and glassy when she turned in Bosley's arms and looked at Grace. "Will that bring back my April?" she demanded, anger and hatred making her voice tight.

"No, ma'am, it won't," Grace conceded. Nothing would bring April back and nothing would ease the pain.

The radio chirped and Grace headed to her squad car, leaving Bosley to ask the standard questions about April. Grace heard the answers—victim was eighteen, supposedly babysitting, not into drugs or with a bad crowd, and trying to get into beauty school. Grace slid behind the steering wheel and the radio drowned out any further conversation between Bosley and Marla.

"Are you ten ninety-eight?" Dispatch asked.

"Negative. We're still here on-site." Grace stared at the many tiny holes as she held the receiver in her hand. A little over a week on the job was about all it took for her to learn the equipment and methods of RPD, and to know she hated how antiquated everything here seemed. Especially with a young woman so brutally murdered. They needed the most modern and advanced equipment to aid in nailing the bastard who did this to the wall.

"I need you en route to Ten Fifteen Ash. Some kids over that way found a body. I'm dispatching an ambulance now," Christy said quickly, her excited voice chirping through the small speaker. "They think she's been dead for a while," she added.

Grace stared out the passenger window when Bosley drove them to Ash Street a bit later. One officer remained on-site where April Monroe was found, instructed to scope the area behind the Dairy Queen and search for her shoes or any other clues that would explain why April Monroe was found back there. Apparently her babysitting job was on the other side of town.

Grace couldn't get the eerie feeling to stop washing over her. It was an odd sense of trepidation, as if someone were pointing out the obvious to her and she couldn't see it.

"I thought the address sounded familiar," Bosley said when he pulled up in front of 1015 Ash. "This is the Brewster house."

"Brewster house?" Grace asked, staring at the plain-looking tract home that matched the other houses on the block, shy of being painted a battleship gray while the house on its left was a faded green and the one on the right a dark blue.

"Ralph and Candy Brewster. Last I heard I think they've got ten kids."

"Ten kids?" Grace couldn't imagine it. Taking care of her daughter was more than a full-time job, although one she wouldn't give up for the world.

Bosley rolled his eyes and pulled to a stop, curbing it with the tires as he parked. Grace jumped out, patting her gun at her waist, then grabbing the flashlight from between the seats, when she immediately heard loud voices inside. Several neighbors stood out in their yard down the street, looking on curiously. They turned away, making a show of talking to one another, when Grace glanced their way.

"Police!" Bosley announced, reaching around Grace to rap on the screen door.

The front door was open and Grace looked inside at a

group of people, all talking loudly. She'd be surprised if
any of them heard Bosley.

"Get your ass upstairs and clean up!" an older man yelled,
looking like someone out of a lumberjack magazine with his
broad shoulders and thick, muscular arms. He didn't look
toward the door but instead opened a glass door to a cabinet
and pulled out a rifle. "What the hell were you thinking,
going and touching a dead body?"

"Maybe it was cursed with some kind of black magic," a
woman said in a shrill voice.

Her comment spawned all kinds of comments, the group
inside getting more and more excited as the talking turned
to yelling.

Bosley stepped in front of Grace, opening the screen door
and entering. Grace followed him inside and wasn't surprised
that the group didn't react to either of them entering without
permission. A couple of the taller boys, both strongly resem-
bling the man with the rifle, gave her a curious once-over.
Grace wasn't worried about them. She stared into the outraged eyes of the man she guessed might be Ralph Brewster.

"Ralph, put the gun away," Bosley said calmly. "You know
you can't just go out shooting up a storm."

"You think I'm going to just sit by and twiddle my thumbs
when a dead body shows up behind my house?" Ralph didn't
put the gun away but held it with one arm, while pointing
toward the dining room table with the other. "The little ones
found it, but then the ones you'd think would have a lick of
sense go and try moving it. All I know is whoever put it
there is going to get to know Betsy here real personal like."
He stroked the barrel of his gun and then looked at Bosley
and Grace, his grin sinister.

"Show us the body." When Grace spoke everyone in the
room grew quiet.

"When did Rockville get a lady cop?" an older woman
asked, who sat at the kitchen table with the younger children
around her.

"Bosley, if you're training her, this isn't the scene she
should see." The young man who spoke possibly was one of

the oldest of the Brewster children, although he wasn't a child, more like a man, in his early twenties. He tilted his head, his scrutinizing stare a mixture of interest and curiosity.

"I joined the Rockville Police Department just over a week ago." There wouldn't be any investigation until she appeased this family's curiosity. Grace focused on the older woman who remained seated at the table as she spoke. "I'm not a rookie, ma'am. I worked for the Washington, D.C., police department for three years prior to moving here. I'm new to Rockville, but not to the ugliness that exists in this world. I'd like to see the body. Whoever she is, her family needs to know."

"What's your name?"

"Grace Jordan," Grace told her.

The woman nodded. "Cindy Brewster. Ralph Junior, go with your daddy out back with the officers. The rest of you get out of the way."

"Thank you, ma'am." Grace worked her way around the younger children, who didn't listen to their mother.

Ralph Brewster and his oldest son walked through the house, Bosley on their tail and Grace excusing herself. The remainder of the family didn't seem to want her to follow the men outside, although possibly it was her imagination. If only they knew the gruesome death she'd just witnessed, hands-on, before coming over here. She stuck her hand out, blocking the back screen door so it wouldn't slap her in the face after Bosley left the house. If he started treating her like she wasn't competent enough to run with the big boys, they would have more than words.

Traipsing over the uneven backyard that was littered with bikes and balls, Grace studied the neighbors' yards that stretched the length of the block. No one had fences up to interrupt the flow of land, making all the yards appear to be more like an open field.

"Shit," Ralph Brewster hissed, and wiped the back of his hand over his mouth. "You're going to get her out of here, right? My God, that's about the nastiest stench I've smelled in a long time."

"Pop, she looks familiar," Ralph Junior said, although when he edged near the dark, shadowy lump on the ground his father grabbed his arm and yanked him back.

"We've got an ambulance dispatched already," Bosley assured Ralph, the father.

Grace pushed the button on her flashlight, noting by the putrid smell that she was smelling death that had aged for at least a few days. The beam lit up a circular area of uneven earth with patches of grass and dirt.

"Over here, Grace." Bosley reached for her flashlight.

Maybe she was being a bit stubborn, but she would be damned if she was going to turn over her flashlight because she had thought to bring one, knowing they would be trudging through a dark backyard, and he didn't.

"Folks, I'm going to have to ask you to stand back." Grace held her arms out, facing the Brewsters and ignoring their sudden disgruntled looks. "Bosley, we need to secure the crime scene."

If Bosley looked just as perturbed that she was barking orders, he would get over it.

"We need to keep the ground around the body as undisturbed as possible," Bosley barked, lowering his voice and probably trying to reassure the Brewsters that he was still in charge. Nonetheless, he did as Grace said and unrolled the crime-scene tape, securing it to one tree and then making his way to another.

"She's been dead three days to a week." Grace walked around Bosley and trained the light on the figure, which was lying on her side facing them. A young woman, more like a teenager by how slender she appeared, was covered in mud, making it hard to tell in the dark what color her hair was. "Do you know who she is?" Grace asked, glancing at the son and then his father, who stood anxiously on the other side of the yellow tape, before training her attention on Bosley.

He shifted his attention quickly and that damned out-of-place smile appeared on his face. "Maybe once she's cleaned up I'll know who she is, although I admit not knowing all of the high school kids."

"Mr. Brewster, are your children out here playing daily?" Grace glanced toward the back of the Brewsters' house. Enough faces plastered the windows in each room facing them that it was almost comical.

Unlike Bosley, though, Grace found staring at death made it impossible to smile.

"Best as I know, all the neighborhood kids play in their yards." Ralph Brewster's demanding baritone sounded deflated. "She's no more than a kid," he added, his voice cracking. He cleared his throat and squinted at all of the faces pressing against the glass panes. "There's your ambulance. I'll go bring them back here. Junior!" he bellowed, regaining control of his demanding disposition.

Ralph Junior didn't hesitate in bounding after his father as both of them headed toward the front of the house where the ambulance parked, its lights enough to turn on a few more lights in the houses surrounding them.

"There's no way she's been lying here since she died," Grace mused out loud.

"I agree. Seems she might have been brought here and dropped off, too."

"Too?" Grace frowned at Bosley.

"You're the one who pointed out April Monroe didn't walk to where we found her in her clean socks." Bosley searched Grace's face before his gaze dropped lower down her body.

"Huh," Grace grunted, following his line of logic but not seeing where it took her.

Training her flashlight on the girl on the ground, Grace covered her mouth and nose and walked around the corpse, then squatted so she could see her face.

She was covered in dirt, blood, or both. Her hair was probably dark and long, past her shoulders, it appeared, from the matted strand stuck to her skin above her breast. Looking closer, Grace detected the outline of a sleeveless shirt torn and leaving her breasts exposed. She was so filthy it took a moment to gain that conclusion.

"I think she's covered in dried blood," Grace guessed,

and looked across the yard when a group of men, two of them carrying a gurney, approached. "This sucks bad. I don't see any gun shot wounds . . . or any obvious wounds, although she's so filthy I'm not even sure what she looked like. No one should have to die like this."

"Come on, Grace." Bosley reached for her. "This is a lot for anyone to handle in one night and you're taking it on like a trooper. You don't need to impress me, though. I believe you're an incredible cop."

"You're right. I'm one hell of a cop." No one belittled her today. Grace didn't want to dwell on his or her characteristics right now though. "This girl, and April Monroe, deserve the best both of us have to offer, Bosley," she said quietly, her back to the Brewsters so they wouldn't overhear. "Two young women were horrifically tortured and killed. Quite possibly the same person did this to both girls."

He was trying to assure her, but it pissed her off. The others reached them at that moment or she would have put Bosley and that stupid smile of his in his place.

"Two murders in one night is a lot to handle." She fought to remain calm and stepped away from their corpse so the technicians could load her onto the gurney.

The M.E. didn't show up for this scene. His technicians played by the book loading the young girl into the ambulance. Grace moved in around them once she was loaded and took advantage of the light to see her better. Definitely young, with a dark substance flaking off her flesh—dirt and blood.

"Can you clean her up or make her look a bit more decent?" Ralph Brewster asked from behind Grace. He rubbed his hand over his mouth as the light from the inside of the ambulance accented the worry lines on his forehead and around his eyes. "Ralph Junior thinks she might be that Margaret girl," he added, giving the corpse a furtive look before focusing watery blue eyes on Grace. "I'd bring my girl out but don't want her seeing her like that."

"I understand," Grace said quietly. "It's not a view I'd

want burned into my daughter's mind, either, but I'm afraid we can't do that. We need to preserve whatever evidence may be on the body."

Mr. Brewster grunted.

Grace focused on the young girl, now strapped into a sterile, white environment with powerful lights making it easier to see the contours of her face. Although it was dirty, Grace saw the swelling in the girl's eyes and the way her lips were pressed together. Grace tried looking past the effects of death to how the girl would have looked when she still had a soul. Long dark hair and a narrow, European-looking nose with a slender neck, and she'd been thin. Probably pretty—and young. Possibly about the same age as their victim behind Dairy Queen.

What if both of them were carried to their final resting spot before being discovered? She needed to turn their coincidences into facts.

Grace stepped out of the way when the ambulance doors were closed, and once again she stood in darkness, surrounded by the people of Rockville, who all speculated on the dead girl's identity. It wasn't the first time Grace saw vividly how that corpse could have been her, with strangers standing around in the street wondering who she was. But she had not died beaten and mutilated. Grace had lived. Rachel had lived. The monster had died.

And now a new monster was on the loose.

Two days later, Grace looked over the autopsy and lab reports, as a cold feeling settled in the pit of her stomach. Margaret Young disappeared July 5th, April Monroe on July 12th, last Sunday. Both turned up dead on the same day, Margaret seven days after she had gone missing, April mere hours after she was reported missing. Both girls were found partially naked and badly beaten. They were raped and stabbed to death vaginally. The semen that was found in both victims was from the same man.

"How is it going?" Sheriff Doug Montgomery stood in the doorway to her office, his calm baritone startling the crap out of her.

"Shit." Grace slapped her files shut and prayed her smile looked sincere. "You startled me, Sheriff. Sorry."

"When I startle a good cop, that tells me they are on the verge of serious revelation." Sheriff Montgomery made himself comfortable in one of the two wooden chairs facing her desk, leaving her office door open as he focused on her with unnerving gray eyes. "Spill your gut, Jordan. What do you got?"

He had a way of looking at a person like he already had the answers and wanted to see if she had it right.

"Two murders," she began, fingering the files in front of her. "Matching semen. Both stabbed to death vaginally."

"Sick motherfucker," the Sheriff interrupted.

Grace looked up into his fatherly expression. His long nose and high-set cheekbones gave him a regal look. Short, silver-gray hair complemented his features.

"Yup," she agreed, blowing out a breath. "Very. And my gut tells me we've got a very serious problem on our hands."

"Two murders is a serious problem." He relaxed in his chair, his expression calm but guarded.

Grace wondered what the worst crimes were he'd dealt with in his career. Sheriff Montgomery had been sheriff of Sherwin County going on ten years from what she'd heard.

"The similarities bother me." She opened both files but then glanced at her legal pad where she'd taken notes, her stomach twisting painfully as she ran her finger over the list she'd written.

"Tell me."

"Both females just finished high school, both were pretty. There are no witnesses to either crime and both girls were tortured, stabbed to death vaginally, and then deposited where they would be found." She paused, staring at the last two similarities while the words suddenly trapped in her throat.

"There's more." The Sheriff leaned forward, his focus on her list.

Grace nodded.

"What?"

"They were both burnt with cigars and smelled strongly of cologne."

"Does that mean something to you?"

"No." Nor would it ever again. She'd killed one monster and she would take this one down, too.

Two murders, even two eerily similar murders within days of one another was not enough to declare that a serial killer was on the loose, but Grace knew without a shadow of a doubt that that's what they had. Her gut was screaming it.

Chapter 2

"What are you trying to pull?" Bosley demanded.

It was too early and her day was already off to a bad start. Grace reached for the coffee pot, letting Bosley's question hang in the air. Rachel had thrown such a fit about wearing the right outfit to school, and then had tripped over a toy in her bedroom, busting her knee wide open, that there had been no time to make coffee before leaving the house.

"Do you really think you're qualified to suggest we have a serial killer in Rockville because two teenage girls show up dead?"

She hated Bosley for ruining her moment of enjoying the rich aroma as the dark brew poured into her cup.

"What are you talking about?"

"I'm surprised big city cops don't read the paper in the morning." He moved in close, too close, and leaned against the counter at the back of the large main room in the station. His strong-smelling aftershave robbed her from enjoying the smell of her coffee even more. Bosley held the thin Rockville newspaper up for her to see. "Or is it that you're used to seeing yourself in the paper?"

"What?" she gasped, spilling hot coffee on her hand and then causing more to drop on her fingers when she put the cup down and reached for paper towels. "Crap," she hissed.

"Jordan!" Sheriff Montgomery bellowed as he entered the station.

"Don't worry. I'm doing damage control." Bosley sounded

too calm when he pulled the paper out of her face before she could see more than her picture on the front page.

"Grace, I need you in my office." The Sheriff sounded a lot less intimidating as he ignored Bosley and nodded at her.

She wouldn't panic. It didn't matter who saw her picture or knew where she lived. Sure, there were monsters, incredibly sick people in the world. But *her* monster was dead. Grace gripped her coffee and willed the nauseated feeling in her gut to go away.

"I take it you've seen this morning's paper." The Sheriff dropped the thin paper, which was no thicker than an advertisement section in the D.C. paper, on his desk, face up, and then walked around his desk.

"Actually I haven't." She edged closer to his desk, the sensation that if she got too close it would reach out and bite her adding to the nausea building inside her.

Sheriff Montgomery leaned back in his chair, his uniform crisp and clean. He clasped his hands behind his head and watched her, his gray eyes more unnerving than usual this morning.

"I won't let Bosley do damage control, if that's what you're worried about." The Sheriff continued watching Grace until she rested her gaze on the newspaper, then his focus dropped to it as well. "But damage control needs to be done. I'll back you because you're from a big city but, Grace, Rockville is a small town. News like this won't go away. Our reporters don't have a lot of news to report. Talk to them about something like this and you've got to know it will hit the paper."

The headline of *The Eagle* read, "Serial Killer On The Loose In Rockville." The article covered the entire front page. Grace spotted the name April Monroe, but then her gaze tripped over Margaret Young. The Sheriff's words hit her before she could figure out how he'd leaked out that the second body found was Margaret's. Had the reporter been intuitive enough to seek out Margaret's mother, who hadn't been overly receptive when Grace and Bosley had visited her yesterday?

"Do you think I spoke with a reporter?" Grace saw the Sheriff's expression change with her question. She slumped into the chair facing his desk and dragged the paper closer. "Lieutenant Grace Jordan doesn't know what to do about two recent deaths in Rockville," she read out loud and then stared at a picture of herself, the picture taken when she first moved here for her photo ID as a county employee.

"Are you telling me you didn't do an interview for this article?"

"I didn't even know about it until I got here this morning," she said, shaking her head.

The Sheriff grabbed his phone on the first ring, obviously irritated. "What? I'm in a meeting," he barked at Christy, the dispatcher.

Grace could hear Christy through the open door behind her. "Sorry to interrupt, Sheriff, but the FBI is on line two."

Two days later, Christy appeared in the doorway with a tall, very tall, well-built man standing behind her and said, "Sheriff, Special Agent Justin Reece is here for your appointment."

Grace stood to her feet as well, her eyes fixed on the man. She felt suddenly as if she had been hit by a 2×4. She'd never seen a more powerfully impressive man in her life. Sandy hair bordered Justin Reece's perfectly sculptured face and green eyes looked at her with an intensity that sent a heat rushing through her. Grace wasn't sure she'd ever blushed under a man's interested gaze, but she flamed to life under Justin Reece's. After the hell she'd endured, living as a slave to a monster for so many years, she was convinced beyond doubt that no man could ever pique her interest to the level where she'd want to do anything about it. Grace noticed Christy sizing the man up as he moved around her and she wagged her eyebrows at Grace before backing up when Sheriff Montgomery turned.

"Thanks, Christy. Justin, welcome to Rockville. Or as I hear tell it should be, welcome home." The Sheriff shook hands with Justin who nodded but didn't smile.

His grave expression didn't faze the Sheriff, who looked at Grace, his professional smile in place. Grace wasn't sure but she swore he looked less stressed than he had a moment ago, as if Justin's appearance took a weight off his shoulders.

"Grace, I'd like you to meet Special Agent Justin Reece." Sheriff Montgomery moved to one of the two chairs that faced her desk and placed his large, calloused hands on the back of it.

Special Agent Reece glanced at her blank walls before focusing his attention on her window that looked out at the large lawn in front of the courthouse and the Dairy Queen across the street. She took advantage of him taking in his surroundings and admired the view he offered. His firm ass and thick thighs were a mouthwatering view. He had long legs, and the faded jeans he wore hugged all that ripped muscle. His waist was narrow and she bet rock solid, and the way he filled out the plain blue T-shirt he wore had her picturing corded muscle bulging in his chest. The kind of chest a woman dreamed of dragging her fingernails over and feeling tiny chest hairs tickle her fingertips.

He had to be over six feet, with broad shoulders and a strong back. He shifted his attention from her small office to her and his soft green eyes brightened, suddenly intense, as his gaze swooped down her and back to her face. She got the overwhelming sensation of being memorized. Not only her, but everything around her, her world. Like with a single sweep he entered her life and put all of it to memory, claiming and taking command of everything surrounding her. It was an unnerving sensation and didn't mix well with the heat that continued swelling inside her the longer she stared at his perfect body.

When he shifted his attention to the Sheriff, Grace studied his profile. A statue couldn't be sculpted better than

Special Agent Justin Reece. He had a slight scar on the edge
of his chin that she hadn't noticed at first. Otherwise, his
straight nose, broad cheekbones, and tanned skin, not from
a tanning bed but from being outside, created one hell of a
picture. Somehow that small scar, which was all she saw
that prevented him from being absolutely perfect, added to
his sex appeal.

"Sheriff, if you don't mind, may I have a moment alone
with Lieutenant Jordan?" Justin Reece's soft baritone was as
sexy as the rest of him.

"We can talk in my office." Grace nodded to Sheriff
Montgomery, intentionally not looking at Justin when she
spoke. Let him see her, take a really good look. If he saw
anything, he would see her strength. Because something
told her if he detected any faults in her, he would zone in on
them and not see what else she might be able to offer.

Working with this man would be a challenge. And one
she was up for. There weren't men anymore who would
sweep Grace off her feet. She'd been to hell and lived
through it. That experience made her stronger today, possibly invincible. No matter how drop-dead gorgeous to the
point of distracting Justin Reece might be, she could shut
down her reaction to him.

"You two get to know each other," Sheriff Montgomery
said, shaking hands with Justin. "It's good to have you
here."

Grace was already out the door, not that Justin couldn't
easily find her. Her office was next to the Sheriff's.

He appeared in her office doorway, a strand of sandy-
blond hair falling over his forehead. His hair was too long
for FBI field agents but one look into those soft green eyes
and she guessed few people countered him. The longer she
stared, the more intense a shade of green his eyes became,
creating a distracting heat that swelled between her legs.

"What brings you to Rockville? Were you compelled by
the two murders?" She wouldn't let his enticing good looks
get to her.

"Now they are two murders and not a serial killer." His

deep baritone gave her chills, in spite of her effort not to be affected.

"There are two murders," Grace stressed.

"Why didn't you say that to the press?"

"I never spoke to the press." She didn't wait to see the disbelieving look he would give her, just like everyone else since she had appeared on the front page of *The Eagle*. The reporter, Jules Giles, was an ass. When she'd approached him and asked why he wrote the article in such a way that it suggested she'd given him an interview, all he'd pointed out was that the facts were accurate. Any conclusion anyone came to as to where he'd gotten those facts wasn't his problem.

Grace had her suspicions. Giles and Bosley went way back to high school. And Bosley did seem out to sabotage her credibility. She'd dealt with worse before. Neither would distract. No man would own her, in any way.

"I believe you." Special Agent Justin Reece closed her office door behind him, which seemed to close him in to her space.

A tingling rushed over her flesh and she moved around her desk, using it as a shield against way too much male sex appeal. "How nice of the FBI to come forward personally and announce they back me."

"Do you disagree with the article?" Justin made himself comfortable in one of the chairs facing her.

Grace watched roped muscle flex against relaxed-looking blue jeans when he crossed one ankle over the other.

"Actually the article is factually accurate." She sat as well, wishing she had more coffee. Her mouth was suddenly too dry and more caffeine would help her stay focused and not drool over him.

"Do you think he'll kill again?" His soft, deep baritone was as distracting as the way his intense green eyes were when they continued to travel over her.

Grace held his attention when those deep forest-green, highly focused eyes looked into hers. Something assured her that staring into his bedroom eyes for too long would turn most women into a puddle at his feet. Grace wasn't most women though. She looked away first, tugging her uniform shirt at the waist and looking out her window at the court-yard and street in front of the station. Usually focusing on people on the street, reminding herself they were hers to protect, kept her grounded. No matter her efforts, the swelling heat inside her turned into a throbbing need she couldn't ignore.

"Both girls were killed the same, by a meticulous monster. Given the opportunity I'd say he would kill again."

Justin captivated her with those vibrant green eyes. "You're right. He will." He leaned forward, resting his elbows on her desk. His face was several feet from hers and his gaze dropped to her mouth when he continued, almost whispering. "I've researched you a lot more than this department has."

"Oh really?" She was proud of how nonchalant she sounded, and leaned back, crossing her arms against her thudding heart. "Why would you research me?"

"Standard procedure." He moved too quietly for such a large man, standing and walking to her window but turning when her attention shot to his perfect, muscular ass. "I know that you were held prisoner in the White mansion as a sex slave for five years."

Justin watched Grace's pretty blue eyes turn a violent dark shade, like a storm settling in quickly and preparing to explode its wrath without mercy. She was the most magnificent creature he had ever seen.

"What did you just say?" she asked, her expression not changing other than the intense glare that pinned him where he stood.

"Your past could have quite an impact on working this investigation." He would bet the long thick red curls she managed to pin behind her head were natural. Her creamy complexion and slender body were more than distracting, not to mention her full breasts, narrow waist and hips, and perfectly shaped, slender legs. He'd never seen anyone make a uniform look so fucking hot. "Two women died horrific deaths, the clues they've given us so far offering insight into the methods of a madman not so unlike the one who enslaved you all those years."

"My past is none of your goddamned business," she fired out at him, her cheeks flushing a beautiful rosy shade complementing the curly strands of hair bordering her face. Grace jumped from around her desk, causing another wisp of hair to flutter alongside her cheek, and reached for the office door. "You can turn around and go right back to where you came from, Special Agent Reece." She made his name sound profane. "I will not tolerate implications from anyone that I don't know how to do my job."

Justin moved quickly, unwilling to let her open the door yet. "I'm not going anywhere," he informed her, keeping his tone cool, his reserve in check. "Would you rather me know about your past and not tell you?"

Justin pressed his hand against the door just over her head and shifted his body, trapping Grace between him and the door. Her outraged expression didn't change. She was ready to take him on.

He'd been leery when his supervisor had given him the heads-up on what front-page news had hit Rockville. But then, taking advantage of the FBI's password-protected search engines, the information he had dug up on Lt. Grace Jordan was enough to request returning to the town he had vowed he would never step in again.

She shot him a look to kill and moved away from the door. Even in her outrage, she obviously had enough sense to know she couldn't physically move him out of her way. He watched her move around her desk and sit down. She tugged at her shirt, pulling and stretching it over her nicely shaped breasts, which made her nipples harden. Justin couldn't pull his attention from them for a moment, the view beyond breathtaking.

"Since you feel it's important to display your extraordinary researching skills, your ability in that department is noted."

The chill in her voice would have lowered the temperature in the room a few notches if it weren't for the way her breasts pressed against her shirt when she sucked in a breath. She wore a bra yet her nipples were distracting hard knobs. He loved a woman with large nipples. "I take my work very seriously, though, Agent Reece. If you take any discussion we have beyond the subject of our victims again, you'll regret the moment you did it. Are we clear?"

He would give her credit, she didn't flinch when he followed her around her desk and parked his butt against her desk.

Justin wouldn't smile. He needed to see how strong she was, and his method of attack had proved successful. Over the years he'd seen time and again strong, successful, and happy people stolen away from their lives, beaten, raped, and humiliated, never to be the same again. It destroyed most people, making them delusional and carrying away their self-esteem, which no amount of therapy could restore. If he'd seen any signs of irreversible damage in Grace from her years in the hands of a madman, Justin would have been forced to have her removed from the investigation.

"My name is Justin. You can call me that."

Grace continued staring at him like she might leap and attack any moment. He stared into her deep blue eyes while she remained quiet and glared at him.

He'd never seen her shade of red hair before. Obviously very thick and curly and long, it fought the restraints it was confined in at the back of her head very similarly to the way she appeared to fight being viewed as anything other than powerful and very much in control. Her dark hair, like the shade of a setting sun, was as captivating and enticing as the rest of her.

A sudden compulsive urge to lean forward and release the hair clasp brought him pause. He didn't think twice about coming to Rockville, in spite of the painful memories he knew would surface by doing so. Regardless of the humiliating mistakes that he hated admitting he wasn't man enough to face, this was *his* town. No psychopath would feed off *his* people, and no cop, who might be so emotionally damaged she couldn't find a job anywhere other than a podunk small town, would head up this investigation.

If Lt. Grace Jordan was damaged goods, she hid the knowledge better than anyone he'd ever known. Not only did she not appear damaged, she was so fucking hot he couldn't keep a respectable distance. Let her scream sexual harassment if she wanted, he would argue to any judge he needed to push her, considering her history, to see if she had what it took to protect Rockville. No one would ever make him admit he leaned on the edge of her desk so he could better see how the light from the window offset the different highlights in her dark red hair, or so he could watch her large breasts press against her uniform. He could sit here all day and drool. Grace was a piece of art, a unique creature filled with as much mystery as she was sex appeal.

"What do you have on these two victims found Sunday?"

"You research me and not the case? You were sent here to assist with it, right?" she asked, cocking one narrow eyebrow.

"Would you prefer we continue talking about you, or the investigation?" He was convinced for the most part Grace would be able to discuss the case. The jury was still out, though, on whether her reaction to horrific deaths would cloud her ability to analyze them properly.

Grace exhaled quietly. When she reached for a spiral notebook he noticed her hands shook, the first indication offered that she was having difficulty remaining composed. Her lashes fluttered over her pretty blue eyes when she focused on her notes, slowly turning pages before leaning back and returning her attention to him. She wore a black belt. That, and how her shirt tucked in to her slacks showed off her very narrow waist.

"April Monroe was an eighteen-year-old high school graduate." Grace straightened, lowering her gaze to her notes, and continued reciting facts he already knew. "She was

babysitting on Monday, July twelfth, and put the two children she was watching to bed. We don't know yet how, or
why she left that house, but her body was found a mile away
behind Dairy Queen. She'd been beaten, raped, and sodomized, and was killed by multiple stab wounds inside her vagina."

Grace flipped the page and licked her lips. Justin doubted
reciting the graphic information bothered her as much as
knowing he watched her. The way she shifted in her chair
and repeatedly tried to get a curly strand of deep, dark red
hair to obey and remain behind her ear was body language
he bet she didn't realize she offered.

"Later that night another body was found, Margaret Young,"
she continued in a matter-of-fact tone. "Apparently this town
is small enough that most knew who she was in spite of a
missing persons report never being filed." She shot him a pensive look, probably determining his reaction to her throwing
in opinion mixed with fact.

Oftentimes opinions solved a case faster than facts did.
"I agree it's a small enough town. Continue," he prompted,
watching her suck in a breath and her buttons stretching in
their buttonholes as her breasts pressed against her shirt and
her nipples once again grew distractingly hard.

"Margaret Young disappeared on July third." Grace
paused and licked her lips again. But instead of looking up,
she pressed a long curl behind her ear and stared at her notes
before continuing. "Her mother is disabled and reports that
her daughter, who was eighteen, wasn't home a lot since
finishing high school. She claims she wasn't worried about
her for the first few days she was gone. Now she's hysterical,
regretting her actions and blaming herself."

"Very normal." Family of victims blamed themselves no
matter the circumstances. He'd seen every instance in the
book.

"Yes, it is," Grace said, her tone still all business. She
leaned over and reached for something at her feet. Produc-
ing her purse, she opened it and pulled out papers, folded in
thirds, and opened them, pressing them with her palm. Her

expression was neutral, unreadable, and not once did she look up at him. "Coronary reports indicate both women were beaten several hours before being killed. They were raped, sodomized, and disfigured."

"How were they disfigured?" He guessed she still fought to contain her anger, and keeping her expression relaxed showed off how smooth her skin was, her face wrinkle free, with no lines around her eyes, and her cheeks soft looking. He really loved the long, slender outline of her neck and her collarbone, visible where she'd left the top button of her shirt undone.

"There were circular burn marks on each victim."

Grace moved away from him, leaving her office but returning a moment later with files in her arms, pressed against her chest. "I happen to know FBI don't make a habit of surprise visits to local law enforcement agencies." She stayed on the other side of her desk but pushed her door closed with her foot. She didn't want anyone hearing her berate him. "These are the case files for Young and Monroe, which I'm sure you've already had faxed to you." She dropped the files on her desk and stared at him. "Cut to the chase, Reece. What do you want?"

"I want to hear your version of what happened."

Not only would she not gain the upper hand by issuing orders, he wouldn't validate her accusation. She surpassed all preconceived notions he had had of her. Now he was curious what such a drop-dead gorgeous woman with more backbone than most cops he'd ever known was doing in Rockville.

"Continue," he prompted.

She opened both files, turning them to face him. "Monroe has two large circular burn marks near each hip bone. My guess is a light bulb, which means she was tortured somewhere where there was power."

"The second victim has similar burn marks?"

Grace nodded.

"Why do you think the marks came from light bulbs?"

She lifted one shoulder lazily. Grace was thin, but not

skinny. In fact, she was damn near perfect, complete with a nasty temper that he was tempted to set off again just to see the way her cheeks flushed and accentuated her incredibly beautiful and unique shade of red hair.

"It's a guess. The burn marks are round, about the right size. They were also cut internally with a knife, or similar sharp bladelike object. Both women were stabbed to death vaginally after having intercourse." This time she did look at him when she finished speaking. Her blue eyes were no longer the shade of a stormy sky but instead bright, vivid, and alert as she stared at him. He sensed that she wasn't actually seeing him, certainly not undressing him with her eyes like she had when he first entered the office, but instead contemplating something.

"Opinions matter," he encouraged her. "Let that be understood between us. I can't properly work this case without you sharing every hunch that comes to mind."

She blinked and he wondered if she had heard what he just said. Something about a gorgeous woman being alone in the same room with him and not seeing him, or hearing him, created a challenge inside him. His preconceived notion of Grace Jordan was grossly inaccurate. He had created an opinion of her based on her distracting good looks and knowledge of her morbid, despicable past. And he'd been way off base. Justin saw now that Grace was all business, almost too much so, and closed down sexually. For some reason that made her even more intriguing. He wondered if he could get a rise in her.

Men his age weren't after virgins, at least not sane, normal men, which he professed to be. But believing Grace had called it quits on men after being abducted and cruelly abused for so many years helped explain why she would attack, admire his body when she believed him not to be looking, but remain cold toward him when all he was asking her to do was her job. Justin's guess was Grace wouldn't let any man near her, ever.

"April Monroe's hands smelled of men's cologne," Grace

said, staring him down while folding the papers she'd removed from her purse and then sliding them into the appropriate file. "I endured being thought a bit odd when I asked the examiner down at the morgue to tell me what Margaret's hands smelled like."

"Man's cologne?"

Grace nodded.

"Why did you think Margaret's would just because April's did?"

Again, Grace shrugged, her attention darting around the room before settling on her hands. When she looked down, the loose curls fell free around her face. She would be beyond gorgeous with all of that dark red hair falling free past her shoulders and over her breasts.

"I didn't know that they would." She didn't move the curls falling free past her jawbone when she looked at him. "But if they did, it might be a calling card."

"Which is typical of a serial killer."

"Very typical."

"For the sake of argument, let's say we are dealing with a killer who's submitted to his addiction. When will he kill again?"

Grace sagged in the chair, shaking her head, and opposite her desk Justin guessed she'd been mulling over this awhile before discussing it with him. "I don't know," she admitted. "We have no prints, and the semen found doesn't match any on record."

"What do we have?"

"A calendar."

"A what?"

Grace grabbed her notebook while he twisted so as to better see the page she opened to. Her eyes glowed when she looked up at him. She glanced down, ringlets framing her pretty face when she tapped her fingernail on the notebook. Grace got off piecing the puzzle together from crime scenes. He wondered what else might get her off.

"We found both girls on a Sunday." She pointed to a chart

drawn on the page. "But autopsy reports show Margaret Young died a week before April Monroe." She slid her finger across hand-drawn boxes similar to a calendar. "So maybe he kills on Sunday. But I haven't figured out why we found April an hour or so after her death and Margaret a week after. Kids play where Margaret was found. They would have seen her."

"She wasn't put there before that evening," Justin speculated.

"That's what I thought. But why?"

"Maybe he wanted you to find her."

Her eyes glowed almost violet when she met his gaze. Grace shook her head slowly, puckering her lips. With the deep, dark shades of so many curls adding to the picture, Grace was nothing short of a goddess. She was the type of woman a man would kill for, and quite possibly already had.

"The Sheriff and I already discussed that possibility, especially after the front page article, which was an obvious set-up to make me appear unprofessional." Grace looked away from him first, studying the time-line calendar she'd devised. Her expression remained undaunted as she spoke. There was a tough shield around her, protecting her because discussing the possibility of these horrendous acts somehow involving her didn't faze her. "No one in Rockville, other than Sheriff Montgomery, knew I was moving here when Margaret was killed. Bosley didn't even know until the day I arrived."

Justin pushed himself to his feet and glanced at her office window. Outside, the perfect landscaped yard in front of the courthouse hadn't changed a bit over the years. He stood, stretched, and moved to the window, brooding and letting the few facts known on the case form a list in his mind.

"The Dairy Queen is where the first victim was found."

"Yup," Grace said behind him.

"Place hasn't changed a bit," he muttered, already apprehensive about being back in Rockville. Not that it wasn't clear as crystal why he was; he knew the territory. Knew it like a bad dream that wouldn't go away.

"You don't sound like a small-town hick."

"I'll take that as a compliment."

"I wasn't complimenting you."

He didn't doubt that. If he stood here and stared out this window too long, though, his mood would sour to the point where he wouldn't be able to focus on this case. There wasn't any point dwelling on how terribly he'd fucked up his life here. What was done was done.

He slapped his hand against his thigh, unwilling to allow the past to haunt him simply because he was back in Rockville. "Let's drive by both spots where the bodies were found, pay a visit to the morgue, and then I'll take you to lunch. If it's still there, I know a wonderful little restaurant that serves the thickest steaks you can imagine."

Grace's phone buzzed and she grabbed it without hesitating, or responding to him, again giving him the impression she wasn't paying attention.

"Jordan here," she said. Grace held the phone to her ear and scooted her chair back to lean down and pick up her purse. Her tummy was flat and probably fine-tuned and firm. When she straightened, the thick pile of hair twisted against the back of her head shifted, again making him wonder how it would look tumbling down past her shoulders. "That's fine; put the call through. You're not interrupting."

He leaned against the wall, crossing his arms and once again getting the sensation Grace had forgotten he was in the room. As he glanced toward the window while she listened to the person on the other end of the line, another woman came to mind, a woman who would just as soon shoot him as let him overhear her have a conversation with anyone. Justin wasn't looking forward to talking to his ex-wife.

"I appreciate your calling," Grace said, her voice smooth and soft, reassuring and actually friendly. The cold treatment was for him, which he had anticipated after exposing her with his opening line. As she spoke on the phone, though, he saw her true colors. She was warm and compassionate. She just had a brick wall built up around her, protecting her while protecting others. "I'll be there in a few minutes. Tell her I'm hurrying."

Grace hung up the phone, grabbed her purse and notebook as she headed around her desk to the door. "You're going to have to enjoy your thick steak alone. I've got to go."

"Wait," he barked, moving quickly, as she was past the dispatcher's desk by the time he was out of her office. "Grace, hold up."

Grace didn't stop but left the building, simply waving at the dispatcher, whose amused expression as he stalked past her didn't help his mood any. It was hard enough coming back here to defend a town that despised him, and now he would be working with a hot-tempered redhead who believed communicating with him was trivial at the least.

"Where are you going?" he demanded, grabbing her arm.

Grace spun around but with him holding one arm and her embracing her purse and notebook against her chest, she couldn't move the strands of hair that fell loose against the side of her face.

"I need to run an errand," she said, yanking her arm from his grasp. "I'm sure the Sheriff can help you with any questions."

"When will you be back?"

In the sunlight Justin could see that her dark red hair had different shades to it. Her blue eyes glowed even as she pressed her lips together. "I need to run to the school and take my daughter a clean pair of clothes. She spilled paint on herself during art class and is upset. She's in a new school and being comfortable is very important to help her adjust."

Justin blinked, surprised. He'd dug deep, unwilling to work with Grace on this case if he'd thought her too damaged to handle it. Rockville might have become a thorn in his side, but nonetheless, it was his hometown, where he was born, raised, married, and had kids. After being shown *The Eagle*, the small, locally owned newspaper, with its horrendous headline about a serial killer, he hadn't hesitated in taking the case. Of course he did his homework. Grace, being new in town, was the first person he checked out. When he'd found a gap in her history, a five-year span when nothing came up on his system, it raised a flag. Anyone researched through the FBI would show activity as long as they were breathing. Cash a check, purchase anything, travel, switch jobs, it was all documented. Go five years without any activity showing up and something wasn't right.

"That shouldn't take you long," he said, recovering from the knowledge that she had a daughter quickly. Justin didn't overlook anything. Grace never gave birth, adopted, or had a foster child.

"Nope. Probably not." She didn't suggest meeting him afterward but headed to her car.

Instead of pressing the issue, Justin watched her walk away, the sway of her ass stirring his dick to life in his jeans. Before he arrived he thought he had her figured out, and within the length of one conversation he had discovered how off base he'd been. Now he saw she was even more of a mystery. He headed back into the station, pretty confident he could clear up this new revelation quickly.

"Lovers' quarrel already?" Christy, the dispatcher, grinned mischievously at him.

"How old is Grace's daughter?" he asked, knowing no matter what he said or how he approached asking questions, Christy Briggs, who'd been dispatching for the police department since they got out of high school, would direct any gossip about him in the direction of her choosing.

"I think she's about ten." Christy ran her fingers through her pale blond hair, not her natural color from what he remembered of high school, and then studied her fingernails. "Grace enrolled her in the summer program over at the school. She figured it would give her daughter a good opportunity to know the kids she'll be going to school with once it starts. She really is a good mother," Christy added pointedly, narrowing her brows when she lifted her head and studied Justin. Then leaning back, she gave him a big, toothy grin. "Her daughter would be the same age as yours, now wouldn't she?"

Like he would give Christy Briggs the satisfaction of knowing he didn't remember what grade his daughter would be entering this fall. Not that his ex-wife hadn't made it clear to the town before he officially left what kind of father he was.

"I'm headed out to the house. You've got my number if you need me," he said, instead of allowing the conversation to dig deeper into family matters.

"Sure do," she said, still smiling. "It's good to see you again, Justin. You're looking really good."

"Thanks, you, too," he muttered, knowing his scowling nature would be enough to get the gossip going. Some things in Rockville would never change.

He decided to run the errands he'd suggested doing with Grace alone. After walking through each crime scene, which were no longer taped off and both now no more than a parking lot and backyard, he headed over to Robert Starkey's office. The older medical examiner was thrilled to see him and catch up on old times but just as enthusiastically discussed both cases with Justin.

More than enough time passed for Grace to be done taking care of her daughter. Justin headed for his F-150, parked on the street. As he glanced down the length of the street, memories of Rockville, of growing up and learning about life, hit hard and he paused, hand on the door handle, and stared at the buildings lining either side of the street. The best times of his life and the worst nightmares of his life had happened right here in this corner of the world. Nothing he could do would change that.

Quite possibly his daughter, Elizabeth, would be in the same grade as Grace's daughter. She would probably have the same wild red curls Grace did. Elizabeth had her mother's coal black hair, but her eyes weren't cold and empty like Sylvia's. Instead, Elizabeth reminded Justin a lot of Clare.

"Clare," he whispered, and climbed into his truck, gunning the engine to life and willing himself not to travel down that particular memory road.

Elizabeth had milky green eyes just like Clare's, eyes that were full of wonder and an eagerness to learn all that life had to offer. In spite of her mother being a coldhearted bitch, Elizabeth glowed with happiness and didn't see bad in anything. In his daughter's eyes, Justin was perfect for keeping the world protected from all bad guys. Whenever Justin found time to see his daughter she'd been there, unlike his son, with a smile and a hug, thrilled to see the father she barely knew.

Justin pulled away from the street. It was time to head out to his ranch and make sure rodents hadn't devastated the place. "You can embrace the hell out of all your old ghosts once you get home," he grumbled, knowing one ghost in particular he'd kill to embrace just one more time.

Clare had thought her older brother was perfect just like Elizabeth viewed her father. And he'd let Clare down. Let both of them down. Gripping the steering wheel, he reminded himself for the hundredth time that even he wasn't perfect. The reminder didn't help much.

He'd let Clare down in the worst way. Five years had passed since Clare's untimely death, but not one minute passed when Justin didn't wish for a second chance. Clare had fought to live in that old apartment building, with locks that didn't work properly and windows too warped to offer any protection at all. The hallways inside the apartment building weren't lit, and there was no lock on the main door. Anyone could enter that apartment building, whether they paid rent or not.

All Clare saw was the adventure, the beauty of an old building, and its strong artsy slant. She was excited about college and called Justin every night to talk about her professors and assignments. There wasn't a more beautiful creature that ever walked this earth, other than his daughter. Clare had been perfect, in every sense of the word.

He still remembered the day Clare had moved in with

him, when she was only ten, after his parents died on assignment overseas. Justin was thrilled to pull her out of that boarding school, and Sylvia sulked every minute Clare lived with them clear up to her eighteenth birthday, when Justin insisted on driving her to the university and her own apartment.

No one knew better than him the foul taste of regret. It made him stronger today, more determined, and left him with knowledge that today no one, no matter how soft and pretty their eyes were or how much they adored him, would ever sway him from doing the right thing. Today he saved the world so that tomorrow he could love those who loved him.

But regret still bit at him for his mistakes in the past. If only he'd insisted Clare live in the dorm her first year at college. If only he'd taken the time, spent his own money, and secured her apartment. Justin didn't give a flying rat's ass about what anyone told him about mourning and all the regret he needed to let go of. It *was* his fault. He had left Clare in that terrible apartment building when all of his training and experience told him it was a crime magnet. If he'd ignored his little sister's enthusiasm and told her how it had to be, Clare would still be alive today.

"I'm sorry, baby girl," he whispered, and saw her lifeless body, raped, beaten, and strangled, her assailant never found.

He wasn't able to save his little sister, but he'd be damned to hell if he didn't stop the monster who had decided to use young Rockville women to appease his disgusting craving for abuse and murder. After getting a feel for the investigation, Justin knew before he did anything else he should call his ex-wife, possibly arrange to see his kids.

His cell rang and he got it on the second ring. "Reece here."

"Reece, Sheriff Montgomery here. Do you have time for a meeting right now?"

Justin slowed his truck, signaling to turn into a gas station to turn around. He'd put his family on hold so long the damage was probably irreparable. Another hour or two wouldn't hurt him any worse than he already was. "I'll be down at the station in a few," he said, and turned his truck around.

Chapter 3

"Grace?"

"In here." Grace faced a bulletin board with thumbtacks in her palm and stared at the pictures of April and Margaret.

"Would you look at you?" Bosley said, entering her office with coffee in hand and then grinning at her arrangement of papers on her board. "You look just like your standard TV cop."

"Thanks, I think," she muttered, and stared at the newspaper article about April Monroe. "This article came out a week before she died."

Bosley moved behind Grace and brought his cup to his lips. He smelled clean, and his hair was cut short, the trim behind his ears and at his neck creating perfect lines. Bosley was the textbook definition of the perfect cop, his uniform impeccable and his appearance in top order. In the two weeks that she'd been here, though, Grace noticed that he didn't appear to do a lot. Not to mention, she still believed he had something to do with her appearing on the front page of *The Eagle*.

Bosley believed he was the top-notch cop in Rockville. Grace wondered if Bosley realized Justin probably wouldn't be here if it weren't for that article. She doubted he looked at it that way.

"Yeah, it did," he said, and then leaned against the wall

by her bulletin board, watching her with his carefree smile that would make anyone believe he was the perfect man, always out to help others and eager to listen to what anyone might have to say. "Are you excited to work with our FBI man?" he asked her, changing the subject.

Grace pinned the newspaper article under April's picture. She'd been a very pretty teenager and, according to the article, had been heading to state finals with the debate team. "I don't mean to sound all big city," she said, turning her attention to Margaret's picture. "But I've worked with the FBI before. Not that I've done much work with Justin so far, though. We met on Friday, I spent the weekend settling into my new home, and now here it is, Monday morning, the town is still quiet, and there's no sign of him."

"Well, our Justin is an incredible investigator. I look forward to seeing the two of you in action." Bosley rocked up on his toes, looking a bit too pleased with himself.

"Our Justin?" she asked, turning and looking at his grinning face. "How is he our Justin?"

"Just a matter of speech." Bosley shrugged, his grin not fading. "Justin grew up here like a lot of us did. I don't know that he knows the area better than I do, but I guess I'm not FBI."

"Does he have family here?" Well, that just slipped out. Like she cared anything about Justin Reece. He was pompous, arrogant, and knew too much about her.

"Yup. He used to be married to the Mayor. Of course now that she's shacked up with Todd Wilkins, who works over in the law office on Maple, things might get a bit sticky." Bosley wagged his dark eyebrows and his eyes glowed with excitement. "Rockville is coming of age when we have a lady mayor who lives with her boyfriend. Sylvia is dynamic enough, though, that no one would dare publicly condemn her. But anyway, I'm sure you being the professional big-city cop and all, you'll keep the scandal to a bare minimum."

"What scandal are you talking about?" she demanded, although it was obvious by the look on his face he ached to know if she was interested in Justin. "Two families are destroyed now because these girls were brutally murdered. You would think the people of Rockville would be more concerned with the monster who did this being put behind bars than who is, or isn't, sleeping with whom."

"Of course they are." Bosley patted her shoulder and then kept his hand there. "Reece will be a good partner for you. I can't imagine him letting any history with this town get in the way of solving this case. And I'm sure you'll do a great job, too, sweetheart."

Grace shrugged her shoulder, stepping backward until Bosley's hand fell to his side. "It really isn't proper for you to touch me like that," she said, her voice a low whisper.

Bosley pulled his hand away from her, his smile fading while his expression turned guarded. "I didn't realize you were so jumpy today. I just stopped by to let you know your computer should be installed later this afternoon. Once it's up and running, I'll show you how to run our programs. I've got some paperwork to finish up. If you have any questions, just holler." There was that confident smile again.

"Don't worry. I'm a mother. Trust me, I know how to yell."

"You yell at your child?" he asked incredulously. His eyebrows shot up quickly, although his gaze traveled down her slowly and didn't quite return to her face.

"If she needs it," Grace said coolly.

"It's just with you being such the politically correct lady and all." Bosley patted her shoulder again.

Grace felt an overwhelming urge to growl, especially after just telling Bosley not to touch her. Instead she moved around him, ignoring his comment and picked up her notes.

Grace decided Bosley's social couth was seriously lacking. He might know how to look good, but when it came to behaving, he'd be the one to put his foot in his mouth before anyone else. "Is there anything else?" she asked, hoping her hard stare made it clear that Bosley was in the way.

Bosley cleared his throat. He offered his usual toothy

grin. "You don't strike me as the mom type." He leaned from one foot to the other, looking awkward for the first time since she met him, which confirmed her newfound opinion of him.

"I work out," she offered, and decided she really didn't care what he pictured a mom looking like.

"Well, if you have any questions, even though I guess I'm not officially your partner anymore, feel free to ask."

"I'll do that." Grace waited for him to leave before returning to the bulletin board in front of her. Two beautiful young women's pictures hung before her, one having accomplished a lot for her age and the other starting out slower into adulthood. Their one commonality being now that they wouldn't become adults, get married, or have kids.

She thought briefly of the child she'd birthed so long ago. The one instantly taken away from her. She'd been a proud parent legally now for two years. That was her secret, though, and she'd take it to her grave. That is, as long as Rachel kept her mouth shut.

Focus on the cases. There were clues in front of her. She needed to find the similarities in these two rape and murders. Moving to her desk, she leaned against it and stared at the bulletin board.

"Okay, both girls were eighteen. Could be coincidental," she muttered to herself, but grabbed her pen and pointed at where she'd documented this fact in the chart she'd created. "Both girls were killed by being stabbed to death vaginally. Probably not coincidental."

If she could match up all the clues and nail this bastard, her new position in Rockville would be sealed for life. The town would love her. She would be their strength, their pillar and security that would allow all of them to sleep well at night and not worry when their children went out to play. Everyone would adore and envy her for her independence and firm resolution to continue protecting them from the evils of the world.

Like goddamned Batman.

Daydreaming wouldn't get her anywhere. She tapped her pen on her notebook, then jumped when the phone on the desk next to her buzzed.

"Special Agent Reece is on line one for you," Christy sang through the phone when Grace answered.

She pushed the button to accept the call. "This is Jordan."

"What are you doing?" Justin asked.

His baritone sent chills over her flesh. "Brainstorming," she admitted.

"Good. Same here. Do you know of any other cases where the victim was raped, sodomized, burned, stabbed to death, and then moved to a new location?"

Obviously Justin was tearing into these cases as much as she'd been. If only he hadn't learned about her past, or mentioned to her so casually that he knew about it.

"No, not any I remember hearing about. Being stabbed to death vaginally is pretty gruesome. I'd remember that one."

"Then, not only do we have a despicable murderer who's suddenly appeared in a town of twenty thousand, but one who already has a calling card."

"What do you think his calling card is?" Her stomach twisted. She'd dealt with insane psychopaths before since she'd become a cop, and knew about their nature all too well. But when a serial killer started leaving calling cards, it meant he planned to kill again. To him it was a game, a challenge from him to the law to see if they could find the clues he left. And when caught, if brought in alive, such killers seldom regretted their actions.

"He deposited both girls where they could be found, and left them visibly marked in similar patterns."

"What patterns?" She quickly shuffled through her papers and pulled out her copies of the autopsies. "And we found them on the same day but they weren't killed on the same day."

"Look at your reports," he said, as if he could see her through the phone and knew she already had them in front of her. "Margaret and April were both burned several times, the object possibly being a lightbulb. There are smaller marks, too. Starkey has sent off for further testing to determine what caused the burn marks."

"You think burning them is his calling card?"

"I think all of it might be. He's methodical. With two women he repeated his actions and then left them where they would easily be found. As you go over the autopsy reports of both women, detail by detail, you start seeing the pattern he used on both of them."

Grace had noticed that, and imagined how it had played out. But that was how her mind worked, visualizing the torture, the pain, and wondering how much endurance each girl had before she cracked.

"Grace?" He said her name so softly it created warm tingles that spread over her like being wrapped into strong, protective arms.

But she didn't need protecting. She took care of herself. "You're right." He wouldn't see her get drawn into the visualization of it.

"I'm still here at my house," he began, but then paused.

"You have a house here in town?" Grace blinked and then pinched the bridge of her nose. The last thing she should do was get personal with this guy. He knew too much about her, which made him dangerous. And just the way he said her name a moment ago made her worry he was ready to comfort her. Letting her guard down for even a moment and allowing that would be disastrous. "That's convenient," she added, stopping him from elaborating on anything personal.

"I grew up in this house," he offered, his voice remaining soft, comfortable sounding, like it did when he spoke her name. "And it's where I raised my family."

"Must make it a comfortable place." She would not ask about his family. And she wasn't so stupid that she didn't see he had set her up to do so. But inquiring about anything might imply interest. Justin Reece was already dangerously good-looking and had the ability to send sparks shooting down her insides even when talking to him on the phone.

Her smartest move right now would be to shift the conversation back to the investigation. "Do you think our guy will strike again?" she asked, pulling the question out of the many she'd asked herself about this case.

"Yes, he will. What I'm trying to figure out now is when," Justin said with enough conviction, the warmth he'd created inside her turned to an icy chill. "April and Margaret were found Sunday night, but Margaret was killed a week before. We know April died Sunday. The pattern could be a day of the week, a location in town, or the time of the day."

"It shouldn't have to be that someone else dies so we can determine a pattern."

Pain tore at her insides. Just thinking about another young lady dying like that made her sick to her stomach. She knew the hell, the agony, the humiliation and abuse. All the bruises, the sick, demented things that bastard had done to her. And to be burned. To smell her own flesh sizzling, the infliction so excruciating it would rob her ability to think, or act, or respond in any way. That made Master pissed, and he'd scream at her until she could scream back. But exerting the effort to talk, communicate in any way, made the pain more acute and intense.

A blurred picture of a cigar burn taunted her. It was as if it floated toward her, a cruel, evil reminder of her haunting past. Grace grabbed her chest, suddenly unable to breathe, as her fingers brushed over the spot on her body that was scarred for life, a reminder of the hell she had lived through. And that too often, especially during an intense investigation, resurfaced to torture her again.

Master was dead. Dead!

No. No, he isn't my master. He isn't a master of anything. He is dead!

Get a grip. She sucked in a breath and realized she gripped the phone hard enough that her fingernails pinched her palm. Grace prayed Justin didn't say something she hadn't heard.

"We can't save the world," Justin said, his deep voice soothing her frazzled brain.

"I sure as hell can try." Just like she could toughen up and take this investigation on full force.

Christy stuck her head in the doorway, her headpiece hanging, unplugged, down her front. "I need to send you on a call," she whispered, looking apologetic.

"Duty calls," Grace told Justin.

"I'm heading in anyway. I'll be there when you get back to the station." He hung up before she could say anything.

"We have a robbery in progress out at the Kwik Mart." Christy gestured for Grace to follow and disappeared from the doorway. "Bosley is heading out," she said, speaking louder although Grace followed her. "If you hurry outside, you can ride with."

"On my way." Grace patted her hip, feeling her gun, and then hurried out the door to catch up with Bosley.

A rusted green Ford Pinto and a silver Taurus wagon were parked in the gravel parking lot outside the Kwik Mart.

Grace and Bosley pulled into the lot as two teenage boys ran out of the store. One of them, a tall, skinny kid with blond curls, held several six-packs of beer while yelling something at the other kid. The second boy, dark-haired, shorter, and a bit chubbier, held a small handgun. They laughed and cheered each other, indifferent to the patrol car in front of them.

A man, wearing a shirt that had the logo of the convenience store on it, hurried after the two boys. He gestured wildly and yelled at both of them. One of the boys flipped him off and started the car.

"Looks like it's time to put an end to their party," Grace said, patting her gun secured to her belt and then checking to make sure her microphone to Dispatch was secured to her collar.

"Afraid so." Bosley either contained his excitement very well or wasn't too excited about bringing in the boys.

"Do you know these kids?" she asked, reminding herself that with a town this small, possibly Bosley regretted having to arrest delinquent boys from good homes.

"Oh yeah." This time Bosley did look remorseful. He pulled the car up behind the parked cars. "Tell you what. This is your show. Let them see what you've got."

"Okay." Grace jumped out of her car and pulled her gun on the two juveniles. "Freeze, right there."

The tall, lanky, blond-haired kid looked at her, then at his buddy, who stood on the other side of the car. The other boy didn't look like he would run. In fact, neither of them looked scared at all—more like cocky. Well, if they took her for some rookie cop, they were in for a shock.

She pressed the microphone attached to the collar of her uniform shirt. The earpiece didn't fit quite right in her ear, but the dispatcher's voice was easy enough to hear.

"Car number seven is ten ninety-seven," Grace told her. "We've got two juveniles; one is armed."

"Ten four."

"Stand by for the plate number. I should have IDs for you here in a minute."

"It's Daniel and the Walters' kid." All of a sudden Bosley stood next to her, looking almost bored when he broke into her conversation with Dispatch.

Both boys noticeably relaxed.

"Are you bringing them in?" Dispatch asked.

Grace wasn't sure what else she would do with them. "They aren't running."

Grace handcuffed both teenagers and then helped them into the backseat of the squad car. Neither boy fought her. If anything, they seemed confused. She couldn't help but think this hadn't been the first stunt like this the boys had performed and they probably sat in shock that they'd been caught this time. The clerk stood outside the store, his arms crossed as he frowned and watched. She shut the door on the two boys when Bosley climbed into the driver's seat.

"You taking those boys in?" The clerk ran his hand through greasy hair as he hesitated just outside the glass doors of his store. "Do I have to fill out a report or something?"

"I'll need to get a statement from you." Grace turned when Bosley remained sitting in the car with one leg out and the door opened. "They don't appear to be hiding their guilt, though."

Bosley looked like he said something to the two boys, then got out of the car with clipboard in hand. "They won't, either," he said when he'd returned to her side.

"It's getting old. I'll tell you that much," the Kwik Mart employee groaned. "They scared the tar out of me with that gun of theirs."

"Do they get into trouble often?" Grace looked from one man to the other.

"Daniel does at least." Bosley nodded his head toward her car. "He's the one with the blond hair. I guess he feels he's above the law since his parents are the Mayor and FBI."

What?

Grace escorted Danny Reece, as he told her he preferred that name over Daniel, into the jail. Bosley walked alongside the dark-haired kid, who was sniffling. Danny didn't say a word but stiffened, forcing Grace to grab his arm, when they entered the jail.

"Look what the cat dragged in," Danny said, bristling at the sight of Justin, who stood at the end of the hallway, looking darker, more dangerous, and very pissed.

"Watch your mouth," Justin growled.

"Or what?" Danny puffed out his chest, refusing to move when Grace took his arm, and squared off against his father. "What are you doing here anyway?"

"Working. What I want to know is what you are doing here."

"Who are you working on?" Danny turned, looking down at her with more arrogance and cockiness than he'd displayed outside the Kwik Mart. "This hot little number, here?"

Grace didn't care whose son he was. If this teenager thought he could mouth off in front of her like that, he had another thing coming. She twisted his arm behind his back and pushed his wrist up toward his shoulder blades, shoving him forward at the same time until he hit the wall.

"You ever speak like that around me again," she hissed, pushing his arm against his back as he growled and his cheek remained pressed against the wall, "I'll kick your ass. I don't care where we are or who is watching. Are we clear?"

"Dad, are you just going to stand there?" Danny's tone changed completely, probably after he tried pushing back against Grace and realized he couldn't.

"I'm waiting for you to answer the Lieutenant." Justin's tone was colder than ice.

"She's hurting me."

"Apologize. Promise to behave, and you can walk on your own to the holding cell." Grace didn't know what kind of family drama existed between these two, but it wasn't her place to care.

"My mom is the Mayor. You're going to regret treating me like this." Danny held on to his pompous attitude, although the punch in his words was gone.

"Apologize," she sneered.

"Daniel," Justin barked.

"I'm sorry. Crap. Where's my mom?"

Grace knew enough about dealing with teenage delinquents to know that was the best apology she would get out of him. Letting him go, she backed up and straightened her shirt, giving Danny time to compose himself and turn around. She turned the boy over to the officer working the jail and headed for the stairs. Justin followed her while Danny yelled behind them that he wanted his mother. Then for good measure he yelled that obviously his father didn't care about him at all.

"I'm sorry you had to deal with that," Justin said when she reached her desk.

Grace shrugged, noting the pain in his eyes that she doubted he'd share with her. It wasn't any of her business what his family life was like anyway. "Part of the job," she told him.

"You handled him very well."

"Thank you."

"Once he cools off I'll head down there and talk to him." Justin ran his fingers through tousled sandy blond hair. He looked at her with tortured green eyes. "I don't have the best relationship with my kids."

She wasn't sure what to say, other than that much was obvious. But seeing the intense pain swirling in his green eyes had her trying for some appropriate comment. "We raise them the best we can," she said, knowing it was true of her and her own daughter.

"You were tough and in his face, in spite of knowing he was my son," Justin said, his expression unreadable when he studied her with those green eyes of his. And with that windblown sandy blond hair, a slightly darker version of his son's, he maintained that dangerous persona that made the room grow warmer by the minute. "It's good to know you can handle yourself."

"You doubted that I could?" Grace saw through Justin immediately, that macho bad-ass lawman who believed the world wouldn't survive without him in it. "Let me tell you something, Reece," she sneered, feeling her heart pound in her chest and fueling the anger that suddenly surged to life inside her. She stabbed his rock-hard chest with her finger, immediately aware of how solid he was. "That teenage boy down there isn't the only type of male I can handle myself against."

Justin grabbed her wrist before she could pull her hand back and held it between them. His grip was solid, but the hard expression he maintained was suddenly fueled by the smoldering gaze that made his eyes appear to glow.

"We've all got hell in our pasts," he said, barely moving his mouth. "But you and I are about to descend into hell again, and we need to be ready."

"Don't think for a minute that because you know something about me that you shouldn't know you can make me submit," she hissed, knowing if she didn't settle down quickly her temper would take over and she'd make a scene.

"No one makes me submit. I run my own show, or there is no show."

"Grace, forcing a woman to submit isn't my style. If there isn't mutual interest to seeing it out until the end, there isn't anything." He pulled her hand closer to his chest. "And since I can tell by your face that you think I'm referring to sex, that applies to working together also."

"Grace Jordan." A tall, sharp-dressed woman with jet-black hair pulled back in an impeccable bun stopped sharply in the open doorway. "Well I'll be damned, look what the cat brought in. Up to your same old tricks, Justin?"

Justin turned, his body still wound tight, and didn't let go of Grace's wrist in spite of her effort to pull free of his grasp. "Sylvia," he said, his tone losing the fire it had held when he talked to Grace. "Hear I was in town and stop by to say hello?"

"Is my son okay?" Sylvia walked into Grace's office as if she owned the place. Ignoring Justin and the way he held Grace's hand, Sylvia stared at Grace with ice-cold blue eyes. "I heard you're the officer who booked him and left him in a holding cell. I know you're new on the force—"

"He's not hurt physically, if that's what you mean." Grace wasn't going to let anyone imply she'd bend the law because someone was the child of prominent citizens in this town, or citizen, since it was becoming more apparent as she met Justin's family that this was the first time he'd been in Rockville for a while.

"Good. The message I got scared me to death." Sylvia flashed a million-dollar smile. What was this woman doing in the heart of the Badlands? She'd fit right into D.C. "I'll go ahead and take him now if you'll release him to me."

"Ma'am, your son had a gun that wasn't licensed to him, and he attempted to rob the Kwik Mart." Grace watched penciled eyebrows narrow with her comment.

The lady turned and placed her hands on her very narrow waist. No way in hell would the million curls twisting around Grace's head ever cooperate the way Sylvia's perfect black hair did.

"Justin, I'm sure that in spite of never being around to watch your son grow up you don't want him behind bars." She pointed her perfect fingernail toward Grace. "You must have some say over this new lady cop here."

Dark green eyes stared at Grace and she swore her body temperature jumped several degrees. Unable to look away for a moment, she wasn't sure if she read disapproval or something else. Either way, he wasn't pleased. Justin's lips formed a thin line and his jawbone flexed when his gaze shifted to Sylvia and then to her.

He grew larger as she watched, muscles pressing against the very large polo shirt he wore untucked. He again wore comfortable-looking jeans but today sported cowboy boots, making his legs look even longer. Justin Reece was mouth-watering eye candy. Dear Lord. She couldn't believe she reacted to him like this.

"I'm not a cop in this town, Sylvia. You know that."

"Are you going to charge him?" Sylvia asked, bringing Grace out of her drool session.

There was no room for eye candy and sex appeal in her life today.

Grace walked around her desk and sat down. She would handle these two the same way she would talk to any distraught parents who'd just arrived because their child was in jail. The law was cut-and-dry and she'd handle the matter the same. Typing Daniel's name into the system on her computer, she kept her expression relaxed, refusing to let them see she struggled with the program Bosley had promised to explain to her and had yet to take the time to do.

Finally, Daniel Reece and his history with the legal system appeared before her. "Your son has been brought in on more than a few charges, but I noticed that he's never been convicted. All charges have been dropped every time." Grace tapped the monitor with her fingernail, feeling her confidence fall into place. She glanced up at Justin and Sylvia, who stood next to each other, both looking at her with very different expressions on their faces. She swore each stared at her completely unaware of the person standing next to them.

"Daniel showed me today that he's got little concern for the law."

Sylvia's jaw dropped and then she turned an accusing stare at Justin, who now rested his arm on the top of Grace's filing cabinet. He shifted his attention to his ex-wife but didn't say anything. The ghosts Grace had seen haunting him earlier over his children were no longer there. She wasn't sure if he were pissed as hell or simply allowing his ex-wife, who probably raised their children exclusively from the sounds of it, to call the shots.

"He's only fourteen," Sylvia said, sounding frustrated when she continued looking at Justin. Her tone changed to a sickeningly sweet drawl when she focused her glassy blue eyes on Grace. "If you'll kindly release him, I will see to his punishment at home."

Grace took a long drink from the water bottle on her desk, needing a moment to get grounded. Daniel's track record was enough to show her that the law in this town looked the other way when it came to the Mayor's son. Grace wanted to keep this job, needed the stability of a solid community that was nowhere near the ghosts that tortured her past so she could raise her daughter properly. If she made the wrong call here, she might never have the opportunity to nail to the wall the bastard who'd killed two young women in this community. And she really wanted that opportunity.

"Mayor, I may be putting my neck on the line here, but I was hired to maintain a low crime rate, and ensure we don't have repeated crimes by catching our guy the first time. When I was down at the Kwik Mart, the man working made the comment that your son had scared him to death. He also said that he's getting really tired of this. I realize I come from a different world where juvenile crime is a daily problem. You don't have a juvenile detention center, and hopefully you won't need one for a very long time, if ever."

"Where are you going with this?" Sylvia's voice lost all civility and turned to ice.

"Maybe I'm not going anywhere with it. I don't have the

final say." Grace sighed, and Sylvia gave her a triumphant smile as she turned to Justin.

"If I may," Grace added quickly, fearing the ground crumbled beneath her. "I've seen this before; in fact, I'm way too familiar with it. We have a young boy, who I'm sure is very intelligent, that's found a way to gain attention from his parents."

"What?" Sylvia turned around slowly, giving Grace a look to kill. "You are not going to leave him down there in that jail cell!"

"Let Grace finish what's she's trying to say." Justin spoke quietly, his baritone blood chilling. "Daniel is fine for the moment."

Sylvia moved gracefully and sat down in front of Grace. She crossed one leg over the other and allowed a fair amount of skin to show through the slit of her skirt. Perfect woman sat there and stared at Grace.

"How are you all too familiar with this?" Perfect woman was also ice woman.

"My father was an FBI agent," she began.

"I see," Sylvia interrupted. "Was he gone a lot?"

"Yes, he was."

"Did you like that?"

"I hated it."

Sylvia turned her head sideways and gave a triumphant look to her ex-husband. "Justin was never around to raise his children. He was gone off and on until we divorced two years ago, and this is the first I've seen of him since." She crossed her arms and gave Grace a knowing look. "Apparently, since Daniel is just his stepson, he doesn't care if he sits in jail and rots."

Not only did Justin look dangerous, as he continued leaning in the doorway, glaring at Sylvia's back; he looked pissed enough to attack. "Don't even begin to imply that you know, or understand, what feelings I have for our son," he growled under his breath.

No matter the personal affair between these two, Grace

fought like a son of a bitch to focus on her job. She ignored Justin's comment and fought to make her point.

"My mother was a criminal lawyer." Grace chose her words carefully. "She wasn't home much, either. Our teenage years were the hardest."

"Our?" Justin Reece raised an eyebrow. "I thought the only family you had was an uncle."

Grace didn't smile when it was obvious that erasing a lot of her ugly past on file had proved effective if an FBI agent couldn't pull up the complete truth on her. Maybe his comment when he first met her didn't go as deep as she feared. Justin might have slipped on a glimpse of the truth and, being the investigator that he was, he tossed out his comment about the White mansion just to see what kind of bite he would get. Grace cleared the speculation out of her head. She would worry about what Justin knew, or didn't know, later.

Sylvia dismissed his question with a wave of her hand. "So you ran wild as a teenager."

Sylvia nodded and gave Grace the once-over, as if by looking at her she could believe this to be the truth.

"Oh no, I didn't run wild," Grace said, and then met the Mayor's hardened gaze. "My brother was two years older. He got into a lot of trouble with the law. Of course, growing up in Washington, D.C., it wasn't as easy to bail him out of trouble all the time. But when the police called, or paged, or contacted secretaries, both my parents would do their best to get to the station as quickly as possible. It was practically the only time we saw them together."

"I get your point." Sylvia almost spit the words out as she stood up and moved toward the door. She reached out a perfect hand toward Justin's chest, and Grace looked down quickly, minimizing Daniel's file.

It didn't matter to her if the woman touched Justin. Just because he was gorgeous as hell and appeared to care about a boy whom he didn't actually father didn't mean that Grace was interested.

"What happened to your brother?"

Grace looked up and stared into Justin's green eyes. Something swelled deep inside her womb, and at the same time she swore she saw something smolder in his gaze. She looked down quickly and noticed her hands were clasped together and her knuckles white. Focusing on the sad memory barely helped cool her insides.

"He got into a fight when he was twenty. I remember both of my parents were home for a change. The fight was gang related, over drugs, or a woman—I don't remember. My dad went in after him. They were both shot and killed." It seemed a thousand lives ago. "Mom died a year or so after that in a hit-and-run."

Sylvia's head fell, and her hand caressed Justin's powerful chest. He still didn't touch her but did look at her. Bosley showed up behind them at that moment.

"I have the statement from the Kwik Mart employee." He spoke to Grace, but then something on Sylvia's face changed his tune. "Should I file it?"

Sylvia stormed out of the office and then turned in front of all of them. Grace stood, acknowledging the sinking feeling that she'd be going down to the holding cell to release Daniel.

"He can't have a criminal record, Justin." Sylvia's tone chilled the air. "That wouldn't look very good for my career." She raised an eyebrow, giving Justin a haughty look. "And if there is any decency in you, and you want to restore any relationship with your stepson, think carefully about what you say to that . . . that woman."

Grace came around her desk, ready to give this woman, Mayor or not, a piece of her mind.

"I'm not afraid of this, Sylvia. I say we send him in front of the judge this afternoon, and see if we can't get some kind of supervised probation, maybe some community service."

Sylvia grabbed a cell phone out of her purse. "I'm calling Todd," she said to no one in particular. "I don't need this from you right now." She glared at Justin and then over his shoulder at Grace. "I really don't need this. I am his parent, his only parent!"

Damn. If Grace exhaled, she was sure she would see her breath. Sylvia chilled a room like a pro.

Chapter 4

Justin pulled into the school parking lot shortly after five later that day. His '68 Chevelle Super Sport rumbled with a rich, powerful sound that invigorated him. Pulling her out of the garage earlier and hearing her purr and then getting her out on the road, feeling all that raw power, improved his mood tremendously. He watched a couple of parents walk out of the school with their children. Once, settling down and being a family man had appealed to him, even to the point of marrying a woman with a little boy already in tow. Sylvia had made that home life hell, though. One good thing about this case—possibly the only good thing—was that Justin would see his daughter again. He wouldn't dwell on how Sylvia fought to make him appear cold and heartless in front of Daniel. Soon, very soon, Justin needed to spend time with his son. He wasn't going to give up on Daniel that easily.

But Elizabeth, who was ten, never seemed to mind that her father was in and out of her life. If anything, his daughter appeared to love him unconditionally, something not even her mother could destroy.

Relaxing his hands on the steering wheel, Justin acknowledged the parents who showed up to grab their kids from the school care that was a new program implemented since the last time he'd been in Rockville. He'd give Sylvia this. She actively endorsed the working mother, of which there were quite a few in Rockville by the looks of the amount of children enrolled in the summer school care program.

Elizabeth hurried out of the school, her backpack flopping over her shoulder and one of her shoes untied. Spotting her father, she squealed loud enough to turn a few heads and ran to him, her grin broad and her cheeks flushed with happiness. At least one of his children was excited to see him. Justin got out of the car and met her on the other side of the street. Elizabeth wrapped her arms around his waist, hugging him fiercely while her backpack tried sliding off her arm.

"How's my beautiful baby girl?" He helped Elizabeth zip up her backpack, after confirming all her papers were neatly tucked away.

"Great." His ten-year-old daughter, with her mother's jet-black hair, pulled on her dad's arm. "You came home just in time, Dad. Come meet my new friend." She turned her head, still tugging at him. "Rachel, come here."

He looked up to see floppy red curls bounce in every direction as the young girl approached him. Rachel had her mother's smile.

"You're the FBI guy, right?" Rachel stood in front of him, ignoring a twisting curl that fell over one eye.

He nodded and smiled. "So you two are in the fifth grade?"

"Yeah, this place is great." Rachel looked at Elizabeth. "You're lucky to have a daddy to pick you up from school."

"He only does it when he's in town; then my mom picks me up the rest of the time. Why don't you have a daddy?" Elizabeth asked.

"Oh, I did. Everyone has to have a daddy or they can't be born." For a moment it looked like she might offer more education to his daughter than she might be ready for. "My dad died before I got a chance to remember him," she said, and then blew her curl out of her face. "For a while I thought these other people were my mom and dad. Then they made me leave the people who weren't really my mom and dad, and stay with my Uncle Charlie. It was called foster care, but I don't need it anymore because my new mom is with me all the time now. I don't think I'll ever get a dad, though."

Justin looked at the little girl standing in front of them. His background search on Grace confirmed she had never signed a birth certificate. Yet this little girl chatting so openly with him was the spitting image of Grace. There was history here not documented. He suspected the truth yet had no proof. Apparently, his incredibly intelligent daughter felt compelled to do his dirty work. He had no problem with that.

"You got a new mom and left your old mom?" Elizabeth narrowed her eyebrows, and he squatted down to their level, anxious to hear the answer.

"No. Well, yes. Daddy burned to death and these other people tried to say that they were my mommy and daddy. Grace, I mean Mom, had to become my mom so we could stay together." Rachel looked past Justin. "Mommy!" she squealed too close to his ear, and he guessed he deserved it.

But what had this girl said? Her father burned to death? Grace had to become her mother so they could stay together? The obvious stared him in the face. Almost always that's how it was.

Justin turned around to see Grace scoop the redheaded girl into her arms. She looked over her daughter's shoulder at him and absently blew a long curl out of her face. He couldn't help but smile. She was so beautiful; in fact, she got prettier every time he saw her.

But the little girl said Grace wasn't really her mother. Elizabeth continued chatting, and he fought to listen while his mind twisted around possible ways to gather the truth out of Grace. If her daughter was ten, like Elizabeth, she would have been born during the time period that was blank on Grace's personal file he'd read over before coming here. That would mean Grace had a child while being held captive in the White mansion. If that was the case, possibly she would have to fight to gain legal custody of her own daughter.

The mystery around Grace grew deeper and more intense the longer he knew her. And he loved a good mystery.

Justin studied the pile of collapsed boxes on the corner of Grace's front porch. A pink bicycle, with a basket hanging over the handlebars and reflective lights attached to the spokes, was locked and lying on its side. At the other end of the porch, a porch swing sat on the floor, waiting to be hung up.

Man's work, he thought, allowing a rush of male domination to fill his insides. Something about Grace brought out sensations in him that he had never experienced with another woman, and sure as hell not with Sylvia.

Justin glanced at the thick hooks already installed in the ceiling before turning his attention to the door again. He knew Grace was renting the place and that she and Rachel had stayed in a motel the first few nights she was here in Rockville before they were able to move in.

Grace was actually living in Rockville when Margaret Young was murdered. Justin knew Grace wanted everyone to see her as cool, calculated, and in control. He'd detected a softer side to Grace though, one he couldn't wait to explore further. It was a terrifying possibility that their killer held on to his first victim intentionally. Justin didn't understand yet why their perp wanted Grace to find both young women. Whether she would admit it or not, she needed protection.

Although it was a damned good idea to make sure the community knew he had his eye on her, Justin should probably do some serious self-evaluation to figure out why he had this urge to let her know he had his eye on her, too. Grace pulled something out from deep inside him, something more than a good hard boner.

He ran his hand through his hair and scowled at her front door. There was no way to see into the house through the closed curtains, which was good. He'd be the first to tell anyone that Rockville was one of the safest communities in the United States, but recently that had changed. He could imagine Grace would hand his head to him on a platter faster than Sylvia ever could if he suggested ways of keeping herself and her daughter safe. There wasn't any doubt in his mind that Grace believed she could take care of herself. And more than likely, under normal circumstances, she could. He rapped on the door, trying not to knock too loud in case her daughter was asleep.

They were working on this case together. And although ever since Sheriff Montgomery contacted the FBI it had been very quiet, he and Grace needed to spend more time brainstorming together, creating MOs, working up profiles, and going over forensic files to see if there were any matches online.

Justin tilted his head, trying ineffectively to see through the curtains covering the window next to the front door. There were lights on inside. Grace's car was parked out front. But no one came to the door. He turned, looking at his Chevelle parked behind her small gray Honda. Then, glancing back at the bungalow-style home, he focused on the single window at the other end of the front porch. More than likely it was a bedroom window. His boots created heavy thuds on the wooden planks in the porch floor as he walked to the other end of the porch. The other window was as well bound by curtains on the inside, blocking all view of any movement in the house.

Which was how it should be, he noted with frustration.

Grace wasn't intentionally not answering the door for him, was she?

Cowardly behavior didn't match the nature of her being as he'd seen it so far. His ex-wife had over half the town successfully cowering at the first sign of her, yet Grace took her on without hesitating. *Oh, hell yeah.* The other day when Grace had told Sylvia to leave Daniel in the holding cell and not run and baby him for robbing a Kwik Mart had turned Justin on more than it should have.

Grace's guts and drive to do her job thoroughly and without being bullied turned him on almost as much as thoughts of being buried deep inside her. Grace had a fiery temper and was motivated and determined to do what was right. No one confronted Sylvia, and Grace had put her in her place as if she did it every day. He'd wanted to pick her up and swing her around the middle of the station after Sylvia left—bend her over and devour that hot little mouth of hers. He hadn't gotten a damn thing done the rest of the day.

The woman was hot as hell. Again, he wondered what

possessed him that he'd consider creating a relationship of sorts with a partner on a case. But God, Grace would be one hell of a hot lover. Thoughts of stretching out alongside her, feeling every curve, caressing and tasting every bit of her, distracted him to hardness.

Justin returned to the front door and tried opening the screen. It was locked. So he rapped on the wooden part of the screen door a bit louder.

No woman ever climbed under his skin like this. Maybe knowing about her past did something to him, too. Although he didn't want to believe that was the case. But believing that underneath that tough no-bullshit shell of her lay a woman who was vulnerable and needed protection also really appealed to him. Her spirit was wild, just like her hair and her personality. Nothing held her back. She was damned near perfect.

In a way, Grace reminded him of his baby sister. Clare had carried that same enthusiasm toward life. And it made him want to protect Grace even more. He'd failed with Clare. But while he and Grace worked together to find their man, Justin would make damn sure she was safe at all times.

He raised his fist to knock again, this time harder, when suddenly the dark wooden door opened wide. There she stood, on the other side of the screen door, hair down, long ringlets falling almost to her elbows. She wore a long T-shirt and her slender legs were bare. She stood barefoot, her nipples hardening against her shirt as she stared at him with bright blue eyes, and slowly ran her tongue over her full lips. There were damp spots on her shirt, which made the material cling to her body.

Surprise and possibly suspicion glowed in her pretty eyes for the briefest of moments. Grace quickly raised her shields and her expression softened, turning neutral and not concerned that he had shown up at her home unannounced.

"Uh, Justin." Grace looked down quickly and pulled her hair back into a ponytail using a wrap she'd had on her wrist. "Hello."

Being alone with him made her wary, which proved his

hunch that there was an attraction there. He followed her to her dining room table, which was littered with files and copies of forms.

"What do you have here?" He was curious to see which files she thought took precedence.

"I didn't have an opportunity to look them over as carefully as I'd like today."

"I wanted to thank you for taking such a firm hand with my ex-wife. I wish she'd be that way with Daniel."

"I'm really sorry about your son." She didn't look up at him.

"He's my stepson, as I'm reminded on a daily basis, and thank you." He tried to keep his tone sounding relaxed, willing her to relax. The only time she did was when they discussed their investigation, which was why he had stopped by. Working alone with her, without fear of interruptions, would get her to drop her guard and allow him to make his next move. "Where is your daughter?"

She licked her lips before glancing down the hallway. "She's asleep. Has been for about an hour." When Grace pinned him with those baby blues, the warning in them couldn't be missed. "But she wakes up easily."

Justin nodded, hiding his smile. Grace knew he had come here to learn more about her and she let him in. They would discuss the case, although his hunch was they would either get a call on another dead body or it would be a few more days before someone screamed rape. Their murderer wouldn't systematically kill those girls and not keep strong repetition in the other aspects of his life. "What files do you have there?"

Her blue eyes glowed when she met his gaze, but then she looked away again. "I pulled files of any rapes in the state, and nationwide, that might match our MO. I tried working on it today, but Bosley insisted I go with him to the school and take turns playing crossing guard. He said it's good politics and will help smooth things over with the Mayor." She flashed him a haughty look. "Not that I care a bit about smoothing anything over with her."

"Is that so," Justin muttered, moving closer to the table and adjusting her laptop so he could see what she was doing. He glanced up when Grace edged away from him. When he did, she lifted her head, staring at him head-on with almost a challenge in her eyes. She was nervous about him being here and didn't want him to notice. "We won't be interrupted here, unless your daughter wakes up," he added, enjoying it when Grace's expression turned defiant.

She frowned. Then blinking, she nodded quickly. "I thought I'd call the lab tomorrow on some of these files. They're old, but there might be some loose ends."

Those pouting lips added to her sensuality. He ached to devour her, taste every inch of that hot, perfect body. Suddenly it was too warm in her dining room. Thoughts like that and she would kick him out just for the raging hard-on that would be noticeable any second now.

"Good thinking. I think we need to brainstorm more on commonalities here. If we can accurately nail the similarities, we'll know when he'll hit again."

"I don't think I like your pessimistic outlook. We don't want him to hit again," she snapped, her cheeks flushing and turning her eyes a bright, intense blue.

"Darling, we don't know enough to stop him. I know these horrendous acts are hitting you personally and—"

"You don't know shit," she hissed before he could finish his thought. "Don't think for a moment that because you managed to dig a little bit of dirt up on me it means a thing."

All of her defenses were up in full mode. Justin didn't doubt for a moment that she could handle herself, but there were monsters out there that even he would be cautious taking on alone. The only way he'd be able to work with Grace was if they established a few ground rules early in the game.

"What I know or don't know about you doesn't matter right now," he began quietly, moving toward her while he spoke. "What matters right now, Grace, is that you're running from me and you need to come to me if we're going to capture the asshole who is out there raping girls and destroying lives."

"I am not running from you," she hissed.

Justin moved closer and had to give Grace credit for digging in her heels and not taking another step backward. Although if she did, she'd be backed up against her wall.

He didn't praise her. It was the last thing she wanted out of him, and he sensed it. "You're working without me and we need to be doing this together. I'll head home, sit at my laptop, and we can discuss this over the phone if you prefer. Obviously you can't handle the sparks igniting between us when we're alone in a room together."

Justin turned and headed toward her door. He was sure she'd shut it behind him, let him leave without another word.

"I've made a complete list of things I want to check out tomorrow," she said hastily, walking out onto the porch with him.

Damn. Maybe he read her wrong. She was a gorgeous woman who had to deal with men coming on to her on a very regular basis. He'd guessed that with a past like hers, being abducted and abused, she hated men. It was a common aftereffect with women in her case. And that knowledge made him wonder if they could work together. Because there was one thing he was sure of: Being around her got him hard as hell. He wanted to explore that, not ignore it. Grace's zest for life, her determination to show him how independent she was, along with her distracting good looks, created a package he'd never found in a woman before.

He stopped before reaching the porch stairs and turned his back on the street, watching her. Her blue eyes were like sapphires in the darkness.

"Good. I want to hear about it." He breathed in her perfume, which wrapped around him like a sensual drug. "There's some gross similarities—"

"I know," she interrupted, her face suddenly glowing with excitement. All anger toward his cornering her, forcing her hand, and drawing her toward him vanished. "I've been racking my brain all day trying to figure out what patterns might lead us to knowing when he might strike again. I admit, though, I've gone over the reports of the two victims, trying to figure out what led him to them so I could eliminate those factors and prevent him from doing it again."

"That would mean eliminating every pretty girl in this town," Justin said quietly, understanding her idealistic way of thinking but needing her to see that it wasn't practical.

She made a face, then rolled her eyes. "Besides that factor," she grunted. "There's got to be something else about those two girls other than their good looks that made him go after them."

Justin reached for her, needing to touch her, feel that soft skin against his fingers. Her mouth formed a perfect circle and she sucked in a breath, never taking her gaze from his. When his fingers brushed over her smooth cheek, her lashes fluttered closed. A moment passed before she backed up and crossed her arms over her chest. He swore the breath she blew out was one of frustration.

"You're right," he offered, loving how her blue eyes were alive with desire when she shot him a quick look. "And we'll figure out what it is that he's after—together."

She nodded once and her expression changed at the same time he heard movement behind her. Grace turned as her screen door opened and a very sleepy-looking girl blinked at him.

"What are you doing out here, Mom?" Rachel asked, never taking her attention from him. "Why are you talking to Elizabeth's dad?"

"I'll be inside soon, sweetheart. Go back to bed," Grace said, reaching for her daughter's wild curls.

Rachel scowled. "I think you need to come inside now."

"I'll be inside in a minute."

"Fine. But I'm waiting on the couch for you," she said, her tone as fiery as Grace's was towards him a moment ago inside. "You know my father wouldn't like you being outside in the dark." Rachel turned, slamming the front door.

If this child had inherited her mother's temper, then he'd better watch out. Although earlier Rachel had said Grace wasn't her real mother. Maybe the child was confused. She was a mirror image of Grace.

"That must be hard on you," he said after the girl slammed the screen door shut and was gone.

"She doesn't remember anything about her father, which is a very good thing. I'm not sorry he's dead." Grace looked so powerful standing there before him—all five feet of her and maybe a few inches more. "But she's developing curiosities, and isn't happy when I refuse to describe her father as a saintly, perfect man."

That bit of information didn't surprise him in the least, that is, if his growing hunch was right. The truth around her daughter and their past wasn't documented anywhere. Rachel's age was right, though. And if Grace really was her mother, then all he could do was hope and pray that Grace told her daughter the truth and that her father really was dead.

"It's tough when your kids strike out at you." He watched Grace worry her lower lip, and when she didn't respond or look up at him he added, "I sure as hell don't have all of the answers, but from what little I've seen, and the raving report my daughter offered, you're doing a good job with Rachel."

"Thank you." She did look up at him then. "Where is your daughter?"

"With Sylvia tonight." He didn't want to discuss bouncing his daughter back and forth between parents. He was the one sauntering into town, and as much as he hated admitting it, he was grateful to Sylvia for letting him spend time with Elizabeth. "I can come back in an hour after you put her down."

"No," she said quickly, but when he was ready to argue, she pressed her palm over his heart. "It will be too late. I'll talk to you about all of this tomorrow."

"Promise not to run from me."

She scowled, and her sapphire eyes glowed brighter.

"And don't tell me you weren't running," he added quickly, and grabbed her wrist when she pulled her hand from his chest. For a moment he considered bringing her fingers to his lips, tasting her, even if just briefly. But in spite of the fact that Grace would dispute his charge, he wouldn't spook her further by moving too quickly. He held her hand between them, not letting go but not moving, either. "I'll be at the station in the morning. If you get a call, I'll ride along."

"That isn't necessary. We wouldn't be able to talk about the case if I end up working an accident or handling another civil or criminal matter."

He brushed his thumb down the side of her hand, noting how her skin was like silk, smooth and soft. Her gaze dropped to their hands and he caught her sucking in a breath.

"Yes, it is necessary." He squeezed her hand and then released it but cupped the side of her face to make her look at him. "We're going to get to know each other better, a lot better."

She didn't say a word, didn't breathe or move. He didn't think he terrified her. And he almost believed he'd intrigued the fiery redhead cop into being too stunned to strike out and attack.

"I'll see you tomorrow." He took the porch stairs two at a time, knowing he couldn't do anything else with her this evening.

Grace shook her head as she shut the door and leaned against it. *Why the hell had he just come over here? God.* And he had touched her. Worse yet, she'd wanted him to—no, ached for him to.

In all the years that had passed since she'd been forced to live with Master, under the same roof with a child who didn't know Grace was her real mother, and enduring torture and severe humiliation, she had never craved a man's touch. In fact, she despised it. What was it about Justin then?

"Will you tuck me in, Mommy?" Rachel asked, looking angelic as she sat on the couch.

"Yes, I will. But if you talk to me like that again, whether we're alone or around others, you will be punished, young lady. Now what do you say?"

"Nothing!" Rachel yelled, jumping up and running to her bedroom.

Rachel wouldn't ever know the horrors that had existed during the time of her birth. She wouldn't know that Grace was tortured, shared with others, and forced to do despicable acts. No one, not even Justin with his incredible sleuthing skills, would ever comprehend the nightmares associated with being spread-eagled, chained to the ceiling and floor, and left there, for any man to take, fuck, or do whatever he pleased with her. No one would know what she had felt, to truly give up on life yet be forced to continue living.

"Good God," she mumbled, shoving curls out of her face and pushing away from the door. "Get a grip on yourself."

She walked into the middle of her living room but then turned around quickly and hurried to lock her front door. Taking just a moment to peek out the window, she stared at where his car had been parked.

"Why was Elizabeth's dad here?" Rachel asked from behind her.

Grace swung around and then quickly put her hands on her hips, at that moment remembering Rachel mentioning her new best friend in school, Elizabeth. "We're working together on a case. You need to get to bed, though. Get moving. I'll tuck you in, but you won't get out of bed again," she said sternly. They could discuss Elizabeth and Justin later. "And you will apologize for the way you spoke to me in front of Special Agent Reece."

Rachel didn't say anything. It was harder for Grace's daughter to apologize than it was for her to remember to make her bed. Grace knew she should probably force her daughter to utter the words, but she wanted sincerity out of her, not recited lines that would get her out of trouble.

"Go get ready for bed. I'll be in to tuck you in soon."

Rachel turned toward the hallway but then stopped, slowly looking over her shoulder. "I think Mr. Reece likes you."

"Go to bed," Grace said, although she couldn't manage a stern tone.

After sitting with Rachel in her new bedroom and talking about school, she climbed into bed, Grace turned off the overhead light and turned on the small lamp by her daughter's bed. As she kissed her beautiful child good night and got a tight, hard, firm embrace for her effort, Grace prayed for the millionth time that Rachel wouldn't hold any of the nightmares from the early years of her life. If Rachel had ever witnessed anything, she never uttered a word about it. Finally leaving her room, Grace walked barefoot into her bedroom.

She tore off the long T-shirt that almost fell to her knees and pulled a flannel nightgown over her head. After making hot tea, she sat down and stared at her simple bedroom. There was a time when she honestly never thought she'd be here.

If it took the rest of her life, she would pull one scumbag after another off the streets. She had to do it. For all women out there who endured abuse like she did, Grace had to see that they got to witness their aggressors suffering and paying for their crimes. Grace never got that privilege. But other women would. She would see to it.

"Good morning, lady," Bosley said, in between chomps of a donut. "Do you drink coffee?"

"Yes, please." Grace smiled, accepting the steaming mug.

"Donut?" he asked, lifting the lid to show her the variety of pastries.

"No thanks." She glanced at Christy and then over at Justin.

Grace's blue eyes were exceptionally bright this morning, contrasting beautifully with her thick curly red hair that she'd managed to confine with a black clasp at the back of her head. Already several strands bordered her face. She wasn't in uniform but instead wore clean blue jeans that hugged her hips. A wide black belt accentuated how narrow her waist was. And the knit short-sleeved sweater she had on stretched over her breasts, offering a mouthwatering view. As conservative as he could tell she tried to dress, she was a knockout, and if he stared at her much longer, he'd be harder than stone.

"I want to gather more information on Margaret and April," she said, looking past Bosley toward him.

"Was there a problem with the information on the reports?" Bosley asked, stealing her attention from Justin.

"No. Not at all." She smiled easily at Bosley. "But we have one girl who had everything going for her and another girl who barely made it through high school and then apparently wasn't doing much with her life. There's got to be more common interests between the two. So far all I'm seeing is they were both eighteen and pretty."

"Maybe those are the commonalities we are looking for," Justin offered, ignoring Christy and Bosley when they gave him their attention and keeping his gaze pinned on Grace. "I know they're very common factors and you're aching to narrow it down to something more unique. The sad truth might be that is all he's looking for, young and pretty."

"Lovely," Grace groaned. "There's no way I can protect every eighteen-year-old pretty girl in Rockville, is there?"

"Remember, though, Rockville is a small town. Honestly, there might not be that many pretty eighteen-year-olds left around here," Bosley said. "But if you put the word out that girls that age need to be watched, you'd be surprised at the reaction in the community. We stay on top of each other's business. You might take that into consideration when you have company over after-hours."

Grace looked up quickly, her eyes opening wide while her lips parted in surprise. Bosley straightened, rocked up on to his toes, and then turned, walking out of the station without saying good-bye.

"Got to love small-town life," Justin mumbled, and moved quickly to follow Grace into her office before she could close the door on him. "How's it going?"

"Okay," she answered. "But it sounds like you'd better stay at arm's reach from me at all times, or the gossipmongers in this town are going to go nuts."

Justin leaned forward, putting his hand over hers. "Or we could have sex and really give them something to talk about."

Grace's phone buzzed and she jumped visibly, then yanked her hand out from underneath his, cursing under her breath as she answered it. Her blue eyes were on fire when she glared at him, although somehow he didn't get the impression that she was as pissed at him as she was at herself for jumping when the phone rang.

"Ten four," she said after a moment. Her expression changed quickly, as she hurried around her desk. "Write down the directions for me. I'll head out now."

"What's up?" Justin asked, standing and moving in front of her when she tried heading out of her office.

"We've got a teenage girl who is MIA. I'm heading over now to talk to the parents."

"I'm going with you," he decided, and didn't balk when she frowned at him. "Don't tell me you're not strong enough to handle idle gossip."

"You don't want to find out how strong I am," she whispered, her tone deadly and loaded with a challenge.

Justin might have to disagree with Grace on that one. He couldn't wait to find out how strong she was.

Chapter 5

Ed and Janelle Straus lived in a ranch-style house on a well-manicured street on the edge of town. The house stood in stately silence as if years of family pride refused to allow it to appear lacking when confronted with such an atrocity. Crisply painted black shutters bordered the windows facing the street, and bushes trimmed in perfect squares gave an impeccably clean appearance. Grace prayed that no ghastly crime was actually committed here. Many times missing teenagers showed up unharmed and embarrassed that forgetting to check in with their parents could result in the police being contacted.

Grace had a fair amount of experience dealing with distressed parents. Janelle Straus was beside herself over the disappearance of her daughter. Her entire body seemed to shiver uncontrollably as she guided Grace into the kitchen.

"This just isn't like her," she moaned for the tenth time since Grace arrived. "Something's just not right."

Grace relaxed in a well-cushioned swivel chair and stared at the handful of pictures the Strauses had produced of their missing daughter. She brushed her fingers over each one, spreading them around over the glass kitchen table.

There was Vicki Straus' class picture, showing a girl with blond hair parted neatly down the middle and flowing like gold over her shoulders. A perfect picture of well-bred innocence sang through like a mockingbird. Next Grace ran her fingers over the family picture, where everyone sat poised stiffly in their Sunday best. She then sifted through a handful of snapshots showing a teenage girl whose beauty glowed in her toothy smile in shot after shot. All showed a very pretty teenager with long blonde hair and a body Grace would have died for at the age of seventeen.

"The last time you saw her was when she left for a Spirit squad practice." Grace reviewed her notes. "And that lets out around eleven thirty?"

"She's always belonged to several clubs." Janelle Straus focused on her hands. "On Tuesdays and Thursdays she comes home from work early and heads over to the high school to help with Spirit practice over the summer. This is her senior year coming up and she's doing a lot of extracurricular and club work before the school year starts to help on her applications for scholarships for college." There was so much pride in Janelle's voice. "No one knows where she is," she added, her voice cracking.

"Vicki is a very responsible young lady. We've never had any reason to worry about her." Ed Straus shot a glance at his wife. Wearing a pin-striped black suit and with silver hair brushed back to hide a bald spot, he fought to maintain dignity and failed, looking across the room as his voice quavered. "She's never disobeyed curfew or come home late for any reason without calling."

"How was she supposed to get home?" Grace asked. "Does she have a cell phone on her?"

"She borrowed my car," Janelle spoke up. "It's missing, too."

"We've called her cell phone over and over again." Ed looked up at his ceiling, sucking in a breath. "It keeps going to voice mail."

Justin called in the information while Grace took down the make of the car, a silver Dodge Aries, and jotted down the girl's cell number as well as the cell phone service they used.

"Any names of close friends, boyfriends, even boys she liked?" Justin asked when he got off the phone.

"Vicki has so many friends," her mother began. When

Mr. Straus named a few, his wife chimed in with more names.

"Good," Justin reassured them, standing over Grace's shoulder while she jotted down the last of the names. "We'll talk to these kids."

Grace closed her notebook and stood, trying to give Janelle a reassuring smile. "We'll find your daughter."

"Find her alive." Ed Straus' expression was pinched with worry. "She's eighteen, with her whole future ahead of her. Some monster has no right to rob her of that."

Grace walked out the door in silence, barely noticing when Justin held her car door for her. She'd been eighteen when a monster had robbed her of her life. And for five years he had forced her to keep living without it. Had anyone voiced those words to police officers after she disappeared? Or would she have been more like Margaret Young, also eighteen with her whole life ahead of her, but with a family who didn't bother to report her missing because it didn't cross their minds that she might be until it was too late?

"What are you thinking?" Justin rested his hand on the steering wheel of his F-150 pickup truck.

Grace quit chewing her lower lip and focused on roped muscle that stretched down Justin's bare arm. "All three of them had their life ahead of them," she mused, not really answering his question.

Meeting his gaze, she could tell that he knew that.

"We're ahead of the game this time." He reached over and squeezed her hand. The warmth from his touch scorched her flesh and sent tingles rushing up her arm and then straight down her body. "Now to figure out when he plans on killing her."

She stared at Justin, not bothering to move her hand while pressure swelled fiercely between her legs. Aware of her reaction sitting so close to him in the confined quarters of the cab, she also heard his words.

"April Monroe died on a Sunday. Do you think we have that long?"

"It's Thursday." He didn't elaborate. But then there was no point. No one but their killer knew his next move.

Grace would find out, though. They would find Vicki before Sunday. Another girl wouldn't endure the hell Grace had lived through.

Rockville had one high school. It didn't take longer than her phone call to Christy to check in before they reached the school parking lot. After a brief wait in the school office, Miss Cunningham, the girls' PE teacher and Spirit Club coach, strolled through the glass door, wearing shorts and sporting a cute ponytail that curled under at her neck.

"Well, they all left the gym together." Miss Cunningham brushed short fingers over her brown hair. "She runs with the same girls most of the time."

Grace jotted down the names. They matched the ones the Strauses had given her.

"I don't think they hung out in the parking lot for too long, maybe five minutes or so." Miss Cunningham chewed her lower lip, shrugging. "I'm sorry I didn't pay closer attention."

"Did you see anyone in the parking lot, or in the gym, that you didn't know?" Justin asked.

"No, it was just the girls." Miss Cunningham shook her head. "It's a real shame. Some of the girls here, if they didn't come home, I'd suspect they were up to no good. Vicki, though . . ." She made a clucking sound with her tongue. "She's a good girl, spending her summer working and on extra-curricular activities. I'm afraid to say it, but I suspect foul play."

Grace knew better than to say she suspected the same thing. Worry and panic in a community quickly turned to hysteria. Best to stay calm and do her job quietly.

"Let's return to the station and make some phone calls," Justin said when they walked through the parking lot back to his truck.

Grace was all too aware of Justin next to her while they drove to the station and then in her office, where he leaned against the edge of her desk, helping with the phone calls to parents of Vicki's girlfriends.

No one had seen Vicki, but all thought it was an incredible shame. More than once, Grace heard a parent say they feared the worst. It wasn't like Vicki to simply disappear without telling someone.

"Grace?" Christy called from the outer office. "Sheriff Montgomery is on line two for you."

Running one hand through already-tousled curls, Grace reached for the phone.

"I need you to come out to County Road Five, just three miles from town," he said. "What kind of car do the Strauses drive?"

"Vicki was in a silver Dodge Aries."

"Well, I can't confirm the color, but this is definitely a Dodge Aries." The Chief's voice sounded very serious and reserved. Something was terribly wrong. "The car's burned to a crisp," he added quietly.

"Let's go," she told Justin, grabbing his arm before giving it any thought. "They've found a car that matches the Strauses' car outside of town. It's burned to a crisp."

"Where is it?" Justin asked, right behind her when she hurried to the dispatch counter.

"Three miles out of town on County Road Five." She stopped at the doors to the station and looked into Justin's deep green eyes. "Do you know how to get there?"

"Yup." He reached over her and pushed open the door, then rested his hand on her shoulder as they left the station. Obviously he'd forgotten about keeping her at arm's length.

Two firemen poked through the inside of a charcoaled vehicle as they walked up to the scene. Pulling on latex gloves, she held them over her nose, inhaling the plastic scent. It wasn't strong enough to block out the hideous odors surrounding her.

For a moment she was rushed back ten years to another fire. The flames sprouted up around her, singeing her eyebrows and making her flesh burn. She clutched a small baby in her arms and felt the sweat trickle down her flesh, making her itch furiously, as she held her daughter to her and prepared to run for her life. And for a second, as fire burned menacingly closer, eager to consume Grace in its wrath, Master glared at her, forbidding her to move. He wanted them both to die that day, or at least her and her daughter.

"We were called to the scene just over an hour ago." The fireman who had spoken earlier walked up to them, glancing at his watch and then squinting at the car.

The firemen doused the fire before they arrived. And their efforts left flattened grass and soaked ground after it was sprayed to stop the fire. She avoided large puddles, although her shoes were obviously not waterproof. Water sloshed between her toes in her socks as she hunched over on soggy ground and peered into the backseat, or what was left of it. Any evidence on the ground around them or the field off the side of the highway had been washed away. An unfortunate necessity to keep the fire from spreading.

"So there are neighbors who saw the fire?" She studied the length of the road, seeing nothing but rugged rocky ground.

"Folks down the road reported smoke."

Justin moved toward them, snagging her attention. "Got everything you need, Roger?"

"I think so." Roger frowned at Grace.

"The tags are melted off the car, but I'd say we've got a good chance of this being the Strauses' car." Justin spoke from behind her. "Can you think of any reason why he'd burn it?"

"It's a message," she mused. "He's letting us know he's got Vicki."

"Agreed." Justin stood next to her, squinting down the road. "But why burn the car? What is he telling us?"

Grace noticed something on the ground and walked over to her car for a Baggie and tweezers.

"Find something?"

She picked up a half-smoked cigar and dropped it into the bag.

"Another message?"

Grace stared at his rugged face, feeling his frustration. The brightness of the day helped outline his strong cheek-

and jawbones. When he dropped his gaze to hers, the swelling she'd felt in his truck returned with a vengeance.

"There were burn marks on the other victims," he said, searching her face.

There was no point in dwelling on the burn mark on her. "Starkey hasn't called yet confirming the cause of the burns."

"I'm running the tests through our system," Justin told her, meaning the FBI. "We'll get results a lot faster that way. I'm going to run all tests through our guys from now on. We need answers faster."

"Must be frustrating at times working with such ill-equipped law enforcement," she said, the small part of her that had always wanted to move beyond being just a cop feeling envious over his connections.

"I don't see anything ill equipped around me," he said, his gaze burning into hers.

"Oh." She turned, focusing on the cigar in the Baggie as she headed to his truck.

"Might be able to pull a print off that," he said, following her.

"Hey, we're through here," Roger yelled from the fire truck.

Justin nodded. "We'll catch you later."

Grace looked up quickly, realizing she and Justin would be alone together out in the middle of nowhere in a matter of seconds. She dropped the Baggie on the passenger seat and then grabbed the notebook she'd used all day. The best thing to do was keep their conversation on business.

Or we could have sex and really give them something to talk about.

Having sex with Justin wasn't an option.

Justin watched the fire truck head out down the highway. "Do you think the cigar is a message, too?"

"It could be," she said. She worried her lower lip between her teeth to distraction. A dark smudge of soot smeared her cheek. He itched to wipe it from her. The sun caused her hair to glisten like dark rubies. "Maybe he's helping us see that he's the man who killed the other two girls."

Grace backed away from the car and wiped off her now-dirty uniform. White dust from the fire retardant foam the firemen used was all over the front of her. She brushed off her shirt and her arms, then lower, stroking her thighs. His muscles ached from forcing himself not to move. And his brain had a field day imagining his hands on her instead.

"The question now is where he is taking them." She glanced up and flashed baby blues that looked cold as ice. "If he kills every Sunday, we've got a few days to find her."

"Why would he choose Sunday?"

"It's a day of rest for the Lord. If he's the Antichrist, maybe it's the day he works." She offered a dry laugh, but something in her eyes showed she bought into her own theory.

Justin moved closer and reached for a curl that was sprung tight alongside her face. "How do we track the Antichrist?"

"He was right here earlier today," she mused, lifting her gaze slowly to meet Justin's. Her eyes were exceptionally blue today and her voice a bit huskier than usual.

"We hit the houses here on this road, see if anyone paid attention to the cars that drove by today," he said quietly, watching how her hair curled tightly around his finger as he toyed with it. The sun reflected on her red curls, which were soft, like expensive silk, and made her strands glow like rare rubies. She was a class act, and standing this close to her affected her strongly enough that he swore he saw her breath come faster, at the same time he was aware her mind churned, plotting and speculating on their next move. "And we hit the streets, questioning everyone, whether they knew these girls or not, about anyone who seems to be acting out of character."

"Leaving no rock unturned," she finished for him.

"Before we head out, there is something I need to get out of the way before it distracts me any further."

She met his gaze before he finished his sentence. Her lips were parted and he took his opportunity. Lowering his mouth to hers, he brushed his lips against hers. She tasted perfectly sweet and enticing. His cock was harder than steel in an instant, and every inch of him stiffened. But he couldn't stop the kiss. In fact, his hand moved behind her head and he adjusted her and deepened the kiss. As he dipped deep into her moist heat, a growl escaped him when her tongue danced around his. Not only did she respond to the kiss, but when her fingers ran up his arms to his shoulders sparks ignited inside him that created even a stronger urge to do more than just kiss her. A hell of a lot more.

A car drove by and honked and Grace jumped, whimpering as she lowered her face. Justin turned to see the back of the car before it disappeared but didn't recognize it. Returning his attention to Grace, he focused on the way her curls twisted beautifully into the clasp confining her hair behind her head. When he stepped back, the view was beyond perfect. Her hair was slightly tousled, with more curls falling loose around her face, and her lips were wet and slightly swollen.

She licked her lips and then brushed her fingers over her mouth.

He gripped her chin, tilting her head so she'd look at him. "We're not done," he informed her.

"Oh." She cleared her throat and then pulled away, turning and hugging herself as she hurried to his truck.

Grace's insides were in a frenzy, her entire body tingling, as she walked alongside Justin up the gravel drive to the second farmhouse on the road where the Strauses' car had burned.

"I don't think the same folks live here that did when I used to drag race up and down this road as a kid." Justin seemed too cheerful, relaxed and all business, when he rapped on the door to the ranch-style home set off the road.

A tall, lanky kid looked wide-eyed at Justin's badge when he answered the door and then retreated into his house to produce his mother, a stout middle-aged woman with gray hair.

"Can't say that we saw anything," she informed them, looking warily from Justin to Grace as she stood on the stoop outside her front door.

Grace's emotions were in as much of a flux as her body was when she nodded her appreciation and headed back to the truck with Justin. By the time they'd reached the fourth house, on the opposite side of the road and closest to town, she had forced herself to focus on work and not on how the air between her and Justin continued to sizzle as he stood next to her waiting for someone to answer the door.

"Looks like no one is home." Justin's eyes were exceptionally dark when he turned from the door and searched her face.

Grace stepped off the front porch first, walking across the yard to the drive where Justin's black truck was parked. She looked toward the back of the house and the large detached garage that had its garage doors opened. Sounds of someone working grabbed her attention and she gestured that way.

"Someone is back here," she said, heading that way and more than aware of Justin on her heels.

His body brushed against hers and then his large hand gripped her shoulder, slowing her pace and causing the simmering heat inside her to skyrocket when he eased her to a stop outside the garage.

"Anyone here?" he called out, keeping her by his side. "No reason to startle the natives," he whispered near her ear.

"Hello?" a deep, bellowing male voice echoed inside the garage.

"Excuse me, we've got some questions," Justin called back.

An older man with a potbelly and overalls appeared from the darkness of the garage, carrying a red rag that he wiped his hands off on. There were smudges of grease and dirt on his arms and face, and as he approached it was clear he could use a good shower.

"Who are you?" The man rubbed his round chin, which was covered with more than a day's worth of whiskers.

Two small boys came darting out of the garage, and then an older girl, possibly in her late teens, appeared slowly, holding on to the shadows, as she also used a red rag to wipe her hands. Under the dirt and grease it appeared possibly she could be a pretty girl.

"FBI, sir." Justin flashed his badge.

It never ceased to amaze Grace how those three letters, *FBI*, could silence anything and everything around them. The older man halted in his steps, gawking at the badge and then slowly shifting his attention to Justin and then Grace. The girl balked in the shadows, also freezing in her steps, and the two young boys stopped in their tracks, staring wide-eyed up at the two strangers.

"We'd like to ask you a couple questions," Grace said, grabbing everyone's attention. "Possibly you saw someone haul a Dodge Aries, silver, along this highway earlier today?"

"The one that burned up down the road?" The girl suddenly appeared animated as she walked out of the shadow.

Her father, or whoever he was to her, held his hand out and she stopped in her tracks. "What do you want to know about it?" he asked gruffly.

"We want to know who put it there," Justin said, his tone just as harsh.

The man nodded, obviously appreciating Justin's serious tone, as he once again rubbed his whiskers. "Don't know who it was," he said slowly.

"So you saw something?" Grace prompted, glancing around the yard and then toward the highway behind them. There was a decent view for a stretch of the road from the garage.

"Daddy said that Buick couldn't tow that Aries," the girl said, stepping closer to her father.

"Don't you have work to do?" the man snapped at his daughter, who immediately retreated into the garage, disappearing from sight. He turned to Justin, his look hard. "I don't know who put that car there," he said. "What do you want him for?"

"Abandoning a car that could have caused more damage to land around here with that fire if someone hadn't reported the smoke for one thing," Justin said.

"The FBI don't come in just because some car burned." The stout man rubbed his whiskers again and shifted his attention to Grace, giving her the once-over. "You two are investigating some crime that you can't tell me about, aren't you?"

"Pretty much," Grace said. "And anything you can tell us about that Buick that towed that Dodge out here would be appreciated. Color? Year? Obviously you're good enough with cars to know those details."

The guy puffed out his chest and rubbed his palms down his hips while squinting at the road behind them. "If you ask me, he probably blew out the transmission towing it without lifting the wheels off the road. Not sure where he wanted to take it. And I didn't recognize the Buick. But it was dark blue, later model, '98, I'd say. Not the right kind of car to be towing another one, even something as small as that Aries. But there are fools born every minute."

Grace turned to stare at Justin's profile when they turned off the highway. "Isn't that the way back into town?"

"We're not going into town just yet." He didn't look at her and his masculine profile remained all business when he slowed again and turned onto a gravel road. "Are you in a hurry?"

"It depends. Where are we going?" She stared at the brick two-story home buried behind hills and trees from the road.

"My house." Justin parked in front of the house on a circular drive and turned off the engine. Then hopping out, he glanced back into the truck when she didn't move. "I can get a lot more accomplished here on my computer system than we can down at the station. You coming?"

Grace followed Justin into his home, lowering her gaze to

his hard, firm-looking ass when he paused to punch in the buttons for his security system. For the most part she imagined folks around here didn't bother much with home security. But Justin, who probably wasn't here much and was a special agent working with the FBI, his security system made sense.

Justin headed into his kitchen, offered her a bottled water and took one for himself, then headed up the stairs. In the hallway, which obviously led to several bedrooms, Grace paused, edging toward the doorway Justin had entered.

"This is your bedroom," she said.

His brooding expression didn't help soothe the fire he'd left burning inside her when he kissed her. If he thought kissing her would help eliminate a distraction so they could focus on work, she hoped it worked for him, because it sure as hell didn't work for her.

"My computer is in my bedroom." He didn't elaborate or continue looking at her but instead focused on his screen. " 'A late-nineties blue Buick' doesn't tell us squat," he mumbled after a minute.

Grace entered his room, brushing her damp palms on her pants, and moved behind him, all too aware of his broad, muscular shoulders and how strong he'd felt when she'd run her fingers up his arms earlier. But when she shifted her attention to the computer screen, her heart stilled. Her father and uncle didn't spend as much time on the Internet when they were agents, but nonetheless, the formality of the site, the logo at the top, the address, all brought back the reality of the moment.

"What are you doing?" she asked, the silence lingering between them making her more and more uncomfortable.

Not to mention the thoughts that popped into her mind, which did a good job of dousing the smoldering need that had raced rampant through her system a moment ago. She wasn't sure why it didn't hit her before. An FBI man was no man to get involved with, at any level. Regardless of whether he had a home here or not, she already knew he wasn't here much and would more than likely be gone as soon as this case was solved.

"Sending a quick e-mail," he said, typing as he spoke. "I'm sure I'll get a phone call as a result of it."

"Okay." She glanced around his room and then walked across it toward pictures in frames arranged on his dresser.

Most were snapshots that he'd framed, and she squinted at pictures of two young children and then a variety more of his son and daughter at different ages. She leaned in, studying a family portrait of a younger Justin, with Sylvia next to him and two nicely dressed children, all posed and smiling for the camera. It didn't surprise Grace that Justin hadn't bothered removing the picture of his ex-wife. More than likely he didn't bring many women here. Because he was seldom here.

"I never bothered to move those," Justin said behind her. "Honestly, I'd forgotten they were there."

Grace tried not looking surprised when she spun around, hating that she hadn't realized he'd moved from the computer. She grabbed a wisp of hair before it fell into her face, hating her ridiculous curls that if she were smart she'd chop off and be done with.

"That says something about you," she said, and edged around him toward the door.

Justin took her hand and pulled the loose curls from her fingers, preventing her from moving and also stepping into her space. "What does it say about me?"

She tilted her head to meet his gaze and forced herself to remain cool, indifferent to that incredible body so close that he practically brushed against her. "Either you don't pay attention to your surroundings or possibly you still wish your family was here."

"Both are partially true," he uttered, his mouth barely moving while he appeared to be devouring her with his eyes. "Something else is true as well."

"What's that?" She backed away from him, but he tightened his grip on her hair and then ran his fingers deep into her curls.

"It's impossible to be around you and not want you."

"Then maybe we shouldn't put ourselves in settings like this." Her mouth was suddenly dry when she realized she would have to fight to be free of him or relax and let him do what he wanted.

She wasn't sure she liked either option. Testing the waters, though, she turned, trying to walk out of his grasp.

Justin not only grabbed ahold of her hair on the side of her head; he also took her shoulder and pushed her against the wall. "I doubt it would make a difference," he growled before pouncing on her mouth.

The amount of heat that pooled between her legs made her forget her concerns about what, if any, relationship might grow between them. She didn't focus on why, after ten years of avoiding aggressive men, predominantly because they didn't appeal to her, Justin's sexually demanding nature created a fire inside her she feared only he could put out.

He pressed into her, making it impossible for her to move with his feral body on one side of her and the wall on her backside. But when he slid his hand between them and cupped her pussy through her pants, Grace jumped, gasping into his mouth.

"You're on fire down here," he hissed, and nipped at her lip. "Let me see how wet you are."

"I don't think," she gasped, letting her head fall back when he created a hot trail of nibbles and licks down her neck. "I mean it would be better—"

"We'll focus on facts with the case, not between us," he told her, the words swimming around in her head and not quite registering.

He had skills. Damn good ones, too. Her jeans were unzipped before she realized it and his fingers eased inside, driving her nuts with the slow, torturous path they traveled before reaching the source of her heat. When he spread her open with two fingers and then a finger pressed against the nub that already swelled with more need than she could handle, Grace cried out.

"Easy, sweetheart." His growl was almost a deadly purr.

Heat rushed over her body, yet she shivered, trapped but for some reason not panicking. She blinked, fighting the urge to ride his hand. The reservations she had dwelt on minutes ago seemed to fade too damned quickly as he applied his seductive moves on her. Worse yet, she liked it. Loved how his body felt against hers, the way muscles rippled under his tan flesh.

"Don't fight coming for me."

Grace focused on his face. Her lips were dry from breathing so heavily through her mouth, and she licked them, feeling a surge of control when his gaze dropped to the action.

"Trust me, my dear," she purred, proud of her sultry tone. "You'll know when I'm fighting you."

"You're not going to fight me." He pulled on the clasp holding her hair back and red curls tumbled around her face.

"I will if you force me to." She gritted her teeth together, fighting to keep her wits about her while his fingers got her wet and then spread her cream over her tender folds. "You can't keep me pressed against this wall all day."

"Now there's a tempting thought." He looked like he liked the way her curls fell in disarray over her shoulders. "But I have another idea."

"What?" She was worried she didn't want to know when his eyes turned dark as night.

But when he moved, stepping away from her so that she almost stumbled forward, and let his hand slip free of her jeans, Grace didn't have time to master control before he gripped the waist of her jeans and yanked them down.

"You are not going to fuck me!" She grabbed his shoulders but ended up simply holding on when he slipped to his knees in front of her.

No man had ever knelt before her in her life. Such a servile position, yet there wasn't a bit of doubt in her mind Justin still controlled the moment. He put his face between her legs, spreading her open with his fingers, and then devoured her like a starving man.

"God damn," she cried, digging her fingernails into his flesh and bracing herself.

He pushed her so close to the edge she couldn't form a single thought. His tongue did magic she didn't know was possible. Over the past ten years, her sexual encounters had been limited at best. For the most part, the men she dared spend time with did little for her sexually. And now she understood. Being able to manipulate a man, conquer him and make him obey, did nothing for her, yet that was all she allowed in any relationships she attempted. Grace was positive that any man who was too headstrong, dominating, and aggressive would bring forth the nightmare of her past that she wanted nothing to do with.

She didn't ask for Justin. Even now, as he stroked her flesh, dove into her heat, and lapped at her cream, she wasn't sure allowing this to happen was such a good idea. At the same time, there wasn't an ounce of resolve in her strong enough to demand he stop.

Not to mention, as he caressed her moist flesh, tantalized and tortured her senses, he created sensations she wasn't used to. The swelling continued, growing and throbbing until she couldn't stand it any longer. She would explode, fall apart and lose control. That wasn't an option.

"Justin," she hissed, dragging her fingers up his neck to his hair and then grasping the sides of his head. "No. I can't."

She pushed him away from her, struggling against the confines of her pants. When she teetered to the side, though, he gripped her ass and buried his face in her flesh. He growled, uttering something she didn't quite catch. Her world turned hot, colorful, while the pressure inside her exploded with a ferocity she couldn't control.

"No!" she screamed, fearing the worst as she pushed with all her strength against his head.

Justin moved with unbelievable speed, standing and catching her as she tumbled forward, her insides exploding with an array of color and a flood of heat that soaked her down her thighs.

"You're okay, sweetheart," he said, his voice unbelievably calm.

He lifted her into his arms, carrying her to the bed and then sitting, adjusting her on his lap and cradling her. "I do believe that might be the first time you've ever had a real orgasm."

Chapter 6

Justin had heard Grace say she wouldn't let him fuck her. He didn't doubt for a minute he could persuade her to do so. And as rock-hard as his cock was right now, burying himself deep inside that soaked, tight pussy of hers sounded better than taking his next breath. He wouldn't push her, though.

The way she lay in his arms, damn near lifeless after exploding like she did, taking his time and showing her the true pleasures of lovemaking would be worth every tortured minute he put himself through.

"Stay here," he said, sliding her out of his arms, although he ached to keep holding her. "I'll be right back."

Taking a moment to glance at how she fell back on his bed, those gorgeous curls of her tumbling past her shoulders, made it even harder to walk away from her. Which didn't make sense. He was the pro, helped write the fucking book and had the T-shirt on how to walk away from women.

Even when he made it to the bathroom and closed the door, splashing cold water over his face repeatedly didn't do shit to soothe the burning craving that seared his insides and damn near scalded his senses so that all he could think about was Grace. He should go back in there and fuck her, devour that hot pussy of hers some more, rip her clothes from her body, and savor every inch of her.

"Crap," he growled, water dripping down his neck when he straightened and reached for a towel. His cock still burned with fierce pain in his jeans.

Grace was so in his system he wouldn't be able to work this case properly if he didn't get a grip. And no one, nothing, stopped him from conducting his investigation. Heaving out a heavy sigh, he scrubbed his face with the towel, forcing his thoughts onto the case.

It wasn't hard. That much relieved him. It was one puzzle piece with many of them still missing, and Grace had gained some knowledge so far today. Rockville wasn't a big town. Their guy was getting cocky, always a good sign. He had let himself be seen during the day, carrying on an activity that would be noticed. Cocky and arrogant. Arrogant enough to believe he could do as he damn well pleased in this town and then continue abusing it.

"Think again, motherfucker," Justin told his reflection in the mirror. Maybe the bastard didn't know whom he was dealing with yet.

Which didn't fit the profile. He was methodical. And most psychopaths not only researched their victims, ways to abuse them, torture methods that would allow them to draw out their "playtime" before killing, but would also research the law enforcement officers trying to capture them.

Justin heard his cell phone buzzing at the same time footsteps sounded outside the bathroom door. Justin opened it and Grace stood in his hallway, his phone in her hand.

"Phone," she offered, her smile pleasant and very guarded.

"His timing is perfect." Justin guessed sending an e-mail to his supervisor would result in a phone call.

"Whose timing?" Grace was dressed and her hair once again wrapped behind her head and secured in her hair clasp.

"My supervisor, Cliff Bogfrey." Justin took the phone from Grace and put his arm around her shoulder, walking with her down the hall while glancing at the phone to confirm his hunch. "Well, maybe not," he added, pausing and deciding whether he should risk answering right now or not.

"Oh?" She looked at the phone buzzing in his hand, instead of at him.

Creating a type of intimacy with Grace seemed inevitable. Especially after tasting her. Even after he had dried his face, her scent clung to him, made him crave her with every breath. Possibly using that intimacy to keep her close would allow them time to work through this case faster.

"I'll head down to the truck," she added, and hurried to the stairs.

"Wait." He met her gaze for only a moment when she turned, her blue eyes bright yet guarded. He wouldn't have that hesitation and worry lining her pretty face. "We'll go down together," he told her, and pushed the button to answer the call. "Reece here."

"Well, who else would it be?" Sylvia said, laughing her professional laugh, which told him immediately that she wasn't alone but performing for an audience—probably her new live-in lawyer boyfriend. Rockville sure had become the progressive town. "I won't ask how long you're gracing us with your presence," she continued. "But I would ask that you not break your daughter's heart when you leave."

"Elizabeth understands why I leave," he growled, confident that Sylvia would pollute his daughter's head and create issues of denial and betrayal if Elizabeth allowed it. "But if you're calling to let me know I can spend more time with her, just let me know when."

"Maybe sometime this week."

"How about I pick her up again after her school program is over." He headed into his bedroom and shut down his computer, then hurried after Grace when she headed down the stairs. "I have a few things to take care of, but I'll call you if I can't make it there by five."

Grace let herself into his truck and focused on her hands when he climbed in next to her and started the engine. "I think we should forget about what happened inside," she said, her voice just above a whisper.

"No," he said without hesitating. His insides hardened with a need to protect, to take away whatever fears caused her to wrinkle her brow when he took her chin and turned her face to look at him. "No, Grace," he repeated. "I'm not going to forget what we did inside, and neither are you. And darling, neither one of us wants to forget."

"But—"

"No," he insisted. "We're going to make a few stops just inside town, see who else saw our Buick towing the Aries. Maybe he stopped to gas up somewhere. When we're done, I'm taking you to dinner."

"You can't." She pulled away from his grasp and looked out her window. It was amazing how well she could wrap all those gorgeous curls into that wooden clasp and even more incredible that it held her magnificent hair in place. "You'll have your daughter tonight."

Two messages caught Grace's eye the minute she sat down at her desk the following morning. First, there was a message to call the fire department. The second message was from the lab. It looked like more results were in. Hopefully today she would know a little bit more about the Strauses' Dodge Aries catching on fire.

The computer buzzed to life when she pressed the button, and she stared blindly at the screen trying to focus her thoughts. It would take at least two cups of coffee before she could enter reports. Another department handled the tedious job when she worked in D.C. Doing it herself took some getting accustomed to. But she'd get to them when she had time. She grabbed her phone and punched in the number for the fire department.

"Roger Swanson, please." Grace read the name off the message slip.

"Swanson here," a scratchy voice said after she'd held for a minute.

"Hi, this is Grace Jordan returning your call. Do you have something for me?" Impending doom surrounded her, although she fought to sound enthusiastic.

Getting answers would bring the rapist down faster. Why was it then that the sensation rushed through her that she wasn't going to like what Roger had to tell her?

"Yeah, just a minute." There was a shuffle of papers and

she visualized a messy desk. "Here it is. The Strauses' Dodge Aries was definitely an intentional fire. We found airplane gasoline saturated through the interior upholstery. It's highly combustible and burns quickly."

She scribbled notes frantically in her notebook. "Thanks, Roger. I really appreciate it." She needed to find out where airplane gas was sold. The average person couldn't go buy it, unless they owned a plane.

"Anytime. And welcome to Rockville. I promise usually we're a quiet, peaceful town." Roger laughed easily. "You'd think some kind of curse descended on our town over the past couple of weeks."

Grace hung up the phone and numbly started entering her paperwork into the data entry program. Her mind raced, however, and finally she sat there with the first form held in mid-air, staring at it but not seeing it.

The conversation she had had with Roger Swanson replayed in her head no matter her efforts to focus on the tedious data entry task. This town had been peaceful prior to two weeks ago. Grace and her daughter had moved here two weeks ago. She wasn't a curse, and neither was Rachel. But what if . . .

"No. It's not possible." She smacked her desk with her fist and felt the sting in the side of her hand. "I don't attract monsters!"

She read over the report in her hand before focusing on her task of entering it on the computer. The commonalities of the two murders were engraved in her brain, but as she typed in the second report, her fingers stumbled over words. Words like "brutally tortured," "burned with two different objects," "raped and sodomized." The *god*-awful truth was that crimes like this happened every day. Master wasn't that original in his hideous offenses. And she wasn't the only one to have survived such terrible crimes.

She sure as hell wasn't a monster magnet.

Grace shook her head hard enough that curls tumbled free of the clasp behind her head. "You're being ridiculous," she told herself. Master had burned to death in a fire ten years ago. If he hadn't, he would have come after her long before now. This was another monster, another freak who needed to be taken down.

Just great—a headache first thing on a Friday morning.

She finished entering the reports and reached for the second message. Pushing the buttons on her phone, she glanced at the clock. Justin had his daughter overnight. Which meant he would take her to school this morning. All morning Rachel had talked about Elizabeth. They were quickly becoming best friends. Grace needed to be strong. When she and Justin solved this case and he left town to take on his next case, his daughter would be upset. Grace sucked in a breath, remembering how he had made her feel in his bedroom yesterday.

God—what he'd done to her. No one ever had tripped her over the edge like that before. She always had maintained control. Something about Justin, about his strong yet caring nature, did her in. And she hadn't seen it coming.

"If I had, I would have run like hell." Even as she muttered the words, Grace wondered at the truth in them. She struggled to put loose hair back into her hair clasp and again glanced at the clock. "Who are you fooling, Jordan?"

She closed her eyes, willing thoughts of Justin and what it would be like to slide down on that rock-hard cock of his out of her head. The more she demanded him to vacate her thoughts, the more she wondered where he was. Elizabeth wouldn't be the only one longing for her father when he left.

"County Morgue." A woman's crisp, professional tone snapped Grace out of her thoughts.

"Lieutenant Grace Jordan here," she said, dropping the report on her desk and looking out her open office door toward the main station. Christy was on the phone, her matter-of-fact tone fading into the background along with the noise of the printer, which was creating a humdrum repetitious sound as it cranked out copies of some file or form Christy was printing. "I have a message here to call your office."

"Yes, Lieutenant Jordan. One moment. I'll put you through to Robert," she said informally.

Grace had barely waited a minute when Robert Starkey came on the line. "Grace, how are you?"

"Good. Do you have a report in for me?"

"Yes, I do. We got results back in on the burns on those two female bodies we have over here. My hunch was right, but with modern science we're required to verify our findings before releasing information."

"Understood," Grace said, picking up her pen and clicking it open and closed while she stared at it. "What did they say?"

"There were chemicals and residue left on the skin where each burn mark was," Robert explained, and she heard him flipping through papers as he spoke. "We've got positive confirmation on the lightbulb. And the tobacco residue left on their skin is consistent with a cigar. We can try sending off for more reports to narrow in on the type of tobacco, possibly a brand, although test results on those are fuzzy and I've never actually submitted forms for one of those tests. But the options are out there if you want to order them."

Grace stared at her pen, no longer opening and closing it, and swore she felt the pain from the ten-year-old scar on her breast. Sucking in a deep breath, she fought for a calming breath. "That's fine. Will you fax the results over to the station?"

Chapter 7

Justin Reece couldn't get the conversation out of his head he'd had with Elizabeth on the way to school that morning. His daughter had been chatting about Rachel Jordan again. Every time Elizabeth brought Grace's daughter up in her rambling conversations, he found himself tuning in with incredible attentiveness. He shouldn't be learning about a woman through conversations her daughter had at school, but his resources were limited right now.

There was an attraction, though. He tried denying it, it would be fair to both of them if he did, but reality spoke too loudly. And life wasn't always fair. Sure, it was physical. Grace was hot as hell with those dark red curls tumbling past her shoulders and down her slender back. But it was more than the way her sweaters stretched over her large breasts or how her blue jeans hugged that perfectly shaped ass of hers. And it wasn't because he believed that trouble was closing in quickly around them and she needed protection.

After sitting in his truck and talking to his supervisor, then putting in a call to the County Morgue to learn Robert Starkey had just hung up the phone with Grace and getting him to update Justin on test results, he let the older man ramble on about how the town had changed. It was hard focusing on the conversation as Justin's mind took in the latest information on their murder victims. If the burn marks were made with lightbulbs, both women had been moved to the locations where they were found. Which he already believed was the case. Lightbulbs needed electricity. So unless their murderer sported some kind of portable lamp or lighting system, which would draw attention to him in both locations, he had killed them somewhere else.

Justin had failed Clare. He wouldn't fail Grace. There was no way Grace would go after this monster on her own. No matter if she'd overcome the atrocities of her past, he wouldn't let her face this guy alone. He would be there for her.

If he hadn't allowed Clare to go off on her own when she was too young to protect herself, she'd be alive today. And if he didn't keep Grace very close to his side, their guy might see she was a better treat than any eighteen-year-old would ever be. Clare didn't make it, but he wouldn't endure that nightmare again. He wouldn't allow Grace to risk getting too close to this madman who could overpower her and kill her the way Clare had died, and the other women.

Justin would be the first to admit to himself that returning to Rockville did have its appeal. Yes, his children were here. Daniel and Elizabeth. And their mother was doing a fine job of raising them, even if Daniel was a hellion who needed a good settling down; was harder to get closer to him than Elizabeth. And Elizabeth understood her daddy needed to work. But now that he was here, meeting Grace and learning that this monster would destroy women just like the one who killed Clare did, Justin didn't want to leave.

"This is for you, baby girl," he said, knowing his little sister was in paradise now and happy every day.

Justin wouldn't deny that if none of this were going on, Grace would still appeal to him. Her gutsiness, her craving to investigate and put pieces of puzzles together, matched his own. He saw her honesty, her integrity, and her compassion. All of that turned him on—her mind and her body.

The coffee smelled good when Justin entered the station. His cell phone buzzed on his belt and he pulled it free, aware of Christy watching him at her dispatch counter. She sat, buffing her nails, and flashed him a flirtatious smile when she looked at him while checking his phone.

It was Sylvia, the last person he wanted to speak to first thing in the morning. Pushing the button to send it to voice mail, he hooked his phone back on his belt.

"One of your girlfriends?" Christy teased.

"She won't ever be a girlfriend," Justin groaned.

Christy laughed easily. "Well, it's nice and quiet here. Grace is in her office, though, has been for well over an hour." She watched him closely as if waiting eagerly to see what his reaction would be to her informing him of Grace's whereabouts.

"Where's everyone else?" he asked, unwilling to satisfy Christy by reacting to being told where Grace was.

"Bosley is off the clock this morning. Some personal matter. So far, fortunately, it's been quiet."

Justin's cell rang again and he pulled it from his belt.

"You're getting more calls than I am," Christy said, her teasing tone in full effect.

Ignoring her, Justin took the call, turning his back on the dispatch counter and walking back to the coffee table at the back of the office.

"Justin, it's Michael Green," Michael said in a quiet baritone. Michael and his wife lived in the house west of Justin, and had longer than he had owned his home. Although he'd only done as much as wave at Michael so far when he'd left his house, it didn't surprise him that his neighbor would call him. The entire town was curious why he was back. "I'm at the office this morning. Think you could stop by?"

"More than likely. What's up?"

"Possibly nothing," Michael said, concern making his voice tight. "You remember the warehouse that is next to my office here in town?"

"I remember we used to go there in high school," Justin admitted, although something told him Michael wasn't calling to reminisce.

"That's the one. Anyway, if you could stop by, it would be easier to talk to you about it in person."

"Is there trouble?" he asked, aware of Christy watching him.

"I'm not sure," Michael said slowly.

"I'll be by." He didn't ask why Michael didn't call the police if something unusual was going on around his office. Getting out and about in the town was a good idea. The more Justin scoped the streets of this town, the sooner he'd stumble onto that late-nineties Buick. He hoped there wasn't more than one in town.

Before he went anywhere he planned on checking in with Grace. He would suggest she ride along with him. He glanced up when Grace walked out of her office. His smile faded, though, when she barely acknowledged him. Grace's eyes looked haunted. She stared at him a moment, making no attempt to hide the worries that crossed her face. Then, in an instant, they were gone. Her eyes clouded over.

"Good morning." She sounded pleasant enough. "Christy, I have some errands to run." Grace dismissed him with one glance.

Annoyance flickered in his gut, but the look that crossed her face next drew concern. Grace looked around the main office, at all the desks, the floor, and the walls, as if she couldn't find something. He was about to ask when the doors to the police station opened. Justin didn't need to turn to know who it was. Perfume introduced his ex-wife's presence.

"You didn't return my call, Justin," Sylvia said, in way of a greeting. She turned and noticed Grace. "Oh, there you are. You're the reason I'm here. Can we talk in your office? Justin, would you like to join us?"

He shrugged, not at all bothered by joining Grace in a meeting, although he wished his ex-wife didn't have to be present as well. Grace seemed distracted as she quietly, with no look of concern, returned to her office.

"I'm glad I caught you," Sylvia said to Grace as she shut his office door behind her back. Grace had walked several feet into the room and turned to face his ex-wife. Her expression bothered him, though. It wasn't one he'd seen before.

"What can I do for you, Mayor?" Grace sounded impersonal, almost sedated.

"Well, I've taken this matter up with the city council and we're all in agreement," Sylvia started, sounding like her matter was of the utmost importance.

Something was wrong with Grace and he didn't want Sylvia bothering her until he knew what it was about.

"What matter are you referring to?" He didn't want to waste time dealing with Sylvia's politics when he and Grace could be out on the streets searching for more clues.

Sylvia shot him a fiery glare, but Grace simply looked at him, then Sylvia, her expression not changing.

"This office is on a budget, Grace." Sylvia put her hands on her hips and sounded like a parent reprimanding a delinquent child. "I'll take this matter up with the Sheriff, but since you're here, I'm going to speak to you, too. Robert Starkey was chatting with the Ogdens, and you know he is on the city council. When Robert told us you might order more reports, just to learn what brand of tobacco some killer smokes, well, I don't have to tell you the Ogdens were shocked at how much that test would cost."

"Sylvia, that's enough." What had he ever seen in her? She was greedy and manipulative, and he wanted her out of his life . . . forever. "You have no jurisdiction here. Grace is top-notch, one of the best damned investigators Rockville has ever seen. There is no way our guy will be caught if we don't learn everything we can about our perpetrator."

He managed to keep his voice level and under control, but the fury mounting within him at Sylvia's outright rude behavior consumed him. He clenched his hands into fists in order to keep them from wrapping around his ex-wife's neck.

"There's no way he's going to be caught with you sitting in this office drinking coffee, either. I'm sure that isn't how you usually work your cases. I can't imagine you sitting anywhere long enough to even pour coffee," Sylvia snapped.

"I am working this case. I just walked in the door to get Grace and we're right back into the field."

"Of course you are. God knows how you worked a case without her in the past."

Justin blinked. Sylvia was jealous of Grace. He shook his head slowly, ready to terminate this conversation.

"It's all right, Mayor." Grace spoke so calmly and evenly that both Justin and Sylvia turned and looked at her with surprise. "There aren't any more tests to order on any of these cases. And I'll hit the streets right now," she added, and started to move around the two of them.

"Well, well, I may have misjudged what's going on around here." Sylvia's smile was triumphant.

"Maybe you have," Grace said, turning and looking at him only for a moment before glancing at Sylvia. Grace's blue eyes seemed dull. Something was seriously not right.

Justin feared he knew what his wife thought might be going on, and he didn't like the way Grace had responded.

"Will that be all?" Now Grace gave a pleasant smile to both of them, but she wasn't able to conceal that haunted look in her eyes. "I really need to get some work done."

"As long as you can use good old-fashioned sleuthing abilities and not spend money this town doesn't have." Sylvia still had that winning smile on her face. He wanted to wipe it off . . . permanently.

"As long as this guy is off the streets before he kills anyone else, we won't need to order more tests." Grace shrugged and edged toward the door.

"Perfect." Sylvia patted Grace on the back and guided her toward the door. Was he wrong or had a glimpse of annoyance appeared on Grace's face? "That's what needs to be done. Of course you know the moment you solve this case, Justin will be out the door. It's what he's best at doing."

Sylvia's laugh curdled his blood. Grace didn't acknowledge the comment but simply offered a limp wave before sneaking out the door.

Justin glared at Sylvia. "You were out of line, and you damned well know it."

"Ha! While I'm Mayor, this town won't go broke. Ever since that little redhead has pranced into this town there have been crimes everywhere. Don't think I haven't noticed that." Sylvia marched out of the office, following him as he tried catching up with Grace. "And I'm doing her a favor warning her about you. She needs to know that you won't stick around, not for a wife or for your kids."

"The next time you call this office, or show up here, it will be to report a crime," he said hotly, not caring about Christy's shocked expression and not giving a rat's ass that Sylvia still looked triumphant. Then hurrying out of the station, he caught up with Grace in the parking lot. "Let's go," he ordered, his voice harsher than he meant for it to be, but he'd be damned if Sylvia would interfere with his investigation, or with him and Grace. "We've got a call to run."

Michael Green owned a veterinary place that he and his wife had run for years. Green's Animal Hospital sat off the road in a nice, clean building and the warehouse next to it didn't look any different than it had since the last time Justin saw it.

"He wanted to talk to me about the warehouse," Justin explained to Grace, more than aware of her cool, silent treatment as they pulled into the vet's parking lot. "And when we leave here, you can tell me why you're so upset. If Sylvia put you in this mood—"

Grace waved him off as she opened her passenger door after he parked. "Your ex-wife doesn't bother me. I think she's a bit jealous, but she's right. You'll be gone soon, so there's nothing to worry about." She closed the door before he could respond.

Justin hurried around the front of his truck and made it in time to pull the door open for Grace. A flood of air-conditioning and strong smells of disinfectants filled the air when they entered the lobby to the vet's.

"Justin Reece, would you look at you?" Norma Green was a beautiful black woman, and he'd secretly had a crush on her back in high school. She'd always had eyes for Michael, though, and it became obvious that hadn't changed when she immediately turned and hurried into the other room, returning a moment later with Michael on her arm. "We really appreciate you showing up so quickly. I'm probably being paranoid. Michael says I watch too many detective shows." Her laughter was melodic.

"What are you talking about?" Justin noticed both of them staring at Grace and put his arm on her shoulder, also aware of them watching his actions. "You two probably haven't met Grace Jordan, Rockville's newest cop. She's straight out of D.C. and probably as good of an investigator as I am."

Grace turned, cocking her eyebrow, while her blue eyes flashed with more life in them than he'd seen all day. "Probably as good?" she taunted.

Norma laughed and Michael grunted. Justin caught Grace winking at Norma. Whatever beef Grace had with him personally, she was a pro in public. He wouldn't be off base to say she was on her toes always.

"Do you want me to walk them over there?" Michael asked his wife.

"I want to go with you. We can put a sign on the door for a minute and we'll hear if anyone pulls up." She pulled out a laminated card, the size of typing paper, with the printed words "Be Back Soon" on it.

If he took liberties and touched Grace more than two investigators might touch each other, Justin was sure she would add that to her list of grievances she'd tell him about later. He didn't mind hearing her rant. It would be done while they were alone; that much he was sure about. Grace wouldn't make a scene publicly. She had more couth than Sylvia. And once he had Grace alone, he planned on seducing all concerns right out of that sexy head of hers.

"There's been a couple times over the past few weeks when we've come down here at night. We're being audited," Michael began explaining as they walked across the grassy area that separated the warehouse from the parking lot. "And last year I bought this warehouse when it went up for auction for back taxes. We haven't had a chance to do anything with it yet, so pretty much it sits here like it has for years."

"Boy, the memories this place brings back," Justin said after helping Michael push open the sliding doors that once were set up for delivery trucks, although the building was abandoned even when they'd been in high school. "Remember when we'd bring the girls back here?"

"You never brought me here," Norma said, shooting her husband a quick look.

Michael glared at Justin, who simply rocked up on his toes. The couple had one of the most secure relationships he'd ever known.

"I never brought anyone here," Michael said, wrapping his arm around his wife's waist and pulling her against him. "You had too much class for a dirty place like this."

Justin wouldn't comment, knowing Michael had been part of their parties on more than one occasion but honestly not remembering whether he had a date or not. Justin had always been too busy trying to score with any girl who would give him the time of day. That was until Sylvia laid her eyes on him and started chasing all the other girls away. If he'd known back then what he knew now . . .

"Anyway," Michael continued. "Norma was sure she saw lights on in here last week."

"Does the electricity work in here?" Grace asked, speaking for the first time since they entered. She'd walked into the middle of the large, dreary-looking area and turned now, facing them and squinting past them toward the walls.

"We don't have it turned on." Michael gestured toward a corner. "But after Bosley came in last week and told us a bit about that high school girl that was found all beaten and dead, Norma started getting these crazy ideas."

"You never said they were crazy," she said, spinning around and putting her hands on her hips as she glared at her husband with large, beautiful brown eyes. "Or are you saying you would call an FBI agent out on a crazy whim?" She winked at Justin and then reached for him. Justin thought the world of Michael and wouldn't abuse their relationship for anything, but when Norma beckoned with her long, slender, caramel-colored arm and wagged her fingers, he approached without hesitating. Norma wrapped her arm around his and patted his biceps with her cool, long fingers. "Michael and I came over here the morning after we saw the lights on in here.

And no, there isn't power in this building. But we did find some interesting items that I don't think have been here that long. They aren't dirty and dusty like everything else is."

"What did you find?" Justin followed her to the far corner of the warehouse.

Most of the windows were boarded up, but sunlight streamed between cracks in the boards and created a thin line of dust bunnies floating in the air when they reached the corner and Norma pointed at a door that probably once led to an office used in the warehouse.

"In there," she said. "Someone's been in there."

Justin stopped her when she reached for the doorknob. "Was the door opened when you two first came in here?"

Norma hesitated. "I'm not sure."

"I think it was," Michael said behind him.

He released Norma and pushed his fingertips against the middle of the old wood and pushed the door inward, then stepped in front of them in the doorway. The first thing that caught his eye was a small generator and a lamp without a lamp shade. One quick glance and he spotted an old lamp shade on its side in the corner. But what grabbed his attention was how the room smelled different, like stale cigar smoke.

"We're going to need a flashlight. Grace, call in to Dispatch. Send out a car fully equipped. We're dusting this room."

Grace hovered over the officer who walked around with his dusting equipment. Nervous energy had sprouted inside Grace the moment she entered the room, immediately aware of the pungent smell of old smoke. A vagrant could have made this place his resting stop, but if so, he or she had enough money to haul in a fairly sophisticated generator, which provided power to the entire room. Once Grace donned gloves, she'd scoured over the room with Justin by her side, and now with the other officers, the trepidation inside her mixed with anxiety and excitement that this possibly could be more than just a pit stop for a homeless person.

"I'm afraid I'm going to have to piss off your ex-wife

some more," she said, picking up the remains of an old cigar and holding it up for Justin. "I want to know if this was the cigar that burned either of those girls."

"We'll turn it in for testing with the FBI." Justin stood in the middle of the room, looking strong and powerful as he scanned its contents before settling his gaze on her. The glow in his green eyes caused her insides to flutter. But she knew his mind was on the case. He loved the hunt as much as she did. "But I have no problem with you leading her to believe Rockville will be putting out for the bill."

"He was here, Justin," she said, ignoring his last comment. There wasn't any point dwelling on Sylvia's behavior at the station. The woman was a spoiled little bitch, but that wasn't Grace's problem. All that mattered was nailing this guy to the wall before he hurt another girl. That mattered a hell of a lot more than the fact that Justin would be gone as soon as they did. "I know he was here."

She stared at an old desk that was so rotten it leaned sideways. Walking around it, she tried pulling open its drawers. The first one wouldn't budge, but the second drawer down slid open easily. Grace squatted, running her finger over the old wood that appeared to recently have been chiseled, probably to help ease the drawer open and shut.

"Look," she whispered, looking past the freshly scraped wood to the contents inside the drawer. "I think this is man's cologne."

She lifted a small bottle, the size purchased when someone planned on traveling on a plane, and stared at the half-full gold fluid inside. Once again her mind spun back a decade to another time, a point in her life when the smallest, most trivial actions done wrong would result in serious punishment.

It was a memory she'd forgotten, but it hit her so hard at that moment it was like it happened yesterday. Staring at the bottle, turning it and reading the brand name, she stifled a shriek and dropped it. The bottle fell into the drawer, landing on its side. She reached to grab it so quickly, to prevent it from spilling a second time, that she racked muscles in her arm.

But it wasn't a second time. That day so long ago when she'd accidentally dropped Master's cologne, spilling it all over his bedroom carpet and causing the room to reek of his cologne for days, was another lifetime.

"Are you okay?" Justin was around the desk, grabbing and lifting her, too fast for her to stop him.

"Fine. Fine." She laughed, shrugging out of his arms, and knew her expression looked sheepish. She came up with the first lie she could think of. "It was a spider. At least I didn't spill it," she said, letting out a sigh that held more frustration than he knew.

Justin reached into the drawer, taking her arm with his free hand and keeping her from being able to move. "Didn't you say something about April Monroe's hands smelling of cologne?" He unscrewed the bottle and sniffed its contents, then held it under her nose. "Same cologne?"

The smell turned her stomach and she coughed, grabbing his wrist and forcing him to let go of her. Grace moved quickly around the other side of the desk.

"It's the same cologne. I'd swear to it." She needed to get a grip on herself. "Bag it up along with the cigar." She ignored his expression when she started giving orders. "I want tests run on the cologne and the cigar. And please tell me we've got at least one print in this room we can use."

She made it outside, following the officer who carried the dusting equipment back to his squad car. Justin grabbed her arm and she fought the urge to throw him off of her and at the same time was overwhelmed with the sensation to walk into his embrace. That bugged the crap out of her. The only one who could offer her security was herself.

"So I haven't watched too many detective shows?" Norma's laugh was so pretty, and she glowed as she grinned from ear to ear and approached them. "Will this help you crack a case?"

"I think you've given us a lot of good leads on an investigation we're working on." Grace crossed her arms over her chest, suddenly aching for a shower as she faced the pretty, clean-looking woman who continued grinning at her.

"Thanks for calling," Justin said, reaching to shake Michael's hand. Justin's baritone was lower than usual when he turned his attention to Norma. "You keep right on watching your detective shows."

Justin's cell phone rang and he pulled it out of his pocket but then pushed a button, sending the call to voice mail. His expression wasn't readable but relaxed noticeably when he returned his attention to Norma.

"I'll try to stop by again soon," he said. "I'd give you a hug, but I think I'm pretty dirty after being in that warehouse for so long."

"Like I care," Norma said, laughing as she walked into his arms. "And you're definitely stopping by. How about for supper? Both of you?"

"Oh, I don't know," Grace began.

"Just give me a call," Justin said, interrupting her.

Grace fought the urge not to head back to the truck while Justin continued talking with the Greens. But once they left she'd be alone with Justin, and right now she'd be better off on her own. Too many ghosts were crawling out of the dark crevices of her brain. And she didn't understand why. This wasn't the first rape and murder case she'd worked. She'd dealt with arson, with abused wives; none of those cases had called forth terrible memories from her past.

When they finally headed out, Grace knew the only way to keep ancient history from creeping into her present was to stay busy. It was time to get Rachel, but Grace needed to keep working. Her next-door neighbor had offered on more than one occasion since she and Rachel had moved in to watch her if Grace ever needed her to. Grace would call her as soon as they got to the station.

"Let's head back and see if we can't push through test results," Grace suggested as Justin turned onto the main road through town.

"I'd put money on the fact that he took April and Margaret to that warehouse." Justin held on to the steering wheel with one hand, and his strong, well-defined profile showed off his powerful features as he stared ahead at the road. "If he tortured, possibly killed them there, we should be able to pick up traces of blood, possibly semen."

"There weren't any prints at all, though. I thought we would at least grab one from one of the girls."

He glanced over at her, his brooding expression making his eyes look exceptionally dark. "I'm going to send a couple boys from the Bureau over there to check again," he said. "We'll run a search for blood and semen, too. Even if our guy is a meticulous clean freak, with better equipment we should be able to pick up something."

"Let's hope so," she said, feeling a wave of exhaustion hit her when his phone rang again. Grace watched him pull it out, glare at it, and push the button again to send the call to voice mail. This time, a moment later it made another sound, probably indicating he'd been left a voice message.

She wasn't going to ask who he was avoiding. His personal life was just that, and best kept that way. No matter that he'd been adamant about them continuing to pursue something outside of work, Grace knew he hadn't been thinking with the head on his shoulders. And no matter what she thought of him or how damned appealing he was, getting mixed up with a man who would up and leave as soon as he captured her heart would be a very bad move on her part.

"Now that we've evicted him out of his warehouse, and taken some of his goods, he's going to need to find somewhere else take his victims," Justin mused. "Fortunately for us, Rockville is a small town and there aren't a lot of abandoned buildings. Those that are, we're going to contact all owners and do a thorough search of each one."

She nodded, her thoughts drifting back to the cologne in the drawer. "Maybe we should contact all stores in town, too. If Man's World is part of his calling card."

"Man's World? You recognized that cologne? I didn't see a name on the bottle."

She knew he studied her, but she stared at the road ahead of them. It didn't cross her mind that the name of the cologne wasn't on the bottle. "It smelled like it. Maybe we should double-check."

"Does it mean something to you if its Man's World cologne?" he pressed, still glancing her way.

She pursed her lips, trying to decide if it did mean anything. "It would confirm that I'm right about the fragrance," she decided. "And if I am, we can contact stores here in town to see if anyone has sold, or does sell, that particular man's cologne in the next day or so. If it's part of his calling card, he'll want some more of it."

"Unless he already has more," Justin pointed out as they pulled into the police station's parking lot.

Chapter 8

Grace pulled herself off the couch later that night and made sure the front door was locked. Rachel had been happy to see Grace when she picked her up next door after getting home well after dark. Grace regretted only having an hour or so with her daughter before she slipped off to sleep, but that only meant the sooner she cracked this case, the more time she could give Rachel.

And Grace would have plenty of time. Justin would be gone. And she'd noticed that other than this case, crime in Rockville seemed to be limited to antics pulled by teenagers, parking violations, and speeding tickets, nothing that caused any of the officers at the station to pull overtime.

She stared at the TV set that she hadn't bothered turning on. It was deafeningly quiet. Stretching, she blew out a breath and shivered uncontrollably. Her stomach was twisted in knots to the point where she couldn't eat. Justin was convinced she had declined having dinner with him because she was avoiding spending time with him other than when working the case. Although there was truth in his accusation, Grace couldn't eat a thing if she tried. The old ghosts were back with a cruel vengeance.

"You've got to get a grip," she scolded herself, hating how her knees shook when she walked to her dining room table. Running her finger over the cold metal of her gun, exposed from its holster on her work belt, offered only a small amount of security. Maybe talking all of this over with Justin would be a good idea. "And he would think I was a raving lunatic," she whispered, staring at her gun and cell phone, both secured in their leather compartments on her belt. "The last thing I need to do is let him see that my past, which he already knows about, is bothering me with this case."

She hated the fact that he had the power to pull her off the case. He was FBI. It wouldn't take more than a phone call to pull in more agents and completely relieve her of her duties with this investigation.

"Wouldn't Sylvia love that?" she sneered. "Miss Perfect Ice Bitch can just rot in hell. No one is pulling me off this case."

Pulling her cell phone free and then on an impulse sliding her gun out of its holder, Grace took both back to the living room. She needed an unbiased party, someone she trusted implicitly whom she could bounce her thoughts off of and who wouldn't laugh at her or cause her to lose credibility with her job.

Grace placed her gun on her coffee table and sat down on her floor cross-legged where she could see her front door and all her windows. The feeling of paranoia was making her nuts; clearing her thoughts would help. She'd had years and years of counseling after escaping Master. Grace knew all the tricks to help put the ghosts back in the dark, reclusive corners of her brain.

It was eleven o'clock on the East Coast. Hopefully not too late to call her uncle. *Please be home, Uncle Charlie.*

"Hey-lo," the old man's voice sang into the phone. His southern accent only surfaced when he had a girlfriend. At least life was going well for someone.

"Hi, Uncle Charlie; it's Grace."

"Well, baby doll. To what do I owe the honor of this phone call?"

"Oh, Uncle Charlie, I really need a friend right now." Tears welled in her eyes, and a sob surfaced before she could stop it.

"For crying out loud, child. It's a Friday night. Don't tell me that back-hills town doesn't have strapping young men fighting over my gorgeous niece. What is it, no babysitter?" He chuckled his deep, raspy chuckle that she loved so much. "Tell your uncle Charlie all of your worries." His voice soothed her.

She breathed deeply and began talking. She told him about the rapes and the murders and the burnt car. She told him about the lecture she had received from the Mayor. She told him what Forensics had discovered, the matching semen, the cigars, the burn marks, and the cologne smell on the victims' hands.

"And Uncle Charlie," she finished after taking another breath, "today we found a room in an abandoned warehouse that we're pretty sure is where he took both victims. There was a lamp with its shade pulled off. Forensics didn't find any burn marks on the bulb in the lamp, but they also confirmed it was a new lightbulb. The room was too damned clean. We're working with a master here." As she said the words she swore she heard herself say, *Master is here.* Dragging in a staggered breath, she closed her eyes, suddenly terrified she was becoming delusional. Uncle Charlie didn't say anything, which reassured her that her mind was having a field day. If she kept talking, she would regain control of her senses. "I think it was the bottle of Man's World that bothered me the most," she confessed. "You know they never found his body in the burnt ruins."

"Grace, what are you saying? Slow down and make sense, sweetheart. They didn't find whose body? And a bottle of Man's World? Do you mean the men's cologne? What does that have to do with anything?"

"Master wore Man's World cologne. I spilled it once," she said, her voice suddenly shaking so much she could hardly get the words out. "The smell of it hung heavily in his bedroom for days. And I was punished severely every day that the smell lingered."

Uncle Charlie cursed and she jumped, her heart pounding harder at the sound of his profanity in her ear.

"Now, sweetheart," Uncle Charlie said after a moment of

silence. "First of all, he's not Master. He was a cruel, sick man who has been dead for many years now. Don't let him control you from the grave."

"I know, Uncle Charlie. That's why I called. You're the only one I can talk to about this. If I talked to Justin, he would pull me off the case in a New York minute."

"Sounds like your perp is leaving some strong calling cards, which is usually a sign of an aggressive, pompous murderer. He is confident enough in his actions that he's leaving messages."

"That crossed my mind. A couple who run a veterinary place and bought that warehouse thought they saw lights on in the warehouse. Of course they didn't check it out until the next day. But he was comfortable enough with himself not to cover the windows to block the light. And that room, Uncle Charlie, it was so clean. Most people can't clean a crime scene to the point where there are no traces of a crime." She stared at her hand, willing herself to quit shaking, and thought about her words before speaking. But the truth was too close to the surface. "We're working with a master," she repeated, hearing herself say the sentence correctly this time. "Uncle Charlie, if Master ever used a calling card, it would be the same as this guy. The cigars, Man's World cologne, and the way the girls were brutalized . . ."

"You're talking to an old FBI man here," Uncle Charlie scolded. "And you know this as well. Many criminals say the same thing. We've got so many movies and TV shows for them to use as examples. It all gets to be like a bad rerun sometimes."

She nodded. Her uncle was right. She couldn't let all of this pull her back into her old way of thinking. "I just needed someone to talk to about this who wouldn't throw me off the case for sounding like a madwoman." Grace yanked the clasp free from the back of her head and shook her hair free. "The crimes committed since I moved here fit the profile of everything Master did while I was in that mansion. Old memories are hitting me hard."

"Do they have you working on this case by yourself?"

"No. Sheriff Montgomery contacted the FBI. They sent out Special Agent Justin Reece. We've been working the case together."

"Justin Reece?" Uncle Charlie had a booming laugh.

She jumped at the sound of it but then cursed herself silently, staring at her gun on the coffee table while she damned Master to hell for the thousandth time at least since he'd died. Her uncle started talking again and she found herself fighting to hear him as visions of Master, of the spilt cologne, and then a new memory, one that hadn't come forth in ages, his cigar box, raised their ugly head.

"I worked with Reece a long time ago. He was just a pup, but a good agent." Uncle Charlie still chuckled. "They sent a damned good man out there. There must be high precedence on this case for them to send one of their better agents to such a back-hills town."

Uncle Charlie hadn't hesitated in saying his piece when she first told him about the job in Rockville, South Dakota. He thought she wasted her talents moving to such a small town and accepting a position at a police department that offered little room for advancement. Her uncle was the only person on this planet who believed she should have chased her dream of becoming FBI. Her behavior right now was proof enough that she would never make it as a special agent. Since she was a little girl and lay awake at night listening to her father talk to her mother about his cases, Grace had dreamed of chasing down the bad guy. Master had ripped that dream clear out of her heart. He tortured and continued verbally abusing her, especially when he overheard her talking in her sleep shortly after he abducted her and learned she wanted to be FBI. For the years she lived as his prisoner and slave, he never let her forget that she didn't have what it took to capture a bad guy. And the many times Master chained her to a wall or outside to a tree, naked and exposed, he pointed out to her that good agents would never have allowed themselves to be in her predicament. Years of therapy had helped her make it into law enforcement. But moments like now reminded her she was grateful to make it this far.

"Justin is from Rockville. He's got an ex-wife and children living here."

"I bet the ex loves you."

"Why would you say that?"

Uncle Charlie snorted. "Tell me Reece hasn't made a move on you and I'll call you a liar."

"Is he that much of a womanizer?" She cringed at the thought of being one in a long line of many.

"Special Agent Reece always put his work before everything else. That wasn't what I meant, sweetheart. You're a gorgeous woman and he's a good man. I can see him taking quite an interest in a knockout redhead who carries a badge and can kick ass with the best of them."

"You're being silly, Uncle Charlie."

"And you didn't answer the question, my dear," he said, his cocky tone ringing through strong over the phone. "I'm glad to hear he is out there. Sounds like you're dealing with a monster. You and Rachel are in good hands."

Grace sucked in a breath and then straightened her legs, wiggling her toes as she focused on her bare feet. "Uncle Charlie, I know the Badlands don't hold a candle to Washington, D.C., but do you think you'd consider coming out for a visit? Just until this case is wrapped up. I'd like you to watch Rachel. School starts in a couple weeks and I've got her in day care right now, but tonight I wasn't able to get her until an hour or so ago. I don't want her home life turned upside down so soon after we've moved here. I'm sure it wouldn't be for much longer than a couple weeks."

She held her breath through the moment of silence, hoping and praying she didn't have to come out and admit she needed him here. If her old ghosts surfaced worse than they had tonight, her uncle was the only one she could lean on to bring herself back to reality. Years had passed since she'd had an episode like tonight, but if Justin saw her break down, it could mean her job.

"Let me check my schedule. I'll get back with you really soon. Sound good, sweetheart?"

"Sounds great, Uncle Charlie. It will be great seeing you

again." Grace hung up the phone and leaned back against her living room wall, fingering the gun that rested in her lap and wondering when she put it there.

"Well, I'll be a monkey's uncle," Charlie Jordan said, chuckling to himself. "Justin Reece. So that's what happened to the lad. And if I didn't know better, I'd say he's got the hots for my niece, which any man with half a brain would, and she's running scared." He continued chuckling as he picked the phone back up and dialed Directory Assistance.

Chapter 9

"Reece here," Justin said after picking up the call that came through the field office and was transferred to his cell phone.

He still steamed with aggravation over his ex-wife's visit. She'd shown up at the house screaming and yelling because he'd forgotten to pick up Elizabeth from school. Getting an earful of how lousy of a parent he was from his ex-wife was bad enough. But when she changed the subject and started accusing him of "banging" the new lady cop, he'd gotten pissed. When she implied that word getting out that Grace Jordan was nothing more than a tramp would cause her to lose her job, he'd enjoyed the hell out of kicking Sylvia out of his home.

"Is this Justin Reece?" an old man's voice said into his ear.

"At your service. What can I do for you, sir?"

"Well, I'll be damned. Justin, my boy, it's Charlie Jordan. Remember me?"

Justin Reece sat up in his chair. His memory flashed back ten years, and a broad smile creased his face.

"I'll be damned, indeed. How are you doing, sir? It's been a long time. What can I do for you?" He pictured the gray-haired man, still handsome although in his early fifties. Wait, that would make him over sixty now. The Bureau required special agents to retire by fifty-seven, so the old guy had to be enjoying the life of leisure by now.

"I don't have much time, so I'll cut the formalities and get straight to the heart of things, so to speak. You've got all the family I have in the world there in your town, and I'm mighty worried about them."

"Your family?" Justin let the words sink in. *Charlie Jordan had family out here. Jordan . . . Grace Jordan. Damn. Why hadn't he made the connection?*

"Wait a minute. Is Grace Jordan related to you?"

"You're quick, boy. Now I'm going to ask you something, and I don't want you feeding me a bunch of bullshit about regulations and crap."

"Okay . . . ," Justin said hesitantly.

"Do you remember working that case outside of Rochester, Minnesota? A rapist killed over ten girls and was never caught. When the White mansion burned to the ground the rapes ended and we were pulled off the case."

Justin knew he should play stupid. Charlie was right. Regulations were very cut-and-dry about not talking about a case. "I remember."

"There was speculation that the owner of the mansion, Rick White, was the rapist. Although his body wasn't found in the remains of the mansion, the case was closed. Any chance he might still be alive and up to his old tricks?"

"I take it you've been discussing our investigation with your niece."

"That isn't a 'no.' That son of a bitch destroyed my niece. You wouldn't have recognized her ten years ago. I can't prove it, but there's a chance she's the only woman who got away from him alive."

"Son of a bitch," Justin hissed, leaping to his feet and bounding across his living room. He wouldn't admit to having learned about Grace's past to her uncle. He wouldn't do that to Grace. But that case ten years ago was one of the most aggravating cases he'd worked in his career. No matter the clues they unburied, their perp remained two steps ahead of them, and then the rapes ended when that mansion burned. "I remember they determined the fire was intentionally set, but no one was ever charged with the crime."

"My niece was held prisoner in that mansion for five

years. We thought she was dead," Charlie sighed. "It took quite a few years of therapy to bring a sense of stability back into her life and today she would kill someone before admitting to any of this. So I'd appreciate your keeping quiet about what I just told you."

Justin cursed under his breath. "You've got my word, Charlie," he said, respecting the old man as much as he wouldn't hurt Grace, not that he'd tell Charlie that.

"Before I hung up the phone with her, she asked if I'd come out that way and play babysitter since she's putting overtime in on this case." Charlie didn't pause long enough for Justin to comment but kept right on going. "I think I'll take her up on flying out that way. But there's a reason I'm calling you, son."

"You name it," Justin told him, padding into his dark kitchen and grabbing a beer out of his refrigerator.

"Whoever this monster is, he's pulled some tricks out of his sleeve that are messing with my niece's head. She won't talk to you about it for fear you'd pull her off of this case. And I'm here to tell you that you couldn't ask for a better partner than Grace."

"I won't argue with you on that one, Charlie. Grace is an incredible woman."

"I thought you'd answer along those lines." Charlie laughed but only for a moment before turning serious again. "Take care of her until I get out there. She's one hell of a stubborn, fiery redhead. Grace needs to keep her head straight and she'll work through this case faster than some agents you've worked with in the past. I've seen her in action and she can brainstorm clues together like a pro. Hell, she *is* a pro."

"Say no more, Charlie." Justin put the unopened bottle of beer back into his refrigerator and headed for the stairs. It was late but not too late for a visit. Especially with her uncle's blessing. Not that Justin would ask for it, but Charlie had called him and wouldn't have done so if he didn't want his niece protected. "I won't let anything happen to Grace or her daughter."

Grace fingered the pistol that rested next to her on the floor. It was close to midnight, but she wouldn't be sleeping anytime soon. Her eyes burned from staring at her laptop screen, but she continued searching for crimes relating to the ones they worked on now. She wanted to know if her perp was new to the scene or simply new to Rockville.

A sudden knock on her front door jerked her heart up to her throat and she choked out a gasp.

Grace grabbed her gun and stood slowly. Keeping it low by her thigh, she moved quietly toward the door. No one would come by here at this hour. Hell, she didn't know anyone in town other than Justin and the other officers at the station, although she wasn't sure most of them knew her home address.

Justin wouldn't come by at this hour, would he?

She edged her way toward the window, careful not to stand where anyone peeking in from outside might see her. A noise behind her caught her attention and she spun around, gun pointed. Her mind raced as she tried to remember how many bullets were in the chamber.

Justin Reece stood in her open back door. Oh yeah, her thoughts were clear as crystal. She'd locked and dead-bolted her front door but forgotten to lock her back door. Dear Lord, was she fit to work this case?

Justin stopped dead in his tracks at the sight of the gun. Slowly raising his hands from his sides, he narrowed his gaze, offering no resistance but still looking like he might leap and attack on a moment's notice.

"Grace, put down the gun," he said calmly.

Grace lowered her gun, her entire body slumping to the point that she staggered. Embarrassment and humiliation burned at her insides, pissing her off.

"Don't you ever enter my home and think you'll receive a different greeting," she hissed, lowering her face so he wouldn't see the tears that burned her eyes.

She almost tripped over her laptop on her living room floor and put her gun on her coffee table with a thud. The last thing she needed right now was Justin seeing her like this. Granted, she'd argued with herself all day, fighting to get all desire for him out of her system, but that didn't mean she wanted him seeing her unprofessional and on the brink of completely losing it.

"Come here," he said, moving toward her.

"Why are you here?" she growled, growing angrier at the softness in his tone. If he thought her weak and needing to be cuddled, she'd kick his ass just to release all the aggravation built up inside her since she came home. And if he had stopped by thinking he could get himself some, she'd knock the crap out of him just to show him exactly what type of woman she really was.

"When you talked to your uncle earlier, did he mention he knew me?"

"What?" When she tried swallowing, her mouth was too dry. "Uncle Charlie called you?"

Justin moved toward her again, but she held her hand out, her palm facing him. "Stay where you are," she insisted, refusing to let him trap her in her own living room. If he got any closer she'd have to leap over her own coffee table to get around him, and she'd be damned if he'd touch her when every inch of her sizzled with a mixture of enough emotions that she damn near shook from the intensity of them. "Did he call you? Is that why you feel you can enter my home at this hour?" she hissed.

"Yes, Grace, he called me. Charlie and I worked a case ten years ago together in Minnesota. A lot of girls were murdered and the bastard was never caught."

A numbness settled over her. Grace stared into his dark green eyes, seeing ghosts of his own surface as he pressed his lips together. He still looked fierce, powerful, and deadly. Justin didn't scare her, though. She was confident her suppressed memories were a hell of a lot more terrifying than anything he could dish out.

"I'm sure the number of unsolved murder cases in this country is staggering," she said flatly.

"No one survived the fire when the White mansion burned in Minnesota."

She did. Her daughter did. Grace stared at him. She didn't

understand why her uncle had sent him over here. Justin was
wound so tight his muscles bulged against his shirt more so
than usual. His body was a fine-tuned weapon, perfectly
skilled in the art of seduction and probably just as skilled in
killing. He would see her as his equal, or he wouldn't see her
at all. Grace knew his kind, the perfect investigator, so loyal
to his work that he wouldn't see anything in his world that
didn't meet his standards.

"The fire burned so long and at temperatures hot enough
that traces of DNA that were never matched with anyone the
FBI had on file at the time were all that was found."

"Why are you telling me this?" She kept her cool, unwilling to speculate with him over events of her past that needed
to be stuffed back into their dark corners. "Justin, unless you
have some breaking news to tell me about our case, there
isn't any reason for you to be here."

"Yes, there is. You're my partner and this investigation is
a nightmare slowly unfolding around us. It's going to get
worse the closer we get, and it's going to affect us both."

"The only way it's going to affect me is with intense satisfaction when I nail that bastard to a cross."

"There's no way learning the abuse those two girls endured before they died can't be causing you to relive your
past." Justin took a step closer, his gaze drifting from her
face to her hair.

Grace realized her long curly mop flew around her face
and probably looked horrendous in its tousled state. Pressing the curls to the sides of her head, she shook her head
adamantly. "You're wrong if you think I can't handle this,"
she told him.

"I'm not wrong and I know you can handle this." He
grabbed her hands and pulled them away from her head.

"You're right. I can." She yanked backward to no avail.

Justin tightened his grip on her wrists, dragging her
closer. She couldn't brace herself when corded, steel muscle
pressed against her breasts. Her nipples hardened painfully
and her breasts swelled, touching his body, creating pres-

sure that sunk deep between her legs until she throbbed all over with need. The moment she tilted her head he pounced on her mouth.

Grace should fight him. He let go of her wrists and her palms slapped against rippled muscle as his large arms embraced her, crushing her against him while he deepened the kiss. His mouth was warm, his actions demanding and aggressive but at the same time possessing a warmth and compassion that damn near made her cry.

She was already teetering on the edge, not only from need but also from so many emotions toppling over one another. And as he impaled her with his tongue, his strong hands flat against her back, searing her flesh through her shirt, Grace cried out, the sound a moan of approval that drew a deep rumbling growl from him.

Justin knew so much about her past—a past she'd so successfully wiped out of all records, wiped out of everywhere but her mind. Forcing him to stop might very well wake up her daughter. Rachel couldn't overhear their conversation. Her daughter had been told a few things while in foster care, the bitter facts that came out on the news. Foster parents with good intentions and no knowledge of the dark, disgusting truth, believed Rachel would grow up well-adjusted with life if she understood, and accepted, that her father burned to death in a house fire. At least there weren't any deep memories torturing her young mind. Grace would kill to make sure there never would be. Her daughter would never know a monster had helped create her.

Roped muscles stretched against Justin's jeans when he moved his leg between hers. He grabbed her hair, tugging enough that the sting made her pussy pulse with a fire she never would believe anyone could ignite inside her.

"There is something you need to believe," he rumbled, his voice a deep whisper that crawled over her flesh, making her shiver.

"What's that?"

"You are quite possibly the most beautiful woman I've ever laid eyes on." His arms tightened around her, wrapping her into a world of protective domination that was too easy to drown in.

Grace stretched her fingers over his chest, loving the feel of him. He was any woman's dream, but she knew he couldn't be hers. He deserved better, and she cared too much to hurt him. Besides, Master—no! Until she successfully wiped out all memories of her tortured past, she was too much damaged goods to burden any man with. Especially a man who would rip her heart out even if he didn't intend to do just that.

"Justin," she said quietly, without emotion. She didn't dare let her emotions get involved with this. She fisted her hands, squeezing her eyes closed as he nipped at her neck, unable to ignore what he did to her body. Once she possessed the power to close the world around her out, to prevent the pain and humiliation from seeping too deep into her soul and destroying her completely.

"You're an amazing man and I wish life were different, but it's not." She pushed her fists against hard muscle, willing him to let her go. "All we can be is friends."

The pain that ransacked her body, her soul, her heart, was too strong to endure. She trembled when he lifted his head but wouldn't open her eyes. She couldn't bear seeing whatever expression might be on his face. It had to be this way. Relationships among co-workers seldom worked out, and neither of them could handle a relationship right now. She assured herself this was the right decision, although her heart screamed that she was a fool.

"We're already friends," he said, so quietly that it almost sounded like a growl.

She didn't open her eyes and so wasn't prepared for his next move. Justin damn near pulled her off her feet. The air slipped out of her lungs when she hit his steel chest. He lifted her into his arms, moving too fast for a man of his size and showing too much agility when he moved around her coffee table and down onto her couch. She was draped over him, cuddled against his warm, rock-hard body, before her brain registered his actions and prepared defensive moves.

"Justin," she complained, twisting but then stilling when

his cock stretched against her ass, a hard, throbbing promise of how things could be.

"This is how it is," he growled, and captured her protest when he pressed his mouth over hers.

Grace knew beyond any doubt that no man ever had kissed her like this before. Justin took, demanding her response, but offered at the same time. As he devoured her mouth, the pleasure he gave her sizzled through her body, igniting a craving so deep, so intense, and so powerful that she didn't have the strength to fight it. Worse yet, she didn't want to fight it.

His hands stroked her back, feeding her with his power, his confidence and strength. She felt his determination and knew it matched her own. Grace wasn't weak. She wouldn't cower or submit to Justin or to any man ever again. But she wouldn't let him destroy her heart when, since being abducted, she was feeling for the first time in her life. Justin ignited something inside her that no man had ever reached before.

"I'm going to make love to you," Justin growled as he broke off the kiss and created a hot path of kisses down her neck.

"Oh." She couldn't form a sentence.

He gripped her ass, lifting and pressing her firmly against him so that she could feel how aroused he was. His actions didn't intimidate her or repulse her. Instead, her body responded, swelling, eager and anxious for him to fulfill his promise.

He lifted her off him like she weighed nothing, and she complied, moving her legs until she straddled him. There wasn't a greater glutton for punishment and torture anywhere on the planet. She owned the title there. When she relaxed against him, resting her arms on his shoulder and blinking to clear her vision and stare deep into the most intense gaze she'd ever seen, her pussy rubbed against her jeans while his cock stretched, swelled, and throbbed with heated promises that wiped all other thoughts out of her head. How long had it been since she'd been filled with what he offered? Grace wasn't sure she'd ever felt like this before. Hell, she knew she hadn't.

"My daughter is sleeping just down the hall." She sucked in a breath and her breasts swelled, large and heavy and aching as much as the rest of her. "And we can't do this, Justin."

"Yes, we can."

She swore she'd never seen so much determination, even in Master's insane eyes that had watched her through that leather mask he always wore. She blinked, refusing to dwell on her past. Justin's hands moved up her back, forcing her to arch her back like a cat. His head moved to her chest and he pressed his face between her breasts, as if he cuddled into her.

"I can't do this." Honesty wasn't something she offered to anyone. Not that she lied, but confiding the truth in another person meant opening up to them. Telling Justin the truth why they couldn't explore or put out the fire burning between them meant giving him part of her she'd offered to no man in her life. "Accept that, Justin. You must."

Justin wrapped his fingers around her waist, squeezing slightly before dragging his hands up her sides until he cupped her breasts. "What did he do to you?"

She wouldn't close her eyes, wouldn't let the memories appear as her mind reached to answer the question in spite of arguing with herself that talking about it would make things worse. "Forget about my past, Justin. It doesn't matter."

"Then why did you call your uncle?"

Grace pushed against his shoulders, damn near falling backward and then fighting not to tumble on top of him when the backs of her legs hit her coffee table. She jumped free of him, of her furniture, and pulled her hair behind her head with her hands while she blew out a frustrated breath.

"Leave, Justin. You need to go now," she said, hissing her words when she wanted to scream.

Justin stood slowly, his cock pressing against his jeans, stretched long and thick. He ran his hand over his blond hair and pierced her with dark green eyes that showed he bared the same amount of pain she did.

"Go home. Go to bed." She couldn't look at him, wouldn't

endure the intensity with which he stared at her. "We've got a bad guy to catch and both need sleep."

Her palms were damp and her fingers trembled when she wrapped them around her doorknob and then quietly pulled her front door open. When she glanced over her shoulder in his direction, she turned and put her hands on her hips as he walked to her back door. As she watched him lock the door, then check the window next to it, it was impossible not to drool over his hard, muscular ass. Even when she raised her focus to his back, the way his shirt stretched over his shoulder blades made the pulsing need in her reach a fiery, dangerous level.

It amazed her that a man his size could move across a room so quietly. He walked up to her and then grabbed her neck, wrapping his warm fingers under her jaw, and tilted her head back for her.

"You're an intelligent woman," he whispered, his green eyes dark and ominous. "You should be frightened. An insane monster is at play in this town and he knows now that you're out to get him. Whether you want it or not, and sweetheart, I know how badly you want it, you have me in your life. I will protect you, and your daughter, and I won't leave you alone."

Until the case was solved. Then he'd be gone. She didn't answer, didn't blink or even nod her head. The numbness she had felt for a mere moment earlier returned, washing over her and giving her the strength to harden her heart and continue to stare at him without begging him to stay.

"Good night, Justin," she whispered, her mouth as dry as her eyes.

Chapter 10

Justin got out of his truck Monday morning and stared at the small blue Honda that pulled into the parking lot and stopped, blocking his path to the station. Sylvia put the car in park and hopped out, prancing around the front of it in her high heels and conservative dress that still managed to prove that after having two children she had looks to kill. And an icy glare to match.

"All I want to know is when are you leaving town?" she asked, coming up quick until she stood in front of him.

"Cramping your style?" He tried walking around her.

Sylvia moved quickly, her high heels clicking against the asphalt, and pressed her small fists against her narrow waist. The morning breeze didn't stir her black-as-night hair that was perfectly twisted in a knot behind her head.

"More like my home life," she snapped. "Your daughter will be better off once you're gone. You stood her up. She's not some little toy you can toss to the side when you get too busy. Ever since you forgot about her Friday she's been pouting and throwing tantrums. And don't even get me started on Daniel. I'm not sure if he hates you more than I do or not."

Justin glared at her, knowing he'd failed as a father and as a husband but hating her for continually rubbing it in his face. "Then if you'll excuse me, the sooner I get this case wrapped up, the sooner I'll be out of your lives, again."

" 'Again' being the key word." Sylvia turned toward her running car. "Your redhead cop really should thank me. She'll fall for your charm and won't see the ugly truth behind those good looks of yours, Justin. Maybe I should point out to her again that there isn't a heart on this planet you aren't capable of destroying."

"You'd be wasting your breath," he told her, and headed toward the station.

"Don't think your sex appeal works on every woman, Justin Reece," she called after him. "I'll make sure she understands how much of a snake you are."

If there was anything about Sylvia he was grateful for, it was that she would never do anything publicly to embarrass herself. No one heard her cruel outburst, no one but the one person she had targeted. Hell of a way to start his Monday morning.

Christy winked at him when he entered the station and he managed a smile for her and headed for the coffee. Filling a cup, he fought not to let Sylvia's words sink in too deep. Maybe he would be better off leaving Grace alone. Probably she was the one woman sharp enough to know he successfully destroyed any female's life who entered his. First his little sister and now his daughter. He didn't destroy Sylvia's life. She thrived on making anyone and everyone miserable. But knowing Elizabeth moped because he hurt her cut deeper than he cared to admit. Solving this case as quickly as possible and then getting the hell out of Dodge might be his smartest move.

He sipped his coffee, staring at Christy's back and her pale, short blonde hair that tapered against her long thin neck. Then glancing toward Grace's open office door, he started in that direction before thinking about it further. Keeping his hands off her might not be an option, but it wasn't like he was asking for a commitment. Grace knew he was out the door as soon as they caught their perp. And she came from a family of FBI. He wouldn't let Sylvia get to him. Someday he'd patch things up with Elizabeth, and hell, who knew, maybe one day he and Daniel would speak, but for now his work came first and Grace was his partner on this case.

Her haunted look when he walked in the door pulled something from deep inside him, something dark and dangerous that heated his insides immediately. Her sultry blue eyes were bloodshot. As he watched, her expression turned guarded before she returned her attention to her computer screen.

"There are three stores in Rockville that sell Man's World," she said in form of greeting.

Justin found himself closing her office door, needing to know what exactly haunted her before he moved forward with anything else. The urge to destroy anything that would make her appear before him, looking damn near defeated, even if she did successfully mask the look in the next minute, hit him with a force strong enough to make him want to hit something.

"I'm going to contact each store and find out if they've sold any bottles of it in the past couple of weeks." She didn't look up at him and her hands remained poised over her keyboard. "Of course if he was smart, he paid with cash. But if we took his stash and he needs more he'll go to one of those stores to buy it. I want to find out if they have surveillance cameras installed."

"Sounds good." He fought the urge to come around her desk and pull her out of her chair. Forcing himself to stay put, he crossed his arms over his chest and watched her watch her screen. "What did you do this weekend?"

She looked like the question surprised her, snapping her attention to him quickly, as if he'd just asked her if she'd strip naked and fuck him on her desk.

"Spent time with my daughter. You?"

She couldn't know how her response was as bad as a slap in the face. "Nothing as productive, I'm afraid."

She caught his double meaning, although the way she searched his face proved she didn't have a clue how close to scorching an open wound she came.

"I'm sorry you can't spend time with your children," she said after a moment of silence.

"I've burned my own bridges, as I was so kindly reminded before I came into the station this morning."

"What?" She leaned forward on her arms, giving him all of her attention. "How have you burned bridges?"

"By forgetting to pick my daughter up from school on Friday."

"Oh crap."

"Sylvia pulled up outside when I got here just now, demanding to know how soon I would be leaving town and reminding me of how much of a snake I am. Don't be surprised if she seeks you out to point the same truth out to you."

"Her truth might not be mine," Grace told him, her deep baby blues turning hard.

Her hair was tumbled on top of her head this morning and already threatening to fall around her face in an array of curls that he itched to run his fingers through. As if she read his mind, her slender fingers went to her head and she dabbed at her curls, testing them, an act she did quite regularly and which drove him nuts.

"She loves the opportunity to point out how anything wrong in her life is my fault."

He wasn't sure what possessed him to talk to Grace about this. She had started the conversation out on their case, and he'd be smart to keep the subject that matter, instead of his personal life. But he had her attention, her undivided attention, as she searched his face and the hardness in her pretty eyes faded.

"I'll remind you next time to get your daughter," she said lightly, and then licked her lips, obviously trying to decide on what to say next. She looked noticeably relieved when the phone rang. "This is Grace," she said, grabbing it on the first ring. "We're on our way," she said a moment later, and then almost dropped the receiver when she tried putting it back in the cradle.

She jumped up, shoving her chair backward and making it shriek loudly before placing her receiver on the cradle properly. Then grabbing her purse she headed around the desk, stopping short so she wouldn't run into him.

"Another girl has been raped and murdered," she offered before he could ask.

There wasn't any keeping his hands off her. He ran them up her arms, loving how smooth and warm her skin was. She looked at him with a troubled gaze.

"What's wrong, Grace?"

"Someone is raped and murdered and you're asking me what is wrong?" She was an expert at putting up a shield to block her emotions.

But he saw through it anyway. "You were upset when I walked in here."

"We've got to go."

"And we will once you talk."

She chewed her lip, studying his face while her blue eyes glowed with emotions she couldn't hide from him. "I didn't sleep well last night. That's all."

Justin moved to the side, and she started toward the door. He gathered her thick curls that hung over the back of her neck into his hands and she froze. Then leaning over, he pressed his lips against her nape and hardened to steel when she shivered against his touch.

"We've got to work," she said, her voice a husky whisper.

Grace brought her hands to her mouth, exhaled, and then stepped forward without commenting on his kissing her neck. Instead she made a show of checking that her gun and phone were secure on her belt.

"What details did Christy just give you?"

"Young female raped and murdered. She's got the name and address out there."

"It's Monday morning," he said, grabbing Grace's attention. Her cheeks were flushed beautifully, offsetting her complexion against her dark red curls that already strayed out of their hair clasp and fell in tightly wound wisps around her face. "If she was murdered yesterday, then our killer is acting every Sunday."

"You're right," she said, then opened her office door and led the way to Christy's desk.

As they headed out the door, Grace handed him the

handwritten information. Daisy DePaul lived on Second Street. He didn't know any DePauls, which meant nothing, but the address would be easy enough to find. When he headed to his truck, Grace walked to the passenger side without question or concern over taking a squad car or riding with him. Whether she would admit it or not, she was comfortable around him. He wouldn't hurt Grace. She understood working an investigation, the need to find their perp, and that nothing else came first.

"One thing before we leave," he said when they got into his truck.

"What's that?"

No matter her defiance, he wouldn't think straight without knowing the truth. Justin grabbed her shoulders, pulling her to him, and pressed his mouth over hers. She opened to him, sighing against his body while her fingers traced lines up his arm. Trusting him implicitly instead of fighting her desire for him would help her think better. It sure as hell would help him keep his mind on task, too.

Grace tasted like coffee, her mouth hot and moist. She adjusted herself to him, tilting her head. He deepened the kiss, kneading her shoulders gently and pushing deeper into her heat.

The moment tension drained from her body and she relaxed under his touch, every inch of him hardened triumphantly. He ached to be inside her, wrap her heat around him until he couldn't stand it another minute. That would have to wait. Right now, knowing he had her, that no matter the nightmares harboring inside her she wanted him as badly as he did her, would have to do.

Justin ended the kiss, nipping her upper lip and then opening his eyes. Her long lashes fluttered over her baby blues, and she ran her tongue over her lips. Slowly her gaze met his.

"We're a team now," he whispered, straightening and caressing her shoulders a moment longer before letting her go. "Now we can leave."

She looked like she would argue but then nodded her head.

Nice stroke to the ego there. He'd rendered her speechless.

An ambulance and another patrol car were parked outside the plain stucco home when they arrived. Grace called in to Dispatch and confirmed another car was on its way.

"Who is already here?" Grace asked, and scowled at the answer. "Ten four," she said, and hung up her phone. "Bosley reported to the scene since he was already in the neighborhood."

She didn't like that Bosley was already here, and Justin didn't blame her. Grace wanted to investigate the crime scene knowing no one else had touched or moved anything prior to her arriving. Justin followed Grace up to the house. The energy radiating off her wasn't just from his kissing her senseless. He knew when a woman wanted him, but that wasn't all he saw in Grace. She craved the chase, the thrill of the hunt, and he would be right there to see the victory on her face when they closed in for the kill.

An older woman wearing a shapeless dress with an apron tied around it answered the door. Her eyes were swollen from tears, and she held the apron over her mouth as she allowed them to enter. Justin donned gloves, and Grace did the same. He glanced around the dimly lit room but was distracted by the metallic smell of fresh blood.

"It's the most terrible thing." The woman's voice cracked as she spoke. "The most terrible. I just don't understand," she continued, sobbing as she led them through the living room.

"Justin, I've never seen anything like this." Bosley walked into the room to greet them. "I've already got the statement from Mrs. DePaul, but I sure hope neither of you has just eaten."

"I found her like that." Mrs. DePaul, the woman who'd answered the door, spoke through her apron. "I didn't touch anything. I couldn't bear to even stay in there."

"You may not want to go in there, Grace." Bosley said, and his hand went to her arm.

"It's my job," she said dryly, but Justin thought he saw a small smile of reassurance on her face, as she patted Bosley's hand, then removed it from her arm.

"Okay, but I warn you, it's pretty ugly." Bosley looked up at Justin. "I've confirmed our Forensics team is on their way. ME should be here soon."

Grace pushed past the two men and entered a small bedroom off the living area. The fierce knot that grew quickly in her gut didn't hurt as much as her heart when it started pounding furiously against her chest. She tried gulping in air and getting a grip, but every inhale filled her lungs with the foul stench from a horrific death. She stared at the room in disbelief.

On a single bed, pushed up against the wall, a woman lay naked with her wrists bound to the bedpost. Bruises and cuts distorted her face and blood soaked her creamy white skin, pooling between her legs and hips. Her eyes were sightless, large and glassy like marbles, while her jaw hung open like her life had ended with her screaming.

A side table was overturned, and a lamp lay on its side next to the bed. The lamp shade had been thrown in the corner. By the discoloration on parts of the naked woman's body it appeared she had been burned by the bulb in several places.

Grace's belly roared and bile rose to her throat. She looked away from the body to give her stomach a moment to settle, and took a moment to look around the room. But when she glanced up at the wall her knees grew weak and she reached for the doorknob to steady herself.

"Oh my God," she whispered, and her hand went to her mouth.

Justin was next to her with his hands on her arms before she even realized he'd entered the room. On the wall, written in blood, were the words "Back off, or it will get worse."

"I can't believe it," she whispered as she realized how the woman had been raped, tortured, and murdered, then her blood was used to write the cryptic message.

No matter how many gruesome crimes Grace had witnessed, emotions strong enough to make her shake bit at her insides. Her inability to stay calm under such hideous situations kept her from reaching her dream. She'd heard it over and over again, and the thought hit her hard when she was sure she would puke. Grace didn't have the strength to be FBI, not when she couldn't handle situations just like this.

"Holy shit!" The lab technician voiced his opinion as he entered the room with a small black suitcase in his hand.

Grace could barely walk across the room. She bit her lower lip and held her breath as she neared the bed. Daisy was drenched in blood. It was dried to her skin and soaked deep into the twisted sheet underneath her. Her hands were bound above her head, and her arms were skinny, as was the rest of her. Grace would guess her to be under twenty, which fit their killer's profile.

Staring at Daisy's hands, Grace walked toward the head of the bed, barely able to stomach the atrocious odor that hung so heavily in the air it seemed to soak deep into Grace's skin.

"What are you doing?" Justin asked.

She ignored him and bent over Daisy's body. It was all she could do to inhale, and when she did her gag reflexes kicked in and she stood quickly, immediately choking. Justin grabbed her waist with both hands and pulled her against his body.

"What are you doing?" he repeated.

"Her hands." Grace coughed and then covered her mouth, scared she would puke any second. "They smell like Man's World."

"How can you smell anything?" the technician asked, pulling out a paper mask and yanking it over his head to cover his mouth and nose. "This is the most disgusting sight I've ever seen," he told them, sounding nasal through his mask.

Grace didn't like the way Justin pulled her away from the bed, letting her go next to the door. The technician's back was to them, staring at the wall, and she prayed their actions appeared professional and nothing else. This was her new town, her new job, and she'd need to get along with these people. There was no way she'd tolerate people talking about her having a fling with an FBI man who would be flying in and out of town.

Justin bent over Daisy, reached for one of her hands, but had to move closer to smell it. Grace had the warped satisfaction of his face looking rather green when he straightened.

"It smells of cologne."

"Dust the entire house," she told the technician as she walked away from Justin and out into the living room. "Or is this your case?" She suddenly realized Bosley had arrived first.

"By all means, you can have it." Bosley looked grim.

He handed the report he'd completed to her, and she read over it as she attached it to her clipboard. Then, ignoring the other officers and technicians, she began walking through the rooms of the house, determined not to let Justin see how disgusted all of this made her feel.

He had floored her back at the station, almost making her come with just a kiss. Now he stood like a rock of composure, unreadable and probably mentally calculating and photographing every detail of this crime scene. More than likely she was the last thing on his mind right now.

The hell with him for kissing her like that. She could do her job, too. After she left the men in the living room, she edged her way around a dining room table that was too large for the small room it was in and entered a small, cluttered kitchen. A variety of smells hit her, coffee, the smell of grease from cooking, and made her stomach churn more. The god-awful sight of Daisy DePaul in the other room wouldn't leave Grace's head. It took more than one try just to pull her pen from her pocket, her palms were so sweaty and her hands trembled so furiously. To make it worse, she couldn't push the button on the tip of the pen to open it. Just standing there for a minute, she fought to shove the nightmares that had plagued her all weekend out of her head.

The only thing to be thankful for when she looked at the older woman in the kitchen was that she seemed as tortured as Grace, sitting at the table with her face resting in her pudgy hands. Grace kicked herself to get her act together. This woman was suffering a hell of a lot more than Grace was right now.

"Do you have any pictures of . . ." She looked at the report. "Daisy DePaul? She lived here by herself?"

"Yes, ma'am." Mrs. DePaul stood slowly, her swollen knees visible past her loose dress. She walked around the kitchen as if she was trying to remember something she was supposed to do. "She's my daughter." She let out a choking sound into her apron. "We were supposed to go to the Laundromat together. I got here at ten, and I always just let myself in. I found her like that and called the police." Fresh tears flowed down the woman's face, and she blew her nose into her apron. "I guess I got a picture of her somewhere at my house. Who would do something like this? She didn't have no men in her life. She never even had a boyfriend, I don't think."

"The report says she was nineteen. I'm guessing you told Lieutenant Bosley that. Do you think she has any identification in the house? Do you know where her purse is so that I can see her driver's license?"

The woman again turned aimlessly around in the kitchen, and then her eyes fell on a purse thrown on the counter.

"Here, let me," Grace said, and prevented the woman from touching the purse with her hands. "Try not to touch anything until the technicians have had a chance to dust for fingerprints."

Grace had entertained a thought and now she realized her suspicions were correct. Daisy DePaul was a very pretty young woman. She had a toothy smile and dimples in both cheeks. Straight blond hair fell behind her shoulders, and spaghetti straps barely covered her thin shoulders as she smiled in the picture.

Grace dropped the driver's license into a Baggie. A pattern was falling into place, and she didn't like it.

"When did you last talk to Daisy?" she asked Mrs. De-Paul.

The woman jumped and looked startled, as if too far gone in her own thoughts and just realizing Grace still stood next to her. "She came by yesterday afternoon," she said, and then turned her back on Grace to blow her nose.

"What time did she leave?"

Mrs. DePaul waved her hands in the air. "I don't know. Oh, this is so terrible."

"It would really help me if you could try remembering."

"She . . . she stayed for supper. I guess she left around six." Mrs. DePaul faced Grace, her eyes watery and blood-shot. "She probably just came home. She works second shift but didn't work last night and has to work tonight." Mrs. DePaul's eyes grew wide and she looked toward the bed-room. She let out a low moan and started crying again.

"Is someone coming to get you?" Grace asked quietly, feeling the woman's pain and hating that there wasn't anything she could do about it.

Mrs. DePaul nodded but covered her mouth with her Kleenex, not commenting. Grace nodded, patting the wom-an's shoulder and then leaving her in the kitchen.

Grace was outside walking around the house when Justin caught up with her.

"What do you think?" He ran his hands through his hair, leaving it standing on end.

"I've got some hunches, but they're just speculation."

"Let's hear them."

"He's striking on Sunday. Daisy's mom told me Daisy was at their house yesterday until around six. We'll know once the coroner report is in the exact time of death, but she's been dead longer than a couple hours. He's going after girls in their late teens. Margaret and April were eighteen. Daisy is nineteen. And we already know his fetishes." She squinted toward the backyard. "We've obviously pissed him off."

"Have you ever seen anything like this before?"

"I've never been called to a scene like this before. I've seen some murder scenes that were pretty bloody, but not with messages left." She watched him as he studied her, and guessed he was trying to determine what had been done to her personally. Well, he could just forget about ever knowing. She would never let him know the humiliations she'd personally experienced.

Forcing her eyes away from him, Grace pointed to a window.

"None of the windows appear to be tampered with. Mrs. DePaul said she just walked in like she always does. I assume that's what the assailant did. None of the rooms are disturbed other than the bedroom. My guess is she was already in there when he attacked her."

They walked back around to the front of the house and stepped aside as the medics carried Daisy DePaul out on a stretcher with a sheet covering her body and red belts strapping her in. Blood had already seeped through some of the fabric.

"I want a copy of the autopsy faxed to my office the second you got it done," Grace told the medics. She and Justin waited while Mrs. DePaul walked in her husband's arms to their car. Bosley gave Grace a salute and wink as he headed to his squad car parked in front of the ambulance.

Justin's cell phone rang again, and he pulled it out of his pocket. He took her arm, holding his cell in his other hand, and started toward the house. "We're going over this scene again," he said, then answered his phone.

It was Uncle Charlie giving the arrival time and flight number. Grace wondered why he had called Justin with the information and not her.

Justin finished writing down the information on a small notepad, then stuffed it into his back pocket after hanging up the phone. "We'll pick up your uncle at seven tonight," he said simply. "Now then, we're going to relive this crime scene."

His green eyes were exceptionally bright today. They pierced her, holding her captive and for a moment making her forget how grotesque their surroundings were until she forced herself to look away.

She sucked in a breath, gathering her thoughts. "Okay. Daisy comes home last night after having supper with her parents. We know her mother enters this home without knocking, so possibly Daisy is relaxed enough in her environment that she doesn't lock her doors."

"The windows aren't locked, or tampered with," Justin pointed out.

"Right. So she doesn't lock her front or back door, either."

"Did he come in the front or back door?"

"There's no parking around back. When I glanced at the backyard, it's fenced in, no garage. Only parking is on the street."

"So front door?"

"We can't prove that with what we know. He either parked out front, not worrying about neighbors in an area where people don't lock their doors, or parked on another street and walked here, in which case he could have walked to the front or back door."

Justin nodded, tapping his finger against his lips as he walked toward the bed. It was clear where the body had been, and the mattress was slightly sideways over the box spring. The fitted sheet was crumpled on the middle of the mattress and the top sheet was still tied to the headboard, although it was clear where the medics had cut it to remove Daisy's body.

"So he enters the house." Justin stood with his back to her. He wore his usual ensemble of blue jeans and T-shirt, but she'd never seen a man make the casual attire look so appealing. Focusing on where the material stretched between his shoulders, she listened as he replayed the event out loud. "My hunch is that she was already in here, possibly in bed. She was naked, and I don't see any clothes tossed on the floor anywhere."

"You're right." She hated admitting that her attention was completely on what was done to Daisy, and the hell she had endured during it, when she needed to focus on the bigger picture, what was going on around her at the time. She walked around the single bed, ignoring the cryptic message on the wall, and studied the dresser and side table next to the bed. "I bet this is where her lamp usually was," she said, pointing to a doily on the side table. "See how it's got a white circle on it? I bet Daisy smoked; that would explain the yellowing on the doily that was exposed around the base of the lamp."

Grace looked around more, opening dresser drawers and then getting down on her hands and knees and tilting her head to see under the bed. She focused on Justin's boots on the other side before narrowing her gaze in on the few items and many dust bunnies before her.

Reaching under the bed with her gloved hands, she pulled out a shoe box, a pair of dirty socks, and a Monopoly game.

"Anything good?" Justin walked around the bed and stood over her.

Grace felt the weight of her hair clasp hanging crooked on the side of her head and reached to fix it but then looked at how dirty her latex gloves were after pulling everything from under the bed.

"I don't know yet," she said, pulling a glove off to fix her hair.

"You search through everything and I'll fix your hair," Justin said, squatting next to her and pulling off his gloves.

"What?" She turned as he grabbed the clasp holding all of her hair. "Justin, you can't—"

"It sucks you have to keep all these gorgeous curls bound up like this," he said, interrupting her, his tone deep and caressing her while he gripped her head and turned it so she once again looked at the objects she'd pulled out from under the bed.

"You're crazy. My hair is insane." She didn't like this. It wasn't right for him to play with her hair. And his fingers dragging over her scalp created sensations inside her she couldn't focus on right now.

"It's gorgeous, sweetheart," he said, his voice husky.

Before she could even fathom a response, he leaned forward and kissed her cheek. It was a comfortable action, way too comfortable, like they were longtime lovers or, even more so, a couple. And they weren't either. At the most they could be lovers, but the amount of discretion needed to pull that joining off would require behavior she wasn't seeing out of him. Not only was he not being discreet around her, far from it. Justin almost acted like he wanted everyone to know she was with him. But worse yet, his behavior right now implied something even more serious, a relationship of emotions, commitment, of love.

"There. Good as new."

She turned her head and didn't need to look over her shoulder to feel her hair securely in place the way it was supposed to be. "Thank you," she mumbled, feeling a fever rush over her skin when she tried concentrating on what she'd pulled out from under the bed.

"Well, hell," she said, picking up the half-smoked cigar that currently was covered with dust from under the bed. "What do you want to bet that this hasn't been under there as long as it appears?"

Chapter 11

After grabbing her daughter from after-school care, Grace hurried into the house with Rachel leading the way. Grace called Uncle Charlie, hoping to catch him and confirm everything before he left for his flight.

"What do you mean, you're staying with Justin?" She balanced the phone between her ear and shoulder while struggling out of her uniform and into jeans.

Rachel leaned against her bedroom door, crossing her arms, looking ready to throw in her two cents. Sometimes her daughter looked way too wise for her years.

"From what he tells me, his house is much larger than yours. He and I were talking, and with all that's going on, it might not be a bad idea for you and Rachel to stay out there, too."

"What?" She almost dropped the phone while struggling with her shirt. "You're kidding, right? We can't move in with Justin."

"Is there something wrong with the place?" Uncle Charlie laughed. "Don't tell me you've never been to the man's home."

Grace scowled, sliding into her shoes and then grabbing her daughter, making her do an about-face and then guiding her into the living room. She let go of Rachel and headed into the kitchen.

"Uncle Charlie, he is a special agent assigned to help me with this case. And his computer system linked to the FBI offers access to information we can't gather at the police station."

Rachel turned and looked up at her. "Whose house have you been to?"

"Justin Reece's," she told her, then pulled out the fixings to make both of them sandwiches.

"What's for supper?" Rachel asked, seemingly unimpressed with the conversation her mother was having.

"Rachel will be safer there, Grace. You're chasing a monster and from what I hear starting to piss him off."

"You know I've pissed criminals off in the past," she argued, balancing the phone between her ear and shoulder while opening the refrigerator and grabbing condiments. "Rachel and I are fine right where we are."

"I don't know that I agree." Uncle Charlie was using that tone he used when he wasn't going to be argued with.

But this was beyond ridiculous. The last thing she could do was stay with Justin. Rockville would have a field day, and at her expense.

"We'll discuss this later, Uncle Charlie. I'm going to get Rachel fed and then we'll be on our way to the airport. Love you."

She and Rachel left for the airport after eating sandwiches and yogurt for supper. Justin suggested he go with them to pick up Uncle Charlie, but Grace needed space from him.

"Someone has to stay in town and keep all the bad guys at bay," she said lightly.

As she drove back to Rockville on the dark county road, silence fell between her and her uncle. Rachel crashed in the backseat and Grace hated that yet again another night her daughter was going to crawl into her own bed later than she should. Soon she would figure out a way for Rachel to stick to a schedule and not continually be falling asleep somewhere else, only to be hauled to her own bed once Grace managed to wind her evening down.

"Tell me, what's going on with your investigation?" Uncle Charlie asked, breaking the silence.

"Well, we had one hell of a nasty murder to investigate this morning. Another young girl was killed after being tortured and raped. And there was a message written on the wall in her blood," Grace said quietly, glancing in her rearview mirror to make sure Rachel still slept.

"This isn't looking good, Grace. What did it say?" His face wrinkled with the worry that she'd only heard on the phone earlier.

"It said: 'Back off, or it will get worse.'" She kept her eyes on the road and white-knuckled the steering wheel.

Uncle Charlie exhaled loudly.

"Do you have all the paperwork in order showing that Rachel is yours?" Uncle Charlie whispered. He startled her with that question.

"Of course I do. You helped me legally adopt her, remember?"

"I just want to know the paperwork is available," he said gruffly.

"Yes. The paperwork is in order." She didn't like the insinuation that she might lose something so important. "It still eats me up that I had to legally adopt my own daughter," she hissed under her breath. "But what does that have to do with anything?"

"I know life has given you some hard blows." He patted her hand, and she wrapped her fingers into his. "There isn't anyone on this planet more than me who wants you to only have to deal with the normal challenges of life from here on out."

"What are you getting at, Uncle Charlie?"

"The murders you're describing sound a lot like murders I dealt with ten years ago in Minnesota right before we found you and Rachel."

"There are a lot of murders that are like what we're investigating," Grace said, keeping her voice low and fighting the bile that rose to her throat at her uncle's insinuation. "Don't even think that, Uncle Charlie."

Uncle Charlie squeezed her hand with his large, rough fingers. "Never rule out any possibility while working a case, Grace," he said too seriously. She looked over at his grave expression in the dark car. "The facts are sitting right there. You're describing horrific, brutal rapes and murders where your perp is leaving calling cards that match what we investigated ten years ago."

"He left cigars?"

"Yup."

"Man's World cologne?"

"No, that one is new."

"Sorry, Uncle Charlie, I'm not going to panic and lose my ability to think straight by allowing a ghost to haunt me." She focused on the two-lane highway ahead of her, pursing her lips with determination to feel the words she had just voiced. There was no way Master still lived. None at all. "Besides, if he were alive he would have come after me long before now."

"Grace Jordan?"

"Speaking," Grace answered, and adjusted the headset she had found at the department store in Rockville, which willingly charged it to the city's account for her. It might be a small, trivial expense, but remembering the pained expression Justin gave her when he more or less conceded to being a terrible father after Sylvia chewed his ass made it worth it to think of Sylvia fuming if she learned Grace was spending her precious city funds.

"Ms. Jordan, this is Dorothy DePaul. Could I talk to you?" The woman's tone alerted Grace. She sounded pensive and almost whispered.

"Of course. What can I do for you?" Grace had diligently entered reports that next day and leaned back in her office chair, stretching and glancing at the clock.

"Not on the phone. I need to see you. Is that okay?"

It was almost five. It would be time to get Rachel soon and head over to Justin's house for dinner. Uncle Charlie was already there and had called to make sure Grace was going to make it for a special meal he'd spent the afternoon preparing for all of them. She couldn't help feeling he was encouraging her to spend more time with Justin. Although

Grace didn't doubt her uncle's heart was in the right place, she knew without any doubt that her heart couldn't handle getting close to such a wonderful man who would be leaving soon.

"I'm getting ready to go get my daughter," she said slowly.

Mrs. De Paul breathed heavily. "Oh, I'm sorry. I can talk to you tomorrow."

"No, that's okay. I have someone who can watch her once she's home." Uncle Charlie wouldn't be thrilled if Grace missed his meal. Of all people, he would understand, though, that work always came first before socializing. "Where would you like me to meet you?"

Dorothy DePaul suggested a local restaurant that Grace hadn't been to yet. After writing down the address, she told Dorothy she would meet her in an hour and then grabbed her purse. Grace experienced a wave of relief on getting out of the meal. She didn't like the nervous rush that ate at her, though, when she put the call through to her uncle but found her thoughts on Justin. It wasn't like she answered to him. If this meeting pertained to the case, then she would call him.

"Thank you for meeting me." Dorothy gestured with her hand, and Grace sat down.

The woman had picked a small diner that smelled strongly of fried foods and burnt coffee. There were a fair amount of people in the place, and the sounds of conversation and silverware clinking against plates created an appropriate background noise as Grace studied the stout woman who didn't look much better than she had when Grace first saw her in Daisy's home.

"It's not a problem." Grace smiled and pulled a small handheld tape recorder out of her purse. Another purchase she'd joyfully charged to the city's account. "Do you mind if I record our conversation?"

Dorothy shook her head and twisted a napkin while she watched Grace place the recorder on the table between them.

"I've always thought of myself as an honest person. And I raised my Daisy to be honest, too. Honest and hardworking . . . that's the kind of people we are." Dorothy choked, looking like she might cry, but then took a breath and continued. "There's something I didn't tell you. With everything else that's just happened, I just don't need this on my conscience. I don't have any concern for myself, not without my Daisy."

"What do you need to tell me?" Grace watched Dorothy glance around the diner. A pimply-faced waiter walked past them with a large tray full of plates of steaming food. The smell of the food turned Grace's stomach.

"I was scared. But I don't care what they do. I want the bastard that did those things to my baby to rot, and if I tell you this and it brings him out of the woodwork, then so be it," Dorothy rambled, and Grace forced herself not to pressure the woman. A minute passed while Mrs. DePaul tore her napkin to shreds and Grace restrained herself from saying anything. Instead she focused on the tape, winding around itself, inside the recorder.

She glanced up when Dorothy put her purse on the table and then dug through it for a minute. The crumpled piece of notebook paper she pulled out looked like it had been folded and unfolded many times. "This was in the bedroom when I arrived. I guess the bastard got my Daisy to tell him that I would be the first one to find her."

Grace took the paper with apprehension. She hated it when evidence at the scene of a crime was removed by a family member. More than likely Mrs. DePaul didn't realize she had handled evidence that could have had the murderer's prints on it. Although in this case Grace seriously doubted it, she held the paper at the corner with her thumb and index finger. The sprawled handwriting was blotched with pale pink smudges on the otherwise plain notebook paper—like whoever wrote it might have been bleeding.

"Is this your daughter's handwriting?" Grace asked.

"Yes, ma'am," Dorothy said, her voice cracking.

Grace's heart started thumping in her throat, and she

fought her gag reflexes when she quickly scanned the contents of the letter, then forced herself to read it slower. The room started spinning slowly around her.

Dear Mama
    I'm hurt bad, and he's not through. He wants me to write this to you so you know he takes breaks so I feel everything and the pain don't run together. He says I'm lucky that he's chosen me because he only chooses the best. He's returned from the fires of hell for only the prettiest girls. He won't enjoy torturing me for too long. He promised me. He's never made a mistake, but he has learned from his experiences. When he returns to hell he will take all that belongs to him with him. He told me to write that.
    I love you, Mama.
    Daisy

Grace stared at the piece of paper in front of her and tried to keep her emotions in check. Tears burned her eyes while she fought to stifle emotions the way a good investigator would.

When he returns to hell he will take all that belongs to him with him.

The words jumped out at her.
"Where did you find this letter?" Grace asked.
"Oh." Her flesh puffy under her watery eyes, Dorothy stared at Grace. "Does that matter?"
"I'm just trying to make sure I know every detail concerning your daughter's death. It will help me catch the guy who killed Daisy."
Dorothy nodded, continuing to stare at Grace until enlightenment made her straighten. "I remember. I'm sorry. Everything about my Daisy's death is quickly becoming a blur."
"That's natural," Grace assured her.

"It was in her hand. I saw her handwriting and took it out of her hand."

Grace looked at the letter again. Holding it a bit closer, she wasn't sure if she smelled anything on the piece of paper or not.

"Mrs. DePaul, did you notice any unusual smells on the paper when you picked it up?"

"Now that you mention it, I remember wondering why it smelled like men's cologne. But the room was so bad . . ." She choked and then broke into a coughing fit, covering her mouth as she stared at the tape recorder on the table between them.

"Thank you for bringing this to me. I think you've helped move this investigation forward a lot," Grace said, reaching out and patting the older woman's plump hand. "I need to take this with me, if you don't mind."

"God, I don't want it. If I think of anything else, I'll call you." Dorothy stood, hesitated for a moment while her hands fluttered around her face, then turned and hurried out of the restaurant.

Grace picked up her tape recorder, turning it off, and put the handwritten letter from Daisy in her purse. As she walked to her car, the words in the letter swarmed around in her head.

He's returned from the fires of hell . . .

Grace shivered against a cool early evening breeze that competed with the warm summer sun. Even in her car she couldn't warm up, though. Jumping out, she unlocked her trunk and pulled an evidence bag from a box of supplies she kept there for times like these. Mrs. DePaul had probably handled the letter to death but there was always a chance they could pick something up off of it.

"Good Lord," she grumbled, remembering as she pulled from the curb that she needed to get her daughter, who was out at Justin's house. "You need to talk to him anyway," she conceded, running her fingers through her hair and not caring that strands fell free from her hair clasp. "It's a typical letter, proof of a murderer's insanity."

When he returns to hell he will take all that belongs to him with him.

What exactly did this madman view as his?

She was proud as hell of herself for finding Justin's house on her own without having to call for directions. That bit of satisfaction uplifted her enough to enter his house with a smile. Which was what Rachel needed to see.

"Mommy!" Her daughter jumped up from the living room floor after Uncle Charlie opened the front door for Grace.

"Hope missing supper was worth your while," her uncle grumbled, standing to the side and then closing the door behind her. "Justin headed upstairs to do some work. But at least these two enjoyed their meal."

"I talked to Elizabeth on the phone. You remember that Justin is her dad, right, Mom?"

"I remember." Grace ran her hand over her daughter's mop of curls and found herself grinning back at her daughter's animated expression.

"She wants to come over, but her mother said no." Rachel's expression grew serious. "Can't you make Justin make her come over? It would be more fun here if I could play with Elizabeth. And besides, she said a long time ago she lived here, so I don't understand why she can't come over."

Grace noticed Uncle Charlie's worried look but focused on her daughter, whose expression made it clear she didn't understand feuding exes.

"We can't make either of them do anything," Grace began, trying to find the right words while her brain was already on overload from newfound information on the case, as well as being acutely aware of her surroundings and how the air seemed to spark with energy from Justin's presence, even if he was upstairs.

Upstairs. God, she needed to keep her thoughts straight.

"But maybe we can have Elizabeth over at our house sometime," she said, glancing at her uncle when he stiffened at the comment.

There wasn't time to determine his reaction. Heavy, solid

footsteps on the stairs raised her blood pressure several notches. And all too aware of her uncle still looking at her, she focused on her daughter, praying he wouldn't pick up on anything going on between her and Justin. Because there wasn't anything going on.

"We should probably get ready to go," she said, deciding it would be easier to talk to Justin over the phone later, after she had her daughter settled in for the night.

"I don't want to leave yet," Rachel insisted, turning and returning to the spot on the floor where she'd been when Grace walked in the door. "Uncle Charlie said we couldn't have dessert until you got here, and this house is better than ours is anyway. Justin has better stuff than we do."

Justin's dark, brooding stare was impossible to read as he stared at Grace in the doorway leading from the hall and the stairs. For some reason, his being barefoot in his jeans, wearing the same T-shirt he'd had on earlier, untucked and hanging over his straight-cut jeans, made him look sexy as hell. His sandy blond hair was slightly tousled, but not even the worry lines apparent around his eyes managed to take away anything from his incredible good looks.

"Looks like it's time for dessert then," her uncle announced, clapping his hands together and then rubbing her shoulder as he walked past her. "Come on into the kitchen and tell us all about this important meeting that kept you from supper."

Rachel ignored all of them as she picked up the controller plugged into the large-screen television and started playing a game. When Grace turned to follow Charlie, Justin fell into stride alongside her.

"Yes, I'd like to also hear what kept you from supper, and from calling and letting me know where you went."

"I didn't realize I was supposed to," she snapped, her guard up quickly even as she met his powerful, dominating expression. She didn't answer to any man and never would for the rest of her life. His protective nature didn't sway her, and she ignored the pattering of her heart when he put his hand on her back and guided her to the kitchen. "And I went to meet Mrs. DePaul," she told him, knowing she did so because it was important to the case and not because he was trying to lay the law down with her.

"Oh really?" When they entered his kitchen Justin faced her and crossed his arms over his muscular chest. Dark green eyes probed deep into her soul, seeming to focus on parts of her she'd rather the world not see. "Why did you go see her?"

Grace refused to drool or get lost in his intense stare. He wanted to control her, and that wasn't going to happen. Moving to stand next to her uncle, she helped herself to a dinner roll and tore it in half while leaning against the counter.

"She called me before I left the station," she explained, and then filled her uncle and Justin in on her visit with Dorothy DePaul at the restaurant. After playing the recording of their conversation, she pushed Stop just as Rachel appeared in the doorway. "Where's dessert, Uncle Charlie?" Grace asked, ignoring his and Justin's anxious expressions and knowing they both wanted to know what the letter said.

Uncle Charlie made quick work of slicing pie onto dessert plates. Justin jumped in, appearing very out of character to Grace as he moved easily around his kitchen and even had Rachel giggling when he carried her plate along with his to his dining room table. Rachel and Uncle Charlie slipped into chairs they probably had sat at during supper, and Justin turned, pulling a chair out for Grace gallantly. She made a face at him and took her seat.

Small talk followed until Rachel excused herself, eagerly taking her plate to the kitchen after Justin suggested she do so. Grace found herself acknowledging a new side of Justin. In spite of his downfalls with his own family, he was good with kids.

"Show me the letter," Justin said, not missing a beat when Rachel left the room.

"It's in my purse." She took Uncle Charlie's and Justin's plates into the kitchen. Then pulling the letter enclosed in the Ziploc Baggie out of her purse, which she'd left on Justin's counter, she turned and almost ran into

Justin's chest. "We're dealing with a really sick mother-fucker," she whispered, even though Rachel was back in the living room.

He took the bag, with the letter pressed flat inside, and then held her arm when she tried walking around him. Uncle Charlie appeared next to them, his gaze locking on Justin holding Grace in place. She could make a scene and make him quit touching her or act like it didn't bother her at all that he wanted her to stand there until he finished reading.

"Good God," Justin grumbled, showing his disgust when he handed the letter to Uncle Charlie. "He's getting more personal."

"Where was this letter found?" her uncle asked.

"Apparently it was in our victim's hand. She was tied to her bed," Grace explained, all too aware of Justin watching her, his gaze darker and very dangerous looking. "Her mother took the letter and then for whatever reasons didn't tell me about it until today."

"Probably slipped her mind," Uncle Charlie said, looking at the letter again. "I don't like this, Grace. Not at all."

"Who would?" She wanted to be busy doing something. This wasn't her house, and turning to rinse the dishes would give the impression she was making herself at home.

"He's sending us a message." Justin crossed his arms, staring across his kitchen. "When he returns to hell, he's taking what belongs to him with him."

"That line grabbed my attention, too." Grace stared at the letter, still in her uncle's hands. The pale blotches on the paper, where she guessed blood smeared the paper, made the pie she just ate turn in her stomach. "What does he think belongs to him?"

"I can't believe this." Uncle Charlie frowned at her. "This man's a raving lunatic. I don't care how many years I was with the Bureau, I'll never get the stomach for stuff like this."

Grace didn't have the stomach for it, either. She didn't have to read it again. The sordid words in the message still swam around in her head.

"Maybe we should try setting him up," Grace suggested,

and both men looked at her with hard, fierce stares. "He's going after eighteen-, nineteen-year-old girls."

"And as drop-dead gorgeous as you are, you don't look eighteen or nineteen," her uncle interrupted.

"You're not putting yourself in the line of fire for this monster," Justin snapped, turning and walking toward her until he stood right in front of her. "He's sending us messages and his cockiness is irritating the shit out of me. We're going to think this through and take a good look at all the clues here," he continued, taking a strand of hair that curled past her jaw and twisting it around his finger. "There's something about that letter," he said, nodding to Uncle Charlie.

Grace backed up, running her hand over her hair and freeing it from Justin's fingers. Uncle Charlie's expression was grave when he watched the two of them and nodded once slowly.

"Personally I think better on a good night's sleep. You're wonderful to put an old man up, Justin." Reaching for Grace, Uncle Charlie pulled her into a comforting hug and patted her on the back, holding her for a moment before letting her go. "Call me once you get to work, my dear, let me know what time to pick up Rachel. We'll get her going on that routine you crave for her to have."

"Thank you, Uncle Charlie," Grace whispered, breathing in his familiar scent as she hugged him back. "Rachel and I are heading home, too."

Her uncle let her go and stared at her, his expression suddenly sad. She wanted to question him, know his thoughts, but he turned, waving over his shoulder, and then called to Rachel to give her great uncle a hug good night.

"I'm going to follow you home," Justin said when they were alone.

"That's not necessary." She waved him off and started toward the living room. Her emotions were too shot after everything that day to be alone with him, even if they weren't completely alone with Rachel and Grace's uncle in the other room.

Just the thought of fucking Justin created pressure deep

inside her that refused to fade regardless of the conversation. And it made no sense that she felt this way. Ten years had passed since she left the sexual prison and torture that her life once was. Since then, no man, no matter how good-looking and cavalier, had stirred her like Justin did—and was doing right now.

"Don't try denying the fact that whoever had Daisy De-Paul write that letter knows right now that it's in your possession." Justin placed his strong, warm hand on her shoulder, which was enough to keep her from walking away. "We're not dealing with just another rapist or murderer here. He's got an agenda. And I'm sure that cryptic message being in your possession is part of it."

"Sweet dreams to you, too." She looked over her shoulder, but the moment she searched his dark, intense green eyes her heart stopped. Nothing he said affected her the way his gaze at her did.

"Grace," Justin said soothingly, too soothingly.

She stared into his deep sensual gaze. Pressure exploded inside her and she almost teetered. If it weren't for her bra and blouse, her hardening nipples that suddenly itched painfully against her clothes would be a dead giveaway of how he aroused her.

"I'm fine," she insisted, shifting her attention to the doorway leading down the hallway to the living room. "We're fine. Besides, as it was so lovingly pointed out to me earlier, he doesn't like older women."

Justin turned her around with enough force she couldn't prevent herself from stumbling. His arms were around her, his protective, incredibly strong embrace turning the smoldering need burning deep in her womb into a full-fledged burning-out-of-control craving that damn near exploded when he suddenly touched her everywhere.

"If you argue with me on this one," he whispered into her hair, and then his lips pressed against her forehead, searing her flesh, "then I'm not going to let you leave."

"Fine," she sighed, completely incapable of arguing about anything.

He grabbed her jaw, angling her face, and then crushed his lips against hers. The fire he fed into her burned with intensity matching the heat already inside her. His kiss was demanding, aggressive, and a day's worth of whiskers scraped over her flesh, igniting even more need that made her skin too sensitive to his touch. There wasn't any point dwelling on the years of therapy that got her past hating most men. And focusing on all of the lectures she'd given herself over the type of man she would and wouldn't tolerate while attempting to date wouldn't do her a damned bit of good. There wasn't a rule book that applied to Justin. Trying to figure out why his dominating, possessive nature practically made her come in her pants didn't change the fact that he did.

His lips left hers, leaving them numb and feeling swollen. She licked them and he growled, and although she couldn't quite focus, she stared up at him.

"Good. Be miserable," she muttered, and then was able to focus quickly when the haze over his eyes cleared quickly. It dawned on her that without coming out and admitting to anything, she just made it clear as crystal that she craved fucking him as much as he obviously wanted her. That was very dangerous knowledge to put in his head and she realized that immediately. "It won't change a thing when it comes to how things must be," she added quickly, her voice a raspy whisper. She prayed her stern expression drove her point home, though. Eventually the fire would go out. It had to.

Justin straightened but didn't let her go. He dragged his fingers down her neck and then flattened his palm against her collarbone while pressing his hand flat against her body. Moving lower, he never took his eyes from hers as he dragged his hand lower until he cupped one breast in his hand. Her breasts were already swollen and heavy with need, but when he squeezed slightly, charged currents of need zapped her insides and her pussy throbbed so painfully she wasn't sure she could move.

"Before the day is out tomorrow, one way or another, sweetheart, I'm going to witness you coming as many times as it takes until that flushed look on your face is replaced with a very sated and satisfied expression."

Her jaw dropped, his statement shocking her enough to stop her world, her heart, and, she swore to God, everything around her. There was so much conviction in Justin's voice that he might as well have just told her that tomorrow was Wednesday or that the sun would rise in the morning.

Justin apparently didn't need a response. He turned her around, his touch sizzling her flesh as his hands moved over her back and guided her to the living room. "Let's get you home," he said with the same soft, authoritative baritone. "You're going to need a good night's sleep."

Chapter 12

"He's striking every Sunday." Justin leaned against the side of Grace's desk, shaking his head with disapproval as he held an autopsy report in each hand. He nodded at the report Uncle Charlie held in his hand. "We've got our proof now."

"Yup. Looks like it." Uncle Charlie tossed the report on Grace's desk. "Time of death for DePaul was twelve hours before she was found, so early Sunday evening."

"And Margaret was dead about a week when we found her. I guess he saved her so we'd find her when we found April." Grace rested her forehead against her palms and closed her eyes. Justin's aftershave filled her senses when she inhaled but simply reminded her that Man's World cologne, the same nasty-smelling stuff Master used, was another clue. "It's almost like . . ."

"What?" Justin and Uncle Charlie asked at the same time.

She looked up and pushed a curl out of her face. "Nothing. Nothing," she repeated. "We just don't have enough information."

Charlie stood, slapping his hand against his thigh and winking at Grace. "Sometimes all the information is right in front of you. You just have to figure out how to piece it together. I'm headed out on the town for a while. Figured I'd check out what Rockville has to offer me."

Charlie walked around Grace's desk as she stood and gave her a peck on the cheek. He offered a gesture similar to a wave to Justin.

"Call me if you need anything," Grace said.

Her uncle grunted and slipped out of the office, shutting the door behind him and leaving the two of them alone. Immediately her heart raced in her chest. There were officers outside the door, the dispatcher, but if Justin touched her, got too close . . .

"I'm going to head out to the two grocery stores and drugstore that carry Man's World cologne," Grace said, sitting again and shutting down her computer.

"Sounds good. We'll ask around more about that blue Buick, too." Justin didn't move from where he leaned on the edge of her desk.

Grace grabbed her purse, and static electricity sparked over her flesh. There wasn't any moving around her desk without getting dangerously close to him. In spite of the case preoccupying her thoughts and distracting her dreams at night, being in the same room with Justin did something to her insides that she didn't know how to handle.

"What's bothering you?" he asked, tilting his head slightly when she lifted her purse.

Grace looked at him, instantly feeling him pull her in with those predatory green eyes. Nightmares about who their rapist and murderer might be, promises from a seductive special agent, trying to be the best mother she could be and get her new job off on the right foot—she sighed heavily.

"What's bothering me?" she began, not sure how smart it would be to unload on him.

"Talk to me, Grace." There was a softness in his tone that appealed as much as his concerned expression did. He didn't stand but continued relaxing on the edge of her desk, putting them at eye level with each other.

"The messages we're being sent bother me. Who this madman might be bothers me. Your thinking I'm promiscuous bothers me."

"Promiscuous?" he interrupted, giving her a roguish grin as he grabbed her waist and pulled her between his legs. "Lady, I've met women before who've been abused, held captive, and forced to do terrible things."

"I'm sure," she muttered, pushing against his rock-hard chest.

Justin tightened his grip on her. "Most of them are cold and frigid—"

"I'm not being cold toward you."

"And you're anything but frigid," he added, and reached for a curl that had already fallen loose by her face.

"I just don't want you to think . . ." She paused, searching for the right words. "I mean, I don't usually do this sort of thing. We just need to forget that anything between us ever happened."

"No." He uttered the one word with so much finality it stole her breath.

She inhaled slowly, taking his scent deep inside her. "Justin, your attention is flattering, but why are you doing this?"

He looked at her for a moment with almost a comical expression, and she grew antsy under his gaze.

"Why?" He stood, letting go of her and shaking his head as he walked over toward the closed office door. "There is nothing easy about you at all, Grace. If you want answers to questions that haven't been addressed yet, I can't help you."

She looked up from his hard ass when he turned around. Her breath caught in her throat at the dark, possessive look in his eyes.

"There's something here. We're going to explore it. And tell me you don't want that and I'll call you a liar."

"A physical attraction could prove very dangerous."

"We thrive on danger, Grace." He moved the files on her desk and picked up a small, flat box she hadn't noticed sitting there.

Her mouth fell open when he held the small, flat gift-wrapped box in his hand.

"What's that?"

"Open it and find out."

Her cheeks burned almost as badly as the heat swarming inside her. He rendered her speechless, so she glared at him. He seemed to like that look, too.

"Open it." He held out the box. She looked at the fine

silver wrapping paper secured with a gray ribbon as it rested in his palm. "Take it. I went to quite an effort to get it for you."

"You shouldn't have—"

"I wanted to."

Refusing a gift would be rude. And damn it, she ached to know what he got her. Slowly she stepped around his long legs, the sensation of approaching a deadly predator making her heart patter off beat. She lifted the box from his hand, ready to jump if he grabbed her. Instead he lowered his hand, not moving from where he sat at the edge of his desk and watched her intently. She tore the paper unceremoniously.

"Oh my." Two Oriental hair combs lay on a square piece of cotton. She brushed the intricate design with her finger, then looked up at Justin. "They're beautiful."

"That's why they made me think of you," he said, and offered her an irresistible smile.

"Justin." She tried disputing his compliment, but he stopped her with one quick, solid movement. Then his mouth covered hers.

The kiss was demanding yet soothing and burning with passion. He pulled her against him, and the only way she could prevent herself from falling on top of him was to grab ahold of him. She dug her fingers into his shoulders, feeling his muscles twitch under her touch. Just when she felt her world tilt to the side, he ended the kiss.

Grace licked her lips, trying to taste what had just been taken from her. Her heart skipped to a beat she hadn't known a second ago, and she met his gaze.

"You are beautiful." He emphasized each word, then added, "Inside and out."

Her eyes must have betrayed her without permission, because he stood and then wrapped his arms around her, tilting her body so that it molded against his, and stared at her for a long moment. When his mouth covered hers she remembered that she forgot to breathe. Too late. The room spun around her while he impaled her mouth with his tongue. She abandoned all thoughts of fighting off his advances.

"Grace?" Christy tapped on the door to her office.

Grace jumped out of his arms and into the chair, her heart suddenly pounding so hard in her chest it would explode for sure. She crossed her legs, then uncrossed them and stared down at her hands. Every inch of her tingled and her lips had to be swollen twice their usual size. Licking them didn't do her any good. She tasted Justin, which sent her insides into a full raging boil. Her pussy throbbed as hard as her heart, and the pressure between her legs would make it impossible to stand.

At the same time, Justin sounded as nonchalant, and looked completely relaxed, as if they'd just been discussing crosswalk duty.

"You're fine, Christy," he said, opening the door. "You're not interrupting anything." She couldn't look up at him; she knew he was smiling.

Christy peeked her head around the door. "Grace, Sheriff Montgomery is on his way in. He wants to see you, so don't go anywhere."

Grace surprised herself with how calmly her words came out.

"Sounds good. I'll be here." She couldn't help but wonder why Christy felt a need to give her advance warning, unless she suspected what the two of them might be doing in here and had to find out for herself. "Just send him in when he gets here."

Justin pulled Grace out of her chair and into his arms the moment Christy closed the door behind her. "I'm going to make love to you—very soon," he whispered.

"Does it get you off saying that?" Her heart raced so fast in her chest she worried it might explode. His expression hardened, like a deadly predator being challenged. "Maybe you should ask if I want to make love to you."

Every inch of him was wound so tight he looked like he might pounce and fuck her right there in her office. "I wouldn't insult you."

She blinked. "What?"

Justin took her hands with the hair combs and brought

them to his mouth. She felt his strength, the predatory domination that singed her skin, the heat swarming between her legs.

"By suggesting you would get so hot for a man who wasn't capable of seeing inside you and knowing what you want."

Heavy booted footsteps sounded outside the door and Grace pulled away from him. "You pompous ass," she hissed, ripping her hands from his as Sheriff Montgomery filled her doorway.

The Sheriff was old enough to be her father, if her father were still alive, with gray eyes that matched his hair. He was fairly nondescript, although his Sheriff's uniform granted him the authority his persona demanded.

"What's the FBI think about these increasing rapes in our town?" he asked as he entered the room.

"We don't like it. But we've gathered a lot of shit on this guy, Sheriff. We were getting ready to head out to follow up on some leads," Justin offered, and glanced at Grace.

She took the lead and filled the Sheriff in on checking with the stores that sold Man's World cologne and then checking around to see if anyone knew anyone who drove a blue late-nineties Buick.

"Good." The Sheriff looked stern, but his tone was gentle. "I don't have to tell you that Rockville isn't accustomed to crimes like this. We deal with the occasional theft, some drunken behavior, and a few speed demons. But rape, and like this." He walked past Grace, seemingly oblivious to the charged energy that sizzled in the air. Picking up one of the autopsy reports, he shook his head. "It's despicable."

"All rape is despicable," she pointed out to him.

"You're right." The Sheriff nodded seriously. "Rockville is a small town. It's hitting the papers. People are talking, and panicking."

"We'll get your man," Grace insisted.

"I hope so." The Sheriff shook his head, and when he looked at her she swore there was sadness that didn't have anything to do with the rapes. "None of this is your fault. But I'm running out of reasons as to why I hired a new officer and then our crime rate quadrupled."

"You're lucky then that you hired her when you did." Justin stepped forward, nodding to the door. "Are you ready, Grace? Sheriff, we'll get back with you."

Sheriff Montgomery nodded, his expression remaining somber when Grace walked past him, following Justin into the outer office. Bosley stood at the filing cabinets next to Christy's desk and turned, giving first Justin and then Grace an appraising once-over.

Bosley studied her as if trying to figure something out, and his expression changed slightly. Something dark and unidentifiable lurked in his gaze. She didn't like it and turned her attention toward the doors.

"Heading out to solve the world's problems?" he asked sardonically.

Grace stopped, aware that Justin already had headed out the doors. "What's crawled up your ass and died?"

Bosley's expression changed instantly, boy wonder reappearing in front of her. His gaze drifted from her face, but he shrugged, then looked her in the face while offering a crooked grin. "Just the stress of watching my hometown torn apart with a monster on the loose."

"I'll get him. You've got my word." Before she turned to follow Justin, she caught Christy's broad grin. Bosley studied Grace, though, again his gaze darkening. It struck her as odd. "Do you have something you want to say to me?" she asked, wondering if that was what she saw.

The doors opened and Justin strolled back in, his predatory nature immediately creating sparks in the air. "There a problem here?" he growled, his focus on Bosley.

Bosley's dark gaze didn't disappear. Sheriff Montgomery walked out of her office, remaining silent but noticing the charged energy, as did Christy when her smile faded. Grace noticed all activity seemed to still in the station as the two men stared at each other.

"Let's hope not," Bosley said, his tone cool. "As long as we don't have the wrong man, or woman, on the case."

Justin gave Bosley a condescending look for another second but then turned, taking Grace by the arm. She wasn't sure she liked being led out of the station with everyone watching. Rockville was growing more and more terrified, and they needed someone to blame. Until she arrested their rapist and murderer, fingers would be pointed in her direction.

Grace's phone rang as they walked across the parking lot.

"Lieutenant Jordan, this is Lieutenant Nelson."

"Yes, Randy." She'd met him only briefly after starting here but remembered seeing him at the DePaul house, dusting for fingerprints. "What can I do for you?"

"We picked up a print at Daisy DePaul's house."

"You did? Kick-ass," she said, grinning at Justin's curious expression when they reached his truck.

"Well, maybe."

She picked up on his wary tone. "What's wrong?" she asked, praying no other wrinkles complicated this case.

"The print belongs to Bosley."

"Crap," she hissed, sliding onto the passenger seat. "Okay, Randy, do me a favor: Don't say anything until I get back to the station."

"No problem." He sounded relieved.

"What was that?" Justin started his truck and put it in gear, his profile etched in stone, bordering on dangerous. He didn't look at her when he headed out of the parking lot.

"Lieutenant Nelson found a print at Daisy DePaul's house."

"Oh?" Now Justin did glance in her direction, his green eyes volatile with emotions she couldn't read.

"It was Bosley's."

"Where did he find it?"

"I didn't ask."

Justin returned his attention to the road. "We'll find out when we return to the station." There was a twitch at the edge of his lips, indication, she thought, that he was angry.

What she wanted to know and ached to ask was what had pissed him off. Glancing at her phone that she still held in her hand, she doubted the same thing upset Justin that upset her.

When they pulled into the third parking lot, of a drugstore that had been in Rockville longer than Justin could remember, he was acutely aware of how subdued Grace seemed. The day wasn't half-over and already she'd questioned his motives for wanting her, and his abilities to protect Rockville were in question. He knew his first concern bothered Grace as well. But he doubted she would understand his second concern.

Maybe his family had disowned him and would be better off if he left, but nonetheless this was where Daniel and Elizabeth were growing up. Sylvia might hate Justin's guts, and personally he couldn't care less. She had brought on her own demise, encouraging him into law enforcement with repeated comments on how much she would love being the wife of a lawman. But then the second Justin took his first assignment, she had her first affair.

Sylvia's infidelity didn't bother him today. She was someone else's problem now. But his kids, even if he was reminded repeatedly that Daniel wasn't really his son, would be safe. They would grow up here like Justin did and know a happy childhood. He would see to it no matter what it took.

"Are you coming?" Grace asked, her hand on her door handle, looking at him expectantly.

"Yup." He didn't give her any indication that it bothered him she had caught him lost in thought for a moment but turned off the truck without saying anything else and got out. "It's going to storm," he said instead, meeting her at the front of the truck and then placing his hand on the small of her back when they entered the drugstore.

"Justin Reece, I'll be darned." Alicia Harvard never was as pretty as her sister, Norma Green. "Didn't anyone tell you that you're supposed to look worse over the years after high school and not better?"

"Obviously you didn't listen to that rule, either." He grinned his roguish smile at her, his hand still on Grace's back. "Alicia, this is Lieutenant Jordan, Rockville's newest cop."

"It's 'Grace,' " Grace offered, shaking hands with Alicia.

Alicia grinned a broad, toothy grin, her cheeks blushing a pretty dark rose against her milk chocolate skin. The years had been good to her, and the big gold band on her finger indicated she had married, although he hadn't heard to whom.

"My sister told me you were quite the looker," Alicia said, letting go of Grace's hand and then winking at Justin. Alicia looked for a moment like she might say more, something probably intended to give him shit. She once had lived to pick on any guy she didn't have her eyes set on. For whatever reason, Justin usually hit the top of that list.

"I wanted to ask you about purchases made in the drugstore over the past few days." Grace saved him from being teased by Alicia, although he wasn't sure by her all-business expression whether she realized that or not. Grace pushed forward when Alicia gave her a blank stare. "There is a men's cologne called Man's World."

"Our cologne for men is on aisle four," Alicia offered, pointing in the direction of the aisle.

Justin followed where she pointed, noting the aisle and then glancing at the ceiling, seeing security cameras and wondering if they were real.

"Our records show you carry it. What I need to know is if you sold any bottles of it in the past couple days, and if so, do you have a record of what time of day? I need to speak to whoever would have sold it if you did."

"We're short staffed right now and close at ten. Unless a bottle was sold over the weekend, I sold it, as I work weekdays, ten to ten," she said, groaning at the admission of her long hours.

"Can you tell us if you sold a bottle on Friday?" Grace asked.

Alicia frowned at her for a moment and then walked out from behind the counter. "If I see what it looks like I might remember. Honestly, people come in and out of here and after a while I don't pay attention to what they buy," she said, leading the way to aisle four and then slowing as she walked down it.

"You would have sold it to a man you've never seen before," Justin said.

Grace glanced at him. They hadn't discussed whether the rapes and murders were being done by a local or not, and Justin could tell by her questioning look that she was wondering why he had determined they weren't looking for someone who was from around here.

Alicia looked at him, suddenly shocked. She pointed at the colognes on the shelf. "Man's World. This one?" she asked. "I sold a bottle."

"Do you remember who?" Grace asked quickly.

"I don't think he told me his name." Alicia tugged her lower lip, glancing at each of them, her expression worried. Then picking up a small bottle that looked exactly like the one they had tagged for evidence, she fingered it as if that would help her memory. "Definitely not from around here," she murmured. "He had one of those demanding personalities that commands attention the moment he enters through the door, you know?"

"Is there any way you can pull up the sale?" Grace asked. "What did he use to pay for the cologne?"

"Okay. Let me check," Alicia said, putting the bottle back on the shelf and heading to the counter.

"What did he look like?" Justin noticed Grace's preoccupied worried look when he followed Alicia.

"He was one of those tall, dark and deadly kind of guys. You know, the 'definitely don't take home to Mama' kind of guys." Alicia walked around the counter and pushed a few buttons on her register. Then with a quick look at both of them she sucked in her lower lip. "I didn't pay close enough attention to him to remember his features, though. Sorry."

"It's okay," Grace said, reassuring her. "Whatever you can tell us will help a lot."

"Is he the guy who killed those girls?" She turned chalky, her brown eyes growing wide as her fingers moved over her mouth and she started shaking.

"We don't know. Please, Alicia, remember what he looked like," Grace said softly.

The door dinged when several teenagers pushed their way through, laughing and talking as they hurried into the store and toward the middle aisle. Alicia watched them, her hand still over her mouth, and then returned her attention to Justin and Grace, her eyes moist.

"He was tall, about your height, Justin. White, black hair, good-looking in a disturbing way."

"Why do you say in a disturbing way?" Grace asked.

"His eyes, they were black, so incredibly dark, like he had no soul."

After Alicia promised not to be a stranger, Justin walked to his truck with Grace. She seemed more withdrawn than he'd known her to be so far. When he hit his brakes hard for some jerk who wasn't looking and pulled out in front of him, Grace looked around disoriented, so distracted by her thoughts she didn't realize they'd almost been hit.

"You didn't even see that," he told her, glancing her way before accelerating after the bastard finished cutting across traffic.

"Good thing you're driving."

"What are you thinking?"

When she looked at him, the hesitation making her eyes glaze over was enough to make him grip the steering wheel harder. Maybe it shouldn't matter to him that Grace hesitated in confiding in him. Once there was time, he'd figure out why in the hell it bothered him so much that she did.

"Grace, something click for you back there?" he pressed. "Because right now, we've got no proof that whoever came into the store and purchased that cologne had anything to do with the murders."

"True," she said, her agreeing with him raising even more red flags. "Maybe we should have asked her if the camera system they had installed was real."

"And we will, once we have more proof whoever came into the store was our man."

"I think it was," she whispered.

"Talk, Grace. Now." He pulled into the station while the most bizarre memory hit him, one of his mother once commenting to him that Rockville was so small you couldn't ever finish a conversation while driving from one end to the other. "I want to know what you're thinking right now."

"I'm sure you do."

The urge to grab her, yank her up against him, and kiss her until she submitted and trusted him implicitly hit him so hard he slammed his truck into park. He turned on her, but when he reached for her, she opened her door quickly and hurried out of his truck.

"Son of a bitch," he hissed, turning off his truck and leaping out, hurrying around the front of it, and intercepting her in the parking lot. "Enough, Grace. Whatever it is, I want to know right now."

"Once I understand it, I'll tell you." She raised her chin, staring at him with enough defiance it made her blue eyes glow and her dark red curls shine in spite of the heavy clouds weighing down on top of them.

She grabbed his wrist when he tried reaching for a curl, but he was done with her pushing him away. "Talk your thoughts out," he instructed, pulling her closer. "Open up to me, Grace," he added, whispering.

Her blue eyes darkened, although he wasn't sure if they smoldered or her temper soared. "When I'm ready to talk to you about my reaction to anything, you'll be the first to know," she hissed, grinding her teeth and making it clear why her eye color had turned as dark as a thunderhead. "And what if someone sees us?"

"Do you think I care what anyone in this town thinks?"

"Yes. I do."

He wrapped his arms around her so fiercely she squealed and stumbled into him. Then tilting her head back, he pounced on her mouth, ignoring the tiny pang in the back of his head that assured him he cared very much what people in this town believed of him. One thing he knew as well: Grace mattered to him. Since he first laid eyes on her, with her fiery curls that refused to behave and her sultry blue eyes always glowing and so full of life that not even a monster could kill, she'd impressed the hell out of him.

She crawled up his chest with her fingers and dug her nails into his shoulders. Her breasts were full and so soft pressing against his chest. When he felt her nipples harden his cock flared to life, forcing him to slow his actions before he really did get the town talking.

Her cheeks were flushed and her lips parted, full, and wet when he raised his head and stared down at her. The way her long lashes fluttered over her eyes and then she slowly lifted her gaze to his was all he needed to know he moved her as much as the kiss moved him.

"Later, my dear. I promise."

She shoved him back, pressing her fists into her hips although her heavy breathing and hard nipples so visible even through her shirt and bra took away from the angry look she tried giving him.

"Don't even think you can know what I might or might not want later," she snapped. "We've got a fingerprint to inspect. Are you coming, or not?"

She marched around him, her ass swaying so delightfully as she headed toward the station that he didn't mind walking a few paces behind her. He caught up with her at the door, though, and reached around, opening it for her.

"You don't need to tell me what you might want or not want later, sweetheart," he whispered into her ear as he held the door. "It's very clear by your actions, not your words."

There was incredible satisfaction that swelled quickly

inside him when she looked over her shoulder, her mouth forming a perfect circle. Grace couldn't shoot back a quick comeback, though. Christy looked up from her desk as he pressed his hand on Grace's back and guided her through the door.

Chapter 13

Grace's mind raced. Did Bosley wear gloves while they were at the DePaul house? Of course he did. They all did. How could his print have been picked up off the railing?

"You picked this up off the railing going into the house but no prints inside?" Justin asked Lt. Randy Nelson.

Randy stood on the opposite side of the desk from Grace. "Yup. Obviously there were a lot of prints on the railing. But this one was very strong and clear. Oftentimes people run their hand along a railing while using it, which would smear prints. He gripped the railing long enough to leave a solid, clear print. The computer pulled up a strong match as soon as I entered this."

Grace stared at the two prints in front of her: the one Randy had picked up and the print on file for Bosley that was taken when he was fingerprinted for the job—common procedure. She just didn't get it. Possibly he had entered the house before he realized the seriousness of the situation. It would be sloppy investigative work, but it could have happened. Maybe he took the gloves off as he left.

"Can you tell if the print occurred when he was arriving or leaving the house?" she asked Randy.

Another thought hit her. What if Bosley had entered the house earlier that day? If he had, he would've walked in on a rape in progress.

Or he could be the rapist.

Chills trickled down Grace's spine. She shook off the ridiculous thought and watched Randy peck at his keyboard as Justin moved to stand next to her.

"The fingerprint is facing the house, which means it occurred when he entered the house."

"Unless he started to leave, took off his gloves, then forgot something and reentered the house," Justin pointed out.

Randy almost looked relieved when he shot his attention to Justin. "Very true," he said, and then turned his worried look to Grace. "The Sheriff goes over all of my reports. He'll know this is Bosley's print."

"Do your job," Grace said. "If Justin's hunch is right, I'm sure Bosley won't be in any trouble."

Randy didn't say anything but returned his attention to his monitor.

Grace guessed his unspoken reaction to this. A cop would be grossly distracted to not wear gloves at a crime scene, no matter what stage of investigating the scene it was.

"The school is calling you on line two," Christy called from the other room.

When Christy shouted, Grace jumped and then sucked in a deep breath. She hated being on edge. Her muscles would be sore as hell before the day was out if she didn't relax and remain focused on the case and not the incredibly virile body next to her who she swore was emitting sexual energy that singed her skin the closer he got.

"Thanks, Randy," she said, turning and heading toward her office. She hurried, waving to Christy when she looked over her shoulder, obviously on another call.

Grace closed her door, reveling in a moment with Justin not so close that he fogged her ability to form a rational thought. Then, reaching over her desk, she grabbed the receiver off her phone and pushed the blinking button.

"Lieutenant Jordan here," she said, sounding calm and relaxed.

"Ms. Jordan," the secretary said pleasantly. "I'm sorry to disturb you at work, but we have your daughter in the office and I thought it was important enough to call you."

"What is it? Is she hurt? What's happened?" Grace

immediately shifted gears. *God. If anything happened to Rachel . . .*

"Well now, I won't say it's not serious, but she isn't hurt or sick." The secretary's voice was too damned calm and pleasant-sounding. "Apparently at recess after lunch she grew very upset after insisting her father called out to her from the street."

The entire room started spinning around Grace.

"Now, I understand that her father is deceased. She's very upset and determined about what she saw and swore this man spoke to her. Understand, please, the school has very firm policy on any strangers being near the school yard. There is a tall chain-link fence surrounding our property and we've never had any problem with anyone disturbing the children. None of the teachers outside saw anyone near the fence or talking to your daughter. But she's so insistent about what she claims she heard some man say to her. She broke down crying when we suggested she might have mis-heard what someone said, or that he wasn't talking to her. I thought it was important enough to call you."

Grace barely heard a word the woman said. Thunder rumbled outside and it grew darker in Grace's office in the next moment.

Rachel wouldn't remember what her father looked like. Hell, Grace didn't even know what he looked like. Other than certain parts of his body, he was always covered in black leather from the top of his head to the tips of his boots. Although there were times when she first got free that she swore a man walking in front of her was Master, she accepted today he was dead. Dead and burning in hell where he belonged.

It was odd; she had less of a problem with Rachel thinking Grace adopted her than the child thinking Master was her father. And as proud as Grace was to have given birth to that beautiful little girl, it repulsed her knowing Master really was Rachel's father.

"Tell Rachel I'll be right there." Grace quickly hung up the phone. She grabbed her purse and then quickly told

Christy she was taking a few hours off before heading out of the station. She would hang out with Rachel until she knew her daughter was okay and then return to work when Uncle Charlie could spend some time with her.

Grace needed to find the rapist. But she also needed to help her daughter accept that life was okay even if she didn't have a father.

It dawned on Grace that she didn't tell Justin she was leaving, not that he probably hadn't figured that out by now. And she would call him, right now, if he weren't already implying that she needed to share her thoughts with him before she even understood the speculation floating around in her brain. Grace didn't answer to anyone. But it was proper protocol to let her partner know what she was doing.

Grabbing her cell, she called Dispatch. "Christy," she said when the woman answered. "Do me a favor and let Justin know I'm gone."

Christy laughed. "Trust me, he knows."

Her response was enough to tell Grace he wasn't pleased with her rushing out the door. "Good. My daughter had a problem at school. Once I can calm her down and get my uncle to watch her, I'll check in. But call me if you need me."

"You don't want to talk to Justin?" Christy sounded surprised.

"Does he have a problem?"

"Well . . ." Christy laughed.

Grace prayed she didn't actually growl into the phone. The last thing she needed was this town thinking they were a couple and then Justin leaving and everyone assuming she would be devastated missing him.

"Okay. Call me if there is a problem." She prayed she didn't sound put out but simply indifferent. Later she'd deal with Justin. Right now she needed to focus on her daughter.

Parking in the school parking lot, Grace hurried inside to the office. She liked how even though this was summer care, children were in the classrooms they would be in during the school year and the atmosphere was just like that of regular school. Her daughter needed structure, and the warm, pleasant atmosphere immediately surrounding Grace as her boots clicked against the tiled floor assured her that Rachel was in good hands here. Grace hoped the incident today was simply the result of her daughter's over-active imagination.

"Mommy!" Rachel jumped off the daybed with bloodshot, puffy eyes, and the way she jumped into Grace's arms and cuddled into her almost made her cry. "I saw him, Mommy. I know you won't believe me. No one here does, either. But it wasn't my imagination. He waved at me, and called out my name. Mommy, he is so handsome. I just know he's my daddy. He's not dead!"

This speech was too much for Grace, and she went to her knees in front of Rachel, tears forming in her eyes. "How would you like to spend some time with me this afternoon, baby?" She couldn't keep her voice from cracking.

"Can we look for Daddy?" Rachel's eyes were pleading.

God, Master! I hate you so much!

Grace tried to respond, but a choked sound came out of her throat instead of words. The secretary and principal, who were looking on, stepped forward simultaneously.

"Lieutenant Jordan," the principal asked softly, "is there someone you would like us to call who could meet you here, or at your house possibly?"

Grace regained composure quickly and stood up. "I appreciate your concern, ladies," she said, and found her professional smile, knowing that like so many others, they misunderstood her reasons for choking up when her daughter mentioned her father. "Rachel and I will be just fine, though. I'm really glad that you called me." She looked down at her daughter and smiled. "This is a good excuse to have some quality mother-daughter time."

The two women nodded, and Grace and Rachel walked out to the patrol car hand in hand. Rachel was quiet in the car, seemingly interested in the police radio that occasionally squawked out instructions to one of the police officers. They drove down the main street of Rockville, appropriately named Main Street, and passed the courthouse.

"Mom, there's Elizabeth's daddy and mommy!"

Grace turned her head in time to see Justin standing on the lawn in front of the courthouse. There were several other people standing around him. Justin easily stood a couple inches taller than the men around him, and the way his jeans hugged his muscular legs and the plaid shirt he wore stretched over his steel chest made him stand out easily.

Many men had approached Grace in the past few years. There were desperate fools everywhere. But none of them came close to holding a candle to Justin. Even at this distance there was an aura around him, something that loudly proclaimed he was in charge. Maybe it was how he stood, or the comfortable expression she knew was on his face even without being able to see him clearly when raindrops started splattering on her windshield. Justin's incredible good looks would make anyone turn and look twice, immediately acknowledging him as a man who would dominate and take care of any situation.

Only one other person stood out equally as well—for very different reasons. And that was Sylvia. Both of them were laughing, and Sylvia had her long, slinky fingers wrapped around one of Justin's arms.

Fire ignited inside Grace's gut—raging to a boil instantly.

That did it!

She kept her eyes on them long enough to see Sylvia look up into Justin's face. Grace was too far away to see Sylvia's expression. Before Grace returned her attention to the road she saw Justin look down at his ex-wife, smile, and pat her hand with his.

It was a look of affection. Grace could tell even at this distance. Divorced or not, there was something still alive between them. A bond existed that had been created over many years of working to be a couple and parents. A piece of paper obviously had not severed that bond.

"Mom, I'm hungry. Can we get ice cream?" Rachel asked, and pointed to the Dairy Queen across the street.

"Ice cream for lunch?" Grace gripped the steering wheel,

so outraged over what she'd just seen that several calming breaths didn't appease the anger growing inside her.

"They sell more than ice cream," Rachel said hopefully.

Grace glanced at her daughter. It was bad enough this case was taking so much time from Grace being a mother. She couldn't let a man she'd already sworn to herself wouldn't get behind the barrier she had securely in place around her heart distract her from what mattered.

"Ice cream it is then," she said, smiling and then turning into the Dairy Queen parking lot.

As the rain started falling harder they ran inside hand in hand and laughed as they shook the drops off of them and then ordered lunch.

"Okay, little lady, why don't you tell me exactly what happened today," Grace said as she stirred soft-serve ice cream in a clear plastic bowl.

"Mom, you've got to believe me." Rachel's red curls were wet in spots from raindrops, and tight ringlets fell past her ears. "I was at recess. I didn't want to play four-square, so I was making clover bracelets in the grass. I just looked up, and this tall man stood on the other side of the fence. His hair was really black, just like his coat, but he wasn't scary."

"And he talked to you?" Grace fought to sound calm.

"He said, 'Rachel, it's me, your daddy.' I wish I would have thought to say something to him, but the bell rang. They called me to get in line, so I couldn't wait."

Grace thanked God for observant teachers.

"Rachel, your daddy is dead. I know how much you want to believe he isn't, but we can't change the past." Grace watched her daughter's eyes fill with tears.

"Mom, it was *him*." Rachel choked on a sob.

"Oh God, baby, I know you want a daddy. And if I could, I'd give you the best daddy on the planet."

"You can't give me another daddy. I have one. And I saw him. He told me he was my daddy. He didn't die in a fire. He's alive."

Grace's stomach twisted in knots as she watched her daughter stare at her wide-eyed, looking desperate for her

mom to believe her. Her heart broke for her daughter and
with the knowledge that the man she was desperate to believe
was alive and well was one of the worst monsters ever to
walk this earth. "Rachel, whoever you saw, he wasn't your
daddy. There are some bad people out there. They may disguise themselves just to get young ladies like you to go with
them."

"He wasn't wearing a disguise, Mom." Rachel sounded
disgusted with the view Grace took on the subject. "You're a
cop. Why don't you find out if it was him?"

"Well, hello, ladies."

Grace looked up quickly to see Sylvia standing next to
their table smiling down at them. The recent memory of
Sylvia holding Justin's arm, the two of them smiling into
each other's eyes, burned through Grace like acid. Her stomach jolted, and she instinctively began stabbing her ice
cream with the plastic spoon in her hand.

"Mayor, it's nice to see you." Grace kept a civil tone and
was pretty sure she managed the smile to match.

Sylvia laughed quietly and locked eyes with Grace. "How
nice of you to say so." Sylvia's voice was soft and husky, almost evil. "Have you decided to take the day off?"

"I'm spending the afternoon with my daughter, yes."
Grace forced her same congenial tone, acting impervious to
Sylvia's behavior.

"I see. Do you always make a habit of taking time off
right after starting a new job?" Sylvia's tone turned absolutely hateful. "I don't know if our budget can afford to pay
the salary for a cop who takes time off while we have a rapist in our community. It seems to me like you have a job to
do."

"I'm doing my job, Sylvia." Grace stood up quickly, looking her square in the eye. "I think you should focus on doing
yours, and let me do mine." Fury raged through her like
there was no tomorrow. She turned and reached for Rachel,
who was staring at the two women, stunned. "Come on,
Rachel. Let's go."

Rachel grabbed her orange drink as her mother escorted

her quickly out of the Dairy Queen. Grace knew she shouldn't have said what she just did to Sylvia. Sheriff Montgomery might have to fight to keep Grace's job for her. At the moment, she didn't care. Storming out of Dairy Queen was smarter than punching Sylvia in her face.

"Are you okay, Mom?" Rachel asked when they both sat in the car.

"Yeah, honey, I'm fine." Grace sighed heavily and looked at her daughter with a sheepish grin. "I think I let my temper get the best of me."

"Uncle Charlie used to always tell me that I got my temper from Mom." Rachel turned away from Grace when she spoke. "But I think I get my temper from you."

Rachel's words tore Grace apart more than the little girl would ever know. More than anything, Grace ached for her daughter to know who her real mommy was. That wouldn't be fair to Rachel, though. Not at this point in her life.

Grace had headed toward the parking lot exit determined to find Uncle Charlie when Justin pulled in. He stopped his car next to hers and rolled his window down quickly. It crossed her mind to roll her window up just as quickly and drive on. Rachel was with her, though, and Uncle Charlie was staying at Justin's house, not to mention her daughter's brand-new best friend was his daughter. Sometimes it sucked having to be so damned mature.

"What's going on?" His eyes sparkled as he searched her face.

Grace simply couldn't match his cheerfulness. "We've had a really bad day, Justin. I pulled my daughter out of school for the afternoon. Christy said she told you." Grace let her voice fade a little. "I'll be back to work as soon as I can."

His concerned gaze searched hers. "I'll meet you over at your house."

Justin accelerated and turned around behind her. He didn't even bother waiting to hear whether she wanted him over or not. Maybe in a better mood she might believe he was relaxed enough around her to feel comfortable about inviting himself over. But she wasn't in a good mood and was even in less of a mood for a man to assume he could make decisions without consulting her.

For years she had endured being a doormat, never being consulted or even spoken to but treated like an object, like a toy that one day was a favorite and another despised. There was a time when Grace had believed her life would be like that always, spoken to only when being ordered to commit some vile act or, worse even than that, when ordered to behave like an inanimate object.

And when she gave birth to Rachel, Master took the baby from her, not even allowing her to hold her. When Grace cried for her, she was beaten. Sluts weren't mothers. Master never explained why he didn't force her into an abortion. Even after all these years, she couldn't find it in her heart to believe that meant he had a soft spot in his heart. For whatever reason, he'd allowed her to give birth but then taken the child and created a birth certificate, filing it with the state of Minnesota, claiming someone else was the mother. Grace was forced to legally adopt her own daughter, after pulling her out of foster care.

Rachel contentedly snuggled up on the couch with an afghan and watched television after they got home. After her needs were seen to . . . a cup of juice and her favorite doll, Grace headed back to her bedroom and called her uncle.

"Uncle Charlie, where are you?" She frowned when he told someone with him to hold on a minute and there was the obvious laughter of several women in the background.

"I'm over at Doris Agnew's house." Uncle Charlie sounded a little louder and more jovial than usual.

"Doris Agnew? I've never heard of her."

"Well, darling, that's because she's not a criminal." There was an incredible amount of laughter in the background after he spoke. Grace assumed he had an audience who found his Jordan charms irresistible.

"Uncle Charlie," Grace sighed with exasperation. "I thought you were going to the library to look at newspapers."

"I did go to the library. I ran into these charming ladies down there. They're all members of the Rockville Book

Club. They read novels and get together once a week to talk about them. Sounds like fun. They say there are no laws against a man joining."

Again, a fair amount of giggling came from the background.

"I can't believe you. You are incorrigible!" Grace rolled her eyes and at the same time noticed a truck pull up out front. Moving her blinds enough to watch, she saw Justin walk with his usual confident stride up to her porch, in spite of the rain. She fought to calm her suddenly pounding heart.

"I know that, sweetheart." Uncle Charlie's tone was way too friendly. Obviously, he didn't want the ladies to know what she just said. "And, you know, these ladies have lived here most of their lives. It's amazing, I think between these women they know everyone in this town and some of the surrounding towns. We were just sitting here talking about those awful crimes that have been happening. I think these ladies should be private detectives. They're nothing more than a bunch of Miss Marples."

The shrill laughter that followed was deafening. But suddenly Grace understood. Uncle Charlie was pumping the ladies for information. She could just imagine that he had spent most of his career in the Bureau charming women out of all their secrets. Move over, James Bond!

"Have you found out anything?" She focused on the floor aware that Justin had let himself inside without knocking, and hearing the quiet, comfortable exchange between him and her daughter. A moment later his heavy footsteps came down Grace's hallway.

"Now you'd be surprised at what these women know." Uncle Charlie still sounded jovial, but she sensed a level of seriousness.

"Uncle Charlie, will you be done soon? I need you." Her last sentence half-stuck in her throat. Uncle Charlie heard the fear in her voice, and Justin was by her side as the words left her mouth. She turned away from him, but her backside tingled even though he didn't touch her. "Something's happened. Will you come over here, now?"

"I'll be right there, sugar," Uncle Charlie said softly. "Are you okay?"

"No, I'm not."

She hung up the phone, fighting for control before turning to face Justin.

"What happened?" Justin asked quietly from behind her.

Grace turned around. Maybe she shouldn't have. Between thinking about Master and seeing Sylvia with Justin, not to mention staring at that bottle of cologne in the drugstore and remembering how much Master loved that particular brand, every nerve in Grace's body bordered on shattering. Justin's brooding expression didn't hold that usual smoldering desire, although she was more than aware of how close he stood, and with her alone in her bedroom. His dark gaze was deep enough to drown in, and he sincerely appeared concerned, worried, as he searched her face and waited for her answer. She needed his strength, those strong arms wrapped around her. She needed him.

And that made her weak.

Which pissed her off.

He was her partner on this case. There was business to handle. She walked around him and down the hallway, smiling at her daughter who was cocooned in her afghan, her eyes heavy and glassy as she stared at the television and barely shifted her attention to Grace and Justin when they walked past her into the kitchen.

"I found out several things today." She impressed herself with how calm she sounded. But the biting coolness in her tone made her shiver.

Justin crossed his arms over his chest, and tendons twitched in his forearms. It seemed he was all over her body language as much as what she said.

"What did she say to you?" he snapped.

"What?"

"Sylvia. That's why you're upset, isn't it?" He walked around the table toward her, and she took a step backward.

"I'd like to keep this conversation work-related, if you don't mind."

"Work related." He cursed under his breath and then glanced quickly at her daughter. "Okay. We'll talk shop."

He grabbed the back of one of Grace's kitchen chairs and lifted it, instead of dragging it, then turned it to face her. Sitting down, he leaned back, crossed one leg over the other, and stretched out in front of her. "Shoot."

"Okay." She hesitated for a moment and then opened her refrigerator, grabbed a bottled water, and closed it, not offering Justin one. Then leaning against her counter, keeping as much distance between them as possible, she unscrewed the bottle slowly while gathering her thoughts. There was no way she'd chew him out with her daughter in the living room on the couch. "I don't understand why Bosley wouldn't have his gloves on at a crime scene, no matter if he just got there, was leaving, or forgot something and entered the house again."

Justin looked at her a moment without commenting, as if he'd expected her to say something else. Maybe he guessed there were other things on her mind, but she wouldn't discuss them with her daughter in earshot.

"I'm sure he'll have a believable explanation," Justin said without much emotion.

"I'm sure."

"There's more, I'm afraid." She would drown in those dark eyes if she stared too long. They were bright with passion, overloaded with enough emotion to make them glow.

"I can see that." And as horrendous as these crimes were, he and Grace could talk shop all day and not touch what had her so upset right now. He'd bet a year's salary on it.

For a moment Grace lost her train of thought. So much power radiated from him, and not just physical strength. He saw how upset she was. As aggressive as he could be, he wasn't forcing her to talk right now but instead appeared incredibly relaxed and patient, like a deadly predator willing to wait for the exact right moment before pouncing.

She focused on the image of Sylvia smiling up at him in front of the courthouse—the same bitch who had just threatened Grace's job. No matter her efforts, pressure built inside her, throbbing between her legs. Justin might possibly be more man than she could handle. She closed her eyes. *Stay focused on work.*

"When we left the station earlier today, Bosley seemed almost too upset that these rapes were putting his hometown into a panic."

"It's normal for an officer to release frustration before a tough case is solved." Again Justin appeared too calm, his lazy drawl only adding to how damned sexy he looked watching her.

"Maybe," she said, not sure she agreed with that being why Bosley was so upset. "Call it intuition, but I don't trust him."

"Why not?"

"Something lingered in his eyes. He was more than frustrated. He looked pissed, and at me."

"He won't get out of line with you. You have my word."

Making a show of being her protector didn't impress her. She sipped at her water, shaking her head. A slightly damp curl fell loose and clung to her cheek. She wiped it away and watched Justin's attention shift to the act. Hunger surfaced in those dark eyes. She saw it and heat swelled between her legs.

"I'm not worried about Bosley," she said, meaning it. "Do you know how good of a cop he is, though? I've never bothered checking his track record."

"Nothing much happens in Rockville for a cop to get an impressive track record."

"Until now. Until I moved here," she added, watching him stiffen at her comment. "When I first arrived here, Bosley was incredibly nice to me, offering to help and taking me under his wing and showing me the town."

"I'm sure," Justin muttered.

"Then when these rapes and murders started, he got more distant. Now he's downright cold toward me."

"He's jealous."

Grace shook her head, not buying it. "He wasn't giving me the kind of attention you are."

"That's good to know."

She sipped her water again, her mouth suddenly dry. His possessive nature should be irking her and not making her insides swell with distracting need. Forcing the image of Sylvia on his arm in front of the station helped a little, and Grace fingered her bottle, willing herself to be immune to the intense stare he continued giving her.

"Sheriff Montgomery even came out and said it, that the crimes in this town quadrupled since I arrived. And then watching the clerk at the drugstore and the way she—" Grace broke off, mad at herself suddenly for almost slipping.

"And the way she what?" Justin demanded.

She pushed herself away from the counter and walked toward him, acutely aware of how he didn't move a single muscle as she approached and then walked around him so she could see Rachel. Relief washed over Grace when she saw her daughter was sound asleep. She was another very important matter to deal with. Somehow, Grace needed to make her daughter believe that her life wouldn't be better if she had a father. Especially *her* father.

"Grace," Justin said, his rough baritone sending chills rushing over her flesh. "Even if the crime rate in Rockville was higher, crimes like these would wrack anyone's nerves. They are terrible, heinous murders. The town is talking, the news is starting to cover them, and it will get worse before it gets better. That's how it is in a small town. And when something despicable happens that a person can't easily fix, it's normal to point fingers. You've got to be tough and immune to talk like that and stay focused on the case."

She spun around, ignoring the curls that fell loose and fluttered around her face. "If you're implying I don't have what it takes to solve these murders, you can get the hell out of my house right now, Justin Reece," she hissed, keeping her voice at a whisper in spite of the overwhelming urge to scream at him.

Justin stood, and although she walked around him, he cornered her against her counter and grabbed her neck. Holding her firmly, yet not so tight she couldn't breathe, he kept her face pinned and held his inches away.

"You are quite possibly one of the strongest, most focused and determined women I've ever met." His calm tone belied the harsh look he gave her. "You're not perfect, though, Grace. None of us are. And there's nothing wrong with allowing someone into your life and trusting that he won't ever hurt you."

"I can handle the Sheriff expressing his concerns. That's his job. But Bosley was out of line. This doesn't have anything to do with trust. I noticed a hard edge in his eyes that shouldn't have been there. He was doing more than expressing his concern over a town he loves. He was mad at me. And I'm not sure why."

Justin had a temper, too. She imagined how deadly he could be if worked up enough. For some fucked-up reason, that got her wet. She chewed her lip, using the quick, sharp pain to stay focused.

"Sweetheart, if he's angry at you, it's because you're giving me attention and not him. If his anger is deeper than that and if those fingerprints on the DePaul railing aren't easily explained, than we have a deeper problem." His green eyes were like thunderheads, ready to explode. "I'll question Bosley, but if he doesn't answer me to my satisfaction, I'd say he's definitely a suspect."

Chapter 14

"Goodness, it's getting warm out there." Uncle Charlie let himself into his niece's house, and the screen door banged behind him. "Oh shoot, I didn't realize Rachel was here." He lowered his voice and walked quietly into the kitchen.

"Hi, Uncle Charlie." Grace studied her windblown, somewhat damp uncle. "I could have come and got you."

Uncle Charlie waved her off. "Nothing wrong with a bit of exercise."

He looked fit enough to endure a brisk walk. After all, Rockville wasn't that big. No matter where he'd been, it couldn't have been that far of a walk to her house. His silver hair, usually parted neatly on the side, was now blown in every direction, making him almost look like a mad scientist.

"I hurried over as quickly as I could." He attempted combing his hair with his fingers, which only mildly helped. "What's going on here?"

"Justin and I were talking."

"So, are you okay now?"

"I didn't mention why I wanted you to come home." She looked quickly from one man to the other. "I thought I'd wait until you got here."

"What's wrong?" both men asked at the same time.

"It's Rachel." Grace looked out her kitchen window at the juniper tree branches that were wet from rain. "I had to bring her home."

Rachel might be out cold, since she didn't wake up with

Grace and Justin talking at the kitchen table or her uncle entering. Nonetheless, Grace wouldn't risk her daughter overhearing this conversation.

"Let's talk out on the back deck. I don't want to wake her." After locking her front door and gazing at the red curls sticking up around her daughter's face, Grace prayed she could keep that innocent, precious look Rachel had right now always there.

Both men followed Grace into her backyard without making a sound behind her. Her deck was no more than a cement slab with a flat roof over it, but it offered privacy, especially with the fat juniper blocking their view of the street.

"Why did you bring her home?" Justin's voice was so low it sounded like a growl. Sunlight beamed through dark clouds behind the thick evergreen growing alongside the back of her house. It made his hair look golden. His expression, though, was etched in stone.

"Rachel told her teachers that some man told her he was her daddy at recess."

"What?" Uncle Charlie hissed.

Grace placed her hand on his arm, knowing her uncle understood how painful this was for Rachel. "None of the teachers saw anyone, but Rachel insists a man stood on the other side of the chain-link fence and called her by name, then told her he was her father."

Just the thought of Master being anywhere near Rachel, even though Grace knew he was dead, gave her a chill she couldn't control. Crossing her arms against it, she scowled at her soaked backyard. "It's not like Rachel to make something like this up for attention. She's never done anything like that before."

"I agree, sweetheart. Who do you think he was?" Uncle Charlie asked.

"I'm worried that our murderer approached her. It's a way to torture me, to let me know he knows who I am and to show me how close he can get to me."

"Who is Rachel's father?" Justin asked.

One look told her he had already guessed the answer. "I

got pregnant and gave birth while being held hostage in Minnesota," she said tightly.

A tiny muscle next to Justin's lower lip twitched. For a long moment he stared at her and she couldn't look away. When he finally yanked his attention from her, it looked like he would pound something.

"And you know who the father is?"

"Yes," she snapped, grinding her teeth and fisting her hands into her waist. "And I know the son of a bitch who got me pregnant is very fucking dead. I watched the mother-fucker burn."

"Did you?" both men asked at the same time.

She blinked, looking at her uncle and all too aware of the intense stare Justin gave her. "He was trapped, Uncle Charlie. There's no way he could have gotten out."

"Damn it to fucking hell." Justin turned to Uncle Charlie. "This is getting a bit too close to home for my tastes."

"Agreed." Her uncle stared across her backyard. "There's something you need to consider, Grace."

"What's that?" She hugged herself, hating the creepy-crawly sensations that plagued her insides when she allowed memories of Master to surface.

"Your perp might try some scare tactics by getting too close to people you love." Uncle Charlie's expression was hard when he focused on her.

"Grace, it would take one hell of some intense in-depth research for anyone to learn who Rachel's father is. If our perp told Rachel he was her father, he knew how much that would terrify you."

She glared at Justin, but he remained undaunted.

Uncle Charlie shook his head. "You impressed the hell out of me, Justin, when you told me how you dug that infor-mation up on our Grace."

"She needs twenty-four-hour protection." Justin didn't appear flattered over Charlie's praise. Instead he scowled. "You said the abuse was pretty bad. It won't fucking happen again."

Grace's jaw dropped open. Uncle Charlie and Justin had

talked about her and Master? How could Uncle Charlie do that to her? She opened her mouth to speak, but her uncle didn't let her get a word in edgewise.

"Good God, man." Uncle Charlie turned on a dime. "X-rays proved several broken bones didn't mend properly. When she escaped the mansion and was picked up, there were bruises everywhere, and I mean big bruises all over her. Her wrists and ankles were raw, obviously from rope burns. It took almost a year before she would open up and start talking. That monster brainwashed her so bad. She's nothing at all compared to the broken, beaten child she was when we got her back." He looked at her, his smile sad. "Most women wouldn't have your strength to return to normal after the atrocities you lived through."

"Uncle Charlie, that's enough." No way would they stand here and rehash her past. She glanced inside the quiet house, praying her daughter wouldn't wake up. "I'm standing right here, you know, and if I wanted Justin to know these things I would have damn well told him myself." She glared at both of them, outraged, but then was actually shocked when Justin turned his pissed-off glare on her.

"Regardless of your personal feelings for me, you have firsthand knowledge that can blow this case wide open. If you can't share that, maybe I should reevaluate your being on this case."

"I would think if viewing one of those crimes didn't affect a person they should be taken off the case." Her mouth went dry and she wished she had brought her water out here with her. There was no fucking way he would try taking her off this case. "Just because you've experienced a god-awful crime firsthand doesn't make you immune to it down the road. These are hideous and repulsive acts we're witnessing."

"Grace, I know you were thrilled to get this job," Uncle Charlie began.

"And in no way are you going to lose your job," Justin continued.

"You're not going to talk to Sheriff Montgomery about anything you've heard just now. I swear to God, Justin, if you do, I'll never speak to you again." She glared at him while her heart beat so hard in her chest she could hardly breathe. "I'm more qualified to find our perp than anyone else in this town, and you damn well know it."

Too many emotions welled up inside her. She started trembling and sucked in a hard breath, focusing on the yard and not either man for a moment before she had a complete and total meltdown.

"Sweetheart, you'll live through this," her uncle said quietly, and then pulled her into his arms. "You need to question Rachel's teachers, see if they saw anyone outside the school yard."

"Alicia saw the man who bought the cologne in the drugstore. We'll compare notes if anyone at the girl's school saw anything."

"I know what I fucking need to do," Grace snapped, damned if either man would think she couldn't focus through all of this.

"I won't talk to a soul about your past." Justin rubbed her cheek with his thumb, his touch impossible to ignore, even in her uncle's arms. "There's one stipulation, though. You and Rachel might not be safe here."

"I can take care of us." She stiffened and then pushed away from her uncle.

"You'd be safer out at my place."

"We're not moving in with you."

"We'll discuss how long you stay there later." Justin's dark eyes bore through the resistance she tried keeping up against him. And the hard look on his face would be terrifying to many. She didn't doubt that for a moment. When Justin made a decision, she doubted many in the past ever swayed him. "But for now, you and Rachel are moving in with me."

"Go load what you can into your car now. We'll help you." Uncle Charlie rubbed his hands together, nodding as he glanced from her to Justin. "I'll take your stuff and Rachel. You two need to get back to work. You can let me use your car."

"Slow down here for a minute." She had the sensation of

a carpet being yanked out from underneath her and didn't like it.

"Grace," Justin said, closing in on her and then grabbing her face, a habit he was too damned good at. He cupped her cheeks and held her face in place, tilted just how he wanted it so she was able to only see him. "You know as well as I do that serious serial killers will often stalk the cops seeking them out. It helps them feel they are completely in control."

"I know that," she snapped, not liking the direction he was taking.

"Your daughter would be safer out at my place and I think you know that. Do you want her to stay with her uncle and you stay here?"

She was tempted to agree just to see Justin's reaction but hated him more when his resolute expression proved he already knew the answer. Grace wouldn't let go of Rachel, not to family, not to anyone.

"I'll get some things packed," Grace said, backing away from him and hugging herself. "Are you sure you have enough room for us?"

"Positive. It's a four-bedroom house."

"I'll sleep with Rachel."

"We can work out the sleeping arrangements tonight."

Rachel clung to Grace when they got out of her car a little over an hour later.

"Sure is a good-sized spread you have here." Uncle Charlie winked at Rachel, then took her hand. "Let's go do some exploring. What do you say?"

"We'll drop this stuff inside the house and then head back into town." Justin pulled open Grace's back door and started stacking suitcases under his arms.

"Go save the world." Uncle Charlie waved them on. "Just make sure we can get inside after we're done exploring."

Grace watched her daughter disappear around the corner of the house with her great-uncle, knowing she'd be dirty and happy once they returned.

"You didn't bring much stuff." Justin led the way across a large deck and then unlocked his home.

"I don't want Rachel thinking this is anything other than temporary."

When he bent over and placed Grace's things inside his door, his hard, firm ass distracted her, proving to be damned good eye candy. He turned quickly, forcing her gaze to take in the slight bulge in his trousers. Heat tore up her insides.

"You can unpack this evening." He moved before she could react, pressing into her even as she stepped backward until he had her against the wall. "Then you'll be too busy to think about my seducing you every chance I get."

He nibbled her neck while he ran his hands down her sides and then gripped her hips.

"I don't want to be seduced."

She searched for the image of Justin and Sylvia smiling at each other. Grace's brain wouldn't register on anything other than hard-packed muscle touching her everywhere and his mouth doing a wicked number on her neck.

"What do you want?" Sizzling heat escalated to dangerous levels as he ran his flat palm up her front and squeezed one breast, massaging it gently until her nipple hardened so painfully it about made her explode.

"I want to be . . ." She choked on the last word, not sure she truly knew what it meant, let alone what it would be like, to be loved.

Her legs were as useful as wet noodles when she squeezed around him. She fumbled with the door and gulped in fresh air when she got outside.

Justin had one hell of a grip. Strong fingers grabbed her shoulders and almost knocked her off balance. Her backside collapsed against his chest.

"Love doesn't happen overnight," he whispered into her ear. "But when mutual interest is this strong, I'm more than willing to explore where it will lead."

He had no clue how much he actually held her upright at that moment. Every inch of her tingled. Her pussy throbbed so hard she could barely stand it. And the pressure mounting inside her made her wonder how the hell she'd make it through the rest of the day. Not knowing what to say, she nodded. Love wasn't a topic she discussed with anyone.

Thankfully, he guided her to the car. Her legs would have embarrassed the hell out of her and given out right underneath her otherwise. She was sure of it.

"I forgot to mention Michael Green called this morning," Justin offered as they drove back into town in his truck. "Norma is having a field day trying to play private eye."

"That's not good," Grace said, staring out the window at the countryside that was incredibly green after the storm.

"What I told him. But she mentioned seeing a blue Buick driving by several times and slowing, looking at the warehouse."

"She get a look at the driver?"

Justin met Grace's gaze when she shifted in her seat and looked at him. "Just that he had black hair."

Grace nodded. "Matches the description Alicia at the drugstore gave."

Justin slowed when they entered town, but when he turned right, instead of left, which would have taken them to the station, Grace looked at his profile. "Where are we going?"

He turned again and her stomach did a flip-flop. He was headed toward her house, and as he slowed on the street before hers the heat swelling inside her was definitely in reaction to the sexually charged air filling the cab.

Grace's home was on the corner and Justin parked in front of her house, his truck easily visible to anyone who drove down the busy side street off her road.

"Why are we—" She didn't finish her question because Justin already was out of the truck.

Climbing out and following him up to her front porch, she pulled her keys out of her purse and didn't look at him when he held her screen door so she could unlock the front door. Her palms were damp as she fumbled with her key, all too aware of his large body so close to hers.

"If our guy is stalking us," Justin said once they were

inside, "there's a good chance he already knows you've rented this place. We're going to set him up."

"Oh?" She turned in the middle of her living room, but Justin was already back out her front door, letting the screen door slam behind him.

Her heart jerked in her chest in spite of watching the door close. She was too on edge, her nerves frazzled, and it wasn't from the possibility of a rapist and murderer doing a drive-by. As she watched Justin hurry down her sidewalk to his truck, the pressure inside her created moisture between her legs just watching his confident stride.

If only he weren't leaving once this case was wrapped up. She straightened, knowing how idiotic it was to allow fantasies to manipulate her actions. Justin could destroy everything she'd accomplished over the ten years since she walked away from that burning mansion. It wouldn't be intentional on his part. Grace was in control of her life today. No one and nothing would take that from her.

Justin headed back up her walk with a black suitcase in his hand. Anyone watching might think he was coming to stay for a while. "I think this is our best window here," he said when he used his foot to open the door.

Grace crossed her arms over her chest, feeling how hard her nipples were and that even her skin, when she touched it, seemed ultra-sensitive. "What are you doing?"

Justin placed the suitcase on her coffee table and opened it. A rather sophisticated camera was inside. "Setting a trap," he informed her, his mannerisms all business. It was like he was barely aware she was there.

He was a jerk to tell her they would have sex and then be alone with her and turn into super agent. As annoyed as she was that he ignored her, a wave of relief also washed over her. No matter how many times she reminded herself that getting too close to him would destroy her, it was impossible not to be acutely aware of his magnificent body.

"I think positioning the camera right here will grab any cars that drive by on either street," Justin said, pulling the cap off of the camera and then checking the settings.

Grace pulled out a collapsed tripod and started snapping the legs until it was almost as tall as she was. "How powerful is the camera?" she asked.

"We should be able to get a good face shot." He put the camera on the coffee table, placed the tripod in front of the window, adjusting her curtains so there was enough room for the lens to peer out. Then he placed the camera on the tripod and snapped it to it. After peering through the viewfinder, adjusting the camera further, he backed off. "Take a look," he offered.

Grace stepped forward while Justin moved around her, locking her front screen door and main door, then stalked across her house to her back door, testing it, too, until he was satisfied. She put her eye to the camera and adjusted her vision. A car drove by and she grinned, easily seeing the woman behind the wheel. "Is it recording?"

"Yup." Justin put his hands on her waist and pulled her back. "Better yet, this little baby will allow us to freeze-frame on any object recorded, photographing it."

He pressed his body against her backside, solid steel touching her everywhere. Worse yet, his hard throbbing cock pressed against her tailbone, raising the temperature in the room drastically. Fucking him wouldn't be so bad if she kept her head on straight. As long as she knew in her heart and her soul that all it would be was sex, she could handle it. She couldn't let her emotions get in the way. But ignoring the charged energy zapping the air around her was too damned hard to do.

She didn't fight him; there wasn't any fight in her. He hugged her and then pressed his hands over her stomach. Pressing against her shirt, he kept his hand flat over her body as he brought it up over her breasts, causing them to swell even more painfully than they'd been for well over a week now. When he reached her neck, she tilted her head, looking over her shoulder at his dark, predatory gaze.

"Once we get a good look at our man," he said, his voice a low growl that sent chills rushing over her flesh, "we're going to hope and pray that he's got some type of criminal record."

He held her firmly against his body and his cock shifted in his pants, torturing her as much as all that rock-hard packed muscle did that touched her everywhere. "Let's hope your idea works."

"It will. I can't go on the word of a child, but if he approached Rachel today, then he's out to scare you, if not worse." His fingers moved over her neck, resting over her vein that she was sure throbbed as hard as his cock did.

"He'll know that your truck is parked outside, too," she pointed out, and her breath caught in her throat when his eyes darkened, while he pressed his lips into a thin line. She'd hit a nerve but wasn't quite sure what she'd hit.

Justin gripped her jaw, forcing her head to turn until her face was close enough to his that his lips brushed over her cheek when he spoke. "You will never be bait for the motherfucker where I can't protect you. He's going to learn really fast that he won't ever find you alone."

"Justin, I won't deny he's very dangerous. And trust me, I know when and how to call for backup. But you need to accept that I'm very well trained to defend myself." There wasn't time to press her argument further.

Justin flipped her around, causing her hair clasp to slide to the side of her head and curls to fall around her face. He moved with an energy and aggression she hadn't witnessed in him before, although she never doubted it simmered just under the edge of his usual control. A growl erupted from him right before his mouth landed on hers.

Instinct kicked in before she could react to his sudden attack. She pushed against his chest when his hands were under her armpits. But to no avail. Justin held her off the ground. Wrapping his steel arms around her, he devoured her mouth and crushed her against his virile body. As he impaled her mouth, her pussy swelled, growing so wet as the need to fuck him consumed her ability to think about anything else.

She grabbed his shoulders and when his hands moved to her ass, gripping her with strong fingers and grinding her crotch against his, her world shifted in a way it never had before. He nipped at her mouth, teased her with his tongue, and then impaled her again.

Grace opened for him, aware that he moved across the room. His muscular thighs moved against hers and she raised her legs, wrapping them around his hips while the fire burned out of control inside her. In spite of the need enflamed and swollen inside her, she hated the disoriented feeling when her ass hit a hard surface and his body no longer pressed against hers.

She grabbed either side of her counter and blinked, focusing while sliding off the edge. Justin backed away from her, quickly removing his shirt. One look at his ripped, muscular chest and she forgot to breathe. He was the perfect specimen of man, his tanned skin covered with a brown sprinkling of chest hair that spread over pectorals and then tapered into a thin line that stretched down his stomach and lower, disappearing into his jeans.

His fingers moved to unbutton his jeans as she watched. "You can take off your clothes or I'll rip them off you," he said, his voice a rough growl.

Her mouth was too dry. But then as she raised her focus to his face, the incredibly determined expression that created hard lines in his features and made his dark eyes glow with a hunger that matched hers at least, her mouth was suddenly as wet as her pussy.

"If we do this . . . ," she began, needing him to understand the only terms she could live with.

"There is no if," he stated, unzipping his jeans and at the same time kicking off his shoes.

Her fingers were on her shirt, but his dominating statement brought her pause. "There are always ifs."

She trembled when he stepped out of his jeans, pulling boxers down with them. Before her stood Justin, looking like a deadly warrior from another time, completely naked yet anything but vulnerable looking.

"Not with me, Grace." He moved in on her and placed his hands over hers, then began undressing her. "Not when it comes to you. There is only the certainty that this is the right thing to do, that there will be no regrets, and that with you and me this was meant to be."

She licked her lips, allowing him to remove her shirt and not saying anything when he dropped it along with his clothes on the ground. He said just what she wanted to hear, what she'd dreamed always of a man voicing to her before making love to her. And it was a bittersweet attack that it came from a man so perfect, so beautiful, and possessing every quality she would use to describe what she wanted. Justin would be any woman's wet dream yet at the same time would break her heart, as his track record already proved. He was a special agent with the FBI and nothing came before his work.

Grace shoved the unpleasant thoughts out of her head. His fingers made her skin sizzle, and the throbbing need between her legs grew until she feared she would start begging him to hurry while she continued removing her clothes.

Grace stepped out of her shoes, holding his arm to balance herself, and then unzipped her pants. Her uniform was a pile on the floor along with his clothes in less than a minute.

"God damn, Grace, you're more beautiful than I even dreamed you would be."

She almost asked if he'd really dreamed about her, but he dragged his fingers over her breasts and she lowered her gaze, feeling the weight of her hair clasp shift behind her head as strands fell loose around her face.

"Take your hair down for me," he asked, his hoarse whisper as seductive as his gentle touch.

His actions didn't match the feral body that was a human weapon capable of damage in more than one way. She looked up at him while reaching behind her head and unclasping the large barrette that kept her hair in place. It tumbled free, falling over her shoulders and tickling her back and chest.

"Gorgeous, absolutely fucking gorgeous."

"Now you're going to make me question your sanity," she teased. "There is nothing pretty about a huge head of red curls that absolutely refuse to behave."

"That is not true!" He dragged his fingers along either side of her head, pulling until she let her head fall backward. He brushed his lips over hers but then straightened, freeing his hands from her curls and dragging them down her front. "Anyone who ever suggested you weren't perfect in every way needs to be shot."

"Too late," she murmured, and caught his gaze darken again. "There's nothing I can do about my past," she told him, knowing the look she saw harden his face was disapproval. "But I promise you it doesn't make me any less of a woman today."

"You're more woman than any I've ever known, sweetheart." He grabbed her hips and lifted her onto the counter.

Grace didn't doubt for a minute that if she commented on any woman he'd been with in the past, he'd dismiss the topic as unimportant. But mention any man from her past and she would see the possessive, dominating side of him surface in a heartbeat. Well, if he wanted to believe her a virgin, she prayed he had one hell of an imagination.

Chapter 15

Justin ran his fingers around Grace's full, round, perfectly shaped breasts. There was a small, circular dark scar just below her nipple and he grazed it with his fingertip. Grace watched his face but noticeably stiffened as if the scar, which didn't look new, was sensitive. He held her gaze, squeezing her breasts and tugging. She hissed in a breath, and his balls tightened painfully.

He couldn't wait to get inside her. There was still hesitation in Grace's eyes, though. As much as he'd work to replace that look with unadulterated lust, it showed him Grace didn't have casual sex. And he'd believe that about her. She was an amazing woman, overcoming a past that would have destroyed most women. But there were scars, emotionally and physically. He spotted another on her leg, a long thin line, but wouldn't ask if the scars were job-related or something else. That conversation would take place another time. Hell, he had more than a few scars of his own to include in the discussion. They were in a tough line of work.

"Perfect," he growled, letting go of her breasts and tracing lines down her flat tummy to her thighs. "Absolutely perfect."

The way she trembled and arched her back when he spread her thighs filled him with an urge to consume her. But more than consume, he wanted to make her scream his name, know in her heart, in her mind, and in her soul that no one would ever make her feel the way he was about to make her feel. As odd as the thought was, Grace impressed him as a beautiful, sensual creature who'd never been properly appreciated. And who'd never truly known the meaning of coming. He would make her explode, bring her to the edge and go over it with her while showing her how perfect an orgasm could be.

"Relax, sweetheart. You don't know how hard I'm trying to make this gentle and perfect for you." Her rich scent drifted to his nose, intoxicating him.

"Don't change how you are for me, Justin," she said, her gaze hooded with her long lashes while her baby blues appeared to glow. She stretched her legs farther, pulling her feet up to the counter and bringing her ass to the edge. Then as she dragged her nails over his shoulders, it sounded like she purred. "You've promised me this; now deliver. I don't want a presentation; just fuck me."

Her candid talk turned him on more than he thought it would. Grace was a mixture of soft and hard, and he'd yet to learn which was the real her. The thought that she was a bit of both, her soft, alluring, and sensual side surfacing when she let her guard down and her tough, ornery, and "hardass" side also the real her when she was ready to attack and take what she wanted, was worth investigating. But for now, he'd enjoy her, learn her body, and push their relationship to the next level.

"This afternoon that's what you're going to get. As for rough, my dear, you don't want me to unleash and let go. I wouldn't do that to you." He ran a finger down the center of her moist folds. "Crap, woman. You're fucking soaked."

She bit her lower lip, pinching his skin with her fingernails while searching his face. The corner of her mouth tilted into an impish smile. "Think you can handle it?" she asked, barely moving her mouth.

"Oh hell, you're asking for it."

"You've figured that out?"

He wanted to taste her, to plant kisses all over her body and watch her come several times at least before diving into her heat. There would be time for that, though; he'd see to it.

Possibly tonight, since she'd be at his house. But for now, taking the edge off, giving both of them what they wanted for some time now, would at least ease the sexual tension that had simmered between them since they'd met.

"Are you asking?"

"Make it more like a demand." She wrapped her legs around him, pulling him closer and adjusting herself so that his cock pressed against her entrance. "Show me what you've got," she whispered.

Justin glided inside her, fighting to keep his eyes open so he could watch her face. He about boiled over inside as he suppressed the desire to slam fast and hard, so damned eager to reach the core of her heat. So many tiny muscles constricted around his cock, easing him in farther and suffocating the tar out of him at the same time.

"God damn," he growled, clenching his teeth so that he wouldn't explode right then and there.

It had been a while since he'd had sex. Jacking off in the shower didn't count. But she was so fucking tight, her insides smooth and soaked and wrapped around him tight enough to drag the life right out of him.

"Fuck me. Now, Justin. Give it to me now." She shifted her rear end on the counter, inching him deeper into her heat. "I want all of you and I don't want gentle."

There wasn't any way he could deny her request. Grabbing her waist, he held her in place and drove deep inside her.

Grace's rich, thick curls fell over her face when she jerked, then tilted her head back and screamed. Every inch of her stiffened, and she dug her nails deep enough into his flesh that the sting pierced right through him, intensifying his desire to ride her even harder.

Justin preferred rough sex. Taking a woman hard and fast, watching her hair fly and her breasts bounce while she cried out and held on with all she had, turned him on more than anything else. And Grace gave him that and more. The way her face glowed with arousal and she clamped down on him, a fiery hot, silky smooth glove, pushed him so close to the edge that his heart pounded furiously inside him. Blood roared through his veins, sounding like a fucking locomotive in his head.

"More Justin, now. More!" she panted, dragging her nails down his arms, creating an enflamed trail with her fingers. "Please. Please."

"You're going to have all of it, sweetheart." He thrust harder, faster, nailing her as he impaled her again and again.

She groaned, the sound more beautiful than anything he'd ever heard before. And he waited for her to clamp down harder, for her orgasm to squeeze all life out of him. Thrusting forward with his hips, feeling her cream soak his balls, coat his shaft, he knew he'd found paradise. But he needed to hold out, to wait for her to join him. It was his right to carry her over the edge with him.

"Come with me, baby," he growled.

"I can't."

He blinked, fighting to focus on her. So many curls fell around her face, draping over her slender shoulders and parting around her full, round breasts. She sucked in her lower lip, breathing heavily, and batted her lashes over her sensual blue eyes while meeting his gaze.

"I want you to spill all over my belly, Justin," she whispered, her voice husky and rough.

It was an image that did him in. A growl erupted, starting deep inside him and rising until he roared. His balls constricted and the energy he had used holding back he now used to release all he had for her. As much as he hated leaving her heat, Justin pulled out and sprayed white squirts all over her firm tan belly.

"What's all this about saying you can't come?" he asked when the blood quit roaring through his brain. "I've made you come before. You didn't fake it."

"That's not what I meant." She waved him off, jumping off the counter, and then ripped a paper towel free from a roll fixed to her wall before hurrying down the hallway.

Justin watched her leave, loving how she looked naked and already anxious to have her in his arms again. As he gathered their clothes and then held them bundled in his arm while checking the camera, something told him Grace had just revealed something about herself that she'd rather he not know. She wasn't frigid, far from it, but she'd probably held back for so many years that she didn't know how to let go. The next time he made love to her, Grace would come.

"Gee, doll, you get all dressed up for me?" Uncle Charlie added an extra dose of sarcasm as Grace walked into the kitchen after putting Rachel to bed later that evening.

He sat next to Justin at the kitchen table, and they both smiled as she entered wearing an extra large sweatshirt and pair of sweats. She had large baggy socks pulled up on the outside of her sweats, with large fuzzy slippers covering them. She brushed out her hair and then put it up in a high ponytail. Her face glowed a beautiful rosy shade, as if she'd just washed it. Even without makeup and doing her damnedest to cover every inch of that hot body of hers, Grace was still a knockout.

"I decided I wanted to go outside and enjoy the country sky. I could see some of the stars out the window when I put Rachel to bed. I'm going to enjoy them for a minute." She smiled at both of them, and it was obvious the grin didn't reach her eyes. "Find anything on the tape?" she asked, nodding to the camera positioned on the table between them.

Justin had noticed she seemed to avoid watching the tape with him, or maybe it was his imagination. After leaving her house, they'd driven out here, Grace checking in at the station and he putting in a call to his supervisor. Grace's daughter wanted to talk to her about her father, and Grace had disappeared with Rachel upstairs, the two of them remaining there until supper. He envied the close bond Grace had with Rachel but fought off the twang of regret that he didn't have the same with Elizabeth. Someday he'd be close to his daughter and, he hoped, Daniel, too. Maybe after they were out of the clutches of Sylvia.

Justin slid the small screen in front of him sideways so Grace could see it. "I didn't want to interrupt you while you were with your daughter, but we got a bite."

"No shit?" Her face lit up for the first time since he'd fucked her, and she moved closer, putting her hand on the back of his chair and then leaning over slightly to see the screen. Her hair tumbled over her shoulder, smelling like strawberries and making his dick stir to life in his sweats. "You should have called me down. That makes the afternoon worth it."

She sucked in a breath as if trying to retract her words but didn't look at him. Justin stiffened, ready to demand what the hell that meant. If Charlie noticed the sudden tension nipping the air around them, he didn't comment.

Justin stabbed the keys on the keyboard, making the DVD they'd made from the recording fast-forward. He counted the cars and when the fifth car passed he paused the DVD.

"There's our guy," he said, and leaned back, crushing her hand as he crossed his arms.

Grace pulled her hand free but then squatted next to him, turning the screen and staring at the image of a man with black hair, his window rolled up but his face still fairly visible as he stared at Grace's house.

"I've already forwarded it on to my supervisor. Hopefully by morning we'll know if he matches up to anyone in the FBI's files."

Grace nodded, standing. "Well, I'm going out back for a few minutes. I'm not used to seeing such bright stars." Once again her smile appeared cold, distant, when she walked past them, patting her uncle's shoulder and then letting herself out Justin's back door.

"I'll be back in a few," Justin told Charlie.

"Figured as much," Charlie snorted. "Give her time, my boy. She really does have her act together. But she's been known to shut down for a time after going through intensely emotional experiences."

There was no way in hell Justin would ask Charlie to elaborate on that one.

The intensity of the stars overwhelmed Grace. She sat down on the edge of the long wooden deck that ran from one end of the house to the other. She couldn't help but wonder if Justin had built it. She imagined him swinging a hammer. Just picturing his muscles bulge against his shirt while sawing wood or hammering created a throbbing pressure inside her. Her mind shifted quickly and she imagined him without his shirt, his hard body over hers while he fucked her. Oh, a man of many talents.

Why the hell did he have to be so fucking perfect?

She shook the thoughts out of her head stubbornly and focused on the stars. She'd never seen so many. And they weren't tiny, either. They were huge—spread out on an immense, black velvet blanket. She quickly identified the Big Dipper and tried to figure out which one was the North Star. She flopped back and lay down on the deck, with her legs hanging down the two stairs leading to the large yard. It was beautiful.

She quickly came to her senses, however, and sat up, then stood, as the back door opened and booted footsteps walked across the deck toward her. Justin appeared out of the shadows, not that she doubted for a moment who it was.

"I'd like to be alone," she said simply, turning her back on him. She'd avoided him ever since arriving at his house, all too aware that he was too good of an investigator for her to keep her feelings from him if he studied her face for too long. And there was no way in hell he'd figure out her mind before she did.

"And I'd like an explanation for what you just said inside," Justin demanded, standing so close to her backside she swore the tiny hairs on her body stood on end from the electrical charge that created sparks in the air around them. "What did you mean by getting a picture of our man made this afternoon worth it?"

"Not what you think." She wanted to enjoy the stars and put everything in her life on hold, even if just for a few minutes. "Don't worry about it. You're good, okay?"

Justin grabbed her shoulders and spun her around. Her red hair flew wildly around her, the weight of it no match for the hair band that held it.

"Good, huh," he said, his deep baritone smooth and very soft-spoken. The hard edge to his expression and the way he gripped her arms showed he was anything but calm. "Suddenly, you're as cold as ice. Lady, what are you thinking?"

"We fucked. We got it out of our systems," she hissed at him. "Let it go, Justin. Nothing is going to come of it."

Justin studied her creamy white complexion and how the moon defined every curl in her magnificent red hair. He'd never known a woman whose looks could compare with Grace's. Yet at the moment she was so cold inside, a mystery. He needed to be patient. It would be worth it. He always figured a complicated woman would be a headache, but she stirred fire inside him. A fire he'd never felt before.

"Nothing is going to come of it," he repeated.

"No," she insisted. "Why were you with Sylvia today?"

"Huh?"

"You know I saw you. Rachel and I both saw you. And you didn't even try to pretend that bothered you."

"What are you talking about?"

"I saw how you two looked at each other, how you touched her and she touched you. And I don't fool around with married men."

He fought the urge to shake her. "I'm not married."

"Yeah, well maybe you should pull that piece of paper out to remind yourself every now and then."

"Now what in the hell do you mean by that?" Justin didn't yell, but it took a hell of a lot of effort not to point out that she was acting like a jealous girlfriend. He let go of her and reached up to straighten a wild curl, but she slapped his hand. He grabbed her hand and prevented her from pulling away.

"She was all cuddled up to you, and you were smiling at her." Grace spit out the words and her blue eyes sparkled with moisture.

"Did you see the scratch marks she left in my arm as she drew blood, trying to bully me into playing her civil servant? There isn't a damn thing going on between me and Sylvia, and there hasn't been for years." Justin pulled her hand to his chest and moved in closer. "If those two special agents had any skills, they got to see firsthand how much the Mayor of sweet little Rockville and I hate each other's guts. She was dripping with sarcasm as she berated the police department's ineptness when it comes to solving crimes. It was all I could do not to slam her to the ground."

The silence between him and Grace became easier to handle after a minute. She looked up into his eyes, searching, aching to believe him. Grace knew abuse. She craved love and was as intelligent, sexy, and full of life as any woman he'd ever met. Justin would not ruin his chance with her.

"Grace, as soon as those two men left to start interrogating our crime victims, Sylvia and I flew into full-force combat. She stopped her attack on me when she saw you and Rachel across the street. I told her to stay the hell away from you and that simply fed her rage and she marched off. I don't know what she said to you, but she did confront you. I'd have been there sooner, but I'm afraid then the Dairy Queen would have witnessed a scene that almost happened on the courthouse lawn." He sighed and she quickly looked down at the ground. "Sometimes I'm not sure I can work in the same town with that woman."

"You don't have to worry about that now, do you? As soon as this case is solved you'll be off to whatever city your next assignment is in." Grace's voice cracked, and anger sparked in her eyes. She tugged her hand free from his.

He stared at her, crossing his arms over his chest and watching until she turned her back on him, appearing to wipe her eyes.

"Justin, I don't have it in me to be hurt again. I'm afraid it would break me altogether."

"I don't want to hurt you."

"Don't worry. I won't let you." Her shoulders straightened, and then when she tilted her head to the stars her ponytail fell in an array of curls down her back. "Maybe there are parts of me that are broken and can't be fixed. But I'm not alone. You can't get close to anyone, either, although I don't think you've come to terms with it like I have."

"You're wrong, Grace."

"Am I?" She sighed heavily but still didn't turn around. "Did you know that your daughter cries in school because she wants her father?"

Grace might as well have turned around and slapped him with all of her strength across the face. "That's Sylvia's fault," he snapped.

Grace spun around, her blue eyes on fire as she shoved her fists into her hips and squared off with him. "No. It's your fault. You've given up trying to mend bridges with your children for whatever reasons. But they are still there, aware that you are still here. I think it's easier for you to run from city to city, solving crime after crime, than it is to risk facing brokenhearted loved ones who want you back in their lives. Well, I'm not going to become a member of that group."

"Grace, I just said I would never hurt you," he insisted, fighting like hell to not let what she'd just said affect him. This conversation wasn't about his children, and he wouldn't let her push it that way.

Grace's over-sized sweatshirt hung over her slender shoulders and her nipples were hard enough to be visible behind the thick material. "What do you want from me?"

"I want you." He'd never been more convinced of anything in his life. After knowing her for two weeks, Justin didn't have a single doubt in his mind. "And you want me. All you need to do is accept that and we can move forward from there."

"Justin," she whispered. "Don't you see? You're no more capable of loving than I am of receiving it."

"You have no fucking idea what you're talking about," he snapped. "Not only do I know how to love; I know firsthand what it's like to lose someone you love with all of your heart. That doesn't make me never want to love again."

"You don't understand."

"No, Grace. You don't understand. Do you think I don't want my daughter with me? I cry for her as much as she does for me. I've lost my world, too, maybe not in the same way you have. But trust me, everything I cared about, cherished, adored, was stolen from me. I can't bring Clare back. I know the pain of loving and losing. But that doesn't mean I'm going to throw in the towel and not even give us a chance."

"Then why don't you seek out your daughter?"

"Is that what you want?"

"It should be what you want." She searched his face for a moment. "Who is Clare?"

"This isn't about Clare." She didn't fight him when he cupped her face with his hands, although she squeezed her eyes closed, continuing to block the emotions he knew existed inside her.

Her smooth skin warmed his hand. Muscles quivered against his touch. She was toned, in perfect shape, but soft in all the right places.

God. What he wouldn't do to take her to his bedroom right now. It would work. Charlie Jordan approved of him seeing Grace. He had the old man's blessing. And if Grace's daughter woke up, Charlie would go to her.

"Don't close me out," Justin whispered.

Grace's lashes hooded her moist eyes when she slowly raised her gaze to his. "What do you want from me?" she asked, her voice cracking.

He took her hands in his. "No one will ever hurt you again."

"That's one hell of a promise."

"You have my word."

She nodded, although it was clear she didn't believe him. "You're safe here."

He tangled his fingers in her hair and pulled her head back. She didn't fight him but kept her eyes closed. Her lashes were moist. He kissed each one of them and then her nose. "Grace," he whispered.

"What?" She didn't open her eyes.

"Look at me."

"Justin."

"Look at me."

Her lashes clumped together and a lone tear slid down her cheek when she raised her lids and stared at him with deep pools, so blue they were like bottomless ponds of sultry desire mixed with fear. Justin swore there wasn't a prettier sight on earth.

"Thank you." Asking more of her right now would be riding on her vulnerability. That wasn't his style.

Justin brushed her cheeks with his thumbs, losing himself in her gaze and, he feared, a bit of his heart, too.

"I'll walk you to your room."

Grace turned, walked into the quiet, dark house, and he followed. Once in the kitchen she turned around and stared up at him. Those blue eyes were on fire. Every inch of him tensed.

"I can make it to my room."

"We both need to head upstairs. You don't want me walking up there with you?"

"Oh. I thought you might want to work a bit longer or something." She turned, shrugging lazily, and headed toward the hallway and stairs.

Justin followed her upstairs, dying to know what was on her mind and seriously doubting she was focused on what kind of parent he was right now. Nor did he think she cared too much about his relationship with Sylvia. Grace had her emotions and thoughts under lock and key and it bugged the crap out of him. Somehow, he would get her to open up to him.

They reached the top of the stairs and he paused outside the bedroom Grace insisted on sharing with Rachel.

"Good night, then," he said, clasping his hands behind his back so he wouldn't touch Grace.

Grace swallowed, nodding. "Good night."

Chapter 16

"Grace, how's it going?"

Grace looked up from her computer as Bosley leaned in the doorway to her office. He looked good on some days and not so appealing on others. Today, he looked good. His uniform fit perfectly on his tall, lean body. His dark closely shaved hair brought out his masculinity, and his smile put a person at ease.

"I'm doing fine, considering I'm knee-deep in paperwork." She wondered if Sheriff Montgomery had talked to him yet about his fingerprint being at Daisy DePaul's house.

Bosley hesitated for only a moment before entering, his hand on Grace's doorknob. His fingernails were clean and neatly trimmed. She had never seen a more well-groomed man. She watched his eyes, his facial expression, unable to tell if he was going to snap at her again or be nice. Bosley appeared to be a bit bipolar, not that she was an expert on the subject or anything.

"Can I talk to you for a minute?" He entered her office and shut her door, then sat lazily in front of her, slouching in the chair and creasing his nicely starched uniform.

She assumed the question was rhetorical.

"What can I do for you?" She stared at the image on her screen of the man in the car that they had taken with the camera at her house and then glanced at Bosley. The man in the car didn't have his hair parted like Bosley did; in fact, his hair was tousled, possibly not even combed. She honestly couldn't tell from the picture whether the man was Bosley or not. If it was Bosley, he had a split personality, one that was impeccably neat and one that was rougher, almost bad-ass looking.

"How's the investigation going?"

"It's taking up most of my time," she answered, not wanting to admit she didn't have enough evidence to pin the crimes on anyone.

Bosley nodded. "I talked to Montgomery about my fingerprint over at the DePaul house. I wanted you to know that." His expression was friendly. She watched him closely, checking her own expression, trying to determine his reaction to what had to have been an awkward conversation.

"You're a good cop." He leaned forward to get up. "Like I said, I just wanted you to know that."

Know what? He hadn't told her whether she upset him or not. She kept her face blank and continued to watch him.

"Thank you, Bosley. I'm sure witnessing a crime like that had to have been hard on you."

"I've been a cop for three years, but these crimes are the worst I've ever seen." He gave her an odd look.

She got the strangest sensation he tried reading her just as she did him. He wanted to see her reaction to his words, yet he hesitated in speaking. She stiffened, suddenly uncomfortable, although she couldn't say why.

"We accept the fact that there are certain people in the world." He stood and turned to the roses on top of her filing cabinet. He touched one of them and began talking again, as if addressing the flowers. "There are certain people who have needs. Even if they're wrong, the needs are real to them."

"It's still a hideous crime." Grace felt a chill and shuddered. "I'll be glad when we catch the bastard."

Bosley turned to face her, and the look on his face was so dark her eyes widened. "What if someone were to say to you that they had permission?"

Grace stared at him, an unwelcome memory surfacing, and at a grossly inopportune time. "Permission to do what?"

Someone rapped on her door and she jumped. As Justin stuck his head inside and then pushed the door open all the way, filling the doorway, Grace caught Bosley's incredibly satisfied expression. Was he fucking with her?

There was no way he knew the dark, morbid secrets of her past. No one—not a single living person—knew the treacherous details and despicable acts she'd endured.

"Everything okay in here?" Justin glanced at Bosley's backside. The Lieutenant didn't turn around to acknowledge him, and Grace continued staring at Bosley. "Did I interrupt something?"

The tension in the room could be cut with a knife.

"What are you talking about?" Grace pushed, growing sick to her stomach when Bosley didn't answer her first question and now studied his fingernails as if all he'd wanted from his question was her reaction. But how would he know what her reaction would be to such a general question?

Memories Grace swore had disappeared forever suddenly tortured her ruthlessly. She didn't hear Bosley right. Or he meant something other than what those words had once meant to her.

No matter how she fought for composure, the memories continued surfacing, like the terrible sensation that she would throw up right in front of both of them no matter how hard she tried to keep the bile down.

Whether she'd been willing or not, from time to time Master had sent men to her. She might have been ironing his clothes, vacuuming in that god-awfully tight and uncomfortable corset he made her wear, or gardening naked. A memory hit her hard enough to knock the wind out of her. One of being on her hands and knees, completely naked, with the sun burning her back, played before her eyes like a motion picture, set on slightly fast-forward and out of focus. The sensations, being dirty and itchy, dirt under her fingernails and stuck to her knees and palms of her hands, and of being grabbed from behind, were so real she rubbed her hands together, suddenly feeling filthy.

I have permission.

She fought. God, she fucking fought with everything she had. And there was laughter. Insane laughter as whoever was behind her seemed to enjoy her more as she kicked and scratched and did her best to get free. She was forced back into the dirt, her face pushed into earth she'd just cultivated. One strong hand on the back of her head, the other between her legs. When he entered her, his dick swollen and so damned thick, it burned. It was like being set on fire and feeling the flames climb within her, taking out one internal organ after another. Her mouth and nose were stuffed full of dirt. She couldn't breathe, couldn't cough with her face shoved in the ground. As she choked and burned alive, the humiliation destroyed her as a faceless stranger fucked her and laughed the entire time.

Master sent them with orders for her to spread her legs, do what she was good at, putting out and getting a man off. He had told her more than once she performed better, fucked better, when she had no notice. The only warning would be a man saying to her, "I have permission."

"I was just making a suggestion." Bosley stared at her curiously.

"Suggestion about what? What are you talking about?" Justin narrowed his brow, crossing his arms over his muscular chest. He didn't look pleased, which told her she'd allowed the terrors of her memories to come too close to the surface.

"Just asking Grace her opinion on something," Bosley offered, not looking behind him at Justin. The grin Bosley offered her looked absolutely wicked.

"None of those women gave permission for the atrocities done to them," she hissed, more than eager to show Bosley that no matter why he said what he did, she didn't like it. "How dare you say such a thing."

Bosley ignored her response but instead turned and

grinned at Justin. "Howdy, Reece." He walked over to her door and patted Justin on the shoulder. "Have a good one." He slid out of her office leaving Justin standing there looking after him.

Justin turned and faced Grace, closing her door again. She'd looked terrified when he'd first walked in here. But now she smiled at him with the look she got on her face when all her emotions were under check. Her green eyes turned dull, almost blank, and she smiled with her lips closed, instead of her cheerful toothy grin that met her eyes and showed her true happiness.

"What just happened?" His protective instincts kicked in quickly.

"I'm fine." She wouldn't meet his gaze, proof of her lie. "But Bosley is a serious trip."

Justin walked over to her window. It scared him that when he focused on her lately all that went through his mind was undressing her and fucking her silly. If anyone annoyed her, Justin wanted to beat the crap out of them. And when she shut herself off to him, he wanted to grab her, press their bodies together, and devour her until he knew her thoughts as well as she did.

"He was in the Sheriff's office with me just a bit ago. We confronted him about the print and he apologized profusely. Apparently he headed out of the crime scene to his patrol car, remembered he'd forgotten his camera inside, and went back in to get it." When Grace didn't answer, Justin turned around, immediately noticing how her hair wrapped around itself in its French braid.

Bosley had said something to upset her. Justin sighed at the realization that getting information out of her sometimes proved worse than interrogating a hardened criminal.

"What did he ask your opinion on?"

Grace didn't answer but stared at her screen. Justin walked up, placing his hand on her shoulder, and she jumped.

"What? Huh?" When she looked up, she was white as a ghost. At the same time, whatever she worked on she quickly sent to the bottom of the screen.

"Your opinion. He said he asked your opinion."

She stared at Justin like he spoke a different language, and then lowered her head, rubbing her forehead. "He wasn't making any sense, Justin. I don't know what he wanted my opinion on."

"You look like you need a break from all that paperwork." A change of scenery might help her open up to him. "Why don't I take you to lunch?"

There was a small Chinese restaurant in the one strip mall the small town had to offer. Only one other couple nestled in the corner of the dimly lit room. The carpet and tablecloths were bloodred, adding to the quiet mood of the place. Justin waited until they were seated and their host disappeared to resume the conversation.

"What did Bosley say to you?" Justin sipped his ice water and watched her play with her cloth napkin.

She warred with her thoughts. He grew exasperated at her unwillingness to talk to him. He wanted her trust and it scared the piss out of him when she acted like she didn't know how to give it. She would let him kiss her, touch her, even make love to him, but not confide in him.

"That's just it." She looked up at him. "I'm not sure what he said to me."

A teenage boy came to the table then and took their orders. He left a pot of tea and Justin took the initiative to pour the hot brew into two cups, then leaned back and stretched his legs. They brushed against her ankles and his cock stirred in his jeans, making him grateful they sat in a booth.

"Why don't you tell me what was said and see if I can make sense out of it?" he suggested, keeping his feet right where they were and noticing she didn't try to move her feet out of his way.

"He asked me how the investigation was going."

"What did you tell him?"

"I said I had a few leads. For some reason, I didn't want him to know I didn't have enough evidence to nail anyone."

"Did he press the matter?"

"No. But that's not what bugged me." She tried to get comfortable on her side of the booth. Her ankles brushed against his pants again, and those sultry baby blues locked with his. "He said after being in law enforcement for a while we accept that some people do hideous things. And even though the crimes are repulsive, some people just have a need to do them."

She looked away first, pursing her lips as she stared across the restaurant.

"Sounds a little callous." Justin idly played with a silk flower arrangement on the edge of the table. "They're still hideous crimes. I hope I never get accustomed to seeing them."

"That's what I said. But, right before you came in he said something really weird." Justin caught her watching his thumb casually move back and forth slowly over the length of one of the silk flower petals. She shifted in her seat but didn't take her eyes off his hand.

"What did he say?"

She finally tore her gaze from what Justin was doing to the flower and searched his face. "He said what if someone were to say they had permission?"

"Permission to do what?"

"I don't know." She sucked in her breath, and when she brought her fingers to her hair, Justin noticed she trembled.

The waiter brought their food and arranged it in front of them.

Grace began dropping Chinese noodles into her hot and sour soup.

"You don't know." Justin didn't touch his food but instead studied her face.

"No, I don't."

Damn it. She was holding out again. Silence weighed heavily between them, which pissed him off. When she didn't look up but continued twirling her soup with her spoon, he focused on his own food. Fighting the urge to yell at her, force her to share her mind through whatever means it took, stole his appetite, and he clanged his fork on his plate.

"I figured he implied the women may have actually consented to something and it got out of hand. But that's ridiculous." She put her spoon down and wiped her hands with her cloth napkin.

"Why the hell would he imply any of those girls gave consent?" Justin demanded.

"I'm not sure. It was so far out in right field, I couldn't even respond." She looked sincere now, her expression relaxing. "And that's when you walked in."

Justin took her hand and folded her fingers over his, studying her filed fingernails and the pale pink polish on them. Those nails had left marks on his shoulders, wounds he carried with pride. Rubbing his thumb over her knuckles and feeling the dampness covering her palm, he still suspected Grace wasn't sharing everything. She was a master at putting on a believable show. Even now, when he raised his gaze to her probing blue eyes, he saw her arousal, which he guessed was intentional. What better way to distract him from asking more questions?

What had him curious now was, why was she withholding information? "So tell me, do you think Bosley's telling the truth about being forgetful and not putting on his gloves?"

"Obviously he's telling the truth about that." She watched his thumb caress her hand, moving slowly in a circular motion. "The question is, when did he touch that railing?"

"You don't buy his explanation?"

"I think his behavior is odd, but I'm not sure how to test it."

Justin didn't say anything but instead continued watching her. When his eyes lowered to her lips she ran her fingers along the side of his hand. He moved his leg under the table, stroking the side of her leg.

"I think the sooner we put our heads together and figure something out, the better."

"That's a good idea." She slipped her hand from his and reached for his fork. "Better eat," she suggested. "Chinese sucks when it gets cold."

Her phone rang at that moment. "Dispatch," she muttered, flipping it open and taking the call. "Ten four. We're on our way."

She hung up the phone and slid out of the booth. "Possible rape," she said under her breath.

Justin was on his feet at the same time she was and threw a couple twenties down on the table and then guided her to the door. "Where are we going?"

"Pastor's Mobile Home Park, number twenty-three."

"I know where it is."

He let go of her hand outside the restaurant and moved his hand to the small of her back. She fought the heat he created inside her. Going back to her house and fucking him again would have been the perfect diversion to clear her head. At the same time, she acknowledged that she'd just finished a serious interrogation from Justin Reece—and passed. Not even FBI would make her break and share the atrocities of her past.

"There's a disturbance going on. Bosley's on his way, but he might need backup. Christy said the lady who called it in thought someone was being raped by the screams." Grace didn't want to think about the town going rampant because they had a serial killer on the loose. "Our guy doesn't act until Sunday, though, so I'm not sure what's going on."

They were out of the parking lot before she secured her seat belt.

"He's proved a bit too methodical to break his pattern, unless something has seriously upset him. I've seen it happen."

"What would have upset him?" Grace licked her suddenly too dry lips while her mind raced at possibilities. Bosley was upset, but then he was also cheerful, his moods bouncing back and forth faster than a Ping-Pong game.

"We could just be dealing with a domestic dispute. No reason jumping to any conclusions here. Rockville isn't a perfect town. Even without rapists and murderers on the loose, shit can happen."

"And apparently does." She studied his hard profile, wondering if she was as difficult to read as he was most of the time.

Within minutes, they arrived at a trailer at the far end of a trailer park on the edge of town. As they walked up to the door, both of their guns pulled, the front door flew open and Bosley pushed a man out in front of him.

The man struggled against handcuffs and his shirt hung on him, unbuttoned. Justin quickly assisted in detaining him when the man lunged at Grace.

"Whoa there," Justin drawled, overtaking him easily. "The car is this way."

"Head on in there, Grace," Bosley instructed. "It's kind of a mess, but I think she needs some help."

Grace entered the plain-looking trailer slowly, her gun comfortable in her hand as she surveyed her surroundings. So far, no mess. "Hello, I'm Lieutenant Jordan. Is anyone here?"

"I'm in here," came a sobbing voice from down the hallway.

Grace walked down the narrow hallway of the trailer cautiously. A young woman sat on the floor in the back bedroom. She focused on her wrists, which were red and chafed. When she looked up, Grace noticed the swelling on her right cheek. She would have quite a shiner. Otherwise, she was naked, shy of a pair of very short blue-jean shorts that were unsnapped and unzipped. Her body was tight and firm, and her breasts proved her youth with their firmness. Grace would put the girl in her late teens. She seemed indifferent to her exposed body.

"Do you think they'll leave a scar?" she asked, still staring at the redness around her wrists.

Grace searched the room until she noticed a T-shirt thrown on the floor next to the bed. She walked over and picked up the shirt. With gloved hands she handed the shirt to the girl.

"I'm Grace Jordan," she said, ignoring the girl's question. "Can you get up?"

"I think so." The girl pulled herself to her feet and then grabbed her shorts to keep them from falling down her narrow hips. After snapping and zipping them, she pulled the T-shirt over her head. "My name is Serena Blazer, and you all arrived in the nick of time."

She attempted a smile but then moved her hand to her mouth as she grimaced in pain.

"I guess I'll be sore for a while, huh." The girl looked at Grace cautiously. "You did catch the guy, didn't you?"

"They were escorting a man in handcuffs to one of the squad cars when I got here. I was called in for backup."

The young lady nodded, then turned and looked at her bedroom. The mattress was almost a foot off its box spring, and the comforter and top sheet were stripped back and almost completely on the floor. There were ropes lying on the end of the bed, and a two-drawer nightstand lay sideways next to the bed. A small lamp with a decorative lamp shade appeared to have fallen from the nightstand. Curtains were pulled closed over the two windows, making the room dark, although the sun shone brightly outside. Otherwise, Grace saw no indication of a struggle as she turned and looked back down the hallway. Several framed pictures hung on the hallway walls. They had been nicely arranged and hung straight. He must have found Serena already in her bedroom.

"Can you tell me what happened?"

"Yes, I think so," Serena said, without looking up. "I guess you'll want to go over this room before I clean it up."

"Yes," Grace said simply, and watched Serena slowly move down the hallway to the kitchen.

"Can I get you anything to drink?" She stuck her head into the refrigerator.

"No thanks."

Serena gestured to one of the kitchen chairs and then sat down in the other one. She opened a can of beer and took a long drink from it. "Well, okay, here it is. I work nights, you see, and I just got off work. I came home, grabbed my laundry, and went over to the Laundromat. It's hard for me to come home and fall right asleep, so I try to get stuff done first thing, and then I crash." She took another drink of her beer and then reached for a pack of cigarettes that was on the counter.

"How long do you think my wrists are going to hurt?" She rolled the sweaty can of beer over the red abrasion on her skin.

"I'm not sure. We'll get you to a doctor right away and take your statement later if you like." Grace watched the moisture from the can trickle down the lady's wrists.

"No, oh no!" Serena looked up, shocked. "No doctors!"

When Grace showed her surprise Serena quickly added, "I just don't think I could let anyone else touch me right now. You understand." She smiled knowingly.

"So, you went to the Laundromat?" Grace tried to direct the young lady back to what happened.

"Oh yeah." She ran her fingers over blonde hair pulled back in a ponytail. Not one strand fell free from the fuzzy ponytail holder behind her head. "Sorry. Okay, so I did my laundry and brought it home. It took two trips to haul it inside, and when I came back to get the second basket, he was standing in the living room. I guess I left the front door open and he came right on in."

"Do you know the man?" Grace asked.

"No! I've never seen him before. I don't think he's from around here. I mean . . . I didn't know him." Serena's hand shook as she tapped ashes into the ashtray. "And well, you know, he attacked me."

"Did he say anything to you?" Grace wrote quickly, wishing she had a tape recorder.

"Oh yeah. He told me he would fuck me and if I behaved, he would let me scream in pain for him. Pretty gross, huh?" She shuddered and then took another drink of her beer. "I could tell right away he was serious. I tried to fight him off, but he got pretty far before the first cop showed up." She sighed and smiled. "That cop was so brave. He tackled the guy, and threw him to the floor. He had handcuffs on the jerk so quickly the guy couldn't fight him off. Then, he untied me and took the guy outside. He said you'd be here in a minute, so I could talk to a woman."

Someone gently knocked on the door, and Serena hopped up to answer it.

"Hey." She smiled and pointed a finger at Justin's chest. "You're Justin Reece, the FBI guy who grew up here. I've seen your picture in the paper. Wow, I feel important."

"Serena, are you sure I can't give you a ride to see a doctor?" Grace watched as the young lady smiled at Justin. He looked down at the young woman and then turned to focus on Grace, his expression unreadable. "I know you've been through a lot, but if you want to press charges, and I assume that you do—"

"Oh, do you think I should? I mean . . . is it something that people do when they get . . . um, you know . . . attacked?" Serena looked down at her wrists. "I guess maybe they could give me something, to make sure I don't get scars."

"I doubt you'll have scars," Grace said casually. She watched Serena carefully as she stood there. The side of her face was turning a two-tone shade of green. She'd been hit pretty hard. Her wrists were puffy with red blotches forming bracelets around both of them. Otherwise, she stood straight, and her shaking seemed to have subsided. Something wasn't right here. "Are you hurt anywhere else?"

"No, I don't think so." Then her eyes opened wider and she nodded. "I know what you're saying. He didn't have a chance to, well, you know, fuck me or anything." She threw a shy smile toward Justin and quickly gave him the once-over. A rather odd action coming from a woman who claimed she didn't want anyone touching her right now.

"Do you have her statement?" Justin put his hands on his hips and didn't look at Serena.

"I've heard enough," Grace said dryly. "Shall I take you to the doctor?"

Justin raised an eyebrow and Serena quickly guzzled more of her beer.

"Oh no, I'm sure you have plenty of work to do putting that guy in jail. Oh, he said he raped those other girls. I'll say that in court if you want." She reached over and grabbed her purse off the counter. "I guess do whatever you have to do," she said, and then opened the door and left.

Chapter 17

Grace studied the closed door for a second before turning her attention to Justin. Her eyes were exceptionally blue, even in their dim surroundings. He took in the drab-looking trailer. Mismatched furniture cluttered the small living room, and a counter separated it from the kitchen. Counters were bare, the kitchen sink dry. For the most part, the place looked unlived in.

"What did Bosley say?" she asked.

"He seemed quite excited that he'd caught the rapist." Justin studied a picture hanging on the wall, a cheap print of a vase with daisies in it. Rather ugly actually. "He said he had a confession."

Justin turned to study her face and read caution, possibly confusion, and definitely doubt. Several strands fell loose from her braid on either side of her face, although she didn't seem to notice. She stared at him, pressing her full lips into a thin line and looking angrier than he'd ever seen her look before.

"What do you think?" he asked.

Grace didn't hesitate. "She's lying."

"Lying?" Justin would bet money on the fact. "That's a pretty harsh statement. I hope you can back it up."

Grace pushed the front door open all the way, leaning out of the trailer until the door crashed against the siding outside. More light drained into the dim room, highlighting dust on end tables and the coffee table. Looking past

Grace, he saw Serena and the small Honda that had been parked outside were gone. Grace left the door open, ignored the living room, and walked down the hallway. Justin followed.

"She said he attacked her in the living room, but she was found in the bedroom. She also said she tried to fight him off." They entered the bedroom and Justin simply stood, arms crossed, and watched Grace as she moved around the room as if looking for something. Her mind traveled a mile a minute. He saw it in her face and enjoyed watching her in action. Her eyes darted from one thing to the next, and he knew she took it all in, not missing a thing.

Grace pointed down the hallway. "If he attacked her in the living room, and brought her to the bedroom, there would be evidence of a struggle. Look at all those pictures hanging in the hallway, all of them perfectly straight."

She then turned and pointed to the bed. The top sheet and comforter hung almost to the floor. The mattress itself was shoved off the box spring by almost a foot. "This doesn't make sense, either. If he threw her on the bed, or even placed her on it . . ." She bent over the bed and pointed at the ropes and headboard. "If he tied her to the bed, she'd still be able to squirm around and try to dodge him. The fitted sheet isn't torn off the bed. See, it's firmly intact under the mattress, even though the mattress has been moved."

She looked around the room again and then headed down the hallway, opening two closed doors. One led to a much smaller bedroom, and the other was to a bathroom. After looking in both doors, she returned to the bedroom and opened the closet to look inside.

"She said it took two trips to bring back all her laundry." Grace turned to look at Justin, who stood, with arms still crossed, watching her every move. "Yet there is no sign of laundry baskets or folded clothes or anything."

"And you think . . ."

"That someone is wasting our time," she finished his sentence angrily.

"Why do you think someone would do that?"

"I think they want us to believe this investigation is solved so we'll drop it." She stuck her chin out defiantly.

"I agree. Come on. We'll take pictures and then see if we can't track down our victim for further questioning."

"I'm going to call in for a full dusting, get Forensics to give the place a thorough once-over," Grace decided, grabbing her phone. "I want all the fucking proof in the world that this was a setup."

Grace followed Justin out to get the camera and then through the trailer, suggesting different angles, as he took shots of every room in the trailer. After that, they touched base with Christy and then headed back to the station.

"Would you conclude," Justin broke the silence as he drove, "that our perp is behind this rape, trying to throw us off guard?"

"I thought we'd already drawn that conclusion."

"What proof do we have?" He turned to look at her for a second. She screwed up her eyebrows and began chewing on her lower lip. Looking at her profile, he enjoyed the long braid that fell, beginning at the nape of her neck. Curls stuck out of it here and there, reminding him of the magnificent bright amber locks that could tickle his body into ecstasy. He forced his eyes back to the road.

"I'm not sure we have any right now," she said hesitantly. "But . . ."

"Yes?"

"Well, I can't even begin to prove this. But what if someone was so devastated by what this is doing to their town that they would set us up, just to get us to drop it and the press to say the case is solved? Put the town back to normal in their eyes. Albeit the rapist and murderer would still be out there, just no longer the focus of gossip." She let her voice trail off as they pulled into the station.

"Holy shit!" Justin muttered.

Fifteen to twenty members of the press stood outside the police station. There were cameramen. Women and men holding microphones were talking into the cameras. Some were in suits while others wore jeans. Justin recognized some of the reporters from the Rapid City channels he watched at times. Several cars indicated they were from TV channels in Minneapolis. Reporters hovered around the steps going into the station.

By the time Grace and Justin parked, she noticed several of them were interviewing Bosley and Sheriff Montgomery. Bosley pointed to Justin's truck and every member of the media turned their attention to him and Grace.

"Fucking crap!" Justin hissed.

"They want a story on the investigation," Grace said unnecessarily.

"I wonder how they found out someone had been brought in?" Justin asked out loud, but they both knew the answer as they got out of the car and the crazed group of reporters headed toward them. Bosley stood on the stairs, watching with his arms crossed.

As reporters surrounded Justin and Grace, he noticed a car pull up to the curb. Great, just what he needed, Sylvia was here.

"Do you have a comment on the young man arrested earlier today by one of your officers?" A microphone was shoved into Justin's face.

"Is it true you were hired simply to catch the rapist?" Another microphone went to Grace's face.

"Do you now view the investigation as closed?" a third voice rang out. "Did you catch your man?"

Justin grabbed Grace and started pushing her through the crowd.

"It's too soon to answer your questions," Justin said loudly. "I'm sure we'll have a statement for the press as soon as we meet with local law enforcement."

"How do you feel about Rockville expanding their budget to hire a new investigator and bringing in the FBI only to have one of our own men catch the guy?" The question caused Justin to stop in his tracks and he looked, knowing who asked it. Sylvia stood, arms crossed, by the entrance to the station with Bosley a few feet from her.

Justin fought to control oncoming rage. He envisioned

wrapping his hands around her narrow neck and squeezing all life from her. It wasn't the first time he'd had such thoughts. It was all he could do to maintain composure and walk past his ex-wife, holding Grace tightly next to him.

The Sheriff was right behind Justin when they entered the station

"Get those reporters out of here," the Sheriff roared to no one in particular, once the police station doors closed behind them. "And I want Bosley's report on his arrest immediately."

Justin continued holding on to Grace as he walked to her office. He escorted her and almost physically placed her in one of the chairs. He hated being made a fool, and in his own town. Someone would pay dearly for this little stunt.

Christy hurried in behind Sheriff Montgomery. "It's his rough copy. He hasn't had a chance to type it up yet. I don't know if I'm going to be able to guarantee your privacy," Christy warned.

Justin crossed his arms and stared out Grace's window at the front lawn. More vans and cars were pulling up outside. This was going to be a media fucking field day before the day was out. And over a fucking hoax. He'd bet his career on it. Grace had called it, and he had to agree with her. Someone had trumped up a staged rape and arrest to get them to back off. Multiple lines rang continuously as the two other officers on duty desperately tried to answer them. The Sheriff said something to his dispatcher, but Justin ignored them. His job just got twice as hard, and the clock was ticking a hell of a lot faster than it had been an hour ago. If he didn't prove damned quick that they didn't have their man in a holding cell downstairs, then he'd be pulled off the case.

Which he was willing to bet was exactly what someone wanted.

"Sheriff," Grace said quietly. Justin turned around when Grace closed her office door and leaned against it. She crossed her arms and gave Montgomery all of her attention. "Someone has gone to an incredibly large amount of trouble to show that this investigation is solved."

"What?" Sheriff Montgomery was a big man and for his age still looked like he could hold his own. He shifted his attention to Justin. "Is that what you think?"

"I agree with Lieutenant Jordan. If you'd seen the crime scene you'd think the same thing, Sheriff."

"He must be scared we were coming real close to discovering something," Grace continued, drawing the Sheriff's attention back to her. "Or possibly he's getting ready to do something so big he needs us distracted in order to do it."

Sheriff Montgomery sat in one of the chairs in front of her desk and mulled over the report Christy had brought him while silence fell over the room for a minute. "You two are making one hell of an accusation here. And you're offering me no proof whatsoever when I have our perp downstairs in a holding cell, a victim who's claiming she was told by her attacker that he killed those other girls, and the fucking media outside my doors getting ready to broadcast that this case is solved."

If his voice boomed off the walls any louder, everyone outside in the station would overhear their conversation. Grace obviously thought the same thing. She sat in the chair opposite him and turned it so she faced the Sheriff, then leaned on her knees.

"I think we should make a statement." She was calm, impressive as hell, and very focused when she spoke quietly. "We need to tell the press we believe we have our man and that we have a signed confession. Give Bosley all the credit and make a big deal out of it."

"And then?"

"Then, we keep our eyes and ears open and see what happens." She leaned back, smiling, although she still looked mad as hell.

"I announce this case is solved and you lose the FBI." Sheriff Montgomery didn't look over his shoulder at Justin but focused on Grace. "I'm not saying you aren't qualified, but at the same time I can't lie to the press. You two have an hour to show me evidence that implies we've been set up."

Grace licked her lips, glancing over the Sheriff at Justin.

He didn't want to hear her tell the Sheriff she would take this case on by herself. Regardless of her qualifications, the odds were stacking up against her. Not only was their killer brave enough to approach her daughter at school—which might or might not have happened, but Justin's gut said it did—but he was driving by her house. And to make it worse, cops inside this station were working against her as well. Justin wouldn't leave her alone to take this all on by herself.

"Sheriff, the FBI can stay in Rockville and keep a very low profile." Justin walked around Montgomery and paused behind Grace, placing his hand on the back of her chair. He didn't give a rat's ass when Sheriff Montgomery lowered his gaze, his disgruntled expression not changing when he focused on the almost intimate action when Grace leaned back and pressed her shoulder against Justin's fingers. "But if you don't go public right now, with the press outside, it will look even worse for Rockville and become an even worse fiasco than someone is already trying to make it."

When Montgomery slammed his fist on Grace's desk, she jumped noticeably and then exhaled loudly. Justin ached to console her, knowing her nerves were wrapped as tightly as his were right now, but he held his ground, letting the Sheriff fume and praying he wouldn't make too much of a scene and allow anyone else in the station to grow suspicious of their plotting.

"I promise you, Sheriff," Grace said, white-knuckling her hands as she clasped them together on her lap. Her voice was as cold as it had been last night out on his deck. Grace barely controlled her temper, but she remained sitting, although she was stiffer than a fucking board. "Whoever set this crime scene up today, I will personally hand them over to you for retribution."

"I want their goddamned head on a platter," Montgomery sneered, glaring at her and then standing quickly, making his chair squeal loudly when he pushed it backward. "I'll go announce to the press that we have our guy. It's going to make me look like a damned fool when you prove we don't. But if we do have our guy, and you're discredited somehow," he said, pointing a finger at Grace, "you're going to start looking for another line of work."

"Sheriff," Justin began, and reached for Grace when she jumped to her feet.

Grace rolled her shoulder, brushing him away from her. "Sheriff," she said at the same time Justin did, and held her hand up to silence Justin and take the floor. "If your officer made a valid arrest, I'll apologize personally. But I'm not wrong. And I will place my career on the line to back that," she hissed, squaring her shoulders, and even with her back to Justin he knew she glared at the Sheriff. "If it makes you feel better, look at the pictures we took." She reached for the camera they'd used, which was next to her purse on her desk. She pushed the button to turn it on, and her fingers shook as she pulled up the recent photos and then held the camera out to Sheriff Montgomery. "Bosley's report probably says she was hauling laundry back to her trailer. It took her two trips and her attacker was in the trailer when she returned the second time. But there're no laundry baskets, no folded or unfolded clothes anywhere. She claims the struggle started in the living room and ended in the bedroom." She pointed at the camera that was now in the Sheriff's hands. "Look at the pictures on the hallway wall, which is a narrow hallway, by the way. They are straight, untouched. Falling into either wall just once would cause those wall hangings to at least shift to the side, if not fall. She was way too cool, too collected, for a woman just attacked, stripped out of her clothes, and tied to her bed by a stranger who allegedly promised to do terrible things to her and told her he'd killed those other girls. She was smiling and flirting with Justin the moment he entered the trailer."

Justin cocked an eyebrow at that comment at the same time that Sheriff Montgomery looked up from scanning the pictures that were still on the camera.

Grace was wound tight and didn't pause or even seem to notice both of them react to her last statement. "She'd been hit in the eye and there was red chafing on her wrists. I'm willing to bet it's going to be hard as hell to track her down for further questioning, and impossible to get her to see a doctor, even if we offer to cover all her expenses. If she were dragged down that hallway, there would have been red marks on her arms. If she struggled at all, kicked, swung out, and hit her attacker, he would have swung repeatedly. The other girls we found were beaten almost beyond recognition. This whole thing is worse than a damned lousy-scripted B movie," she hissed, keeping her voice low throughout her tirade but finally throwing her hands up in the air and marching out from between both of them and over to her window.

The Sheriff returned his attention to the camera, viewing the pictures on the small screen.

"Sheriff," Justin said, glancing at Grace when she spun around as he spoke. "I'm going to call my supervisor now. I'll brief him on everything that happened today. Already we've got a few other agents here in town. They've checked into a local motel, but I can put them up out at my place to keep things quiet. And since I do live here, remaining here for another week or so won't appear odd to anyone. We'll keep things quiet and our eyes and ears alert. Go make your announcement to the press, and then come back in and we'll interrogate our guy downstairs together."

Justin remembered graduating from high school and approaching Sheriff Montgomery about a life in law enforcement. Goddamn if that didn't seem several lifetimes ago. Yet the man standing before him, with his all-knowing gray eyes and his harsh glare, appeared the same man who told Justin he couldn't go wrong upholding the law.

"All right, Justin," Sheriff Montgomery said, exhaling noticeably, and his wiry frame deflated, yet he was still in good shape in spite of his age. "Get on the horn with your supervisor and let me know what he says. I'll round up Bosley and we'll make a statement to the press. But then I want to hear what you two have against one of my better cops." He turned then, leaving the room without saying anything else.

Grace's office felt like a fucking cage. Justin fisted his hands, fighting the urge to slam the wall, send something flying, anything to ebb the mounting outrage threatening to blow up inside him. He headed around her desk to her computer, aware Grace stood to the side of her window, scowling at the ground. There wasn't any doubt her own ghosts tormented her.

"I really am worried about Bosley." She bit her lip, still not looking at Justin but hugging herself and continuing to stare at the floor.

"He's made his own choices, Grace. Don't feel sorry for him if he made the wrong ones." Justin moved her mouse and her screen came to life.

"No," she said before he could ask her about what was on her computer. "The reason you saw me looking shocked when you walked in on Bosley and me . . ."

"You?" He looked up from the altered image of the man they'd photographed driving past her house yesterday.

She opened her mouth to speak but then focused on him with hooded blue eyes. They looked so haunted he wondered if what was on her computer screen had something to do with her holding out on him all day. Obviously her thoughts were going in different directions than he originally thought.

"Bosley suggested those women gave their permission. Is that what is bothering you?" He wanted to ask about her screen but held out to hear what she would say first.

"No," she corrected him, not budging from where she stood next to her window. "He asked, 'What if someone were to say to you that they had permission?' "

" 'What if someone were to say to you that they had permission?' "

Grace's eyes widened and she chewed her lower lip, suddenly looking so forlorn his anger faded. Pushing away from her desk, deciding calling his supervisor would wait, Justin walked over to her.

"Tell me what that means, Grace."

"It was a code phrase," she whispered. "It meant that Master had given someone permission to fuck me. He would simply show up with no notice and tell me that he had permission."

"Fuck!" he hissed.

Grace tried pulling away. But he wasn't going to let her distance herself from him when she'd just opened up. Justin grabbed her, considering only briefly that he might be too rough and that she was upset. He dragged her into his arms and held her against him until she relaxed.

"I didn't know the men and never knew when Master would send them. But when they said, I have permission, if I fought them, it just went harder on me."

"Oh hell." Justin lifted her into his arms like she weighed nothing. "Sweetheart. Don't let Bosley get to you. I'm sure he didn't have a clue that those words meant anything to you. There's no way he could have dug up the information I did on you. He wouldn't have access to it. Hell, I wasn't supposed to have access to it."

When she shoved curls out of her face and gazed into his eyes, which were mere inches from hers, the look she gave him weakened his defenses. He hated seeing the pain etched on her face.

"Why did you search so hard to find out what you did?"

He could tell she needed the truth. Grace had pulled off some pretty creative permanent file editing to alter the paper trail of her life. Most wouldn't have a clue how to do it. "It's not normal for a person's life not to start until they're twenty-three. In your case, though, there was no sign of a check cashed, credit applied for, of anything until you were twenty-three. I would have done the same if I found that on anyone—I had to know why."

She let out a sigh, nodding once. "My life didn't start until I was twenty-three, and even then it was rocky. Master stole me while I was putting groceries in the back of my car. I was eighteen."

"He's not your master anymore."

"You're right." She pushed against Justin's chest and he reluctantly let her go. "No one is, nor will they ever be again. I'm in charge of my own life."

"As it should be," he agreed. "But that doesn't mean you should close yourself off to someone who cares about you."

She gave him a skeptical look. "What are you going to tell your supervisor?" she asked, pointedly changing the subject.

That dull sheen that covered her eyes when she was blocking Justin out wasn't there. Instead her expression glowed with so much emotion, of which he was sure the dominating one was still anger. Looking away from her first, Justin walked around her desk again. He wouldn't push her. Although her admission just now had him curious whether she didn't hold more information in her head that could solve this case than she realized.

"I'm giving him the facts, just as I always do." Justin leaned against her desk, watching Grace while pulling out his cell phone. He'd had it on Silence and noticed that he'd missed a call. Apparently Bogfrey, his supervisor, already had tried reaching him. There was voice mail and he pushed the button to listen.

"Reece, report in immediately," Cliff Bogfrey snapped through the phone. "I've already spoken with Sheriff Montgomery and I want you both on a conference call now."

Justin cursed, deleting the message and feeling his temper soar again that the Sheriff took the time to go over his head before making his press announcement.

"What's wrong?" Grace asked, walking around her desk. She started to sit in her chair but then saw her computer monitor and didn't grab her chair properly, instead damn near falling over it. "Oh my God. Crap!" she hissed, her face turning white as a sheet as she all but crawled over her chair before Justin could get around to her.

"What is it? What's wrong?" He grabbed her, picking her up as she continued battling her office chair, which rolled in a half circle away from her as she started fighting him. "Grace, cool it. What the fuck is the problem?"

"That . . . there." She pointed at her screen, her finger shaking as bad as her voice when she tried speaking. "On the screen. Shit!"

He was fighting her and her office chair behind her desk and all but picked the chair up and threw it to the other side of the office before managing to grab Grace and grip her by her arms. He gave her a quick shake. "You're not making any sense. Are you saying you didn't do that to that picture?"

She shook her head, tears streaming down her cheeks while she shook so hard he worried she would fall into a fit of hysterics he wouldn't be able to calm without drawing attention to them from outside the office.

"Get a grip, Lieutenant," he said coldly, making his voice harsh enough that she stilled.

Justin swore all life drained out of her when she straightened, her entire body suddenly stiff as a board. "Let go of me, Justin. And forgive me. I'm fine. It just threw me off guard."

Justin held on to her with one arm and grabbed her office chair, twisting it around to face him, with the other. Then sitting in it, he pulled Grace, using a bit of force when she hesitated in coming to him, until she collapsed on his lap. Even then, she twisted around against him trying to get back up.

"No. Stay put," he ordered, moving the mouse and staring at the altered picture on the screen. "You didn't color this mask in on his face?"

Grace shook her head, rubbing her hands over her face. "Justin, that's Master."

Justin stared at the screen and the picture. What once was a picture of a man staring out his car window as he drove by had been altered. Someone had used black to cover his face, all but his eyes and mouth, so it appeared he wore a black leather mask that completely covered his face. Justin remembered Grace mentioning once that she didn't know what the man who abducted her looked like because he always wore a leather mask. Obviously someone knew more about her past than just Justin.

"Let me up." She slapped his arm when he hesitated in complying. Grace hurried around her desk to her door. "I'm finding out right now who was in here while we've been gone."

He couldn't get around her desk fast enough before Grace left him alone in the office.

"I hope I didn't seize your limelight." The voice caused her to jump and she turned quickly.

Grace squared off and faced Bosley in the middle of the station, ready to take him on right there and demand to know if he'd been in her office. Bosley looked extremely happy and very relaxed. If anything, when he started frowning at her expression he looked confused, not suspicious.

Grace watched Justin storm out of her office. Sheriff Montgomery called for him, beckoning with his arm, and Justin gave her a warning look before turning toward the Sheriff's office. Justin was headed for a meeting that wouldn't include her, but she'd be damned if she would comply with a stern look from him across the room. She looked away first and relaxed her features, sighing and then smiling as she shook her head, giving Bosley all of her attention.

"Of course not, Bosley." She smiled as reassuringly as she could. "We're a team here, right?"

"I just know how hard you've been working on this. You don't have any doubts, do you?" He raised an eyebrow as he asked. She also noticed his eyes lower . . . to her mouth?

"Well, I've asked permission to question the guy you brought in." She glanced at the station doors where two cops stood outside with their backs to the doors, keeping the press outside. "Once this escapade is over."

"You shouldn't question him alone. But I'm sure Justin would agree with that one easily enough." This time she was certain Bosley was looking lower than her lips.

Grace wasn't going to ask Christy who might have been in her office with Bosley on her tail. She headed back toward her office and cringed when Sylvia pushed her way around the two officers at the door and let herself into the station.

"Is this a private conversation?" she asked, following Bosley into Grace's office. There was enough of a sting in Sylvia's voice to send warning signals off in Grace's head.

"No, of course not." Bosley turned and moved so Sylvia

could share the space in the doorway. Grace thought she saw him give Sylvia the once-over as well. "We were just expressing our relief that this nightmare is over."

"I bet you're just eaten up with envy that Bosley was the one to bring him in." Sylvia didn't hide her vindictive tone.

"You don't miss a single opportunity," Grace returned, not willing to kiss ass at the moment.

"Now, ladies, let's keep it peaceful." Bosley smiled at both of them, almost as if he enjoyed the thought of the two women sparring.

"I'm actually glad Bosley was able to get there as quickly as he was, or we wouldn't have caught him before another girl was raped and murdered." Grace smiled, although she fought the urge to get up and physically throw the woman as far away from her office as she could. The thought was actually rather satisfying and Grace's smile grew.

"I saw you show up with Justin." Sylvia wouldn't back down. "I assume you were out working on another case."

"That's none of your business," Grace snapped, more than willing to take her frustration out on Sylvia. Grace leaned against her desk, unwilling to walk around and see that picture on her screen again.

"Well now." Sylvia raised an eyebrow and turned to Bosley. "Wouldn't the press love to know that you caught our rapist while Special Agent Reece and his own investigator were gone on some unknown rendezvous?"

"I think the press would be more excited to catch a few shots of Rockville's newest investigator throwing the Mayor out of the police station on her ass," Grace spit, and jumped away from her desk toward Sylvia.

Sylvia stepped out of the office but laughed. Bosley reached out and grabbed Grace, holding her by the arms.

He turned to the Mayor. "That's enough, Sylvia. I think everyone's adrenaline is a little pumped right now."

Sylvia waved a couple of hot pink–colored nails in a facsimile of a dainty good-bye. She then turned on her heels and walked toward the back door.

Bosley turned to face Grace, and she attempted to yank

herself free. He held on tightly, though, and let his gaze travel down her slowly. When he looked up, she saw an un-leashed fire that sent terror through her.

"You are one hot redhead, aren't you?" he whispered, and she knew he didn't want anyone else to hear what he said. "Just remember, little lady, I have permission."

Her outrage must have flooded her eyes, because an evil grin appeared on his face. "I knew you understood the first time," he said, and let her go.

"Get the hell out of my office," she hissed at him. "You don't have permission to do fucking shit."

He walked backward a step or two once again surveying her body, then turned and left her office. She slammed the door shut and returned to her desk.

Holy shit! Bosley had somehow found out about her past. She didn't doubt for a moment that he was the one who had altered the picture on her screen. But how did he find out? This wasn't information that she had deleted from her past. Justin had learned she'd been in hospitals, under respite care and psychological treatment. From there he probably had pieced together the facts. But the sordid details that took place while Master held her captive at his mansion weren't documented anywhere. There was no proof other than her sordid memories.

Chapter 18

Justin walked out of Sheriff Montgomery's office, the adrenaline and anger rush he'd held on to earlier now dissipated. Heading home for a cold beer and letting all of the crap around him settle sounded like a damned good idea.

Cliff Bogfrey wasn't thrilled at all with the angle they were taking on the case. Just because their latest rape didn't fit the standard profile at the crime scene didn't mean they hadn't nailed their guy. If Justin heard Bogfrey ask one more time why he bought into the argument of a police officer who had three years' experience behind her, and a shaky past prior to that, he would have yanked that speaker box off of Montgomery's desk and hurled it out the window.

It would come down to him confiding to Bogfrey about Grace's past just so he would understand Justin's motivation. Justin wouldn't do that in front of the Sheriff, but if he didn't, he would be yanked off the case and it would be filed as solved. Then his hometown would suffer under the hands of a madman who would have a fucking field day when he learned the FBI were successfully booted out of town.

Justin growled out loud when he discovered there was no coffee.

"Bad day, Justin?" Christy eyed him over her paperwork.

"I've had better." He allowed a growl to creep into his tone, but Christy wasn't daunted.

"You should cheer up," she said without hesitation. He

turned to glare at her, but she just smiled. "One might think you don't believe the guy we have down in the holding cell is the right man."

He blinked as if she just slapped him across the face.

"You're either worth your weight in gold or a royal pain in the ass. I can't decide which." It took effort to make his facial muscles relax enough to smile.

Christy waved her hand at him and giggled. "What a charmer you are, Justin. And you know, I'm a little bit of both."

He did smile then, and turned to make the coffee. There were serious problems, though. The Bureau would pull him off this case if he didn't come up with something.

How could he explain to Grace that he would have to leave when they assigned him to another case?

"Where's Grace?" The coffeemaker burped and he leaned against one of the empty desks, staring at her office door, which was partially open, and obviously dark inside.

"She headed out to pick up her daughter about thirty minutes ago," Christy spoke from behind him at her desk, but Justin didn't bother to turn around.

He thought about Grace telling him how Elizabeth cried for her daddy at school. That thought didn't cheer him up much. He accepted that he wasn't the best of fathers. Elizabeth was yet another reason, though, why he needed to piece the puzzle together here. If not for Grace, this town would be safe for his daughter, and for Daniel. A pang of regret twisted in Justin's gut and he wondered where both of them were right now, probably home with their mother getting an earful over how inept their father was when he didn't catch the bad guy who'd ransacked their happy town.

"Is our perp still down in the holding cell?" Montgomery agreed with Bogfrey that they would move him to a larger jail in the morning. If Justin wanted to talk to the man, he needed to do it before they hauled him to a larger facility.

"He'd better be." Christy made a face at Justin. "It would suck if Sheriff Montgomery had to make another statement to the press off-the-cuff."

"Off-the-cuff?" Justin crossed one boot over the other and relaxed on the edge of the desk, facing her. "What do you mean by that?"

"You know, Justin, just because all I ever amounted to was a dispatcher at our police station doesn't mean I'm stupid." She sounded offended.

Sheriff Montgomery came out of his office at that moment, closing his door behind him and then locking it. Not a bad move and something Grace should consider doing as well—obviously. Although if Justin had any say in the matter, she'd be working among a much more reliable team before all was said and done on the matter, with a team around her who were trustworthy and not ready to stab her in the back the first chance they got.

"I'm told supper is on the table," Montgomery announced, looking tired and older than he had earlier when he was in Grace's office. His gray complexion matched the shade of his hair, and instead of standing tall and proud like he always had, he slumped, his shoulders hunched as if he'd just endured one of the worst days of his life. The thought of possibly lying to the press probably was the older man's foremost concern. "Make sure I'm notified of anything and everything," he told Christy, heading toward the door. "And Justin, get out of here. Go spend time with your family. Clear your head. That's what I'm going to do. It makes things easier to figure out. Take my word on it, son."

"Sounds like a plan, Sheriff," Justin said, wishing it were an option. He filled his cup with coffee and walked back to Christy's desk. "You off soon?"

"If you're hinting for a date, darling," she said, smiling broadly at him and showing off her large pearly white teeth, "I've already got plans for the evening. But yes, I've got ten minutes before night dispatch shows up."

Justin didn't smile at her joke. He just didn't have the energy. Instead, reclining against the desk next to hers, he stared at her almost white, short haircut and her pointed long nose. She hadn't been the prettiest of teenagers but had a personality that made you forget that she wasn't attractive. That same quality existed in her now.

"Can I ask you something, Christy?"

Her smile faded and she turned her chair so that she faced him, obviously sensing he was burdened with too much, and willing to hear what he might have to say or unload. And in truth, she'd probably be one hell of an ally to create for his side. Christy was loyal, an incredible dispatcher, and he would bet good money that not much got past her.

"Who was in Grace's office today while she was gone?"

Christy didn't ask why he asked but instead wrinkled her nose and tapped her thin lips with her finger. "Well now," she said, hesitating while giving it some thought. "Bosley was in there for a while earlier. He said he needed to use her computer."

"What's wrong with his?"

"He complained it wasn't running properly and wanted me to call in someone to look at it."

"So did you?"

Christy shrugged but then narrowed her alert gaze on his. "I checked it out myself. There's nothing wrong with his computer. Why did he want to get on Grace's?"

This time Justin shrugged, and when Christy leaned back, visibly disappointed that he wouldn't enlighten her with any juicy information, he decided it wouldn't hurt to test her loyalty.

"Can I trust you, Christy?" he asked, point-blank.

She straightened, taking him seriously. "You bet you can, Justin. This is my town, too, you know."

"I know." He made a show of giving it some thought while she moved to the edge of her seat, her eyes wide as she waited for what he would say next. "I want you to call me, call my personal cell phone," he added, pushing away from the desk and grabbing one of her Post-it pads. After scribbling down his number, he pulled the paper free and held it out to her. "If anything happens around here that seems odd, anything at all."

"Like Bosley going in Grace's office?"

"Yes, like that. Or anything else. This is your station. You know everyone here. If any odd phone calls come in, anyone says something that sounds weird—I don't care how many times you call me. I want to know."

"Okay," she said, staring at his number on the yellow paper that was stuck to her index finger. "Justin," she asked without looking up, "do you think Bosley is our rapist and murderer?"

Justin hung up his cell phone, barely remembering the phone call he just had with Sylvia. His mind still spun around Christy's out-of-left-field question she nailed him with. The night dispatcher showed up as soon as Christy asked, saving Justin the trouble of trying to think of a good answer. But at the same time, he couldn't drill her as to why she would ask such a thing.

Not that the thought hadn't crossed his mind.

When he'd picked up his phone, he planned on calling Grace. But she'd picked up her daughter. Sheriff Montgomery's words came to him. God only knew why. But then maybe they came to him for a reason. Instead of calling Grace, he'd called Sylvia. And it hadn't surprised him at all that she picked up on the first ring, laughing and sounding way too jovial.

It did surprise him that she'd agreed to let him see his kids. He pulled up in front of her house, a large, pretentious-looking thing that he guessed probably belonged to her new lawyer boyfriend. As Justin put his truck in park, the front door opened and Elizabeth ran toward him so fast, her arms extended, that all he could do was sit and stare. The strangest sensation ran through him, tightening his insides and growing until his throat felt like it was swelling shut.

Justin got out of his truck as Sylvia started out of the house. "Elizabeth!" she yelled, her shrill tone hitting that pitch that meant she wouldn't make a scene until they were behind closed doors.

Elizabeth ignored Sylvia and plowed into her father when

he reached the front of his truck. She hugged him fiercely, jumping up and down at the same time. Justin ended up walking to the curb with his daughter attached to his hip.

"I'm going with Dad, Mom. I'll be fine." Elizabeth didn't let go of him but only turned her head to yell at her mother. "I'm going with Dad," she repeated.

As if she worried the invitation to spend time with him might be revoked, Elizabeth continued hanging on to him with all of her strength.

Justin hadn't picked his daughter up in years, but he did so now. He couldn't move. And as little as he wanted to hear anything Sylvia had to say right now, it was clear she was going to have her say before letting him spend time with his children.

Looking past Elizabeth, he straightened when Daniel stood in the doorway, scowling at him. The last thing he needed was more headaches. But he wouldn't let Daniel think he wanted to spend time with Elizabeth and not him.

"Are you coming, sport?" Justin yelled.

Daniel stepped out of the house, his tall, lanky frame hidden by the baggy clothes he wore. He was in dire need of a good haircut and overall looked like the thug he was probably desperately trying to be.

"I'm not your sport," he said, his voice squeaking, although Daniel didn't flinch like Justin used to do when his voice gave out on him during his teenage years.

"Fine. Daniel. Want to come along for ice cream?"

"Plan on buying our love?"

Sylvia rocked up on her heels, obviously content to let his son berate him and save her the trouble. She looked thoroughly pleased with herself when she looked at him pointedly, waiting for his answer.

Justin knew he didn't hold ground to discipline his son. Worse yet, Justin saw clearly that Sylvia made no effort to discipline Daniel either. Maybe exerting a bit of effort to spend time with him and Elizabeth would do both of them some good.

"Can I afford it?" Justin asked Daniel.

He stopped next to Sylvia, standing a good several inches taller than she did. "I doubt it," he sneered.

"Then I guess I won't." He put Elizabeth down, although she slipped her hand into his and held on firmly. "So you coming along for ice cream?" he asked again.

"Sounds boring to me."

"What sounds good to you?"

"How about a six-pack and letting me drive?" Daniel's smile bordered on cruel. He wanted to hurt Justin and would do his best to push buttons until he felt he'd succeeded.

Justin shook his head, smiling easily and coming around the passenger side of his truck. "Maybe, and it's a really big maybe, I'll let you drive. Do you have a license?"

"I've got my permit. Mom lets me drive."

"Daniel is a wonderful driver." Sylvia put her hand on her son's shoulder and smiled at him as if she saw no wrong in him at all. When she returned her attention to Justin, her loving look faded quickly. "You'd better have them back in an hour."

"It might be longer than that." He opened his passenger door and helped Elizabeth climb in. "But that depends, too, on how well Daniel drives."

Justin turned in time to see his son's face light up. For the first time since Justin had come back to Rockville, he saw the boy who used to adore him. The tough teenager was still there, but the eagerness in Daniel's eyes brought Justin hope. Again that strange sensation, a pressure in his chest that he didn't want to guess as to where it came from, made it hard for him to speak for a moment. So instead, he held the keys out to his son, saying a silent prayer that Daniel wouldn't wreck his truck.

Daniel snagged the keys out of Justin's hand and hurried around to the driver's side. Sylvia backed up on the sidewalk, crossing her arms and looking worried. Justin realized at that moment that getting close to his kids again would irk her more than it would hurt him to make the effort to try to do so. Suddenly he felt that he might enjoy his evening after all.

"Scoot over, sweetheart," he told Elizabeth, grabbing the

passenger door. Then turning to Sylvia, he ignored the pout that now appeared on her face. He and the children needed to get the hell out of there before she laid a guilt trip on her children for leaving her for their father. "We'll be back in a few hours," he told her, then climbed in and closed the passenger door, giving thanks for his soundproof truck, which blocked out her response.

He wasn't thrilled about going to Dairy Queen any more than Daniel was. Although he had never commented on the murdered girl found in the parking lot there over two weeks ago, he made it clear that only nerds hung out here. Elizabeth, however, was announcing what she wanted to order before they pulled into the parking lot.

Justin seriously doubted his daughter would be able to eat half the food she carried away from the counter. He also would believe his son could pack away the food he carried on his own tray as well as everything Justin and Elizabeth ordered. At Daniel's insistence, they didn't sit outside but in a booth in the corner of the dining area, where he immediately slouched and started devouring his burger.

"Can I stay the night with you, Dad?" Elizabeth asked after finishing her burger, and started picking at her French fries while her ice cream slowly melted.

"Grow up, kid," Daniel said, nudging her with his elbow. "He's just here tonight because he's out of here tomorrow. This way he can say he spent time with his kids."

"Who said I was leaving?"

"Ouch. That hurt," Elizabeth squealed.

"Not as bad as it's going to hurt if you get too close to him and he walks out on you like he always does," Daniel said, looking down at his little sister, who was scrunched in the corner of the booth. "If I were you, I'd eat your food and stay quiet."

"You're not going to walk out on me!" Elizabeth damn near tried crawling over Daniel.

"Crap," Daniel shouted, jumping out of the booth when her orange drink toppled over and started leaking onto their food.

Justin grabbed the drink and slapped a handful of napkins onto the spill. "*I'm not going anywhere,*" he stressed.

"I'm out of here," Daniel announced, grabbing his fries, and then started walking away.

"No one is going anywhere." Justin grabbed his son's arm and was surprised at how easy he could flip his son around.

Justin held on to Daniel so he wouldn't topple over. But when Daniel spun around, his fist came up. Justin stiffened, staring his son in the eyes and barely needing to look down to do so.

"Take your hands off me," Daniel sneered.

"Daniel, you're going to make him mad and he'll leave!" Elizabeth shrieked, drawing attention from the people working behind the counter and the few other customers sitting across the dining area in the other booths.

"He's going to leave anyway." Daniel yanked his arm free and then rubbed it.

"I've told you twice now I'm not going anywhere."

"You will eventually."

"Daniel, sit down. We're going to talk this out."

"What's the point?"

Justin drew in a long breath. He should have expected the resentment, the anger, and pain that his son had building inside him since Justin had left. Daniel hated him for leaving, but the pain in his eyes, the intense anger, showed Justin there just might be a small amount of hope. Hope that possibly he could mend the rift he'd created between him and his son.

"The point is I want to spend time with you. I don't want to walk away from you. And if you're game, I'd like to know you again."

"Why? So you can throw me in jail again?" Daniel continued staring his dad in the eye, although it was obvious now he was shaking.

Justin fought to remain relaxed, non-threatening. It worked when dealing with young criminals, oftentimes when he needed them to open up and talk to him. Justin hated using tactics he'd use on a perp on his own son.

Shaking his head and wondering if he could even pull this off, Justin held his hand out, gesturing that Daniel sit again next to his anxious sister. "So that I can help you never go to jail," Justin told his son truthfully.

"I'm not hungry anymore." Daniel tossed his fries on the table.

Elizabeth jumped and then started sobbing.

Justin was making a fucking wreck out of this. Running his hand over his head, he blew out an exasperated sigh. Going home to a cold beer sounded better now than it had all day.

Turning from Daniel, Justin ignored the curious onlookers and rubbed Elizabeth's back when she scooted across the booth on her knees and wrapped her arms around him.

"Let's get this cleaned up and we'll head out," he decided.

Daniel turned toward the door.

"Daniel, come back here and help clean up."

He turned around, glaring at Justin. "You're not my father. Don't even try telling me what to do."

Justin peeled his daughter off of him and walked up to the only person he'd ever called Son. "You are my son, whether you like it or not," Justin said under his breath, fighting to keep his cool and feeling a throbbing headache come on as a result of it. "I've raised you, and even though your mother and I are no longer married, I still love you."

Daniel snorted. "Whatever. If you loved me, you'd be around more."

Justin couldn't believe his ears. Did his son want him around more?

"I do love you. And I'm not going to let you walk away from a mess." He doubted his son caught the double meaning in his words, but at the same time he heard himself speak and knew he couldn't, either. "Let's clean this up. If you calm down, I might consider letting you drive again."

Daniel sulked but helped grab food and threw it on his tray, then walked it over to the trash can by the door. He headed outside to Justin's truck and leaned against it, crossing his arms, and scowled at the ground.

"Don't worry, Daddy," Elizabeth said, walking alongside him to the trash. "He is mean to Mom, too."

Elizabeth didn't know how much better that made Justin feel.

Chapter 19

Grace stood in the dark kitchen, realizing she stared at the refrigerator's contents. Something she'd yell at Rachel for doing. Grace found a large plastic cup in the cabinet advertising a local convenience store and filled it with ice. Then closing the refrigerator, she filled the cup with water and took a long, soothing drink.

It had been a long day, and she should be exhausted. But even after spending the evening with Uncle Charlie and Rachel, not discussing the case at all, and then helping Rachel get ready for bed and listening to her talk endlessly about Elizabeth, Grace still was too wound up to head to bed.

Not to mention, she was dying to know where Justin was.

It didn't matter. He shouldn't be on her mind. He wasn't her concern. And he sure didn't answer to her.

But you're staying at his house. Was he just letting her stay here because it was safer during this investigation?

An investigation that was supposedly over.

Downing more of the water, Grace had an urge for something stronger, a lot stronger—like a stiff drink. "Which isn't an option because the investigation isn't over and you know it." She glanced toward the two dark doorways, one leading down the hall and the other into the dining area, and then turned to the back door. Maybe she could lose herself in those stars she couldn't enjoy last night. Her uncle and daughter were sleeping upstairs, and Justin was MIA. Heading upstairs, she slipped into leggings and a baggy T-shirt, then wrapped her work belt around her waist. Just because she wanted to lose herself for a while didn't mean she would do it without protection. Checking the safety on her gun, she secured the clasp around it on her belt and then let her T-shirt fall over it. Smiling at the floppy red curls sticking out over the blanket Rachel was buried under, Grace slipped out of the bedroom, down the hall and stairs, and out the back door.

It was the same position she had assumed last night, lying flat on the deck with her feet on the stairs leading into the yard. She adjusted her gun and cell phone on her belt so they wouldn't push into her hips and set her cup of water next to her. The chilled night air and beautiful black sky created an atmosphere that was just what the doctor ordered. Blissful, tranquil, breathtaking.

Grace reached for the sky. "I can snatch you off your black blanket," she whispered, and then tilted her head when she thought she heard something.

There it was again. The sound of tires popping over gravel.

She sat up, instinctively patting her hair, although putting it in place was never an option with this mop. A vehicle stopped on the other side of the house, but then silence wrapped around her once again. Other than a cricket that suddenly was distracting instead of musical, Grace didn't hear a thing.

Hopping to her feet, Grace couldn't decide whether she should go inside, move to the back door and listen, or just lie back down and resume her tranquil moment without worrying about Justin finally coming home. Like she'd be able to lie down and relax now. Just knowing Justin was in close proximity sent a rush of heat through her that quickly swelled and moistened between her legs. Riding him hard and fast right now would beat the hell out of staring at the stars.

Opting to move to the back door, Grace stood silently, remaining outside, listened, and waited for lights to turn on. Nothing happened. She remembered seeing his security system, a setup that wasn't purchased from some security Web site. Justin had the real deal protecting his pad. And it would beep when he opened the front door. She didn't hear a beep.

Prickles of anxiety poked at her spine as she looked around the dark backyard that spread out toward the Badlands. Suddenly she regretted not taking Uncle Charlie up on a walk with Rachel earlier. At least then Grace would have a feel for the spread of land. Right now she was not only out of her element but also on strange soil that she wasn't familiar with.

Something popped on the side of the house. Grace reached for her gun and unsnapped it from her belt before walking silently along the length of the deck. She had no idea whether Justin had security bugs in his yard or not, but if he did, whoever walked alongside the house wasn't triggering anything she could hear.

Like she would rely on some unfamiliar security system when she was at a home she wasn't familiar with and all the family she had in the world upstairs sleeping soundly. Grace reached the edge of the house and pressed her back against the rough exterior of Justin's home. Her hair stuck to the siding and pulled when she turned her head, but she ignored the sting and tried to focus into the darkness spreading out before her.

Again she swore something popped on the ground. Whoever it was, they were going to extremes not to make a noise. Well, if they thought her being here alone, with her uncle and daughter upstairs, made this house an easy target, they would soon learn otherwise. Grace raised her arm, gun in hand, and released the safety. Maybe they didn't know she was here but just knew Justin wasn't home. Either way, someone was about to get a very nice eye-opener.

Grace measured the height of the railing going around the deck in her mind and gauged how high she would have to leap to jump onto the railing and then hit the ground on the other side. Not to mention stay on her feet.

Something cracked just around the corner. Definitely footsteps.

"You want a piece of me?" she hissed, leaping onto the

railing, hitting it square on with one foot and jumping off of it immediately, then landing on both feet.

Adrenaline rushed through her like a favorite drug. Her heart raced and the tightening in her gut and hardening of all of her muscles as she bent her knees and at the same time extended her arms, clasping her gun in front of her, added to the natural high that was incomparable to anything else she'd ever known.

Justin slowly raised his arms. "Well, since you asked," he said wryly, the shadows from the house hiding most of his expression.

"Shit," Grace exhaled, lowering her gun and almost experiencing a twang of regret that she couldn't take all of her pentup energy out on some out-of-line stranger. "It's you."

"Sorry to disappoint you." Justin closed in on her, trying to take her gun.

Grace backed up, keeping a firm grip on it, but then setting the safety and sliding the gun back into her belt. Justin moved faster this time when she looked down, sliding his fingers around her waist but then easing them under her belt and working loose the belt loop.

Grace looked up, his face inches from hers, but didn't have time to react when he kissed her. She wasn't the only one with energy aching for a channel. He undid her belt and tossed it to the ground next to them, pressing his tongue past her lips at the same time.

His kiss was savage, hungry, and his hands warm when they moved under her shirt and found her bare breasts and squeezed. She moaned into his mouth, not even giving thought to stopping him but instead stretching against that rock-hard body of his and pressing her fingers into his shoulder muscles.

When she moaned he growled, sounding fierce, demanding. Heat swelled inside her too fast for her to give thought to anything but getting him out of his clothes. She wanted to overtake him, shove him to the ground, and mount his hard cock. She wanted to ride him until she was spent, to feel him buried deep inside her and know that he would give her all the pleasure she needed and at the same time release the craving running rabid inside her to overcome and manipulate.

There weren't enough times in her life when she was in charge. And right now, with him, outside and blanketed by the night, she would rule the moment. And he would be damned if he even tried to stop her.

Grace moved her hands over his collarbone until she felt the top button on his shirt. It had mere seconds to cooperate or it was going to go. She didn't care if she tore his shirt, sent buttons flying, or had to physically wrestle him to the ground. In fact, the thought of doing so made her even hotter.

But when she pulled on the button, Justin grabbed her hand. He wouldn't stop her, though. She bit at his lip, causing him to growl even more fiercely this time. It took her a minute to realize he tried stopping her, because he was pulling her shirt up her body. Justin let go of her arm and simply yanked the shirt over her head, blinding her for a moment. Unwilling to relinquish control, Grace ripped his shirt open, almost coming as she heard his buttons pop free from the fabric.

"Why, you little . . . ," Justin growled, and exerted enough force that he overtook her, bending her over forcibly.

Grace took advantage of being bent over and reached for his belt, managing to pull it free from the first loop before he grabbed her.

"I'm the one with the gun," she hissed. "You're going to do as I say."

"You forget, my dear, I unarmed you." Justin's baritone rippled from deep in his chest, causing his words to come out on a growl.

Grace straightened, giving way to him taking her shirt, and stood before him, topless in the darkness, and didn't worry about her hair that was half out of the already too-loose ponytail holder at the base of her neck. She glanced at her belt on the ground and then gave him a sideways look.

"Don't underestimate my abilities." She could growl, too, and actually liked how it sounded.

Apparently Justin did, too. He cocked one eyebrow, looking very much up to the challenge. "I'm more than willing to see what you've got," he said, and the side of his mouth curved into a smile so dangerous looking she knew right now that he'd made more than one criminal cringe in his lifetime.

"Think you can handle it?" She was charged, on fire, ready to spring and attack and more than willing to make him her conquest.

"Darling, I know I can."

Now she cocked one eyebrow. "Maybe cockiness might be your downfall in the end."

Grace didn't hesitate. She didn't think about whether she might hurt him or herself. Adrenaline surged through her, and the frustration building up throughout the week, hell, since she'd arrived here, was taking its toll. She felt the fire in her veins, the buzzing in her head, as her blood pumped through her faster than it probably should. And she didn't care.

Grace leapt at him, hitting him full force and feeling like she'd just voluntarily slammed herself into a brick wall. There was one difference. This brick wall moved. Justin caught her, wrapping his arms of steel around her, and took her down.

Grace grunted loudly when she hit the ground, and feeling the sting when the uneven earth underneath her scraped against her bare back, she used her training and twisted quickly. No way would he overtake her. No fucking way would she submit tonight.

Justin would put out. On her terms. The way she wanted it. And she didn't feel like asking. She would take, demand, conquer, and claim victory.

"You're not going anywhere," he hissed when she managed to come up on her knees.

"Maybe not. But you are." She turned and shoved against his chest, forcing him to the ground.

If he didn't use all of his strength and allowed her to slam him to the ground, she didn't care. He was where she wanted him, and she wasn't done with him yet.

"Unless you want your jeans destroyed, too, I suggest you get out of them."

"Bossy bitch, aren't you?" he said, not sounding the least bit put out by it.

"Damn straight, and you'd be smart not to forget that." She moved just enough to shove her leggings down her legs.

But before they were off her body, Justin pulled a fast one. With his jeans unsnapped and unzipped and his cock springing free and making a mouthwatering sight, he sprang forward, tackling her with her leggings twisted just above her ankles.

"Bitch!" she howled.

But he captured her mouth, preventing her from making too much noise, and impaled her with his tongue. His hunger matched her own, and although he came over her, pushing her once again to the ground, dragging her nails over his back to his shoulders and hearing and feeling his growl rumble through him made it worth it.

"You'll learn soon who's the boss," he growled into her mouth.

If he was trying to get her riled, he was doing a damned good job of it. "You think?" She reached between them, grabbing his cock and then stroking it while blinking to focus and see his face.

His eyes were dark and focused. Not only hunger but determination and something else stole her breath. She damn near drowned in those intense round orbs. But losing herself in him, although it would probably guarantee her incredible satisfaction, wasn't what she was after right now. Adrenaline still burned in her veins, and feeding off him wouldn't fulfill her as much as conquering and taking what she wanted would.

"Here's how I see it," she whispered, not once looking away from his brooding, sensual eyes. Her fingers were wrapped around his cock, and as she stroked his thick shaft, feeling the satiny smooth skin move over the steel underneath, the desire to not only make him understand her motives but also get him to submit to them fed her fire. "You're going to do as you're told, and you're going to like it."

"I'm sorry to disappoint you, darling," he drawled, not even so much as blinking. "But I've never been too good at following orders."

"Me, either," she said without hesitating, and then squeezed his cock as hard as she could while coming up off the ground, nipping at his shoulder when he tried blocking her, and then using her entire body to shove him backward. "And tonight I'm getting what I want."

"You'll get what you want, my dear," he growled, grabbing her by the waist. "And more if you keep this up."

"Oh yeah?" She loved the challenge in his tone, fed off of it, and let go of all of her inhibitions.

There wasn't any doubt in her mind that she'd never been this free with a man before. Even as she wrestled Justin to the ground, grunting and almost laughing once, when he was blinded by her hair when her ponytail fell over her shoulder, she knew dwelling on that fact would pull her back into her shell. Tonight, if never again, she would let go, forget about her past, the present, and the future, and take this moment. For as long as it lasted, time would stand still, not rolling forward or dumping ancient history in her way. She would fuck Justin, ride him just how she had imagined, and take all she could from him, with no regrets.

Justin grabbed her hair, finding her ponytail holder, and pulled it free from her thick curls. Grace shook her head, doing her best to keep her thick strands out of her face, and pressed her hands against Justin's chest.

"Lie down," she ordered, sensing he would pounce on her if she took her hands off his chest. He was wound so tight his muscles bulged under his warm skin.

"I'm not wearing you down already, am I?" His grin bordered on dangerous.

She stiffened, prepared for anything. "Think that if you want," she said, and then straddled him, moving down his body and yanking his jeans down his legs. With his shoes on there wasn't any way to pull his jeans off his body, so she left them crumpled below his knees, deciding incapacitating him a bit would only be in her favor. "But I promise I'm not to be underestimated," she said, dragging her finger up the length of his shaft.

He growled when she touched him, which fed her power. At the same time, taking a minute to adore his perfect body made her crave him even more.

"You'd better not underestimate me, either," he growled, and dragged her over him.

Grace spread her legs, loving how she'd confined him with his own jeans, and grabbed his arms. When she adjusted herself over his cock, he overpowered her, not trying to get up off the ground but moving fast enough to grab her wrists and knock her off balance.

"What did I just tell you?" he whispered roughly in her face when she fell flat on top of him.

At the same time, his cock slid against her soaked pussy and he found her entrance. Justin thrust inside her, filling her with his swollen long, thick cock.

"Oh God!" she cried out, struggling against him, which only helped ease him in deeper and causing him to stroke muscles that weren't used to such intense attention.

"Behave, sweetheart," he growled.

She pushed herself off of him, straightening and exploding almost immediately when he sunk in even deeper. He held her wrists, but she used his strong hold on her to balance herself, closing her eyes and letting her head fell back while riding out the incredible sensations rippling through her.

"*I am in charge,*" she said, stressing each word, when she could finally speak.

Justin let go of her wrists, and she slapped her palms against his chest, adjusting herself and using her thighs to lift herself off of him just far enough so she could enjoy sinking down on him again.

Justin reached for her, trying to ease his hand around her neck, and she slapped him away. Her hand made full contact against his forearm, and the cracking sound forced her to open her eyes. She loved the sound of it.

"In charge, huh?" he said, managing to grab one of her nipples and tweak it.

She grabbed his wrist. "Yes, I am. You're going to be-have," she hissed, even though when she wrapped her fin-gers around his thick wrist, while staring down at him, he pinched harder and smiled wickedly. "And I've got my work cut out with you."

His smile broadened and he let go of her nipple, although the sensations rushing from her breast to her pussy still pulsed as she sunk down on him again. Justin gripped her waist, but when she slapped at him again he pulled her for-ward, pinning her there with one arm, and then smacked her ass.

In the ten years since she'd been free, not once had she ever allowed a man to spank her. And although the memo-ries surfaced, the brutal beatings she had endured, they didn't bother her and faded quickly as the heat on her flesh soared through her, building the pressure deep inside her womb until she was on the edge again.

"Does this work for you?" he whispered into her ear.

"Trying to control you?"

He smacked her ass again. It created fiery heat that she swore singed her skin. Grace started riding him harder, mov-ing her ass up and down and creating a moving target for him. Justin brought his hand down on her rear again, the sound of his hand hitting her flesh as hot as the way it made her feel.

"You don't need to control me, sweetheart," he drawled into her ear. "I promise I'm not a man who can be put on a leash."

"Like I would even want to do that," she drawled back, and forced him deep inside her.

Justin pressed his arm down on her back, making it hard for her to pull off of him, and thrust his hips up. He hit a spot deep inside her that pushed her over the edge and she howled. Then to stifle the noise she bit his shoulder, burying her face in his warm skin. Right where his shoulder met his neck—and his smell, a mixture of aftershave and his de-odorant, filled her senses, helping her ride over the edge as she shook from the intensity of her orgasm.

"That's it, sweetheart," he whispered next to her ear. "You're going to come again and again for me. Soak my balls. I want all of you, everything you have."

"Sounds like it's you who want a leash on me," she teased.

"There's a nice ring to that," he said too quickly for her to believe he was joking.

"Like hell," she muttered, but couldn't say more when he thrust again, and again.

Justin fucked the shit out of her, holding her so she couldn't move, with her legs spread wide over his body. The heat building between them grew to where she swore she would burn alive, or pass out, from the extreme intensity of how he fucked her.

When he wrapped both arms around her, no longer preventing her from moving but hugging her against him, she turned her head enough to brush her cheek against his rough cheek. His unshaven face stroked her flesh, which was suddenly so ultra-sensitive that she rubbed against him again. Sparks ignited inside her, turning her world upside down, and showing her at that moment that she'd never truly made love to a man before in her life.

"Grace," he grumbled, saying her name while grunting as he continued impaling her. "I don't want to pull out."

No matter his banter with her, claiming to be unattainable and making a show of overpowering her, his simple statement, laid on the table for her to accept or veto, filled her heart in a way it had never been filled before. Something broke inside her, or possibly awakened for the first time.

"Come," she whispered, and managed to raise her face enough to find his mouth. "And kiss me, now," she instructed.

He turned to her, opening up while the heat continued burning out of control between them. And as he kissed her, not aggressively and with demands but slowly, painfully and tortuously slowly, he exploded inside her, spilling everything he had with a low, carnal growl that damn near made her cry.

Justin ran his hands down Grace's bare back, lying on the uneven ground and staring up at the stars. "I can honestly say that is the first time I've ever had sex in my yard."

Grace lifted her head, her red curls tangled around her face, making her look sexy as hell. He didn't stare, knowing without a doubt if she even guessed her appearance right now she'd hurry to pull her hair back and keep that gorgeous mane from spilling around her face. He loved how she looked right now.

"Really?" She looked at him wide-eyed, not quite smiling but definitely looking pleased.

He gripped her ass, squeezing and giving one final thrust. "Really," he whispered, watching her face flush when her lashes fluttered over her pretty baby blues.

"So where were you?" she asked.

He fought a grin, her tone sounding way too much like that of a possessive girlfriend demanding an explanation for his coming home late. Grace raised her eyebrows, meeting his gaze head-on and not backing down or adding anything to tone down her inquiry.

"I took my kids out."

"How did that go?" She didn't look surprised or judgmental, even when he groaned.

"Not very well."

"They'll push your buttons as long as you let them." She eased herself off of him and stood.

"What do you mean by that?" There wasn't a better sight in the world than Grace standing naked outside. His cock got hard again watching her stretch before she looked on the ground for her clothes.

"They know you're trying to win their affection and they'll use that against you. Until you establish yourself as the one in charge, they'll take advantage and have you doing what they say before you realize you've done more damage than good."

"You sound like you're reciting some textbook," he mumbled, reaching for his jeans and then pulling them up his legs as he stood. "I didn't know you were a psychologist, too."

Her laughter was too sincere for him to get grumpy, although the accuracy of her words didn't sit too well with him.

"There's no psychology to it. I was your kids," she stated, pulling her T-shirt over her head and then sliding one leg, than another into her leggings. "Whenever Dad came home from an assignment, we pushed and pushed, knowing he wasn't in charge. Mom was. We could get anything out of him."

"How did it change?"

She had her back to him when she picked up her belt, double-checked her gun, then slid it around her waist. "It didn't. I was gone by the time I was eighteen," she added, letting her last words fade away.

He couldn't help himself. Grace didn't want sympathy. Her aggressive lovemaking just now proved even further that she regained her sanity by embracing life, refusing to let anyone see that she was scarred from what she'd endured. And he never doubted there were few other women on this planet who could pull off as much as she had.

Wrapping his arms around her waist, he nibbled her neck and grew even harder when she shivered. "Well, he did something right. You're one hell of a woman."

She twisted in his arms, then reached back and started fighting with her hair. "You're lucky I didn't kick your ass."

"Seeing you with that gun got me hard as a rock, lady."

"You're a sick motherfucker." She smiled, though, believing, and it was true, that she was a good cop, her skills finely tuned.

"Come on. I think showers are in order for both of us." He wrapped his arm around her, liking the fact that she'd been here when he came home. Even when he'd confessed the nightmare he'd had with his kids, she didn't judge or accuse. He'd come home to a gun pointed in his face any day if it resulted in being able to fuck Grace.

Justin sat at his computer the next morning and reached for his coffee when he heard the bedroom door across the hall open.

"Grace?" he asked, leaning far enough to see her. He was hard as a rock instantly. She'd showered the night before, although she'd refused to shower with him. This morning, though, her hair wasn't as curly as usual and, although it was pulled back in a ponytail, the holder was halfway down her back, causing her hair to pouf around her face. She was barefoot, in shorts and a T-shirt.

"Yeah?" she asked, not turning to him but heading to the stairs.

"Get your coffee and come here. We need to talk."

Grace grunted but didn't say anything else as she padded down the stairs. Another bedroom door opened and Charlie appeared in his doorway a minute later, his gray hair tousled, giving him a mad scientist look. He was dressed for the day but needed a shave.

"What's the news, Justin, my boy?" He stepped into the room, still barefoot, and moved behind Justin to see the computer screen. "Never was an expert with one of these things. Seems to be the way of the world, though."

"Yup." Justin switched screens, not wishing to discuss shop with Charlie until Grace returned. "Looks like the world made it through another day," Justin announced, pulling up Yahoo's main page, which showed headlines on current events.

"Nothing more than a glorified newspaper," Charlie grumbled.

Justin heard Grace coming up the stairs and muttered his agreement, glancing toward the hallway when she appeared at the top of the flight and met his gaze over a steaming cup of coffee. He lifted his own cup and silently toasted her. Her grin against her mug made his heart swell. God, she looked hot as hell first thing in the morning.

"Well, I know when three is a crowd." Charlie rocked up on his toes, looking anything but upset at his niece's flushed expression. "I'll get Rachel ready to go for the day and we'll be out of your hair in no time."

"You don't have to leave on my account," Grace said, her voice sounding sleepy and way too damned sultry.

"Can't let that daughter of yours sleep in too long. It makes her cranky." Charlie headed toward the door but turned back and winked at Justin. "Just like her mother."

"Uncle Charlie," Grace snapped, glaring at him.

"Told you three was a crowd." He walked out of the room, whistling loud enough to make it echo in the hallway.

"I want to show you something," Justin said, reaching for her after her uncle disappeared back into his bedroom. "Come here."

"What?" She was back to edging away from him.

Which wasn't acceptable. He took her wrist, pulling her to him. She was forced to take the seat on his lap or spill her coffee.

"Read over this."

"What is it?"

"Read," he demanded, running one hand up the curve of her back to her shoulder. Even though she hadn't showered yet, she smelled good, and he nuzzled his chin against her nape, moving her hair out of the way to reach skin.

She shrugged, shifting away from him, but then sucked in a hissing breath. Grace hopped off his lap like she'd just burned herself and pointed at his computer, gasping.

"That's right, I need you with me." He watched her turn so pale she looked for a moment like she might pass out.

"You're signing me on to help the FBI?" she gasped, her blue eyes so wide while her lower lip started trembling "Me?" she gasped. "Are you sure?"

"I need you, Grace. We're in this together."

Grace's jaw dropped. Exhaling the breath she'd been holding, she suppressed a smile by biting her lip. Justin pulled pages off his printer and handed them to her.

"Read and sign those." He stood up to stretch.

She couldn't help watching before glancing down at the papers she held.

"Oh!" The single word was more like a squeal. She shot a look up at him and gasped for breath. "Is this for real?" she whispered, afraid she'd break whatever magic must surely be at work here.

Grace barely managed restraining her excitement. Justin wouldn't understand her losing her cool, though. No one knew her dream, her craving to be more than just a cop. The letterhead at the top of the faxed page said simply: "Federal Bureau of Investigation." She knew the Washington, D.C., address all too well. She didn't know the name of the man who wrote the letter, but it was addressed to Justin.

The letter referred to her. It acknowledged the request to enlist Grace Jordan as a deputized agent in matters of the investigation of the South Dakota serial killer. A security check and drug screen needed to be done, along with some paperwork. She would answer directly to Special Agent Justin Reece. She was surprised to see that he was GS14. The highest level was GS15. Justin Reece had done all right for himself with the Bureau.

Justin watched her for only a moment before his cell phone rang. Grace paced the length of his room, reading the documents, while he communicated with his supervisor. More than once she noticed Justin hesitated in commenting. It wasn't something she was unaccustomed to. She was part of a Bureau family. Even if he'd been her husband he wouldn't be able to tell her everything.

Her husband? What was she thinking? Infatuation and kick-ass sex didn't create love ever after, for life.

Chapter 20

Justin spent time at the field office in Rapid City the rest of the week. As many times as he'd been there, going with Grace made the trip a hell of a lot more tolerable. They'd met with several other agents in the area and brainstormed all angles of the investigation. Grace impressed more than him.

"Sheriff Montgomery is being very cooperative so far," Cliff Bogfrey told Grace when they stood to leave the conference room.

"I've managed to keep up with all my shifts." Grace had a winning smile that didn't get past Bogfrey. He never smiled, and Grace had him grinning and nodding when she shook his hand. "As long as I show up for my cross-guard shifts and make a show of doing the rounds in town every day, no one has said a word."

"Good. If we end up moving in on that police station, we're going to need you right there."

Grace straightened but didn't look intimidated. "If there's a bad cop, he goes down. I'll never have a problem with that."

Bogfrey nodded and Justin knew he was satisfied.

The sun had almost disappeared on the horizon when they headed back to Rockville. Sunday morning and all was quiet. Way too quiet.

"There's the Fall Dance in Rockville this upcoming weekend," Justin said, breaking the silence and watching Grace snap her attention his way.

"You want to take me dancing?"

"More than anything," he muttered, picturing her on his arm when he walked into the Knights of Columbus hall where the dance had been held every year since he'd been in high school. Grace would be the first woman he took to the dance other than Sylvia, and that had been years ago. "The whole town comes out for the event. I want you on my arm when we enter that building."

"Oh?" She glanced ahead of them when he slowed to the speed limit as they entered town. "You know what day it is, don't you?" she asked, changing the subject and not agreeing to go with him, he noticed.

"Yup. Sunday."

"Think our guy will make a move today?" When her cell phone rang she frowned and pulled it off her belt, glancing at the number before answering. "Jordan here," she said, her apprehensive tone alerting him. Reaching down between her legs, she pulled paper and pen out of her purse while wisps of curls fell around her concerned expression. "Roger that," she said, scribbling something on the paper. "No. I'm in town. I'll be at the station in a minute and then will head out."

She hung up her phone and looked pale when she glanced at him. "I spoke too soon. Looks like a girl was raped and murdered at the Ogden home."

Justin cursed and accelerated as he turned toward the station.

The Ogdens lived in an elegant country home, complete with white pillars and a very wide front porch. The property was gated, and ducks swam peacefully in a small pond off the side of the house. A swimming pool, large enough to be visible from the front, glowed with light behind the house. A middle-aged woman with hair wrapped, as if she'd just come from the beauty parlor, opened the door.

"Oh, Justin, how nice of you to come yourself." She smiled as if years of breeding prevented her from doing anything else when she greeted someone at her door.

"Mrs. Ogden, I'd like you to meet Lieutenant Grace Jordan." Justin stepped to the side and presented Grace, making it sound like they'd come for tea.

"I've heard good things about you, dear." Mrs. Ogden smiled. "Please, come in. W-we found Jensen, but we can't find Erica. We weren't even gone that long." She began wringing her hands and her voice cracked when she continued speaking. "Please, come this way."

Grace noticed the large living room seemed undisturbed. In fact, it was in absolutely immaculate condition, with white leather furniture and black brass end tables.

Mrs. Ogden stopped when they walked around a long formal dining room table with a chandelier hanging over it that had to have cost a lot of money. Mrs. Ogden pointed, shaking her head. "I can't go in there," she murmured.

"Nor should you have to," a tall, good-looking silver-haired gentleman said from behind Justin.

Everyone turned and Mrs. Ogden moved into the man's arms, her body trembling when she buried her face in his neck.

"Glad to see you here, Justin," the man said, and shifted his attention to Grace. "I overheard the introductions. Lieutenant Jordan, I'm Fred Ogden." He swallowed, taking in a deep breath, before nodding to the doorway behind Grace. "Jensen is in there," he said, his voice cracking as he obviously fought to maintain composure. "I've called for our doctor, who should be here soon. Marlene here won't make it through the evening without a good sedative. I'll answer any questions you might have."

"Make your wife comfortable, if you can. You mentioned only one of your daughters is here?" Justin asked.

Grace left Justin to talk to Fred Ogden and walked through the doorway. The kitchen was also meticulously clean, with sparkling chrome everywhere. Dark green marble countertops were polished to a shine. In contrast to the meticulous environment, on the floor, in a pool of drying blood, a teenage girl lay facedown, naked and beaten, and very dead.

Grace pulled on her gloves and unclipped her cell phone, calling in to Dispatch. "I need an ambulance, ME, and

Forensics sent out to the Ogden house," she told the night dispatcher. Already Grace had learned that for the most part, she didn't need to give addresses in Rockville. Everyone knew where everyone lived. She prayed that meant, in a neighborhood like this, someone had recognized a car that didn't belong here.

Justin entered the kitchen when she hung up the phone. "Son of a bitch," he growled under his breath as he moved next to the body and squatted next to her. "Sick motherfucker."

"Tell me about it." Grace lifted the girl's hair that clung to the dried blood on her face, and stared at the horrified expression still on the dead girl's face. "She was so young," she whispered.

"And she suffered before she died," he added, donning gloves while his pained expression took in the rest of her body.

"More burns," Grace said, pointing to the large marks that appeared to have been left by a lightbulb the same as on the other girls. Just thinking how much pain Jensen Ogden had endured before she died made Grace sick to her stomach and pissed her off to no end. "We've got to stop this bastard."

"I hate saying we've got our proof that the man they shipped out earlier this week wasn't our killer."

"You knew he wasn't as well as I did." Grace let go of Jensen's hair and stood slowly.

The doorbell sounded and both of them turned to look at the kitchen doorway. Moments later soft voices could be overheard in the living room, but then Fred Ogden called for Justin. Grace followed him through another doorway that led down a wide hallway, which opened into a laundry room and a narrow flight of stairs that was probably not the main flight.

"The girls' activity room is in there." Fred Ogden had loosened his tie but still looked very much the stately gentleman, as if, it being Sunday and all, he and his wife had spent the day in church and then visiting acquaintances. "This is beyond a nightmare," he said stiffly, glancing at Grace but then giving Justin his attention. "We moved to this small town years ago to raise our daughters in a good, small community. Up until an hour ago I would have sworn there wasn't a more perfect community anywhere."

Grace didn't comment on the other rapes. It was too common for individuals to ignore hideous crimes around them until something terrible happened to them.

"Rockville is still a good community," Justin said, stiffening and sounding very much like he meant it. "We're going to catch this guy."

"I thought you already had," Fred Ogden said, scowling and crossing his arms. He then nodded toward the closed door. "Go take one look in the girls' activity room and tell me you caught your man."

Grace might have only been here a month, but she knew with a glance that Justin fought to keep his cool and not attack the man who more than likely had struck out at Justin out of grief and pain. He nodded, reaching for the door handle, and opened the door inward, then walked into the room. Grace didn't look at Fred when she followed Justin into the room. Immediately she smelled something bad.

The innocence of the room provided an eerie backdrop for the destruction and violence that had obviously occurred in here. A computer had crashed to the floor. Pictures were torn from the walls. Curtains had been shredded, and dressers, as well as a small glass table, lay sideways on the floor. The two posts at the head of the bed had clothesline tied to them, the rope twisted in its knots and then hung with six inches or so, where they'd been cut.

More clothesline hung from the posts at the bottom of the bed, their ends frayed like a knife had sawed through them. Grace walked over to them, touching the ends with her gloved hand. The ropes looked like dead snakes.

"There weren't rope burns on Jensen's wrists," she mused under her breath.

The quilt, top sheet, and fitted sheet were all crumpled and hanging off one corner of the bed. She turned around, rubbing the back of her neck, and cursed under her breath. On the rose-papered wall, written in what looked like blood, were the words "You can stop this!"

Two other officers appeared in the doorway and Justin beckoned them in. Each of them carried a small briefcase, and Grace listened when Justin instructed them to dust every inch of the house.

"I want every inch of this room photographed," Grace added. "Where are the Ogdens?"

"They're out in the living room being questioned. They're still missing their other daughter," the lieutenant said as he pulled out a digital camera and turned it on.

Grace took one last look around the room before leaving. Something caught her eye outside the window. It had grown dark outside, and with the lights on inside, she couldn't see much other than blackness. Had something moved out there?

She headed back into the kitchen in time to see medics covering Jensen with a white sheet. Glancing back, assuming Justin was right behind her, she saw him outside the girls' room talking to Fred. If someone was outside who shouldn't be, there wasn't time to waste not finding out who it was.

"I'm going to check around out back," Grace told the medics, then stepped around them as they nodded. "Let Justin know where I am."

"Where's Lieutenant Jordan?"

"She said she was going to check around outside." Pete Forrest looked up from where he squatted next to Jensen's body. "She said to let you know she's out there."

A rush of panic hit Justin hard enough that he almost staggered but managed to move calmly to the back door, which stood open. It was all he could do not to rip the door off its hinges or scream at the medics for allowing her to go outside by herself. Remembering how cocky she'd been earlier this week when she'd pulled a gun on him outside his home didn't help matters any. In fact, he damn near shook with anger and worry when he stepped outside into the darkness.

Out back, a large wooden deck spread across the back of the house. He could see the shimmering blue of the water in the pool. On the other end of the yard was a shed, with siding that matched the house. He didn't see Grace anywhere.

He stepped off the deck and out of reach of the floodlight. The yard was well groomed, and there were few obstacles to block his path. A white fence surrounded the property. Beyond that the Badlands stretched endlessly. But up until the fence, the grass was mowed and the area open.

Where was Grace?

He walked toward the front of the house along the paved driveway that circled the house. When they had arrived here, the sun was just setting. Since then, it had grown dark, but no one had shut the blinds. He could see clearly into the living room. Two officers stood in the middle of the room while Mr. and Mrs. Ogden sat hand in hand on the couch.

A little voice inside his head taunted him. *If you'd pushed to have Bosley detained or at least suspended from the force and gone public with an investigation, possibly none of this would have happened. And you know those girls were probably virgins.*

Someone could stand outside and watch every little detail going on inside without being noticed. The front yard was dark and quiet, shy of three police cars, an ambulance, and the forensic team's dark sedan. It was quiet, too damned quiet! Justin turned and walked toward the back of the house again.

Grace, where are you?

A click-clicking sound, followed by an almost inaudible high pitch, interrupted the silence. Every hair on Justin's body stood on end. A large bush behind him moved furiously, and several branches fell to the ground.

Justin's heart exploded. Instinct took over and he crawled crablike to the back of the house, avoiding the glare of the floodlight.

Someone just shot at him! And whoever it was had access to a silencer.

Grace stood, back pressed flatly against the outer wall of the shed, and held her breath. Did someone just shoot a gun with a silencer on it?

When she saw the message on the wall, once again written in blood, fury almost burned her alive. Minutes later she saw the man standing in the backyard. He wore a black leather jacket, black jeans . . . and a ski mask. All that mattered was she get her hands on the son of a bitch. She hadn't bothered checking to see if Bosley was working tonight. But if he was out here, he wouldn't live through the night if she got her hands on him.

"You got a message, say it to my face, motherfucker." She glared at the darkness around her.

Someone loomed in the shadows by the edge of the deck. The glare of the floodlight made it impossible to make out features.

She reached for her cell phone and pulled it from her belt, almost dropping it before steadying it in her hand. Flipping it open, she dared look down long enough to punch in Justin's number.

Justin about jumped three feet. His mobile vibrated against his hip. What timing! Who in the hell was calling him right now? He knew his service would take a message after three rings. He squatted down, pulling his mobile from his belt, and after a quick glance at the number flipped it open.

"Where the hell are you?" he whispered.

"Please tell me that's you standing by the corner of the house."

He searched the yard, trying to locate her. He'd give her this: She was well hidden.

"*Where are you?*" He emphasized each word.

"I'm right here." She walked a foot or so away from the shed. "Look at the shed."

He hung up his phone and straightened. A figure stepped

away from the shed. He walked toward her, ready to wring her neck and then kiss it in relief. A whistle, so high-pitched it almost pierced his eardrum, sounded right by his head. He slammed his body to the ground. Several gunshots exploded in the night air, and he realized Grace had shot at someone. Within seconds he scurried across the ground until he was able to grab her. He literally used her to climb to his feet and pulled her into him protectively, allowing only her arm holding her gun to be free. His chin fit nicely right above her head. With one large, powerful arm he'd wrapped her up and held her body tightly in front of his. They appeared as one shadow. In his other hand he, too, held his gun poised, ready to shoot.

Footsteps thundered from either side of the house and three officers raced into the yard, armed and anxiously looking around them.

"I don't see anyone," Grace moaned as she struggled with darkness to see beyond the white fence into the rolling earth beyond.

"Why are you out here, Grace?"

"I saw a man wearing a ski mask standing on the deck."

"And you didn't—"

Screams broke through the air, and people started running from the house. Justin nearly flipped Grace under his arm as they ran, almost as one, around the shed and toward the house. The three other officers darted around the deck and ran toward them, guns pulled.

It was Mrs. Ogden screaming. And she was still doing it repeatedly, slicing through the black of the night. One of the officers pulled out a large flashlight and turned it on in her direction. Mr. Ogden had his arms around his wife and looked in horror at the same thing she stared at. As Justin and Grace came around the other side of the fence they stopped in their tracks as they, too, saw what made Mrs. Ogden scream.

A young woman had been spread-eagled and pinned to the wall of the shed. Long kitchen knives ran through her hands and feet, stretching her naked body across the wall several feet above the ground. Her eyes were wide open, glassy, and frozen in terror. Her mouth hung wide open, and something that looked like underwear had been stuffed into it. Her body looked as if it had been submerged in blood; every bit of her, including her hair and face, was red. Next to her, written in blood, were the words "Come to me and I'll stop."

Grace's hands went to her mouth as the urge to throw up overwhelmed her. Never, never had she seen so much blood. How could anyone do such a thing to another person? Their murderer's craving for violence was beyond out of control. Grace attempted to pull herself together when Justin started barking orders.

"Get them out of here," he instructed the gawking officers as he waved to the Ogdens. "I want this entire area sealed off. Every inch of it. No one comes in or gets out. Do you understand me?"

"Who could do such a terrible thing?" Mrs. Ogden wailed when she'd finally quit screaming. "Oh, my babies, my beautiful babies."

Her heartbroken wails tugged at Grace's heart.

"Let's get you back inside," Grace said as she moved to her. "Is there anywhere your family can stay tonight?" She looked toward Mr. Ogden.

"This is all your fault!" Mr. Ogden turned to her and started waving a finger in her face. "Rockville never saw violence like this before you came to town. You brought this monster with you!"

"What are you talking about?" Justin looked down at Mr. Ogden's finger, still pointing at Grace.

"Justin, I know they put up quite an argument over at city hall to hire another officer. And I admit, I voted for it." Mr. Ogden shook his head. "You made a press statement saying you had the rapist. Now we've got a rapist and a murderer in our town leaving terrible messages. I bet it's you he wants to come to him," he added, sneering at Grace. "I'm putting in a call right now. Young lady, consider your position with the police department terminated."

He cuddled his wife then and started walking toward the house. "I'm serious," he said, and then disappeared into the kitchen.

Grace glanced over at Erica's crucified body, then back toward the house. There was no way she could look at Justin. His silence spoke volumes. He might be FBI, but he couldn't control the town leaders if they decided to terminate her position. She stared across the pristine yard, wondering if whoever had fired those shots had overheard Fred Ogden. Tears formed in her eyes as she scanned the endless Badlands.

Chapter 21

"Why do I have to go to school and you get to stay home?" Rachel sulked as Grace handed her backpack to her.

"We've been through all of this before." Grace wasn't sure she had any more tears left. Besides, the pain of having her job yanked out from under her feet over something that wasn't her fault had now changed into outrage. And she wouldn't take that anger out on her daughter.

"You'll be here after school to pick me up?" Rachel looked outside the car nervously.

"Of course I will," Grace promised. "Now don't worry. You've been coming here for a month now. It won't be any different now."

"Before was the summer program. Now it's school for real." Rachel's expression picked up when a Lexus pulled up in front of them and Elizabeth jumped out, immediately turning and waving to Rachel. "Oh well, wish me luck."

She leaned in to Grace for a kiss and hug, then pushed open her car door and hurried outside to her friend. Grace watched her daughter hurry to the group of children waiting outside the school and noted all of the teachers waiting with them. Please let her daughter be safe.

Pulling away from the curb, Grace slowed to allow the Lexus out in front of her. Even with tinted windows, she knew Sylvia was inside, sneering at her and probably grinning with intense satisfaction.

Part of her had died the night before. Mr. Ogden was on

the city council and would get word to Sylvia of the bloody messages and his decision as to whom the messages were meant for. Justin had predicted she would be breathing down his throat gleefully. Sure enough, he and Grace hadn't been inside his house five minutes when his phone rang.

"Justin, I want her out of this town. She brought that beast with her and you know it. All of this started after she moved here!" Sylvia had screamed through the phone so loudly Grace could still hear the bitch's shrill voice in her head today.

What sucked was that without her position Grace couldn't even head over to the morgue or check in with Forensics to see what they'd come up with. She was now heading back out to Justin's house, where all she could do was sit at the computer and search for work.

Charlie greeted her in the living room when she walked into Justin's house. She noticed now that Charlie wore a new pair of blue jeans and a large T-shirt that said: "Classic."

"Uncle Charlie, I think South Dakota is treating you well."

He winked at her. "I admit I like the town. So, sit down and have a cup of coffee with me. I'll tell you some of my old FBI stories."

By law, he couldn't tell her what he had done while in the FBI. But Uncle Charlie was a rebel, and at his age he said he didn't have enough energy to break the law other than by telling some stories. He often suggested that he changed the truth just a little, to liven it up a bit. She never knew whether he told her the truth or not. Most of the time, she didn't care. Uncle Charlie's stories of his adventures as a special agent were better than most good detective novels.

"I don't think so." She smiled weakly. "My brain isn't focusing too well today. Last night was really bad."

"We see a lot of ugly things." He patted her arm gently, his expression and smile as reassuring as she'd always known him to be. "And sometimes we even get thrown in jail. It's all part of the job. You'll get through this and forget all about it when the next ordeal enters your life."

"That's encouraging." She attempted a laugh, but it came out sounding more like choked-back tears. "I think I'm going to go upstairs and surf around for a while. Justin said I could use his computer."

Justin's bedroom smelled like he did. The musky aroma of his aftershave filled the room. It wasn't like she would snoop, but the last time she was here she was preoccupied with other things.

His room was longer than it was wide, and so spacious. It spread the length of the house from one end to the other and had three windows with window seats. She walked its length, admiring the soft gray swirled wallpaper. So masculine, yet done with impeccable taste, giving the room a regal yet dominating atmosphere. There were two tall wooden dressers and a matching clothes bureau. She ached to open the bureau to see how he stored things.

The king-size four-poster bed sat in the middle of the room in between two of the windows along the front wall. The patchwork comforter that spread across it fell on either side within inches of the floor. Opposite the bed was a modern desk, standing out among the colonial-style wooden furniture. His computer sat on top of it. At least she wouldn't have to stare at his bed.

Looking at it now reminded her of Justin seducing her, going down on her and damn near causing her to make a fool out of herself. Odd, though, she considered, standing there staring at the patchwork comforter's pattern, remembering how she had attacked him outside, taken him on, and fucked him until he exploded didn't bother her at all.

"Don't get yourself all worked up," she ordered, muttering as she forced her attention away from his bed. She needed to stay focused, keep her reality in check. The simple truth was that she had to concentrate on her daughter and figuring out their financial situation now that Grace wasn't employed. "Damn that fucking city council to hell and back anyway."

Getting comfortable at Justin's computer, she ordered herself not to hold grudges. At the same time she prayed for a kick-ass job that she could flaunt in Sylvia's face. *The bitch.*

The next couple of hours passed quickly. Grace didn't feel like she accomplished much. Her résumé was on her own computer. And searching for work in the area proved depressing at best. They could move, relocate to another city somewhere in the U.S. and start over—again. That thought soured her mood even further. There wasn't anything local in law enforcement.

Uncle Charlie bounded up the stairs, and she prayed her expression didn't give away her sour mood.

"Doris Agnew just called me. She left her headlights on last night, and now her car won't start. She wants me to give her a jump."

Grace looked up to see his gray hair combed back and detected aftershave lingering in the air. "You like this woman, don't you?"

"You're not the only family member that sees what they want and goes after it."

"What am I going after?"

"Are you, or are you not, sitting in Justin Reece's bedroom after only living in this town for a little over a month?" He grinned wryly.

"I sleep with my daughter," she argued quickly.

"Are you telling me you've never slept with the man?" He raised an eyebrow.

"That, sir, is none of your business." She fought the blush that was coming on. She and Justin hadn't actually slept together—just had incredibly hot sex.

"I thought so." He shook his head but grinned his approval. "I'll go get her car started and be right back. It won't take me more than thirty minutes. You could come with me."

"Oh no. Three is a crowd. You just make sure you set a good example for me." She wagged a finger at her uncle.

"Looks to me like you've learned well," he shot back, and took a look around her at the bedroom she was in. "I promise I'll hurry. All the windows are locked, and I'll make sure both doors are locked before I leave."

"Don't worry about me," she said, waving him on.

She listened to him walk through the house downstairs and then out the front door. The soft click let her know he'd locked the dead bolt. The phone rang almost immediately.

"Reece residence," she said politely, still smiling.

"You make it sound like I have a maid." Justin's dark, commanding baritone sent shivers rushing over her skin.

"Well, you don't," she snapped, trying to sound stern.

"Where's Charlie?"

"He left for a few minutes." She hesitated, knowing the reaction she'd receive.

"You're there alone?"

"He'll be right back. He went to give Doris Agnew a jump."

She heard Justin curse.

"Is the house locked?"

"Yes. It's locked. Trust me, your house is safer now than it's ever been," she added smugly. "Anyone tries breaking in here they'll regret it. I've got energy to burn, and beating the crap out of some derelict sounds just fine to me."

"I have a beautiful woman sitting in my bedroom, who just told me she's got too much energy and needs a way to burn it off, and I have to go to a meeting." She heard him growl his frustration.

Grace couldn't keep from grinning. Maybe when he came home she'd jump his bones, if they were still alone. "How long will it last?"

"I don't know. I don't want to hear any of their crap anyway. The second they get on my nerves I'm out of there. And I'm really grouchy." He chuckled, but she knew it was forced. "I'm coming home as soon as I'm out of there."

She closed the phone, hoping that would be soon. A minute later she heard the alarm beep once as the dead bolt was unlocked and the front door opened and closed again. She cocked her head to listen. Footsteps crossed the living room floor and started up the stairs.

"Uncle Charlie?" she called out, but the silence that followed chilled her blood.

Jumping out of the computer chair, Grace ran across the hallway to her bedroom and then to her utility belt. She grabbed her gun and turned around just in time for a fist to hit her square in the face. She fell backward onto the floor. Slapping tangled ringlets out of her face, she looked up quickly to see her attacker.

"I told you I had permission." Bosley grabbed the gun from her hand before she could get the hair out of her face.

"You don't have permission to do shit!" she screamed, but her mouth swelled quickly enough that it was hard to speak. "Get the hell out of here or I swear I'll kick your ass."

"Un-uh." He reached down and pulled her to her feet by her arm. "This town was better off without you in it, Grace. Apparently losing your job isn't enough to make you leave, though, is it?"

"You lay a hand on me and you'll never work in law enforcement again." She tried to yank her arm free of his grasp, but he tightened his grip and pulled her to him.

"I'm not the one who got booted off the force." The venomous smile she'd seen on his face once or twice before appeared again. "And I hear you're being stalked by a psychopath. That can make a person mentally unstable. You may have a hard time finding a job in any field."

He tossed her gun onto Rachel's bed and wrapped his other arm around Grace. She got a glimpse of it lying where her daughter slept and her stomach clenched, nausea and outrage making for a bitter taste in her mouth.

"Not that you're going to need to work," he added with a laugh.

She could hardly move her arms—his grip on her was so solid. When he lowered his mouth to hers, she fought with everything she had, but he simply was stronger than she was. She finally bit his lip, and he pulled back.

He slapped her across the face, knocking her backward, but she kept herself from falling. Her head spun from the impact, but losing her sense of surroundings, her grip on reality, would give him the advantage. And that wasn't going to happen.

"You're an idiot, Bosley!" She leapt in the air, kicking him square in the stomach and causing him to crash into the bedroom door. "I warned you!"

She tried lunging at him, but Bosley moved faster than she thought him able to do. Leaping to his feet, he body-slammed her. Grace tumbled backward, unable to keep her balance.

"Son of a bitch!" she howled, hitting the floor hard enough to knock the wind out of her.

Bosley grabbed her arm, yanking her to her feet with enough force she felt like he dislocated her shoulder.

"Personally, I don't like it rough, but if that's what turns you on . . ." He shrugged. "Anyway, let's go."

"Go? I'm not going anywhere with you." Her biggest chance of rescue, if she couldn't overcome Bosley on her own, was Uncle Charlie or Justin arriving here soon. But beyond that, never again would someone steal her away from her life.

"You think I'm going to enjoy you in Reece's house? I have more respect for the guy than that." Bosley started dragging her out of the room.

Grace dug in her heels. "You obviously don't have respect for anyone or you wouldn't have killed those girls." What she wouldn't do for a tape recorder right now.

Bosley laughed, although there was little humor in his dark expression. "Look here, bitch. I'm not a murderer. I prefer the blood pumping through a woman." He grabbed her hair by the roots and she howled when he yanked her into the hallway. "Now I said, let's go!"

"Whatever, Bosley." She held on to his hand, which had a painful grip on her hair. "I know you killed those girls. And I'm not the only one."

"You're wrong. I didn't kill any of them." He shoved her forward, pushing against the middle of her back, damn near sending her toppling down the stairs.

Grace dug into his hand, desperately trying to get him to let go of her hair. But she was forced to let go and balance herself when she started down the stairs.

"I told you I have permission. You figure it out from there," Bosley continued as he pushed her down the stairs. "Of course, you're probably in too much denial to figure it out and your knowing the truth now really doesn't matter. It's a shame when you think about it. And I do feel sorry for Reece. His hands are tied by too much bureaucracy, and he's pussy-whipped by his ex-wife. Plus, now he's made the mistake of falling for the wrong woman."

She didn't say anything but instead tried to maintain her balance until they made it to the bottom of the stairs.

When they reached the bottom of the stairs, Bosley let go of her hair and turned her to face him. "How long will your uncle be gone?" he asked, running his hands over her hair.

"A couple of hours," she lied, backing away from him touching her and pressing her hand where he'd held her hair.

Bosley moved so fast she swore she didn't see it coming when he slapped her across the face.

"Stop it! Please!" she howled, landing on her hands and knees and spitting the metallic taste of blood out of her mouth while the room spun quickly around her.

"It's simple. Don't lie to me. Do as you're told. And you won't get hurt." He pulled her to him again and kissed her gently on the lips. She didn't kiss him back, but she didn't fight him, either. Primarily because he had her hair wrapped tightly around his fingers. "Now that's a good girl," he said softly as he pulled back and smiled into her face.

She needed to stall him. As long as they were here, at Justin's house, she had a chance of help showing up. But if Bosley took her somewhere, God only knows how long they would be undisturbed. She needed to get a confession out of him. With her head pounding and the room still spinning, she couldn't gather her thoughts.

"Bosley, I don't understand why you're doing this? You've been in law enforcement long enough to know you can't get away with it."

His grip on her hair tightened, and she squealed from the pain. Memories surfaced that she didn't need to be thinking about right now. There wasn't any method of handling pain.

She'd learned that a long time ago. Pain was pain. But this time she fought for more than maintaining her freedom. There were other girls in this town, girls with futures, with hopes and dreams. Each and every one of them would see those dreams out if Grace played this scene right. Not to mention there was Rachel—and Justin.

"It's just that you're a good-looking guy," she tried again. "And, up until ten minutes ago, I thought you had a pretty nice personality. You don't need to do this to get a woman."

"What if the woman I want is you?" He started moving both of them toward the front door.

"There were other ways you could have told me that. You didn't need to do this." She held on to his hand with both of her hands. She pretended that she couldn't walk well with him holding her hair. She fell several times in an attempt to slow them up.

"I wasn't given much of a chance. I've never seen Justin Reece move as fast as he did with you," Bosley grumbled. "Although can't say I blame him."

"You never gave me any indication."

"Like that would have mattered."

Bosley opened the front door, after peering through the lace curtain on the window next to the door. "Now, sweetheart, let's go," he hissed into her ear.

"Bosley, I'm not leaving this house." She let go of her hair and elbowed him as hard as she could. Her aim hit right below his rib cage, and he doubled over when she knocked the wind out of him.

Grace bolted toward the stairs. If she could only get to her cell phone or at least farther into the house so he couldn't force her to his car. She screamed when he tackled her and the two of them landed on the first few stairs.

"Don't try that again."

He had her down on all fours, with the stairs pressing into her body causing excruciating pain as he lay on top of her. Someone pulled into the driveway. The noise of gravel popping and then the slight squeak of brakes never sounded better. Bosley obviously heard it, too, for he yanked her back up to her feet. She screamed willingly from the pain. A hand clasped her mouth.

"Damn it. Shut up," he growled into her ear. "I should have known he would send someone to check on you. Fucking asshole said he had my back."

"Who has your back?" Any kind of conversation at all right now would give the driver of that car more time to get here.

She looked at the window by the front door and saw two men getting out of the car. They looked familiar. Had she seen them before?

Bosley ignored her question.

"You answer the door and get rid of them." His mouth was right next to her ear.

She shook her head stubbornly. The two men walked toward the door. Bosley pulled her back and relentlessly pulled her hair until she was sure it would come out with skin attached.

"Get rid of them or you'll regret this day instead of possibly enjoying it." He continued to drag her back out of the living room.

Forcing herself to ignore the pulsating pain emitting from the side of her head, she forced her mouth open and bit his hand. At the same time she forced her bare foot down on his shoe as hard as she could. She knew she didn't hurt his foot as much as her teeth hurt his finger. He howled and pulled his hand away from her mouth. She took advantage of the brief moment and screamed as loud as she could. The unlocked door flew open.

"FBI! Hold it right there."

The two men stormed into the living room with guns aimed directly at Bosley, who stared at the two men in complete disbelief. He let go of her hair, and she flew to the couch on the other side of the room.

"Who are you?" Bosley looked so confused it was shocking.

"Special Agent Phillips with the FBI. Now, slowly move your hands straight out, and then place them on your head."

Bosley did as he was told. Phillips approached him and brought his hands down behind him, then cuffed him. The other agent stood motionless, holding a gun on the bewildered police officer. Grace was almost amused at the incredibly astonished look her would-be rapist had on his face. Her head throbbed and she was too dizzy, but it struck her as odd that he appeared so surprised to be stopped.

Was he confused because he was caught or because they were FBI agents? Had it struck him as odd that there were more FBI agents in town other than Justin? Which of course helped her remember where she'd seen these two men before. They'd stood on the courthouse lawn with Justin and Sylvia the day Grace took Rachel to the Dairy Queen. Certainly Bosley would have known that the agents were in town. He was a good cop—or he was up until he arrived here.

It was too hard to think, and Grace's vision kept blurring, which made her fear she might have a concussion. As she glanced toward the front door, it looked like a third man stood by the still-running car.

"Come on, let's go." Special Agent Phillips pushed Bosley on the back with one hand while holding his gun on him with the other. Bosley didn't look at her as he was escorted out of the house.

"Are you okay?" The other agent stood by the doorway and studied her carefully.

"Your timing was perfect. I'm fine." She rubbed her head but looked up at the man and smiled.

"Good." He pulled a cell phone out and quickly pushed numbers.

"Reece? Gowsky here. Good thing you asked us to stop by. She had company." He paused. "One of the cops from here in town, I'm afraid. Bosley." He nodded silently and hung up the phone. "I'll stay until Reece gets here. He's on his way." Special Agent Gowsky once again studied her carefully. "Are you sure you're okay?"

"Really, I'm fine." She stood up and faced him. She needed to concentrate on everything that was said between her and Bosley while he was here. At the moment, none of it made sense.

"Maybe we should find some ice for that lip," Special Agent Gowsky decided, and turned to look for the kitchen.

He ended up following her, but when they reached the kitchen, he instructed her to sit and walked to the refrigerator. He applied several pieces of ice, wrapped in a paper towel, to the side of her mouth and instructed her to hold it there.

She could tell when Justin got home by squealing tires, then loud, heavy footsteps bounding across the front porch. Special Agent Gowsky stood in the kitchen door and turned as Justin entered the house. Justin walked right past Gowsky and took her in his arms. He held her at arm's length and narrowed his eyes as he looked into hers. She saw the worry, the concern, and unadulterated outrage as he stared into her eyes. He looked for answers to unspoken questions. Just staring into his gorgeous face made her feel better than she had in ages. After a moment, he pulled her into his arms again.

"I'm sorry, babe. I really am." He wrapped his comforting arms around her and held her to his iron chest as he turned to the special agent. "I don't know how to thank you enough, John. I guess I owe you now."

"I'll think of something." Gowsky laughed dryly.

She half-listened as Special Agent John Gowsky told Justin how he and Phillips had walked in on her and Bosley and now had him cuffed in the car. Gowsky laughed as he said Phillips was a good old boy and would have enough dirt on Bosley in the next ten minutes to send him to prison for life if Justin wanted it.

She didn't care what they talked about. She never felt better than she did right now in Justin's arms. He didn't loosen his grip, and his thumb on his right hand caressed her shoulder gently. She could stay here forever. When was the last time she felt this safe?

"Special Agent Sam Milton is out there, too. We'll drive Bosley into Rapid City and hold him there." John Gowsky made a clicking sound with this tongue. "If there's a group who can get a confession out of a man, it's those two."

For a moment, Grace wasn't sure whether she was hiding under the covers in her room where Master kept her or still in Justin's arms. Her worlds were colliding and the room wouldn't quit spinning. The throbbing in her head grew, pounding like someone taking a hammer to the side of her head.

Wait a minute! Sam Milton? The conversations she'd overheard when Master talked on the phone while she . . .

Sam Milton?

Master didn't believe in friends. She'd heard that enough times in her lifetime. But Sam Milton came around plenty of times—and he always had permission.

Chapter 22

Justin would wring old Charlie Jordan's neck. How could her uncle leave her alone in Justin's house when they knew the investigation wasn't over? He couldn't suppress his growing anger when Grace suddenly sagged against him. Her clothes were undisturbed, but she'd been knocked around some. Her face didn't look good.

"What's going on here?" Uncle Charlie called as he entered the front door.

Justin's blood boiled. "I'm taking her upstairs and calling the doctor," he told Gowsky. "Tell your men to head out with Bosley and call me once they have him locked up. I'll question him myself."

"Oh, baby. I'm so sorry." Uncle Charlie froze when he entered the kitchen and saw Grace.

"Where the hell did you go?" Justin demanded, not surprised that being yelled at didn't faze Charlie. Justin headed up the stairs, carrying Grace, with Charlie right behind him.

"Doris Agnew called and told me her car wouldn't start. But she wasn't there when I arrived. I thought it odd that there was no note or sign of her anywhere. But when I pulled in here . . ." He caught Justin's eyes. "I was intentionally lured away."

"Are you sure about that?" Gowsky asked, entering Justin's room behind Charlie.

"That was just it." Uncle Charlie rubbed his gray tousled hair and watched Grace when Justin laid her on his bed.

"She's never called me before. It sounded like her and she needed my help. I didn't think I'd be gone more than twenty minutes."

Justin pulled out his cell phone and called his family doctor, explaining to his secretary that they had an emergency and he needed the doctor to make a house call. One of the many wonders of Rockville: There were still doctors who made the effort to come to you.

"Oh, my sweet little girl," Charlie said, moving to her side and gently cupping her chin. Grace didn't wake up when he touched her. "I hoped I'd never see you like this again."

"I need to wake her up." Justin stepped around Charlie and dared him with a look to stand between him and the older man's niece. "If she's got a concussion, we can't let her stay asleep."

"We'll drive Bosley over to Rapid City and hold him there. I'll make sure you're notified when he's checked in over there." Special Agent John Gowsky nodded to both men and left the room.

"Get me a cold washcloth," Justin told Charlie, and sat on his bed, pulling Grace into his arms. "Sweetheart. Wake up. You can't sleep right now."

He cradled her in his arms and talked to her until her eyes blinked. Then, taking the cold cloth from Charlie, he dabbed her face carefully.

"I'll go make some compacts." Charlie stepped out of the room, leaving the two of them alone. If the old man felt guilty, well, that was just fine.

"Talk to me, darling. What do you remember?" Justin asked when he was sure Grace focused on him.

She whispered so quietly he asked her to repeat herself twice before he understood. "Special Agent Sam Milton is an old friend of Master's."

"What? I just sent him off with Bosley for Rapid City." Justin wanted to hit something and felt his muscles tighten and shake while adjusting pillows behind Grace.

"Hold me, Justin," she whispered.

He closed his eyes, wrapping her in his arms until Charlie walked into the room again with coffee and toast. Justin needed to question her more. God, she took a hell of a beating to be this out of it. As bruised as her face was, he assumed a concussion and prayed it wasn't anything worse. His cell phone went off and he reluctantly let her back against the pillows and then took the call from the doctor's office.

By the time the doctor showed up, Grace had shared what had happened, her conversation with Bosley, and his continual insistence that he didn't kill the other girls.

"I want to question him," she said, her face now an array of blues and purples and greens and her mouth so swollen it was harder and harder to understand what she said.

"You can't question him." Justin didn't want to remind her right now that she wasn't employed as a cop any longer. "But I'll make sure you're nearby and can listen when he is questioned."

Many things happened throughout the rest of the afternoon. All of them without Grace's help. She sat on the couch with a bowl of popcorn, her big fuzzy socks on her feet, and watched as first Justin, then Uncle Charlie talked to Cliff. She got the impression that Uncle Charlie simply wanted to say hello. Although Justin's doctor gave her a mild painkiller, informing them she had a slight concussion but should be fine if she didn't overdo it, Grace felt more alert than she had all day. She was also very relaxed and didn't have a desire to move at all.

Justin had his laptop on the dining room table and communicated with several agents in the state, sharing information and preparing strategies. The worst news was that Milton had headed to Rapid City alone with Bosley and now couldn't be reached on his phone. She barely blinked when Justin pounded the wall with his fist over the news. Pain medication had its advantages.

Depression threatened to take over more than once, watching the excitement but not part of it. Uncle Charlie brought Rachel home after school. Rachel ran to her mother, hugging her and asking questions that Uncle Charlie wouldn't let her answer. He whisked her daughter upstairs with promises of pizza and that her mother would be fine, but they needed time to catch the guy who had done that to her.

"Are you sure you'll be fine?" Rachel asked, her large blue eyes and soft red curls adding to her innocent appearance.

The look she gave Grace more than broke her heart. She needed to get better, quickly, and to find a way, regardless of whether she had a uniform to put on or not, to catch the bastard and kill him herself if she couldn't arrest him.

"I'm going to be fine," she swore to her daughter. "Go with Uncle Charlie and I'll come check on you in a bit."

And just to encourage her recovery, after her daughter and uncle were upstairs, Grace pushed herself to her feet, feeling only a bit dizzy, and took small steps, grateful no one saw her, toward Justin's back and the dining room table.

"Do you recognize this man?" Justin asked without looking up when she'd almost reached him.

There wasn't any point in groaning that he knew she had worked her way across the room. He didn't yell at her for doing so. Which would have been bad, because she wasn't sure she could yell back right now. She reached for the chair next to him and didn't argue when he moved quickly and then helped her into it.

"Do you recognize this man?" he asked again after situating himself next to her and relaxing his arm behind her chair while stretching his long, muscular legs under the table.

"Sam Milton," she said without hesitating, and then fought not to cringe at the grotesque memories that staring at his pictures surfaced.

That's when she noticed the handheld tape recorder that Justin pushed closer to her while she stared at the glowing small circular light on it.

"How do you know him?" Justin asked her, his soft baritone barely easing the despicable pictures that flashed before her mind's eye.

"He was a friend of . . ." She hesitated, staring at the tape recorder. Going on record, confirming her past that she'd so successfully wiped off her record and kept any employer from ever knowing about, was about to rear its ugly head. She licked her lips, more than aware of the consequences that would follow. Her testimony might help bust a bad agent and get rid of a sick cop, but it would also destroy her. "He knew a person I once knew."

"Grace," Justin said.

She slapped the tape recorder, moving quickly when she glared at him. The room could just fucking spin. She wouldn't destroy her life. "There's got to be another way," she snapped.

His green eyes never looked softer, deeper, and such an incredibly enticing shade. He searched her face, the worry lines around his eyes more obvious and a day's growth along his jawbone adding to his roguish good looks.

"*If I say how I knew him,*" she stressed, needing Justin to understand, "the world will know about a part of me that I successfully erased once. With today's computer technology, you know as well as I do it would be impossible to erase it twice. I won't be able to work again."

"Your testimony can take down a serial rapist and murderer," he said softly.

"Who continually repeated that he wasn't our guy," Grace stressed. "Wouldn't Milton not showing up with Bosley in Rapid City be enough to shut him down?"

"He did take him to Rapid City."

"What?" She rubbed her forehead, immediately touching bruises that she was sure made her face look beyond disgusting. "He turned Bosley over to the FBI?"

She stared at the picture but then closed her eyes. Grace opened them again quickly, her memories closing in on her when she shut herself in darkness. Instead she returned her attention to Justin.

Justin glanced at the tape recorder but didn't turn it back on. "What time period did you know Milton? Can you give me dates and locations?"

Her head pounded the more she tried thinking. But relaxing, leaning her head back against Justin's warm forearm, she did her best to accurately remember. "It was during the last year or so that I was in Minnesota," she began. "So approximately ten years ago and for over about a year's time period."

"That matches the time when he was there," Justin told her quietly. "He worked with me on that case to capture the rapist and murderer that was killing girls up there."

Grace nodded, tilting her head so she could stare at his face but not lifting it from his arm.

"We never caught our guy back then," he added, but then leaned forward and brushed his lips carefully over hers. *"He's not going to get away this time,"* he emphasized, his warm breath smelling like coffee.

"Get a confession out of Bosley," she said.

His eyes darkened when he backed away from her only a few inches. "If he's our guy."

"You don't think he is?" she asked incredulously.

"I hope he is," Justin told her but then moved his free arm and tapped at his mouse on his laptop.

"Do you recognize any of these names?" he asked quietly.

She read a list of fifteen or so names that appeared on the screen of his laptop. "No, I don't."

"Okay. Several agents are on their way over. If any of them are familiar to you—"

"I'll let you know." She watched his eyes fall to her lips when she spoke.

"You are so beautiful," he whispered, and gently kissed her. He was very careful not to apply too much pressure, and his tenderness sent sparks flying inside her. "Soon," he whispered.

"Yes," she uttered, and swore she'd never seen one word make a man look happier.

She remained at the dining room table when the agents arrived until Justin came and got her. Three men and a woman sat on the couch and chairs, talking quietly. They stood up as the two walked into the room.

"I'd like all of you to meet Grace Jordan," Justin said, and she felt the inquiring eyes take her in. "Grace, please meet Special Agents Steve Applebee, Jeremy Miller, Lance Hoffman, and Jan Overbey."

Everyone shook hands and exchanged polite greetings. Justin included her as he explained everything to them and answered questions.

Grace could tell none of them were new to the force. They'd brought down dangerous criminals before—hell, it was all in a day's work. They spent the next thirty discussing the case and asking questions. One thing grew apparent as Grace sat and mostly listened. Apparently Bosley's declaration that he wasn't their killer carried more weight than she thought. In fact, while they spoke Justin took a phone call from Rapid City, where they learned Bosley was being shipped back to Rockville, where he would be tried by a local judge. Grace would have to press charges, and even at that, Bosley would be out on bail before the end of the day. Justin was sure of it.

Less than an hour later, she found herself alone in the kitchen, listening as several vehicles pulled out of the driveway, Justin's being one of them. When Uncle Charlie came down the stairs, she put on a cheerful look for him.

"It's not the end of the world," he said, seemingly unimpressed by the pleasant expression on her face. "You'll be back out there nailing the bad guys in no time flat."

"If I can find another job after this nightmare is over."

"Why don't you go on and call it a night," her uncle said, leaning against the doorway. "I'll call it a night myself here soon."

"I'm not sure I could sleep."

And I'm tired of sleeping with my daughter. I want to go curl up in that large bed upstairs, but I wasn't invited.

"You'll surprise yourself. Put that pretty head of yours on your pillow and I bet you'll be out in minutes."

Reluctantly Grace dragged herself into the bedroom where her daughter already slept. It was only nine thirty, and sleep was the last thing on Grace's mind. She stood in the darkness, staring down at her beautiful sleeping daughter who was her responsibility, and shuddered at the thought that she didn't have a job. Maybe she'd check the Rapid City classifieds. Would Justin be willing to commute to see her?

Who was she fooling? He was FBI. Justin would travel to his next assignment. Why would he want to travel more just to see her?

Oh, dear Lord!

Was she actually contemplating a future with Justin Reece?

With so many thoughts racing through her brain, she would never be able to sleep. She slipped into her knee-length silk nightgown and pulled her fuzzy socks back on. The house stood dark and quiet. She headed to the kitchen and grabbed a Diet Coke. Like she needed the caffeine at this hour, but what the hell. The pain meds had worn off and she couldn't sleep anyway. Nor did she want to fog her brain by taking another pill the doctor had left for her. Might as well be coherent while she remained awake.

The only available computer was the one in Justin's bedroom. Feeling her stomach tighten, she bit her lip and headed for the stairs to start looking for work.

"Grace . . . hey, beautiful, wake up," Justin whispered, very close to her head.

"Huh? What?" Grace blinked at the glaring computer screen, then straightened, pressing her hands over her cheeks and immediately feeling her bruised and swollen face. "I didn't mean to fall asleep. What time is it?"

"It's almost midnight." Justin sounded tired as he walked over to the edge of his bed, sat down, and pulled off his shoes.

"What were you doing?"

"Bosley managed to get a judge out of bed who granted him bail, which he promptly posted," Justin groaned. "I stayed to watch the fireworks, and to be there when he walked to his car." He cursed as he pulled off his socks.

"What did you do?" She wasn't sure she wanted to know.

"Sometimes even a special agent needs to take the law into his own hands." He stood and untucked his shirt, then began unbuttoning it. "I doubt he ever bothers you again."

He stripped off his shirt.

She stared at the tiny dark blond curls that covered his muscular chest. "You beat him up?"

"I don't take too kindly to another man touching my woman."

Grace swallowed, hearing his words and at the same time watching him shed his jeans until all he wore was boxers. His woman? Did he just say his woman? Her heart beat so hard she felt it in every bruise on her face but for the first time since her attack didn't feel the pain. As wonderful as his words sounded, she couldn't come up with a thing to say in response.

If anything, she felt his words but couldn't comment on them. He was so gorgeous, so perfect, the epitome of everything a man should be.

"I'll head to bed," she muttered, knowing if she sat there a moment longer she'd start to cry. That or simply drool like an idiot over his naked body.

It wasn't fair. She would attack him, wrestle him to his bed, and show him how much she wanted him to be her man. But her face throbbed, and there were other muscles in her body that ached. More than likely, once she got out of her clothes and took time to inspect herself, she'd find nasty bruises all over her body. Like she was in any hurry to stare at herself in the mirror looking like that again. She'd seen enough of herself beaten and bloodied for a lifetime.

"No." Justin pulled her out of her thoughts. "Stay here."

His green eyes were heavy with desire. He pulled her to him hard enough that she almost lost her balance. She landed against his steel chest. All that muscle and his warm, smooth skin somehow made her not hurt so much. He stroked her curls with a large gentle hand, willing her to lean her head back until her lips opened in invitation. He stared down at her silently for a moment. Tiny wrinkles at the edges of his eyes proved evidence of the pressures of his job, but she also saw his desire and concern for her. Did he read her just as easily?

Slowly, he lowered his mouth to hers, never quite closing his eyes, watching her intently as he brushed his lips over hers.

The heat between them jumped drastically. Justin swore sparks flew from that kiss. She felt so soft, so vulnerable, and she needed him. All of his protector instincts dominated his senses. He swore to himself as he stared down at her that she would never look like this again. He should have killed Bosley tonight. As it was, going after him in the parking lot outside the police station, not giving a rat's ass who saw or tried to stop him, was so damned satisfying Justin couldn't wait to get home to Grace after placing a few choice bruises on Bosley.

It didn't surprise Justin that no one stopped him and no one was around when he finally let Bosley go and watched the weasel run to his car and drive off as quickly as he could. This was his town, God damn it. And Grace was his woman. No one would mess with either one of them—ever again. He would tell her through his lovemaking that never again would she feel pain. Never again would she be abused. He would see to it. He would take care of her.

He quietly pushed the door closed with his foot, then slid her bathrobe off her shoulders and let it fall to the floor. Her nightgown glided like silk over her body as he pulled it off of her and dropped it to the side.

Justin picked her up, then gently placed her on his bed. "You are beyond doubt the most beautiful woman on the planet." He stood over her, just staring at her naked beauty in awe.

"You're making me nervous." She smiled and reached a graceful hand up to him.

"I think it's normal to be nervous the first time you make love to a man."

He lay down next to her, propping his head up on one

hand. He ran his index finger from her chin down the center of her body to the curly hair just a shade lighter than the hair on her head.

"I thought I was the one who took a few knocks to the head," she said, attempting a grin with her swollen mouth. "This is not the first time you and I have had sex." She shivered under his touch, than drowned in incredible warmth from the hunger in his eyes and the victorious grin on his face.

"My sweet Grace, I'm not going to fuck you. I am going to make love to you." His mouth brushed hers, just a gentle touch. "I promise I'll be gentle. I won't hurt you."

Grace reached for him, pulling him down on her. "I don't want gentle. I want you."

Her nipples hardened against his chest, torturing him, and he lowered his mouth to adore each one. Nibbling at first and then sucking like a starved man, she cried out underneath him, arching to give him better access.

Justin stared at her closed eyes, at the way her long red hair curled and twisted like a royal robe. She moved her head from side to side, her bruised face showing him now how strong she was, how invincible. Grace wasn't a quitter. And he'd bet her loyalty ran as strong as her commitment to her work. If he could test that, know beyond any doubt she'd never cheat on him, then he'd know he'd found his soul mate. He continued watching her while she reached for his headboard and hung on as if somehow she worried she might fall off.

But the view she offered blew him away. He continued caressing her breasts with his hands and lifted himself off her enough to appreciate how damned sexy she was stretched out underneath him.

He ran his fingers down her middle, noting another large bruise on her hip bone that hadn't been there before. He didn't touch it but studied its oblong shape while again feeling a surge of anger peak inside him.

"I want to be able to do this every day," he confessed, unwilling to let her see how pissed he was that she'd been unprotected, defenseless. No matter how much she wanted him to see her as tough, able to handle any situation, the simple truth was she couldn't. And he didn't want her to have to. From this point forward, Grace would know a life without worry or concern about being attacked like she had been today. He'd see to it if he had to hire armed guards to watch her when he wasn't here. "I want to be able to enjoy you whenever I want," he whispered, dragging his finger over her thigh and watching her shiver and stretch into his touch.

"You and me both." She opened her eyes and they glowed as she focused on him. "Are you going to take off your boxers?"

"Best idea I've heard all night." He moved to his knees, unwilling to create too much distance between them, and quickly unzipped his pants.

He'd never been so swollen, so fucking hard. He managed to slide out of his boxers, though, and kick them off the bed.

The look she gave him almost melted his insides. Never had a lady adorned him with so much appreciation as she did with her small smile and her flushed cheeks. His insides pulsed with need that would push him over the edge quickly if he didn't fight for some control.

She lifted her knees and stretched her legs, opening for him, offering herself. Her pussy glistened, moist and soft and so incredibly feminine. *God*. He throbbed with enough fucking need that he could come right then. His balls ached for it, hanging heavy and full, hard, just like the rest of him.

He adjusted himself between her legs, running one finger over her soaked opening. Grace jerked, swallowing her cry as she grabbed her hair.

"I need you." She sounded like she begged him.

"I know," he whispered, focusing on her vagina, at the way her swollen lips parted and glistened with her moisture. "And God knows I need you."

His cock weighed a thousand pounds. More than anything he wanted to thrust deep, fast, and hard into her heat. In spite of what she told him, he couldn't get rough with her tonight. He wouldn't bring her more pain—only pleasure. But he could bring her to the boiling point that matched the raging temperature inside him.

Slowly he eased his fingers inside her and then hissed and sucked in his breath. He didn't remember her being so damned hot, so soaked and tight. She thrust her hips up, aching to take him deeper. Her stomach hardened, and her full breasts trembled while her lips parted. In spite of her fat lip, her mouth trembled and almost sent him over the edge. Everything about her was so beautiful, so perfect. And she was his—his woman. The pain of that knowledge ripped at his soul. He prayed he could handle losing his heart to a woman, although for the life of him he never remembered any of the feelings he once had for Sylvia matching what he felt right now.

Justin pushed inside Grace farther, watching her face, her muscles contort while she struggled to keep from coming.

"Let go," he whispered. "I want to watch."

"I can't, Justin," she said, sounding like she regretted the fact. "I can't come just because I want to."

"You can, and you will for me."

She blinked a few times, holding her breath, while every inch of her stiffened like a board. Her inner thighs clamped against him, and she started shaking. He shoved his knuckles against her pelvic bone and twisted his fingers. Her inner muscles twitched and closed in on him.

Grace's deep blue eyes glowed with lust. Her lips parted and then her mouth slowly formed a small circle. At the same time, moisture soaked his fingers, dripping over his knuckles.

"God. Justin," she gasped, shaking her head from side to side and breathing so hard her face turned red. But then she jumped off the bed, pulling her body away from him. "I can't," she whimpered, panting. "I can't let go."

"My sweetheart." The heat swelling inside him made it

damned hard to talk. But she needed to know. He wanted her to know. "You aren't letting go. You're giving yourself to me. Trust me and let me show you I'm worthy of that trust."

The face she made at his words was absolutely priceless. But this wasn't time for conversation. Even though she shook her head slightly, he wasn't going to take time to convince her he was right. Instead he moved, adjusting himself between her legs, and then lowered his mouth to hers for a soft kiss while his cock pressed eagerly against her entrance.

"I won't ever betray your trust," he told her.

Grace's eyes grew moist, but she didn't look away. Instead she wrapped her arms around his neck and pulled him closer, opening her mouth and deepening their kiss.

With a quick, thorough thrust, he filled her, giving her every inch of him. Every inch of him tingled. The heat tearing at his insides craved an escape. He hardened, from his toes to his fingers, every inch of him.

"You're so beautiful," he praised her, wanting to say so much more but finding it damned hard to talk.

"I've looked better." She tried laughing, but it turned into a moan when he sunk deep inside her again. "But this is part of the job."

"I don't want you hurt again."

"I'm fine." She sounded convincing.

He couldn't think of anyone ever attacking her again. It didn't matter that this was part of the job. He didn't care that there might be times when a perp got too close. If Justin could do it, he'd seal her away from the world, protect her from all evil. Something told him he'd have a worse fight on his hands trying to do that than he would keeping all bad guys away from her. Even as he convinced himself not to think about it but simply to enjoy how damned good she felt, Justin knew he wouldn't be able to handle anyone touching her again. Bosley got the crap beaten out of him. The next guy would die.

"Justin," she whimpered, digging her nails into his shoulders.

If he slowed down, he would explode. If he took her any

faster, it would be over. But riding her as he did, feeling her pussy stroke his cock, her muscles vibrate against his shaft, took him over the edge no matter his effort to prolong it.

"You're too damned good," he growled, releasing everything he had deep inside her.

"And you're perfect," she whispered, her body trembling underneath his.

He held on to her when he rolled to his back, managing to pull her on top of him and stay inside her. His cock had softened considerably, the unbearable pressure and weight quickly subsiding. Oxygen slowly returned to his brain and he held her close to him, feeling her slowly relax and mold into him.

They were damned perfect together. Somehow, he needed to figure out how to keep her in his life.

Chapter 23

Justin pulled into the parking lot at the grocery store, slowing when he noticed several cars parked at angles and his son one of a small group of kids laughing and talking to one another. Daniel was growing up so fast, standing with his friends, and quite obviously the best-looking young man in the lot. He wasn't perfect, he definitely had an attitude, but Justin remembered himself at that age, and putting his parents through hell, too.

He parked and got out of the car, willing to go into the store and leave his son alone. Justin remembered how humiliating it would have been if his parents had walked up on him while he was hanging with his friends. He grabbed a cart inside, shifting his thoughts to the steaks he planned on grilling tonight. Maybe he'd pick up some flowers for Grace as well. She was a pro at hiding her emotions, but he saw how down she was. Being attacked took more out of her than she wanted him to see.

After almost a week, the bruising on her face had faded considerably, but she still moped around his house. The only time she appeared animated was when Rachel was around. They were coming up on another Sunday and the Fall Dance. Bosley was suspended from the force for thirty days without pay and would have a court date to face charges for assault and attempted rape but was still out on a PR bond. Justin felt his blood pressure rise just thinking about Bosley forking out cash for a personal recognizance and then the judge approving it believing since Bosley was "usually" a model citizen that he wasn't a flight risk.

"You always go around looking that pissed?" Daniel's question startled Justin, and he stopped short, staring at his mop-headed son, who offered him a crooked grin in return. "I hear you beat the crap out of that cop. That's pretty cool. They don't dare take my dad to jail."

Daniel had a petite blonde on his arm who stared up at him like he'd just said the most clever thing in the world. Justin thought about explaining that if Bosley came forward and said who had laid him out, Justin would have been charged. The weasel didn't dare, though. Not to mention, hearing his son sing his praises felt good. Really good.

"We take care of our own," he told his son, and immediately saw his son's eyes darken. The Reece family trait Daniel was his own, and in his son's eyes Justin hadn't taken very good care of him. "You two hungry?" Justin asked, figuring more brownie points were in order.

"For food from here?" Daniel wrinkled his nose, shifting his attention to the aisles in front of them.

"Yup. I have no problem throwing a few extra steaks on the grill." He grinned at the little blonde clinging to Daniel's arm and was rewarded with a shy smile in return. Justin would show his son where his charm came from. He noticed the girl squeeze Daniel's arm and give him a quick nod when he looked at her. "Shop with me. You can help pick out what else we might need."

"I guess I can go with you, if I can choose what I want to eat."

Justin didn't have a problem with that at all. In fact, he was quickly reminded the easiest way to a teenage boy's heart was through his stomach. Although Justin spent over twice as much as he planned, he was convinced by the time they were loading groceries in the back of his truck it was the best time he'd had with his son in ages. Justin caught hell for stopping at the florist for flowers but didn't care.

"We should see about getting Elizabeth over here," Justin said when he pulled up in front of the house.

"Why? She's annoying." Daniel climbed out of the truck and walked to the back of it, eyeing the house and land around it and ignoring his girlfriend, who still hadn't said a word since they'd been together. "Besides, Mom won't let her come over here."

"It would be a family affair if we do," Justin argued, getting out on his side and then reaching into the back of the truck and handing groceries to his son. "And I'm sure Sylvia will let her come over. Why wouldn't she?"

Daniel looked at Justin like he'd just grown two heads. "She won't let her come over because you want her to come over," he said simply, suddenly sounding a lot wiser than he looked.

Justin nodded, understanding but not liking it. The thought of Sylvia using their kids against him pissed him off. "Thanks for the advice," he said dryly, and then helped haul the groceries into the house.

Charlie jumped in to help with groceries, while Daniel inspected what food was already there and explained to his girlfriend how this used to be his house.

"Why is she here?" Daniel asked, stopping in his tracks after finding a box of crackers in one of the cabinets and helping himself to them. He gestured with the box at Rachel, who stiffened at the question, while standing in the doorway to the kitchen.

"Rachel and her mother are staying here." Justin wasn't going to offer lengthy explanations that would be argued and analyzed. This was his home and everyone would get along, or else. "Rachel, where is your mom?"

"She's upstairs. She said we should stay out of the way."

"Nonsense." Justin was all too aware of the scowl on his son's face. "I'm going to call to have Elizabeth come over, too. Would you like that?"

"Why are you asking her? It's not her house," Daniel snapped.

"Be nice, Daniel," Justin growled. Maybe Daniel's mother was dominated by the boy, but Justin would be damned if Daniel would manipulate him for attention. And he told his son as much with a look. "Elizabeth and Rachel are in the same grade and are friends."

"Best friends." Rachel stuck out her chin defiantly, obviously oblivious to the rivalry for ranking of children. "And yes, I'd like that a lot. I'll call her if you want."

Daniel made a snorting sound, but Justin didn't need his help answering the question.

"I'll have to call her, Rachel. I'll need to clear it through her mother," Justin explained.

"And she's going to say no," Daniel added, plopping a cracker into his mouth. "What's there to drink?"

Charlie was smart enough to stay out of the conversation but did open the refrigerator and pulled out two cans of soda pop. He handed one to each teenager and then mumbled something about checking the grill.

"Rachel, go get your mother and tell her to come down and join us," Justin told the young girl, who quickly nodded, forcing her red curls to bounce around her face, and then turned and bolted up the stairs.

"So what's going on here?" Daniel demanded before Rachel reached the top of the stairs. She ran down the upstairs hallway, her small feet pattering on the floor and reminding Justin of a day gone by when his own children had raced through this house. "Are you banging that redhead, or what?"

"Daniel Reece," Justin growled, glaring at his son. "You're out of line, boy. You want me to ask if you're banging this girl?" he hissed, pointing at the blonde, who turned beet red when Justin gestured at her.

Daniel's face hardened, his mouth forming a straight line, while he took a moment to consider an appropriate comeback. Instead of consoling his girlfriend, Daniel looked down at her, apparently ignoring her imploring expression, probably that the two of them leave now, and instead thumbed in the direction of the doorway leading to the dining room.

"Go on in there and watch TV. I'm going to talk to my dad."

"But Daniel," she whimpered, her soft voice matching her pretty young features.

It occurred to Justin that this girl, who still remained nameless, was probably fifteen or so. Almost the age of the girls being raped. The thought that their perp might see her with Daniel and view her as a target to attack closer to home made Justin's blood boil.

"Go on," Daniel encouraged.

The girl lowered her head and pouted as she left the kitchen. Daniel squared off, facing his father.

"That was a low blow, Dad." Daniel tossed his head, forcing his too-long blond bangs to shift across his forehead and out of his eyes.

"If you're going to mouth off to me, you're going to get it right back." Justin decided now was as good a time as any to lay down a few quick ground rules. "You're not going to do as you please and say as you please around me without facing consequences."

"What the hell does that mean?" Daniel snapped.

"It means that every action has a reaction. You get out of line with me, you're going to know it. You respect your father and you'll get the same in return."

Daniel stared at him for a long moment. "You've walked out of my life one too many times for that speech, Dad."

"Daniel, I've never walked out of your life," he answered without hesitating. "I divorced your mother, not you. But it's a two-way street here, man. If you want me in your life today, on a regular basis, you're going to understand my rules. Take them or leave them. But you'll never walk all over me like you do your mother. Respect me, Son, and hopefully, with some work on both of our parts, we'll become good friends."

"Who says I want to be friends?"

"You're here, aren't you?"

"You're feeding me. Like I wouldn't get that at home," Daniel muttered, rolling his eyes. His features relaxed, though, and he didn't look as ready to attack as he did a moment ago.

Justin decided for now he'd take what he could get. He'd made his terms clear and wouldn't insult Daniel by repeating them and making him feel stupid.

"Yup. And when I'm in town, I'll feed you every night if you're up to it," Justin proposed. "But you're also going to understand that when I leave, I'm not running out on you. And I'm completely open to keeping in touch while I'm on cases in other cities."

Daniel shrugged like it didn't matter and finally popped open the can of pop in his hand. "If you want," he said, like he didn't care one way or another.

"I think it might be a good idea." Justin walked around Daniel, feeling the tension dissipate around him and pretty proud of himself that he'd made yet a bit more headway with his son. "Go hang out with your girlfriend," Justin said, pulling out a bottled water and unscrewing the cap. "I'm going to call your mother and prepare these steaks."

Daniel grunted and started out of the kitchen.

"And Daniel," Justin said.

His son turned around, looking at him warily. "What?"

"Keep an eye on her, okay?" Justin said, not surprised when his son bristled defensively. "She fits the profile our perp is seeking out," he added quietly, speaking to his son as if he were the adult Daniel craved to be. "And we don't want her getting hurt."

"No, we don't," Daniel said seriously. "I'll keep an eye on her."

Justin nodded, and as his son walked out of the room Grace appeared in the doorway from the hallway.

"How long have you been there?" Justin asked, and then noticed Rachel appear behind her mother.

"Just for a few," Grace said, shrugging but looking concerned. If she'd heard most of his conversation with Daniel, she didn't appear to disapprove. "Rachel said you were fixing food for everyone."

"I'm going to see what I can do about getting Elizabeth over here, and then yes, I thought it would be nice to have a big family meal."

Grace barely moved her head when she nodded and chewed her lower lip, just watching him. Whatever was on her mind, as usual, he would have to pry out of her. Turning, he knew one way to relax her, and picked up the flowers. The look on her face was priceless when he turned around.

"Justin," she whispered, grinning when he moved closer and then held the flowers out to her, just under her nose so she could breathe in their perfumed scent. "They are beautiful."

"Which is why they made me think of you," he said, and then leaned forward and kissed her on the forehead, deciding whether she agreed or not, her daughter could handle seeing that much affection between them. "Put them in water and I'm going to call my daughter."

Talking to Sylvia soured his mood. It pissed him off that he was fighting so hard to get back into his kids' life and she was going out of her way to make it harder for him. Hanging up the phone, he fought the urge not to throw it at the wall. At least he had placed the call in his room, not wanting Daniel, or anyone else, to hear him arguing with Sylvia. Justin wanted the evening to be relaxed, comfortable, and a success. Now he needed to go face two kids, one who would gloat and the other who would be upset just because his ex-wife was a bitch.

"Let me guess," Grace said from the door. "She won't let Elizabeth come over."

"Nope." He wasn't sure if Grace was just really good at sneaking up on him without him noticing or if he was so distracted trying to figure out where he stood with his kids. "It's damned hard to make headway with my kids that I haven't seen forever when she is fighting me every step of the way."

"She probably feels threatened," Grace said quietly, taking a step into his room. The comfortable-looking faded jeans she wore and pale green tank top with no bra were breathtaking. Her hair was pulled back in a loose ponytail, and long, tight curls fell to her practically bare shoulders. "But you're doing a good job, Justin. That's what counts."

"Sometimes I wonder why I even bother," he grumbled, needing to get rid of his anger somehow. It wasn't Grace's fault that his ex was a royal pain in the ass. "Daniel's right. I'll be heading out of town again on to the next case. Why hurt those I love?"

She chewed her lip, nodding and appearing to give what he said some serious thought. Her pretty blue eyes were focused on him, but her gaze drifted away and then she looked down at her fingers. "I guess if you love them then it's important that you let them know that while you're with them," she said so quietly that he barely heard her.

Justin closed the distance between him and Grace and pulled her into his arms. "That's exactly what I'm trying to do," he said, and rested his chin on her head while tucking her in against him. She felt so fucking good there and for a moment words formed in his mouth that he hadn't said to anyone in years. He swallowed them quickly. Now wasn't the time.

Grace didn't remember when she'd last been so nervous. So far, she couldn't have asked for a better weekend, even though she wasn't convinced she would enjoy it when it first started. Overhearing Justin point out to his son that he would be leaving Rockville soured her already melancholy mood. But the flowers and the little comments he'd whisper when he kissed her forehead, or pulled her in for a comforting hug, sent her a very different message. Justin was fucking with her head, which was the last thing she needed right now.

"So why the hell are you doing this?" she asked herself for somewhere around the tenth time as she drove into town alone and headed for her house.

The side streets were dark, and her house looked even darker when she pulled up in front of it and parked. If she was going to the town dance with Justin tonight, though, the few nice clothes she had were still here. Grace stared at her home, the house she barely had time to make a home before rushing out of it for the protection of herself and her daughter.

But staring at it now, Grace saw an empty shell. She stared at the dark, black windows, remembering fucking Justin inside. Then the camera set up in her living room capturing their perp on film interrupted her thoughts and sent shivers down her spine.

"Sitting here in the dark isn't going to calm your nerves any," she told herself, and unsnapped her seat belt.

Once inside, she turned on most of the lights and then went back to her bedroom to decide on a dress to wear. There weren't many choices, but she opted for a pale green dress, plain in the front, with a low-cut back. It was a straight cut that fell just above her knees. Conservative, yet sexy. Just what she wanted.

"Oh, and for the final touch," she said after turning around both ways and straining to look over her shoulder at herself in the mirror. "The combs."

For a moment she couldn't remember where she'd put the pretty Oriental hair combs that Justin had given her. Was this relationship that she panicked might be setting her up for serious heartbreak not as real as she thought it was?

"God. You would think I would remember where I put a gift if it mattered to me." She turned slowly in her room and then spotted her purse on her dresser. "It does matter to me. There's just too much shit going on right now."

Heading over to the purse she hadn't used since she started staying with Justin, she pulled out the Oriental combs and slid them into her hair.

"Perfect. They're perfect." As was everything about Justin. Which was what confused her so damned much about him.

Grace walked back to the bathroom and surveyed the results of her primping in the mirror. She wore no makeup; her hair would stay damp for a couple of hours, ensuring neat curls. The underside of her hair was darker red, almost mahogany. The red mahogany, in contrast with lighter red curls flowing down her back, looked impressive. She studied herself in the mirror—when did she start thinking of herself as attractive?

"I've never seen a more beautiful creature in all of my life."

Grace jumped, screamed, and almost fell into the shower curtain. Justin moved to her and grabbed her before she could fall.

"What the hell are you doing in here? I didn't even hear

you come in." She gasped the words. Then, embarrassed that he successfully caught her off guard and looked damned pleased with himself for doing so, she snapped, "I told you to give me an hour to come over here and get ready. It hasn't been close to an hour."

"I knew it wouldn't take you half an hour to look gorgeous." He let his gaze fall lazily down her, creating a heat inside her and making her skin tingle the longer he stared at her. "And God damn, darling. You look perfect."

He stood just inside her bathroom door, wearing a dark brown jacket that made his shoulders look even broader than usual. Underneath, the forest green button-down shirt tucked into dress trousers showed off his muscular physique and long, powerful-looking legs. Justin was mouthwatering, sexy as hell, with his dangerous good looks and roguish grin.

"I guess the green dress was a good choice," she said, touching him before she realized it. There wasn't any keeping her hands off of him, and she ran her finger down his strong chest, swearing she felt sparks explode inside when she touched him.

Justin answered by pulling her to him roughly and kissing her with so much passion she felt dizzy. Even barefoot, it was hard to maintain her balance. She struggled to breathe when he put her at arm's length.

"Get your shoes." He walked out of the bathroom back toward the living room.

Grace stared at the doorway where he'd been a moment before. In one moment he had swept her off her feet and she had fallen into his arms without a thought in the world. The next, he was gone. Maybe he was just in the other room waiting for her. But his actions reminded her that he would do this to her again—there one moment and gone the next.

If she could just hold on to her heart and not lose it completely, the pain wouldn't destroy her when he left. Even as she repeated that to herself, her heart continued feeling heavier and heavier until she could barely breathe. Hurrying into her bedroom and slipping into her brown closed-toe two-inch heels, the only pair of dress shoes she owned, she forced her thoughts off of Justin. And this time she heard him come down the hall.

"So what if Bosley is at the dance tonight?" she asked with her back to Justin.

Justin stood in her bedroom doorway and watched as she bent over to slide on her shoes. She was absolutely the most gorgeous creature he'd ever laid eyes on. And she was his date for the dance. More than that, Grace was his woman. This did a job on the old ego. She would turn every head in the hall when they walked through those doors.

"There's something we both need to take into consideration."

"What's that?" she asked, turning around and running her hands down her dress. The rich green material hugged her breasts, showing off how full and round they were, and then clung to her narrow waist and curvy hips.

"That picture we caught on camera here wasn't Bosley."

"You think he has an accomplice?" The combs Justin had given her pulled back her hair, showing off the different shades of red that made her look even prettier than usual. Something he wouldn't have believed possible.

"You said he told you that he wasn't the murderer."

"True."

"There's a chance he's not our man."

Grace stared at Justin a moment and then her blue eyes widened. "There's a chance," she muttered. "With no prints at any crime scene other than Bosley's and sperm and DNA that doesn't match any man we have on file, there will continue being a chance until we can force him to submit to being tested, or catch someone else in the act. What's your point, Justin?"

"It's Saturday night."

"Yes, and?"

"In a few hours it will be Sunday." She was following everything he said; he could tell by how she looked at him. Either she didn't want to let her thoughts travel in the same direction as his or she wanted him to spell it out for her. He opted for the latter to save them both time. "We've got to

accept the possibility that with the dance distracting everyone, our perp might very well strike again tonight."

"I don't think he will," she said without hesitating. "Because we think he might, he won't. He's methodical. We
know that. But he is also incredibly intelligent. If our man is
Bosley, and I am saying 'if,' he toyed with us when he attacked me. You didn't see how confused he was when everyone showed up. He honestly didn't think he'd get caught."

"So he thinks we expect him to attack tonight."

"I'd say yes."

"Then he goes one of two ways. He attacks, or he doesn't.
Either way we're going to be prepared." Taking her warm
small hand in his, he guided her out of her bedroom, reaching for her bedroom light and turning it off, then leading her
to the living room. "I'm going to wire you and you're going
to do the same to me. Regardless of what happens tonight,
or what doesn't happen, we're going to be ready, sweetheart."

"I don't have a problem with this," she said, watching
when he let go of her hand and picked up the small black
suitcase he'd left on her coffee table. "But why are you wir-
ing me? If our perp isn't Bosley, I'm a bit too old for him."

"No matter what happens tonight," Justin said, deciding
he wouldn't share his worst fears with her, that whoever
their guy was, he might very well go after her just because
he had a vendetta on the two of them now and knew that at a
crowded town dance with everyone's guard down Grace
would be an easy target. "I'm going to make sure you're
protected. No one will hurt you again."

She had to take off her dress, and when he touched her,
fire scorched his insides. He fastened the bugs to her, fighting with all his power to keep his hands off her breasts. Of
course, she wouldn't be wearing a bra. Justin sported a noticeable hard-on when he finally finished his task.

"I'm going to be the one to take that dress off you when
this evening is done."

"I'd like that, too," she whispered, her thick lashes flut-
tering over her sultry, glazed eyes. She looked ready for him

to fuck her right now, and it was almost too appealing of an idea to let slide.

"I'm tempted to take it off of you right now," he said, brushing his lips over hers and wondering how he'd make it through the dance with the throbbing hard-on in his pants. "Unfortunately, we need to go if we're going to make our fashionably late entrance. Before we leave, though, I want you to wear these."

She looked down between them when he opened his palm at two dangling pearl earrings.

"Justin, they're beautiful." She looked up at him and he couldn't help but smile.

"Don't take it the wrong way. I'd love to surround you with beautiful things, but these are special."

Her hands trembled when he helped slide them into the small holes in her earlobes.

"If for any reason you need me, squeeze the left earring and it will alert me." He indicated an almost unnoticeable black box attached to his belt loop.

"Do you really think this is necessary?" she asked, readjusting her hair, which didn't quite hide the earrings.

"I'm praying they aren't necessary. Let's go." *Damn it.* When had he reached the point where he didn't think he could live without her?

Chapter 24

Rockville's Fall Dance took place at the Knights of Columbus hall, half a mile out of town. They pulled into the large gravel parking lot stuffed full of parked cars. Justin parked his Chevelle alongside the building instead of in the parking lot so they wouldn't have to walk as far. He was taking his lady out on the town, and they were going to go in style.

"I didn't expect there to be so many people here." Grace looked unsure when she glanced at the parking lot full of cars and the couples who were heading inside.

"You two are definitely the most handsome couple here," Christy greeted them, once they were inside, giving Grace a hug. "I've missed seeing you down at the station," she said into Grace's ear. "I heard what Bosley tried to do, the creep."

"He didn't have time to do anything. But it was shocking for me, too," Grace added, forced to speak louder than she probably wanted to over the noise in the hall.

Justin placed his hand on Grace's bare back, knowing everyone around them was eagerly eavesdropping and Grace being attacked would be the topic of conversation for the rest of the evening. Nodding to Christy on the pretense that it was too loud to continue chatting, he guided Grace across the room toward the bar. She looked up at him as heads turned to watch them pass. Grace didn't like being the focus of everyone's attention, but tonight it was inevitable. Not only was she by far the most gorgeous woman there, but she was on his arm. And he had no problem letting the town know she was his girlfriend.

Bypassing a giggling couple, Justin put his arm around Grace and they entered a clearing in front of the bar. The first person Grace saw standing there had to be Sylvia. Grace wasn't sure if Justin stopped because he felt her body freeze or because of his own reaction to Sylvia's presence. She stood talking to an older woman with silver hair wrapped elegantly on top of her head. By the amount of jewelry the old woman wore, Grace could tell she was quite wealthy . . . or trying to look that way.

Justin's arm tightened around Grace as he began leading her toward the other end of the bar. Good, he had no desire to speak to that woman, either. Sylvia turned her head just in time to see them as they passed her. She stopped whatever she was saying in mid-sentence. Her lips pressed into a flat line, and she eyed Grace from top to bottom with little concern for her obvious actions. To make matters worse, she rolled her eyes, tossed her head, and stormed off without saying a word to the woman she'd been talking to. Grace fought the urge to roll her own eyes. Sylvia was making a fool of herself.

Justin rubbed Grace's back, and she turned quickly to look up at him. His gaze was flat, unreadable. Either he was hiding his anger or he'd shut his emotions down concerning his ex-wife. He studied Grace for a minute, and then his gaze turned, and she followed it. The old woman Sylvia had left standing at the bar clasped her hands in front of her and stood expectantly, waiting for Justin to approach.

Every muscle in Justin's body hardened and he seemed to move mechanically as he guided them over to the older woman. The song ended then and Grace was able to hear him speak clearly over the DJ's voice.

"Hello, Mrs. Hawthorne; may I present Grace Jordan?" Justin said with stiff formality.

"Well," she breathed heavily, and Grace detected the strong smell of cigarette smoke. "I guess you had to be seen with her publicly sooner or later."

Grace fought to keep her expression pleasant and extended her hand. "It's very nice to meet you, Mrs. Hawthorne."

The woman accepted Grace's hand and shook it limply. "I'm sure." She didn't smile but instead looked up at Justin, releasing Grace's hand quickly. "Shouldn't you be out working instead of socializing? That is why you're still in Rockville, isn't it? Because you have a case or something to handle? We all know you don't stay around just for loved ones," she added crisply, giving Grace a very cold once-over.

Grace stiffened, ready to defend Justin, when at the same time she argued with herself to stay quiet and hear his defense. As much as she wanted to hear it, she wanted to slam this ice-cold bitch into her place as well.

"I am working, ma'am," Justin said simply.

Mrs. Hawthorne turned her gaze to Grace and then back to Justin. "I meant at catching the rapist. We all know it isn't our dear Eugene Bosley. He wouldn't hurt any decent, respectable person in this town."

"You are out of line," Grace hissed, stepping in between Mrs. Hawthorne and Justin.

"If you'll excuse me." The old bat turned and disappeared into the crowd.

Justin put his hands on Grace's shoulders, possibly because he worried she would leap and attack. Which sounded pretty damn appealing.

"That was Sylvia's mother," Justin whispered into Grace's ear. "She made it quite clear when I returned to Rockville that she didn't approve of our divorce. She pointed out to me more than once that she stayed faithfully married for twenty-seven years until she was widowed last spring."

"She's a coldhearted bitch," Grace hissed, resenting the implication that she would have done anything to deserve being attacked.

"Mr. Hawthorne slept with every available floozy in three counties." Justin's face grew hard. "His daughter inherited his habit."

Grace didn't know what to say. Justin had never told her why he and Sylvia got divorced, and she never felt it her place to ask. The look on his face made it clear that sympathy wasn't what he wanted, and so she said nothing.

Justin ordered a ginger ale for himself, a Diet Coke for Grace, and then they mingled through the crowd. More and more people arrived, raising the noise factor in the large, high-ceilinged hall. He and Grace hadn't been there half an hour when she was sure her ears would ring well into the next day from how loud it seemed in there. As Justin held her close, moving through the crowd and speaking politely to almost every couple there, Grace spotted her neighbors whom she'd barely had time to get to know before starting to stay out at Justin's. They paused in front of one another just as the song stopped, allowing them the few minutes' break to have a conversation before the next song started playing.

"You are easily the most beautiful woman here," Lucy Nicholson said, smiling when she stopped with her husband next to Grace and faced her. "I love your hair down. I guess you can't wear it like that in your line of work."

"No, it's considered being out of uniform." Grace smiled, noting how relaxed and happy Lucy and her husband appeared to be and wondering if that kind of life was ever in the works for her. As a cop, though, Grace had vowed to protect people like the Nicholsons so they could continue leading their happy and relaxed lives. "But you look fabulous, too. I guess we're not accustomed to seeing each other dressed up."

"No, that's what I love about these things. You get to see everybody at their best." Lucy Nicholson was a breath of fresh air, and Grace couldn't help envying her innocent outlook on life. "You aren't staying at your house anymore. We've missed you and your daughter."

"Special Agent Reece felt we weren't safe there," Grace told her, knowing Lucy was politely trying to determine the accuracy of the gossip flying around town. "You know, with that murderer I was assigned to track, well, he thought Rachel and I would be safer, er, uh, if we stayed with him."

"So, it's still 'Special Agent Reece'?" Lucy's eyes twinkled.

"Lucy, of all people, I didn't think you'd listen to all that slanderous gossip," Grace teased, and felt bad when Lucy's cheeks turned scarlet. "Rachel and I share a bedroom. His house is quite large, you know. I promise you, he's been quite the gentleman."

She noticed Justin give her a quick glance as he carried on a conversation with Robert Starkey, the medical examiner. She also noticed Miss Marble stood next to the ME. Grace knew Justin had overheard her comment, and his eyes danced with delight at her concern over their reputation.

"I don't usually take to gossip." Lucy looked so earnest. "I can't help but hear it, especially at the checkout lanes. You know how it is."

Yes, Grace knew. She imagined how her presence here with Justin tonight would fuel those fires.

"Now mind you, I haven't heard anything mean about you. Oh, his ex-wife and her cronies have tried to stir up trouble, but her sinful ways are her reasons for her misery."

Grace hoped Justin hadn't been in Rockville to endure an unfaithful wife.

"I know when I heard how Justin beat up Lieutenant Bosley after he tried to attack you," Lucy added, moving closer when the next song started and speaking next to her ear, her breath smelling like mint, "of course it's wrong to fight with anyone, but that was so romantic. He's a good, honest man, Grace. You could do a lot worse."

"Thanks for your blessing." Grace couldn't help but grin. "I honestly can't say that there is a lasting relationship between us." And that was the truth. She leaned forward, and talking next to Lucy's face, she was sure Justin was paying more attention to her conversation than his own and, knowing him, could probably hear what they said over the music. "I agree that he's a very nice man, though."

Lucy giggled and then turned when her husband put his arm around her shoulder. He commented that they needed to greet some folks on the other side of the room, after nodding and smiling at Grace.

"We sure hope to see you in church more often," Lucy said seriously before her husband escorted her off. "If not for you, it's good for your daughter."

"We could really get this town talking if we took both our daughters to church together," Justin leaned and whispered to Grace after the Nicholsons had walked off. She elbowed him in the side, and he grabbed his side as if she'd hurt him.

The dance floor lights dimmed, and a slow love song began. Dr. Starkey escorted Miss Marble to the dance floor and Grace caught Justin staring down at her. His fingers trailed up her back and she shivered noticeably.

"Dance with me," he said, and leaned his head close to hers.

"I'd be honored," she told him, and allowed him to escort her to the floor where other couples were already embraced and moving to the melody.

Grace was impressed by how comfortably Justin moved her around the dance floor. The man's skills never ceased to amaze her.

He held her close, like they were two lovers who were very comfortable with each other's bodies, seemingly unconcerned that as far as the town was concerned, this was their first date. Although at first she tried to distance them at a respectable arm's length, he tucked her against his chest and rested his chin gently on her head. She relaxed her cheek along the edge of his shoulder. This was quickly becoming one of her favorite places to be.

The song ended way too soon.

"Darling, there's something very dangerous about dancing with you." Justin's breath wisped through her hair.

When she looked up, the fire smoldering in his gaze raced through her, making the crowded dance floor seem suddenly way too warm.

"I do believe you'd have fun starting scandalous talk about us," she accused, but couldn't hide a smile.

"All of it's just gossip anyway." He brought her fingers to his mouth and nibbled the flesh on her knuckles.

"They don't have any proof right now," she pointed out.

He pulled her into his arms and lowered his lips to her before she could stop him, then kissed her possessively, right there in the middle of the dance floor.

"There." He smiled as he pulled back, looking mighty proud of himself. "Now they have their proof."

"I suppose I should walk away from you at your attempt to tarnish my reputation," she threatened, although she wished he would kiss her again.

"I'd follow you, and then we would make a scene." He grinned and kissed her again before sweeping her around to dance to the next song.

"We need to go outside for some fresh air," he told her as he escorted her from the dance floor after they'd danced to several more songs.

"Actually," she said as she looked around the crowded room, "where are the bathrooms?"

He escorted her through the different groups of people, aware of the many looks they received, most of them approving. They passed a table where Sylvia sat with her mother and Todd Wilkins. Justin felt sorry for the guy, having to sit there and listen to the two women berate everyone else in the room. God, Justin had heard enough of those conversations for a lifetime. His sympathy for the guy faded when Justin realized the lawyer was giving Grace the once-over. Justin's grip on her arm instinctively became more possessive. *My woman.* If they accomplished anything tonight it would be that the good people of Rockville would know Justin Reece had a new woman in his life.

"If you're in there longer than five minutes, I'm coming in there," Justin told her when they reached the entrance to the women's bathroom.

"I'll try not to primp too long." She patted her still slightly damp curls and turned, putting an extra shake in her walk as she pulled open the bathroom door. Grace glanced over her shoulder at him and grinned broadly before disappearing into the small room that appeared packed with women. He would be standing here waiting for her for a while.

Grace swore she was in the bathroom forever and had to desperately use the facilities by the time it was her turn. She didn't know anyone in the public restroom and most conversation was about people she didn't know. Pushing open the door and walking into the crowd and noise again, Grace saw that this wasn't her town, this was Justin's town, even if he was hardly here. Everyone knew and respected him. What a wonderful feeling it must be, knowing no matter when you returned to your hometown, it was there, waiting for you, like a sturdy rock that would never crumble away.

Grace spotted Justin talking to Roger Swanson from the fire department, who had ahold of Justin's arms and grinned as he spoke. Justin's gaze met hers as she walked out of the restroom. Apparently, Roger was telling him a joke or something, because Justin laughed and slapped the fireman on the back.

She glanced around the room before closing the distance between them. Everyone had loosened up as the alcohol began taking its toll on the crowd. She noticed more laughter, and the room seemed noisier, like an echoing boom. Going outside for some fresh air sounded like a really good idea.

There were three sets of glass doors at the front of the room, and Justin stood near the closest one to her. People moved between them, blocking her view of him and then opening up, so she easily could see his relaxed stance, those dark eyes continually looking in her direction, waiting for her. The best-looking, most respected man in the room, and he was hers.

Her man.

Grace floated, feeling exceptionally pretty in her dress and heels, with her hair flowing over her shoulders and her ornate combs actually keeping her hair in place, as well as the earrings that she could feel dangling from her ears. Granted she was bugged and knew work was never more than a breath away, but for that moment she indulged in the fantasy of no cares, no worries, other than returning to the side of her perfect man.

"It's time to go, Grace." The voice that hissed in her ear at the same time cold fingers gripped her arm sounded vaguely familiar. Like a nightmare trying to shove its way in on her perfect fantasy.

"What?" She tried turning and at the same time pulling away from whoever had grabbed her.

"You heard me the first time." His cold, heartless tone hadn't changed in ten years.

The possessiveness she'd felt from Justin, and had enjoyed, was nothing compared to the manipulative, belittling tone that whispered like the devil in her ear. But there was no way. She looked at the man who held on to her arm strong enough to cut off her circulation and led her through the crowd to the door at the other end of the room.

"Who are you? And wait a minute." She dug in her heels when they were at the other side of the dance floor, staring at the black hair on the back of the head of the man who pulled her to the door. "I'm not going anywhere with you. Let go of me right now before I make a scene."

"You wouldn't dare," he hissed, turning and glaring at her.

Grace stared into a man's face she'd never seen before. But his size, his voice, and those black eyes that were colder and meaner than anything hell could possibly offer stole her breath. Cold sweat spread over her flesh and when she tried making a sound it came out as a squeak. In that one moment that she panicked, while her mind tried to figure out who she was really staring at, he yanked her out the back door. He was so aggressive that she stumbled over her own feet and fell into him as the back door to the hall closed behind them, trapping the voices and music of the dance.

"You always were such a stupid, stupid slut," he growled, dragging her across gravel toward a running squad car.

"Who are you?" She'd never seen this man before. Her mind was playing tricks on her, telling her that because of his harsh tone, his brutal grip on her, and the evil look on his face he could possibly be a dead man.

"Like I said, stupid bitch. Get in the fucking car." He yanked open the back door to the squad car—to a Rockville sheriff's department car—and grabbed her hair, yanking her forward until she doubled over. Then he shoved her into the backseat. The smell of cigar smoke turned her stomach. "What a joke that they let you become a cop. Proof of how fucking stupid most people are. Goddamned cunt. Move over."

Grace tried to look away. Her level of confidence and feeling that she was pretty seemed to be fading away faster than it had arrived. She wanted to look at Justin, be reminded that she was beautiful. She wanted to see the passion in his eyes. She wanted to see how much he wanted to give her.

But no, she saw Master. Heard Master. Her hands slapped against the leather bench seat and the side of her cheek pressed against the seat. She reached up to adjust her left earring and squeezed it, then fought to move to a sitting position. Her stomach churned.

Grace grabbed the door handle of the other back door and wasn't surprised that it was locked from the front. She was trapped. The man climbed in next to her and the door closed. Before she could right herself, the squad car's tires squealed over the gravel and then hauled ass out of the parking lot. She saw Justin's Chevelle, parked alongside the building, as they drove by.

God help her! This time she would kill the motherfucker for good.

Chapter 25

Justin managed to smile and laughed politely again while Swanson told yet another lewd joke. The man had had one too many beers tonight. He was off duty, and Justin knew Swanson's wife would drive them home. The guy worked hard, put in long hours, and had a high-stress job. Didn't they all? It was fair that he had an opportunity to unwind like this from time to time.

Justin looked toward Grace. A group of people walked into him, heading outside for fresh air. He held the door for them, wishing they would move faster, and stepped to the side just a bit to keep his eye on Grace. He brushed into one of the women heading outside.

"Come on now, Justin, you can do better than that, can't you?" The young lady batted her lashes at him.

Another time, in another life, he might have stayed and flirted with the outgoing young women. Not tonight . . . not anymore. An incredible redhead would be by his side in the next moment. And Justin didn't want any other woman than her.

He let go of the door when the last of them left and moved toward Grace. She wasn't there! Where the hell was she?

The small box that he'd slipped into his trousers buzzed. The vibration tore through him like a vicious storm. All his senses went to red alert. Grace had squeezed her left earring. She needed him. *Where the hell was she?*

People laughed and talked, but there was no sign of Grace.

He moved quickly to the entrance of the bathroom and scanned the group of mingling people surrounding him. There was no sign of her. The woman simply couldn't disappear into thin air.

The narrow black box vibrated again.

He grabbed his cell and quickly contacted one of the officers on duty out in the parking lot.

"I can't hear you, so just listen." Justin barked instructions as he pushed through the noisy crowd toward the middle of the room. He stood facing the three sets of glass doors. "Grace is missing. I saw her less than two minutes ago. I want officers outside every entrance. Detain her on sight, and arrest anyone she's with."

Justin scanned the crowd in front of the doors. There wasn't any sign of her anywhere. This just didn't make sense. Turning slowly, he scanned the dance floor, wondering if possibly someone had hauled her out for a dance. She wouldn't push her earring because she didn't want to dance with someone, would she?

Suddenly Justin's heart leapt into his throat and lodged there while every inch of him tightened to stone. There she was! He was positive. Disappearing out the back door with someone holding on to her. Justin damn near knocked everyone in his path out of his way as he rushed to the back door, shoving it open hard enough that it banged against the wall next to it. He leapt into the night air just as a vehicle squealed around the corner of the building.

Justin couldn't believe it. His eyes were playing tricks on him. All he saw driving away was a squad car. He raced around the building as far as his car while flipping his phone open once again.

"Someone identify that squad car leaving the Knights of Columbus parking lot right now," he yelled, feeling a vein pulse painfully in his temple.

Grace fought to keep her thoughts in order. She squeezed her earring one more time for good measure and prayed Justin had his eye on her and on the squad car. The listening devices attached to her skin itched terribly. She would have to plug the man next to her for information. Get as much out of him as she could. *Anything you say will be used against you in a court of law.*

"Why are you doing this?" She adjusted herself in the seat and tugged her dress toward her knees, then dared look at the man sitting next to her.

His arm came around her, and although she scooted as far from him as possible, there wasn't anywhere to go in the backseat. He hugged her against him, wrapping his arm around her neck and then covering her mouth with his hand. She breathed in Man's World cologne and the faint smell of cigars. God, she was going to puke.

It couldn't be. There was no way this was . . .

"Not so fast, my love," his voice purred, sounding so familiar that the past ten years seemed to disappear from her memory. "Don't say too much until we get those bugs off of you. Now don't look at me like that. I know you're wired. Reece isn't stupid." He took his hand off her mouth and moved it down to her neck, keeping his touch sickeningly gentle. "No, he's not stupid at all. He found the best that there is, and tried to claim you as his own. Problem is, you're already mine."

"No, I'm not, you son of a bitch; now get your hands off me." She glared at him, and he pulled his hand away slowly, looking offended.

When his hand went down to her leg, she said quickly, "We're in a police car, headed west."

"You stupid little bitch!" he snarled, and slapped her hard across the face.

Grace screamed from the pain, but that was nothing compared to the pain as he grabbed her lower lip and twisted it, pulling her to him. Try as she would, she couldn't talk with her mouth held open and her lower lip pulled out. All she could do was whimper in pain. "If things get rough for you, remember you're the one that started it. I'm an innocent man and your paranoia has ruined my life. Well, it's going to end, tonight!"

He reached into his coat pocket and pulled out a piece of paper. "Remember this?"

She looked at the paper as he shook it open, and her eyes jumped from it to his face. He let go of her lip, and her hands went to her mouth. It felt like her lip was several inches larger.

"Read it. Let Reece and whoever else might be listening hear the truth for themselves." He shook the paper in front of her face.

"What is it?" She stared at it, baffled, while hysteria built inside her. She couldn't think straight from the pain, and he shook the paper so violently that she couldn't see the words on it.

"Read it," he yelled. "It's time you faced up to the truth."

She blinked tears out of her eyes and focused on the piece of paper being held out in front of her. At the top of the page the red stamped word "Duplicate" caught her eye. She looked down the page and saw the small typed words "District of Columbia." Below that, in fancy calligraphy were the two words "*Marriage License.*"

"Tell me what it is," he said, using that calm tone he always used before administering serious pain.

Grace trembled so hard she could hardly speak. "It's a marriage license," she stammered, her mouth hurting worse than when Bosley hit her.

"Good girl. Now read the names on it out loud. This is for your own good, Grace." He turned in his seat so he faced her, and all she could see was blackness out the window behind him. It was all a nightmare. She'd had so many of them, and this was just one more.

He snapped her back to reality.

"Read it." His stone-cold voice sent chills down her spine.

She read, " 'Groom's name: Richard Lee White. Residence: Washington, D.C.' " She paused, and then looked up at him in terror. "This is a lie."

"No, it isn't, sweetheart. Keep reading." He spoke quietly, but with the smoothness of ice. "Tell me who the bride is."

"You forged this."

"No, I didn't. You were there. It's the real thing." His eyes burned her while his voice brought chills. "Now read it out loud so we can end this crazy ordeal."

Tears fell down her face, blinding her vision. This was worse than any nightmare.

"Who is the bride?"

She shook her head violently.

"Grace, tell me who the bride is on this marriage license." His free hand went up around her neck, promising more pain with the gentleness of his touch.

"It says 'Grace.'" She blurted out. "But it's a lie. I'm not your wife."

"Yes, you are, and you have been for over ten years now." His fingers twined through her hair.

"No, I'm not. You're insane. But this time, I'm going to be your worst nightmare." Grace prepared to be hit again, but he simply shook his head sadly.

"Poor Grace. No, dear, you aren't a nightmare. And neither am I. Once the FBI investigates all of this a bit further, they'll see that they foolishly let their rapist out on his own recognizance. When I learned that you were here, in the same town as that insane cop who was raping women everywhere, I hurried to get you as soon as I could." He ran his hands through her curls, and she slid away from him.

"None of this will hold up. You've forged that piece of paper. Your crimes are too numerous for a stunt like this to get you out of them. You're a murderer, a kidnapper, and a rapist."

"There's nothing I need to hold up, as you put it, dear. I didn't rape or murder anyone. I can see how you led Reece and the rest of this town on with your disillusioned thinking. I would have thought a year and a half with that psychiatrist would have gotten you through all this. He was the best one I could find for you. When you disappeared on me with our daughter, it took me a while to figure out where you were. Is Rachel okay?"

His words had her head spinning. Nothing he said made

any sense, but at the same time his calm, chilling tone made it even harder to make his words register in her mind. The eyes. The voice. His hand. His body. All of it matched the man who had abused her for so many years. Richard Lee White. The White mansion. It was him. It couldn't be, but it was him. She stared into those heartless, cold eyes.

"You keep my daughter out of this," she snapped at him.

His smile scared her to death. "I'm sure Reece will verify every word he's heard here, Grace. He has the ability to access our daughter's birth certificate. In time, we'll get you back to your normal self. I love you, sweetheart, and I know we can work through this." He patted her hand, and she pulled it back.

"I watched you burn to death," she hissed at him.

"Good girl. Some of it is still in your memory. That's good." His calm, sadistic tone wasn't half as evil as the cruel, menacing look he gave her. "Now if I didn't love you and my daughter as much as I do, wouldn't I have pressed charges for you burning my home to the ground and trying to kill me? Once we get you back on your medication, all will be fine."

"You're fucking insane," she growled, praying Justin heard every word they said. "And you're proving it by coming forward like this. But that's okay. I don't mind watching you rot in prison after you're arrested."

"No one is getting arrested. There won't be any lawyers, and there won't be a courtroom. You know as well as I do that a wife can waive her right to testify against her husband."

So, that's why he did it. He still believed she would do as he said. Grace looked down at her hands. She held them together so tightly that her knuckles were white. He tried cuddling her against him and she pulled away and then turned to look out the window. He wouldn't get her compliance . . . not this time.

They entered a parking lot on the far side of town. They were in a car lot, and they parked along a row of mobile homes. The driver, dressed in a police uniform, although Grace didn't recognize him, opened the driver's side door and walked away from the car into the darkness.

"Where's he going?" Grace continued to stare out the window. She hoped something would be said that would identify where they were.

"He's securing the area."

A moment later the cop appeared along the side of the trailer. "It's all good, Rick."

"Let's go." Rick pulled her across the seat, digging his fingers so deep into her arm she swore he pressed bones together. Pain shot up her shoulder as he practically dragged her from the car and across the parking lot and then pushed her up aluminum stairs into a small living room.

She realized the mobile home had been secured by nailing black towels over each window. It would be difficult to tell that there was anyone in the trailer from the outside once the lights were turned on.

"Everything's done," the small man said as he walked to the door.

"Call me at once if anyone enters the parking lot—no matter how harmless they may appear," Rick instructed, and then, without a response, the man left, shutting the door behind him.

"Now then, beautiful, let's get those bugs off of you." Rick didn't smile and he didn't move.

Grace's mind raced. Was there any way out of this? She would have to take her dress off, and other than silky green underwear, she wasn't wearing any other clothes.

"What makes you think I'm bugged?" She matched his cold glare. He would learn quickly she wasn't a fucking doormat anymore.

"Grace," he said soothingly as he moved toward her. "I've seen you without clothes on a million times. And I hardly think Reece would bring you out without some kind of insurance that he could protect you. God knows I would."

She backed away from him, grateful that her eyes were too dry for tears. The backs of her legs hit the couch, and she struggled to maintain her balance. Rick grabbed her arm and spun her around before she could regain her balance. He unzipped her dress, sending chills down her spine.

"That was pretty clever of you to put black towels over all the windows to make the trailer appear abandoned. I hope you didn't waste money on designer towels." She needed to find things to say to enlighten Justin on where she was without clueing Rick in on what she was doing. Master wasn't an idiot, though.

God. No! Not Master! Never, ever again her fucking master. He might be an insane, demonic asshole and dangerous as hell, but if she stayed calm, remained levelheaded, she would win.

Not to mention, losing this time wasn't an option.

"Why did you forge the wedding license, Rick? I'd really love to know what insane thinking twists around in that brain of yours."

He ripped the listening devices from her body and dropped them into a small black bag. He then spun her around and forced her arms to her sides, causing the dress to fall to her waist.

She lowered her head, feeling the same humiliation she'd experienced for so many years in his presence. He slid the dress past her waist and let it fall to her ankles. He then pulled her underwear away from her rear end and reached around and pulled it away from the front of her. Apparently satisfied there were no more bugs on her, he let her underwear slap back up against her body and picked up the small black bag and walked to the kitchen.

She quickly stooped down and pulled her dress back up, then struggled to zip it back up. Rick put the small black bag into a larger backpack and then zipped it closed. It was then that she realized he wasn't wearing any gloves. His fingerprints would be all over her body as well as in this trailer. God, she hoped Justin had her bugged long enough to figure out where they were.

"Why have you done this, Rick?" she asked, collapsing on the couch, and then crossed her legs casually while glancing around at the sparsely furnished living area.

"You're not that stupid, are you?" He grunted and moved to the fridge. "Good, they remembered to get beer."

He pulled out two imported beers, twisted off the lids, and brought one of them to her. When she simply stared at the outstretched beer, he shrugged and placed it down on the side table next to her. He then sat in the reclining chair next to the couch and took a long drink from his bottle.

"We shouldn't have to wait more than twenty minutes or so," he said, and then gave her a close look. "You know, Grace, I know you hate my guts—"

"That's the understatement of the century," she snapped at him.

"You've always known when to shut that stupid brain of yours off and simply do what you're supposed to do. That's what always made you beautiful. You know how to be a slut." He actually sounded sincere. "No other girl ever possessed your skills. I told myself for years that you were too old, too used up, to come after. But God damn it, Grace. You're too fucking beautiful, too good and well trained, to turn over to a dimwit like Reece."

"Oh, so now I'm beautiful?" She balled her hands into fists and leaned toward him. "I honestly don't know that I'll ever truly understand the mind of an insane man, Rick. My brain has never shut off. I've never been a slut. You're sick. Do you see that? Do you realize at all how incredibly sick you are?"

Rick grinned. "You've always been beautiful, and perfect." Apparently he didn't hear or register any of her other comments. "I require obedience. A woman who can't blindly obey and please her master doesn't deserve to live. You'd be amazed, Grace, at how incredibly patient I am. Every woman I've ever taken in, I've given her the opportunity to show me she could be my slave, serve me and obey me the way a slut should." He shrugged indifferently, as if somehow all of this were common knowledge to anyone. "I regretted killing every one of them. But when I came here and knew you were here, I wanted you to know it was me. I knew if I doused each one of them with my cologne you would remember. And with your memory revived, so is your training."

Grace wasn't qualified to play psychiatrist and decipher

why Rick thought and believed what he said. One glance at his face, though, showed he was more serious than a heart attack with everything he said. For some reason, Rick really believed women should be owned and used as he saw fit. Unfortunately, he saw fit to rape, abuse, mutilate, and kill them. "Where are we going now?" she asked calmly, as if they were discussing nothing more serious than the weather.

"You're going to love our new home. It's actually larger than our old home, and it's finished now. That's why I decided it was time to get you." He relaxed in his chair, crossing one leg over the other, and smiled at her.

She ignored his joviality. "How many women have you raped and murdered so far?"

He leaned forward and looked at her shrewdly. "I don't want to hear you mention any other women ever again. I'm serious, Grace. There's no reason for you to be jealous of them at all. Do you understand?"

"Not really." She returned his intent stare. "Why do I have to go with you then? What's in it for me? I might not like the state you've chosen, or the climate. Not to mention I have a daughter to raise."

Rick stood up and paced across the room, then turned and faced her. "Your getting pregnant was an accident. Those were your words, if I remember correctly. I did everything in my power to keep you from getting pregnant. That kid isn't my fault. She's with family. Your uncle will see to her."

Grace wanted to lunge at him for his indifference toward the daughter who mourned his supposed death.

"And I have a beautiful mansion that sits in the middle of fifty acres. You'll have servants to see to your every need. We'll move in the circles of the extremely wealthy. There's no lady in this world for me other than you. I want you at my side. We can even get married for real if you like."

"I thought you already saw to that." She glared at him as she spoke. "You're a creep, Rick. A scum and a lowlife. I'll never be the way I was before . . . no matter how much you hurt me. You might as well kill me right now. I will not go anywhere with you."

"But you would stay here and raise my daughter with another man. A daughter you wouldn't have if it weren't for me." She watched his expression change and the cruel, heartless monster reappear.

"Rick, I really have nothing to say to you." She crushed herself into the corner of the couch and started rubbing her left earring. The town wasn't that big. Justin had to be close.

The sound of a phone ringing made her jump and almost caused her heart to explode. She thought she heard Rick stifle a laugh before he answered his mobile.

"Well, dear," he said when he hung up the phone. "Looks like we need to hurry if we're going to catch our flight."

"Our flight?" She looked up at him.

"Yeah, there's a handy deserted airfield just north of here." He smiled and walked over to her.

Damn, if only she were still bugged.

Chapter 26

"I don't understand, Reece." The young agent sat inside the unmarked FBI van parked at the outer edge of the Knights of Columbus parking lot. They'd set up a makeshift console in order to listen in on Grace and Rick's conversation. "We heard him talking while he disabled the bugs you planted. How are we still hearing him?"

Justin paced outside the van. The music from the dance strayed outside, but he only focused on the bantering between Grace and Rick. Justin hardly heard the rookie's question.

Rick wouldn't slip through Justin's fingers.

"Reece?" the agent broke his train of thought. "How are we hearing this?"

"She's wearing hair combs with monitoring devices in them." His mobile rang and he grabbed it.

"Reece," Special Agent Applebee said. "Do you have a confirmation on where the local police patrol cars are in town?"

"They're all over the place." Justin pinched the top of his nose. "What's the squad number?"

"That's just it. It says seventeen, but I thought you told me there were only eleven cars. I'm in a trailer park."

"I know where it is. Do you see an officer?" Justin bolted out of the van and slid in behind the driver's seat of his car, gunning the engine to life.

"The car is back in the darker part of the lot. I couldn't tell you if there's anyone in it or not."

"Check it out. I'm sending backup." Justin put in a quick call to the local dispatch to advise of a potential car disguised to look like one of their own. Applebee cut in before Justin finished talking to Dispatch.

"Wait a minute; we've got activity here."

"What's going on?"

"Hey, Reece!" the agent in the van broke in over Applebee, his excited tone making his voice crack. "We've got a location."

"What?" Justin leapt out of the car. "Where? What did they say?" Immediately he was cursing himself for missing out on some of the conversation.

"White just said something about a deserted airfield."

"They're headed there now?" Adrenaline pumped furiously through his veins. *I'm going to nail you to the wall, you son of a bitch.*

"Yup. White just said they need to hurry or they'd miss their flight."

"Keep monitoring." He jumped back into his car. He called back Applebee and told him to stay on them, but be sure to keep out of sight. This was his fucking bust.

For once he was actually glad he grew up in this part of the country. He knew the country roads like the back of his hand and flew out of the parking lot in a cloud of dust, ignoring the few locals who hurried to their cars thinking they could keep up with him and witness a show. He quickly made several calls, issuing orders and answering questions. All the while, he mindlessly zigzagged from one county road to another, confident no one followed him, until he came to an open field that he knew bordered the runway.

He parked his car and walked through the field toward a small private plane. The small plane rumbled, but no one stood outside.

His heart pumped, and his thoughts raced as he considered all possibilities. The only way to know the plane's destination was to get on board. Rick and Grace would be showing up any minute, and Justin had to decide what to do quickly. He could arrest the man on the spot. He had motive, witnesses, documentation, and the manpower.

The son of a bitch would go down tonight! Grace would be safe. Rockville would be safe. His children would be safe.

Applebee parked on the other side of the field. Special Agents Miller and Hoffman also waited in ambush. Cliff Bogfrey had five other agents reporting to the scene as well.

One loose end remained. Justin wanted confirmation as to whether Bosley was connected with White or not. If he was, two men might die tonight. Justin could save the state a hell of a lot of taxpayers' money if there wasn't a trial. As outraged as he was right now, killing one or both of them sounded like a beautiful plan to him.

Justin reached the side of the plane just as headlights beamed in his face. The car was still quite a ways down the road but would be here in minutes. Justin raced up the portable stairs attached to the side of the plane.

He found himself in a small, comfortable room set up like a living room, complete with a wet bar and a large-screen television. Pulling his gun, he moved toward the cockpit.

"Hold it right there." He aimed his gun at the empty cockpit.

The plane was empty! He scanned the navigational equipment and then pushed the buttons on his phone.

"Applebee, I'm in the plane. There's no one here." His heart pounded adrenaline through his body as he kept his attention on the entrance of the plane.

"The squad car I saw at the car lot just pulled up, and five people entered the terminal," Applebee told him. "We've got men outside the building. We can take them down right now if you want."

Justin pinched his nose again. A migraine threatened. He couldn't wait too long and risk Grace being hurt. "Give it a few more minutes. I want any accomplices working with White. We're going to clean this up once and for all."

"No. We've identified Rick White and Grace Jordan. There are three other men. There's the driver of the car, and the other two appear to be the pilot and co-pilot." Applebee also sounded strained from all of this. "Justin, just say the word and we can all go home."

"Damn it, I need to know if Bosley or Milton is working with White," Justin growled, but then forced himself to calm down. He needed to think clearly. "Wait until they board the plane."

He scanned the equipment again, wishing he knew better how to determine if the plane had a pre-plotted course. Where was White's new home?

"Heads-up, Reece. They're headed your way."

Justin looked around the cockpit quickly and slipped into a small coat closet just as they entered the plane.

"Get us out of here, boys. I've got faith in Reece. He'll figure this out sooner or later. Fortunately, he has a history of always being later." Rick laughed and Grace squealed.

Justin tightened his fists and forced himself to stay put.

"Sorry, darling, but you picked the wrong knight in shining armor. I told you he would be nothing but a disappointment to you."

Justin heard the doors of the plane being closed.

"You men are fools working for this man," he heard Grace say. "Don't do this and I know I can get you out of any felony charges."

"Shut up, sweetheart," Rick snarled. "Boys, get this beast off the ground, and give me some time to make our unhappy guest more comfortable."

Two men were laughing as they entered the cockpit and shut the door behind them.

"That one is quite the beauty." A large man, obviously the pilot, sat down and began flipping switches.

"Yeah. White says she's his girlfriend, but she doesn't

seem too impressed with him." The co-pilot sat down and secured his seat belt.

"White is full of shit. But, whatever, he pays well. I just ignore the rest." The pilot snorted.

"Yeah, I try not to pay attention to what is going on. There will always be dirty cops and dirty government men. Anyone working for that insane motherfucker needs his head examined, though."

"He's paying you," the pilot said, laughing.

"Fuck you, man."

Justin stepped out of the closet and pressed his gun into the back of the pilot's head.

"I'm Special Agent Justin Reece with the FBI," he whispered calmly. "Listen carefully: You two cooperate, and do as you're told, and we'll keep you out of prison."

"I've got a family." The co-pilot raised his hands in surrender. "I'll do whatever you say."

"That's what I need to hear." These two would be no problem. "Now, do I have your cooperation, sir?" He nudged the gun into the pilot's neck.

The pilot nodded quickly.

"Good choice. Now, sit tight, gentlemen." Justin lowered his gun and reached for his phone. They wouldn't be any trouble; hired help seldom was.

"Applebee, the cockpit is secured." Justin plugged his earpiece into his phone so his hands were free. "And I do believe that I have all of my answers." He smiled at the two terrified-looking pilots.

"Stand by; Bogfrey wants to talk to you."

Justin heard a click and knew Applebee had established three-way when Bogfrey's voice came through.

"Reece, what's going on?" Bogfrey sounded annoyed.

"The cockpit is secured, sir. The pilots are willing to cooperate."

"Does White know you're on board?"

"Not yet."

"Applebee, the airport is secure?"

"Yes, sir."

"Good. Reece, bring White in."

"Ten four." Justin mentally made a plan of attack and then focused his attention once again on the nervous men sitting in front of him.

"Okay, boys, this is a wrap. Shut this beast down. Don't try anything foolish, or your wives could end up widows." Both men looked up at him before quickly diverting their attention back to the consoles in front of them.

He watched momentarily until he heard the engines shut down. Justin knew this would trigger Rick's attention and made his next move quickly. He turned from the pilots, feeling comfortable with the fact that they wouldn't try anything foolish.

"Okay, Applebee, bring your boys in." Justin opened the door behind him.

His attention riveted to Rick leaning over Grace on the couch. She'd shoved herself into the corner. Her hair was disheveled, and the side of her face was swollen and bruised.

"Get the hell off of her!" Justin growled with enough ferocity to make Grace jump and scream.

Justin grabbed Rick by his shirt and yanked him backward. But Justin got no resistance and stumbled at the sight of blood everywhere. Grace jumped off the couch and backed up quickly. She held a bloody knife in her hand and pointed it angrily at Rick.

"You're never going to touch me again, you scum! You bastard!" For a second she didn't seem to notice Justin was in the room. Then slowly the knife in her hand began to quiver, and her entire body began to shake.

Justin held Rick up while the man's hands went to the puncture wound in his stomach.

"Why, you little bitch!" He seemed surprised that she'd overcome him, and apparently with his own knife. He turned to look at Justin as the outer doors of the airplane opened up and the room filled with FBI agents. Justin released him to the agents, who grabbed him quickly

"Better call paramedics," Justin said into his earpiece.

"Well, I'll be damned." Rick looked up at Justin while the men who held him forced him toward the door. "I didn't think you had it in you, Reece." He snorted, then gave Grace a parting glance before he was escorted off the plane. "You take good care of her, you hear?"

"Get him the hell out of here," Justin snarled, and then turned his attention to Grace. "I'm sorry I took so long," he whispered, and gently reached up to stroke her hair.

"Oh, Justin," she cried, collapsing in his arms.

Chapter 27

"Can you be here by five?"

"Uncle Charlie, I just feel weird about coming over to Justin's house when he's been in D.C. for the past week and you're the one doing the inviting." Grace sat at her kitchen table and stared at the classified sections from several different newspapers. She doodled absently in the margin of one of them. "What time did he say he was getting in?"

"He said he should be here around six, and he wants you and Rachel to be here. The man's been gone a week. I would think you'd want to see him." It sounded like Uncle Charlie was playing with pots and pans in the background. "I'm roasting salmon. We'll have fettuccine Alfredo and a spinach salad. Oh, and I got some fillets for the kids."

"Sounds awesome." Not that she would be able to eat a bite.

Justin had called her once while out of town. He'd left early the next morning after Rick White, Eugene Bosley, and Sam Milton were arrested. Serena Blazer was also arrested, charged with obstructing the law and faking a rape to help out her boyfriend, Bosley. Justin left the day after all the arrests were made, as did all the FBI agents.

Grace simply had no idea where she stood with him. She was unemployed and having little luck finding work. She wouldn't be able to stay in her house much longer without income coming in. It bothered her to pull Rachel out of school during the school year, but Grace was about to the point where she would have to look elsewhere for employment. The whole situation really sucked.

"It's all Justin's idea." Uncle Charlie chuckled mischievously. "You'll be here, won't you?"

"Of course we'll be there."

"You know, Sylvia even agreed to have Elizabeth here for tonight."

"What time will she be there?"

"She said she'd have her here by five." Uncle Charlie knew that would do the trick.

"Fine. We'll be there at six. I have no desire to see that woman," Grace said defiantly.

"Good. So, how's the job hunt going?"

"There's nothing out there, unless I want to go into clerical work. You know I can't sit at a desk all day." Her pen ripped a hole into the newspaper. "I'm afraid I'm going to have to go national to stay in law enforcement."

"Well, it'll all work out, sweetheart. Now, get that little girl of yours in order, and pretty yourself up." Uncle Charlie blew a kiss through the phone and hung up like the true easterner that he was—without saying good-bye.

Justin would be home tonight!

She took a hot bath with some of her fragrant bath beads and helped Rachel into clean clothes. Nerves tingled all over her.

In the past month and a half something had ignited between her and Justin. They'd moved to hot and heavy quickly. Now a week without him and she had no clue where she stood.

Rachel was incredibly helpful. She couldn't wait to spend time with Elizabeth. Rachel and Grace were finally clean and in order and it was only five thirty. It wouldn't even take ten minutes to drive out there, and she wasn't going to show up early.

So she spent the time in her bedroom changing from outfit to outfit, trying to decide what was appropriate. She didn't want to look too promiscuous, but she didn't want to look drab, either. Rachel lay on Grace's bed offering advice until they mutually decided on a pair of jeans with a black cashmere sweater.

"Okay, let's go. We're as ready as we'll ever be."

"I've *been* ready." Rachel rolled her eyes.

And as predicted, they were out at the ranch house within ten minutes. Rachel jumped out of the car, racing for the house as if she'd finally come home.

Rachel charged in the front door without knocking, leaving Grace to shut their doors and follow her. There were incredible squeals and shrieks when Rachel and Elizabeth collided inside the front door.

"Didn't you two see each other earlier today at school?" Justin never thought he'd love the sounds of happy children in his home as he did now.

"Yeah, but we like it best when we're together here." His daughter gave him a quick hug and then ran out of the room with Rachel at her heels.

"I'm glad to hear that," he said after them, then turned to the open front door.

Grace stood in the doorway. All the stress from the past week drained from his body at the sight of her.

"Hi." She nibbled her lower lip, searching his face with those glowing blue eyes he'd dreamed about nightly while away from her.

"Hello there. You look beautiful."

He ran his fingers down her damp curls, then pulled her into his arms. She collapsed into him, swallowing a cry that came out like a sigh. An electrical charge rippled inside him when her hands glided up his chest. Every muscle inside him twitched, need hitting him harder than if he'd been punched in the gut. He lifted her chin and melted at the moisture that pooled in her eyes.

"I missed you." He needed to say more, tell her that he loved her, how terribly he had missed her. She loved him. He saw it in her expression, in the tears of joy she fought to contain, in the way her heart pounded and her nipples hardened.

An explosion of heat scorched his senses the second he brushed his lips over hers. He wrapped his arms around her, unable to get her close enough, and she opened her mouth to him. So many things needed to be said at once. Tasting her had to come first, though.

She broke the kiss, breathing heavily as she pressed her lips to his chin. "I missed you, too."

The strangest sensation tripped through his insides. For a moment it terrified him, and he straightened, clearing his throat. He blinked moisture from his eyes and stared over her head until he found control again.

"It's great to be home for a while."

"Where are you going next? So now what?" She stepped back, a rush of worry plummeting through her.

Now they would spend the rest of their lives together.

"Now, we enjoy some fabulous food." He wrapped his arm around her and led her to the kitchen, knowing he hadn't just answered her question.

Uncle Charlie didn't mention that Doris Agnew would be joining them as well. The older woman moved around the kitchen like an old pro while she and Uncle Charlie put the final touches on the meal. The girls sat at the kitchen table, eagerly wiping their fingers across a mixing bowl. Already their faces were covered in chocolate.

"Well, it's about time you got here." Uncle Charlie beamed when he turned around and saw his niece standing next to Justin. He tapped Doris' arm and she turned away from the stove and smiled. "Doris, have you met my niece?"

"I've heard so many wonderful things about you, dear."

Grace shook hands with the petite silver-haired lady. The woman wore a blue button-down dress with a thin black belt that showed off a rather nice figure.

"You were right, Charlie." She turned and nudged Grace's uncle. "They do make a darling couple."

The Reece household experienced more family merriment than it had ever seen. Rachel and Elizabeth dominated the conversation throughout supper. Daniel sat next to his girlfriend and, although he chided his sister and Rachel, seemed to be in exceptionally great spirits.

Uncle Charlie presented a feast in wonderful serving dishes he'd found wrapped in newspaper in Justin's basement. The girls laughed over the cloth napkins, and Uncle Charlie scolded Grace and Justin for not properly exposing their children to the finer things in life. At the end of the meal, Uncle Charlie and Doris disappeared into the kitchen and returned to the dining room with a tray of glass dessert dishes. Each one was overloaded with chocolate mousse.

"I don't see how they can move," Justin said as the girls ran out of the room after taking their dishes to the kitchen counter. "God, it's good to be home." He reclined back in his chair, patting his stomach.

Grace shook her head at him but couldn't help smiling. "You relax, and I'll clean up the dishes."

"I'll help you." Doris jumped up and grabbed her plate as well as Charlie's.

"Uh . . ." Justin leaned forward.

"Not to worry, son." Uncle Charlie held up his hand. "Grace, we'll clean up."

"But Uncle Charlie . . ." Grace began.

Justin hadn't been this full in months, but he managed to move around the table and take Grace's arm before she retreated with dishes into the kitchen.

"Not another word," Uncle Charlie said, using an authoritative tone and relieving her of the stacked plates in her hands. "You two go do your talking. We'll mind the store while you're gone."

"Come help me get a fire going." Justin escorted her out of the room, enjoying her puzzled expression.

"So, how's the job search going?" he asked a few minutes later while she sat at the edge of the fireplace watching him. He stacked wood and stuffed newspaper between the logs.

"I've submitted several résumés but haven't heard anything back yet."

"I see. Are any of the positions around here?"

"No." She looked down at her hands, and long curly locks brushed over her shoulder. The hair combs he'd given her held the bulk of her hair in place, and it streamed down the curve of her back. He loved that she wore them tonight.

He stared at her for a minute and then reached up to tug on one of her curls playfully. She rubbed her cheek against his hand, but her expression had sobered.

"Do you want to stay in Rockville?"

"Are you going to be here?"

"This is my home. But you know a special agent does a fair amount of traveling."

She nodded, making a face that he guessed she hoped hid her emotions.

"I haven't had a chance to tell you yet. I wanted to tell you in person." Justin pushed the button on the long lighter and ignited newspaper. "Cliff Bogfrey credits you for the capture of Rick White."

She grinned. "He does?"

"Uh-huh. You assisted the FBI on the capture of a criminal wanted in several states. You helped take down a bad cop and a bad agent. That will go far for you. He's documented it and faxed a copy. You can attach it to your résumé. Not to mention I've seen that it will be placed on your personal record as a police officer. Sheriff Montgomery didn't give me any flack. I have a feeling if you went down there, they would have little choice but to hire you back."

She shook her head and stared at the growing fire. The glow from it brought out the different shades in her hair. *God.* How fucking hard was it to simply open his mouth and let two simple words—"marry me"—slip out?

"You're an incredible officer and any department in the country would jump at the chance to have you." Justin ached to pull her into his arms, to drag her upstairs and make love to her until she forgot all about trying to hide her feelings from him.

She looked down at her lap, nodding. "Thank you."

There had to be a simpler way to do this. He stood, pulling her up with him. "I want to show you something," he said seriously. "Come on."

He led her to the stairs, and Uncle Charlie appeared in the hallway.

"Have you told her yet?" her uncle asked, and his eyes beamed.

"Not yet." Justin began climbing the stairs.

"Told me what?"

No one answered her.

"Watch the girls for us for a while, will you, Charlie?" Justin called over his shoulder while he pulled Grace up the stairs.

"What is going on here?" she asked when he led her to his bedroom and then shut the door behind him.

"Not what you think," he said, poking her nose with his finger and loving the blush that spread over her cheeks.

"I wasn't thinking anything."

"Now listen to me." He sat down at his desk, pulling her onto his lap. "What job would you like to have if you had your choice?"

"Oh, I don't know." She fidgeted in his lap and he clamped his arms around her. No way could he do this if she drained every ounce of blood straight to his cock. He had no desire to let her up, either. He would deal with the pain. He wanted her close.

"Well, I do." He picked up a packet from his desk and handed it to her.

"What's this?"

"Way too much paperwork." He wrapped his arms around her waist, adjusting her so she sat sideways and he could see her face. "But it's necessary to apply to be a special agent."

She opened the large manila envelope and let a bunch of papers slide into her hands. Applications and questionnaires for the position of Special Agent for the FBI.

"We've already scheduled the polygraph. Basically, the paperwork is a formality. You know, they want to know if you've used drugs and if you've had contact with foreign intelligence officers. I've already done the background check, and we'll take care of the written and oral tests next week when you take the polygraph. That is, if you still want to work for the FBI."

"Oh shit! Justin!" she cried out, then attacked him, kissing his cheeks, his mouth, his nose, his forehead.

"I take it that's a yes." He gripped her hips, knowing she had to feel his rock-hard cock pulsing furiously under her soft ass.

"You know it is." She wrinkled her eyebrows together, her face so close to his. "But what do you mean, I could take the tests next week?"

"I hope I haven't been presumptuous here, but I've already made arrangements for us to fly back out to D.C. next week. I said this was all simply a formality. Bogfrey wants you on the team. You've got skills we can use, and the necessary experience." He paused for a moment to outline her lower lip with his thumb. Dangerous warning signs hardened every muscle in his body. Hold her like this much longer and he would have to fuck her, kids in the house or not. "There are sixteen weeks at the Academy in Quantico. It's a big decision, and we'll have to make sure you're comfortable with the arrangement for your daughter."

She nodded slowly, obviously trying to digest everything he just threw at her, as she looked down at the paperwork lying on his desk.

"Justin?" Uncle Charlie could be heard coming up the stairs. "You've got a phone call."

Justin forgot he had left his cell phone on the counter downstairs. Grace tried scooting off his lap, but he tightened his grip. Uncle Charlie didn't need to see firsthand how his niece affected Justin.

"Come on in, old man," Justin called out.

Uncle Charlie pushed open the bedroom door. Charlie didn't have the phone in his hand and gave the two of them an ornery grin.

"It was Bogfrey. He wanted to know if you talked to Grace yet and I told him you were doing that right now. Just give him a call back when you're ready." Uncle Charlie winked at his niece and then looked at the paperwork on Justin's desk. "So what do you think of this turn of events? You always were cut out to be FBI."

"We'll leave next Tuesday for D.C. She can take her written and orals, and I'll give her the tour of the Academy," Justin explained, all too aware that the old man wanted in on the conversation. His excitement for his niece showed in his eyes.

"Don't you worry about Rachel, okay? I'll make sure she gets to school on time and scrubs behind her ears and all that stuff." Uncle Charlie beamed as he went up on his toes.

"Are you going to stay here with her?" Grace looked up quickly.

"Uncle Charlie is my new boarder," Justin explained. "I'm away from this place a fair bit, and Rachel needs stability in her life. When you're through with the Academy you can come back here for a while before you get your first assignment."

The room got real quiet; in fact, it seemed silence crept through the entire house. Either the kids had gone outside or they were eavesdropping in the next room. Grace ran her fingers over the papers while her expression turned grave.

She tried again to get up off Justin, and this time he released her. She walked across the room and stared out the window.

"Uncle Charlie, could I speak to Justin alone for a minute?" she asked without turning around.

"The other option is taking Rachel back to D.C." Uncle Charlie spoke to her back. "You said yourself it wouldn't be right to uproot her during a school year."

The old man had gone to bat for Justin. Charlie liked the ranch house and the Badlands that surrounded the place. It was a beautiful home, a wonderful place to raise children, and a perfect place for an old man to retire. When Grace didn't say anything but continued staring out the window with her back to both of them, Charlie gave Justin a reassuring nod and backed out of the room.

"Well, I'll be downstairs. Let me know what you decide,

sugar. I need to make plans after you tell me what you want to do." The door closed and Justin stood, hesitating before moving toward her.

"What's on your mind?"

She turned around and frowned at him. "Why don't you tell me what you're thinking?"

He pulled her into his arms and engulfed her with his body. She collapsed into him willingly, and he lowered his mouth and claimed hers. Their kiss moved beyond erotic or sensual. Love existed between the two of them. It tore apart his insides, leaving him numb when he didn't have her by his side. She needed the words, though. Women were like that. No matter how much he showed her what she meant to him, she needed to hear it, too.

"I want you to stay with me," he said in heavy breaths after he'd released her lips. "I want you in my life. Your daughter is happy here, and regardless of the experiences you've had since you've been here, it's a good town to raise a family."

"Raise a family?" She choked on the words, searching his face while her tears pooled in her eyes.

He stroked her cheek and placed a very gentle kiss on her lips. He didn't answer right away but instead played with several of her curls, and cocked his head while he memorized the glow on her face. He saw fear, too, and uncertainty. She wanted him to spell it out to her, and it was time to do just that.

"I'm not asking you to make any hasty decisions," he began, wishing it were easier to voice the many emotions climbing around inside him. "I won't even ask you for a commitment—not tonight. But Grace, I love you. Given some time, I'll probably ask you to marry me. I know we haven't known each other that long, and you'll be gone for almost four months. After that, if you're willing, you'll be assigned to me for your first few years. We'll work together, we can live together, and this is a great place for your daughter."

"We'll work together?" Her jaw dropped, but the grin spreading across her face showed him he had said what she needed to hear.

"You have an inside knowledge into the thoughts of a psychopath, a stalker, a rapist. That appeals to the Bureau. I'll be in charge of a special unit sent into cities to assist in bringing in criminals that fit that profile. We're both loaded with experience, and I already know we make a great team."

"I think we'd make a great team," she whispered. "And oh, Justin, I love you, too—so much. All this time while you were gone, I fought to be levelheaded, accept that we'd have to move so I could work. No matter how hard I tried, it made me sick. I don't want to live without you."

His heart fucking exploded in his chest. He'd known it. The way she looked at him, made love to him, hell, even the way they argued—he'd been right. This was love. And it would only get better. He scooped her up into his arms and walked over to the bedroom door and locked it.

"Justin, what are you doing?" She giggled but wrapped her arms around his neck while kicking off her shoes.

He didn't answer but instead walked to his bed and placed her down on it, then knelt down over her and released his hunger when he kissed her. She pulled him to her, then pushed her hands under his collar, stretching her fingers against his skin.

"I think I remember something about Charlie saying they would take the kids for a walk after supper," he told her, pulling away from her long enough to unsnap and then unzip her jeans.

He slid his hand into her jeans and she arched herself to him. As his fingers found their way inside her she groaned in ecstasy.

"I think you two conspired against me," she accused, biting her lip and arching her neck while her lashes fluttered over her eyes.

"Your uncle approves." He pulled his fingers away from her heat, leaving a trail of moisture over her skin.

He took his time undressing her, and then Grace moved to sit facing him, naked, and was torturously slow as she took off his clothes.

"He approved of you before he even moved here," she

told Justin, focusing on his chest while running her fingers over his chest hair.

"I'm a hell of a lucky guy."

"I hope you say that years from now."

His heart constricted. *Years from now.* Damn, he liked the way that sounded.

He took his time kissing her, running his tongue over her body, nibbling and tasting her soft, smooth flesh. Every inch of him throbbed when she insisted on doing the same, moving and pushing him to the bed so that he stretched out underneath her. She paid incredible attention to detail, taking her time while her hot, moist mouth focused on his mouth, then his neck, then lower.

When she gently wrapped her fingers around his cock, lifting the rock-hard shaft until she held it upright, his balls stiffened so painfully that he squeezed his eyes shut. He wanted to experience everything she offered him, enjoy her lips on him, her tongue stroking his length, and the heat of her hot, moist mouth when she sucked him deep inside her. God, she had skills like he never dreamed possible.

When she took her mouth off of his cock, the coolness that suddenly attacked it stole his breath. He barely could focus when he looked up at her, certain his gratitude beamed in his face.

"Don't move," she instructed, her lips moist and full from giving him head.

He doubted he would be able to get up at the moment if he tried. Staring up at her while her long curls draped over her breasts, he watched her stretch her legs and mount him.

"God. Grace." He grabbed her hips to control her when she slid down on his cock.

Her soaked muscles contracted around his shaft, sucking him in deeper. He lifted her slowly and she leaned forward, kissing him, while she fucked him with everything she had.

Justin's entire body constricted when he exploded. Light sparked in front of his eyes while the room spun around them. She drained him so thoroughly it took all his strength to wrap his arms around her and hold her while she draped over his body, breathing heavily and going limp on top of him.

Apparently, Uncle Charlie must have decided to respect their privacy, because as she lay in Justin's arms he heard car doors and voices outside. Doris and Charlie were taking the children, leaving Grace and Justin to enjoy the first moments of the rest of their lives together.

"They already sound like a family," he whispered as they heard children's laughter and car doors shutting. "Our union has brought happiness to a lot of people. I hear two happy young girls, a teenager more content than he was when I first arrived, and an old man and woman that were lonely and now have a large family to spoil."

"We won't be together always," she pointed out.

"Our love will make this family strong, whether we're with them or on assignment."

"I love you," she whispered, not moving an inch but relaxing further on top of him.

"Oh, baby, I love you, too." He found her mouth and took his time kissing her until his cock danced to life inside her. "How long did I say I would wait before I asked you to marry me?"

He whispered the words over her lips, and when he opened his eyes she was smiling.

"I . . . I don't remember," she said finally.

"Well, I've decided. When you return from the Academy, lady, you may expect a marriage proposal."

The groan of pure satisfaction and pleasure that escaped from her throat sent blood rushing to his groin.

"Well then, Special Agent Reece, you'd better get a ring, because I plan on accepting that marriage proposal."

Long, Lean and Lethal

Special Agent Noah Kayne with the FBI stood in the middle of his motel room, squinting against the bright light coming in through the open door.

"I've got a car on the way for you," Police Chief Aaron Noble told him. Although probably close to fifty, the chief looked like he was in good shape. He also looked like he wished he were anywhere but here. "As soon as it's here, you can follow me to the station."

"I've already briefed myself on the case." The file proved interesting reading on the plane, and while he waited for a ride to come get him, since they didn't have a rental car for him at the airport. "Three murders so far."

"So far? Is that how Bureau people are trained to think?" Chief Noble scrubbed his forehead with thick, long fingers.

Noah didn't expect anything different out of the chief. He'd yet to be sent in to aid an investigation and not found at least one person with the local law bitter that he was there. But he also knew, according to what he'd read in the brief, that there would be another murder, probably soon, if he didn't get a handle on the situation and put some shock tactics out. It was a tricky business—scare the perp too much, and he'd never catch him, but let the murderer think he still controlled the situation and more people would die.

Noah watched the Chief walk over to the curtains and then mess with them until he found the long narrow wand that opened them. More light flooded into the room when he pulled them back and also gave them a view of the large parking lot outside. He empathized with Chief Noble's frustration. Noah hated admitting he needed help. It was a fault, a character defect, but he'd been told more than once he had many.

The Chief nodded once. "There's your car and your new partner."

"Partner?" Noah caught the Chief's smug look but refused to take the bait. "I work alone. Always have. It's in writing."

"Call your supervisor, and yes, I do have her number," Chief Noble said smugly. "I know your track record, Kayne, which is why I requested you. You aren't married, are you?"

"No," Noah said sharply, refusing to think about the matching rings that were still in his top dresser drawer at his apartment in D.C. He focused instead on Brenda committing him to an arrangement that fell outside the accepted parameters without discussing it with him first. "And I'll call Brenda right now."

Brenda Thornton, who might possibly be the closest he had to family in this bitter world, knew him sometimes better than he knew himself, which pissed him off to no end. They'd discussed these murders, all happening in three different cities, and all with parallels that were uncanny. It was decided that an agent would go to each town, move in, and get acquainted with the discreetly quiet group of swingers in each community.

"Feel free to call your supervisor." Chief Noble walked over to the door and opened it. When he turned and looked at Noah, the brightness outside created shadows on his face that made his smug expression seem almost demonic. "And good thing you aren't married. Bigamy is a crime in this state and you're about to meet your wife."

Noah reached for his phone, but his hand was suddenly too damp to pull it free from his waist. "What did you just say?"

"Your wife," Chief Noble reiterated. "You're going undercover and we're investigating murders among married couples in a swinging community. Only makes sense that you would need a wife."

Brenda never said shit about a fucking wife. "Like I said, I work alone."

"Not on my case you won't," the Chief growled, nodding to someone outside. "Rain, there you are. It's about time you got here."

"It took longer at the car rental place than I thought it would." A lady with a soft, sultry edge to her voice, like she'd just woken up, spoke just outside the room. "I don't do minivans and it took a while to change the paperwork."

"You're entering into the world of middle class suburbia. And what's wrong with a minivan? My wife loves hers." Chief Noble stepped forward and reached for the person just out of Noah's view. "Come inside first and meet your new partner," he coaxed.

"We've discussed this already," she snarled under her breath and walked into the motel room. "I'll get cozy with your killer, but I'm doing it alone. And why did you want me to meet you here? This isn't suburbia, unless you think we're dealing with cheating spouses and you want to set me up as one."

Noah took advantage of the moment while she adjusted her eyes to the dimly lit room. Most tall women tended to slouch a bit, as if being tall embarrassed them. Since he stood over six feet, it was something he'd always noticed and it bugged him.

But Rain, who probably was a good five ten, held on to every inch with pride. She didn't have an athletic build, or a voluptuous one. Instead, curves faded into hard, flat planes that stretched until they softened and filled out into perfectly rounded hips, the kind a guy would grab on to when taking her from behind. Her faded jeans were snug, helping to round out her curves, and her plain blue, sleeveless shirt hugged her slender waist, ending just before her jeans began and giving him a peek at those hard abs.

She wasn't buffed out, although she looked like she could hold her own. Her shoulders were smooth and round. Straight, thick black hair was gathered in a clasp at her nape, showing off her long, perfectly curved neck that he stared at for a moment, focusing on that soft curve just above her collar bone. He bet she would feel like silk.

Her breasts weren't small, but not too big either. Although he noticed the outline of a bra under her shirt, as he watched, her nipples hardened. Rain sensed his scrutinizing gaze. He'd bet damned good money she was aware of him appraising every inch of her. And his attention affected her. It affected him, too.

But when he shot his gaze to her face, her expression was hard, and her focus was on the Chief.

"It makes no sense whatsoever to bring the FBI in on this case. An outsider isn't going to help." Rain didn't lower her voice, focused on Chief Noble, and ignored Noah. "This is my case, Chief, and you know it. You think I'm not capable of bringing down our guy alone?"

"He's got the expertise. You've got the knowledge of this town and the community. Both of your skills are superb." Noble sounded like he'd rehearsed for this exact moment.

"Find someone else." Rain turned to leave, still not having given Noah as much as a second glance. She tried walking out the door.

Chief Noble must have been on a fairly good basis with his officer. She didn't look shocked when he took her arm, escorting her back into the motel room.

"Noah Kayne, meet Rain Huxtable, your wife." The chief rocked up on his heels like he was witnessing two kids on their first date. For the first time since he'd arrived at the motel room to meet Noah, the chief looked very pleased with himself, like he pissed off two for the price of one.

Noah would rip Brenda a new one first chance he had to speak with her. Rain turned her head slowly, and then raised one eyebrow, giving him a quick once-over.

Noah didn't consider himself a Greek god. More times than he counted, he'd been told he had that bad boy look. Whatever that meant.

It still stung a little when she said, "Right, whatever," and returned her attention to Chief Noble without as much as a blink of an eye.

"This is Special Agent Noah Kayne," the Chief offered, stressing his title.

This time when Rain looked at him, her gaze traveled over him more slowly than before. He quite honestly couldn't say that he'd ever seen such soft baby blues look so incredibly defiant.

"Head down to the station," the chief continued, turning toward the door. "I want a break-down by five on how you plan on nailing our killer."

Rain followed him out the motel room door, leaving Noah to grab his key card and bring up the rear.

"We're already in the process of interviewing," Rain told the chief. "I've got reports that I've put on your desk that have statements from friends of our victims who were interviewed when they came into the station. I've read the reports. There are some good leads in there. You don't think I can break this case on my own?"

Chief Noble reached his squad car and looked over the hood, squinting against the bright afternoon sun. "Your partner might have ideas. Brainstorm together and let me know what you come up with."

It seemed he ducked into his car quickly and took off just as fast.

Maybe the chief ran from his detective because she might have too abrasive of a personality, and he wasn't in the mood to deal with it. If Noah were a compassionate man, which he wasn't, he might feel sorry for the detective when she stood there for a moment, watching the squad car leave the parking lot. Noah didn't care that this tall, sexy detective felt betrayed. Hell, he'd been given the shaft too.

"Where's my rental?" he asked, keeping it civil. For now, they were stuck together and there was work to be done.

She had one hell of a fine-looking ass. "It's the green Taurus. But it's not your rental; it's my rental."

She kept walking, offering a view that won over searching the parking lot for his car. When he finally did glance up, Rain held keys in her hand and paused at the driver's-side door of what he guessed was a brand new Taurus.

Noah stopped next to her and held his hand out for the key.

Rain looked at his hand and her disdain didn't leave her face when she lifted long, thick lashes and graced him with her baby blues. "I'm driving. Get in on the other side."

"I always drive."

"Not with me you don't."

Noah knew a test when he saw one. Rain probably challenged anyone who crossed her path. If he'd known he was going to have the sexy Amazon cop tossed in his lap, he would have researched her. But sometimes there was something to be said about first contact and initial reactions.

"Detective, you can give me the keys, or I'll take them from you. But if we're going to be partners, you might as well get accustomed to shotgun."

She rolled her eyes, looking disgusted, and turned to slide the key into the keyhole.

Noah wrapped his fingers around her arm, and Rain spun around, a long strand of black hair flying free from its confines and drifting over her face. Her eyes turned a stormy, turbulent shade of blue, and her parted lips were a soft red, full and moist. Her sudden quick breath and the fiery flush that spread over her cheeks proved one thing; sparring with him got her off.

And he found that he wasn't exactly immune either. Damn it.

Rain tried shoving her way around him. Almost against his will, Noah found himself moving in closer until she was pinned between him and the car. Because he was so tall, most women leaned their heads back, exposing their necks to him whenever he was this close to them. But Rain barely adjusted her head to glare at him.

"Are you getting your rocks off, Bureau man?" she said, moistening her lips as her tongue darted over them.

"Trust me, Cop woman," he said, his voice low and gravelly with desire, "you'll know when I do."